DEAR FUTURE ME

"Suspenseful and thought-provoking. I will read whatever O'Connor writes next—she is the talent of a generation, and this is the perfect book group thriller."

—Gillian McAllister, *New York Times* bestselling author of *Wrong Place Wrong Time* and *Just Another Missing Person*

PRAISE FOR
THE CAPTIVE

"Stunning. Staggeringly original, chilling, ELECTRIFYING. I raced through the final chapters with my heart in my mouth."

—Chris Whitaker, author of *We Begin at the End*

"This GRIPPING page-turner has a terrifying concept at its heart. Part thriller, part a dark, unpredictable love story, it asks some big questions about crime and punishment. Tense and disturbing, I think it would spark great book club debate."

—Adele Parks, *Platinum* Magazine

"INGENIOUS. A smart, pacy, and highly entertaining thriller."

—T. M. Logan, bestselling author of *The Holiday*

"Oh my god, it's FANTASTIC! Highly original, thrilling, and

emotional, *The Captive* is set to be one of the best books of 2021. I ADORED it."

—Jo Spain, bestselling author of the Inspector Tom Reynolds series

"This original concept thriller is SO GOOD."

—*Heat* Magazine

"KILLER CONCEPT, brilliantly realized, and beautifully, satisfyingly plotted. I loved it."

—Amanda Mason, author of *The Wayward Girls*

"A great concept. Impressive, compelling storytelling as well as a FANTASTIC mystery."

—Gytha Lodge, author of *She Lies in Wait*

"Original, deft, and clever, *The Captive* certainly had me in its vise-like grip throughout."

—Phoebe Morgan, author of *The Doll House*

"Readers will become totally HOOKED within pages of starting this hugely original and entertaining thriller."

—*Irish Independent*

"With an ARRESTING beginning, this dystopian tale draws the reader in immediately... The story rattles along at a cracking pace."

—*Woman & Home* Magazine

"A super smart, sophisticated, and highly original tale, which packs a POWERFUL punch on so many levels. Entertaining, fast-paced, and clever, *The Captive* will hold you prisoner right through to the shocking dénouement."

—*Lancashire Post*

PRAISE FOR
MY HUSBAND'S SON

"Staggering—I absolutely tore through it."
—Holly Seddon, bestselling author of *Try Not to Breathe*

"Gripping"

—*Daily Mail*

PRAISE FOR
THE DANGEROUS KIND

"Brilliantly compelling."
—T. M. Logan, bestselling author of *The Holiday*

"An absolute triumph."
—Holly Seddon, bestselling author of *Try Not to Breathe*

Also by Deborah O'Connor

My Husband's Son
The Dangerous Kind
The Captive

DEAR FUTURE ME

DEAR FUTURE ME

a novel

DEBORAH O'CONNOR

Poisoned Pen
PRESS

Published by Poisoned Pen Press, an imprint of Sourcebooks
P.O. Box 4410, Naperville, Illinois 60567-4410
(630) 961-3900
sourcebooks.com

Cataloging-in-Publication Data is on file with the Library of Congress.

Printed and bound in the United States of America.
PAH 10 9 8 7 6 5 4 3 2 1

For Charlie

Twenty years from now, you will be more disappointed
by the things you didn't do than by the ones you did.

Mark Twain

Chapter 1

All across the seaside town, envelopes whisper through letter boxes. They seem benign—boring, even—the white rectangles dropping down onto the mats alongside electricity bills, seed catalogs and dental appointment reminders. But as the recipients rip them open and read what is inside, it is like a series of bombs going off.

Boom.

Some of the addressees are in the middle of preparing breakfast, juggling a search for their youngest's gym clothes alongside the application of mascara, but as their eyes rove across the handwritten pages, they find themselves rooted to the spot. Others scan the first few lines and, sensing they may not like what comes next, retreat to the bathroom and perch on the closed toilet seat, pulse quickening as they confront words they'd penned to themselves twenty years earlier.

"Dear Future Me…"

The letters had been a class assignment. A harmless exercise in creative writing.

Or so they'd thought.

When they were done, they'd sealed them inside an envelope and handed them in, just as they did all their other schoolwork. The teacher hadn't told them the letters would be filed away, that two decades later he would return these missives to their older selves.

The postman continues to progress through the sand-flecked streets, circling the avenues and cul-de-sacs the same way the teacher once weaved around the classroom, collecting the messages that now sit wedged in his shoulder bag.

———————

Leighton Walsh is sweaty and out of breath, not long back from a run along the vast crescent of beach that defines this section of coastline, when his letter arrives. Ribs heaving, he pulls open the envelope so carelessly he almost severs the contents in two. At first, he has no idea what he is looking at. Twenty years is a long time. Finally, though, something clicks, and as it does his stomach falls, a sickening roller coaster drop.

Kitty Plaige is one of the rare classmates who had given her letter more than a second thought. She regrets the private things she committed to paper that afternoon, had wished she could take them back. Away for a few days at a conference, when she comes home, she is reunited with her pages. Afterward, she presses the envelope to her chest like precious cargo.

The teacher could not find a recent address for Melvyn Arkwright, and so his letter is sent to his parents' house. His father bends down to collect the post, and on seeing his son's name, he tenses. Before he has even returned to standing, he is already wondering how he might pass it on without having to see or talk to Melvyn, whether it's possible to drop it off at a time when he knows for certain he will not be in.

Robbie Rooke's letter comes sandwiched between the usual crop of constituency correspondence, embossed invitations, and a Coutts statement encased in the bank's trademark cream vellum. He assesses the teenage jottings wryly, makes light of them with his wife, but when he goes upstairs to shave, he sees his face is wet with tears.

Miranda Brévart's letter is the last to arrive. Her barn conversion is inland, a mile outside town, and so to get there, the postman returns to his van. As he drives down lanes just starting to thicken with cow parsley, Miranda is making blueberry pancakes; her children, Enid and Edward, are playing fetch by the kitchen table with their cavapoo. Miranda is a messy cook, and so she's plaited her hair and tucked it into the back of her top, but her hands are covered in dried batter, and as she works the spatula against the edge of the pan, her knuckles crack and flake. The dog retrieves the ball from under the sofa and the dust incites a cartoonish canine "A-choo!" The sneeze makes the children giggle and Miranda looks up. She locks eyes with her husband and they share a smile that says, "See how lucky we are?"

Miranda tells the kids to go and get changed out of their pajamas, but they ignore her; they are having too much fun. Ordinarily she would shoo them upstairs, but then another giggle rings out, and she decides that today she will not scold them, that today it does not matter if they are late for school.

The van comes and goes.

Her husband collects the post from the mat and brings it through to the kitchen. After placing it on the worktop he reaches past her for the coffee tin, his other hand brushing her hip; then he faces the espresso machine.

Miranda puts down the spatula, opens the envelope, and reads. She's confused at first; then she laughs and holds the pages at a distance, turns them this way and that, as if they are some curiosity she is trying to identify. The initial paragraphs are sweet and speak of a more innocent time. She brings them close. Reads the first page again, faster.

The top of the coffee machine is stacked with tiny cups and saucers that rattle as it pumps out hot liquid. The kids tire of the dog and flop on the rug. The cooking pancakes have sweetened the air, and they complain that they are hungry.

Miranda is almost finished when her phone beeps. She looks from it to the letter.

Everything is the same, until it isn't.

Enid feels it first—a sudden tightening at the back of her neck, like the moment before she takes a run-up to the balance beam at gymnastics. Then the dog whimpers, and its tail disappears between its legs.

"Mummy?" Enid says the word quietly, not sure what she is asking.

Miranda does not reply. Still in her pajamas, she leaves her phone on the counter and heads for the front door. Her husband looks up briefly. He thinks she's gone to retrieve a forgotten water bottle or some errant part of their uniform from the car, but then he hears the engine come to life.

———————

Huntcliff is lovely in the early light, the land meadowy with wildflowers. The air is sun spangled, the grass underfoot spongy with dew. Miranda walks to the edge. The rock face is pocked with nesting kittiwakes. A hundred meters below, the tide is out. The exposed boulders bake in the sun.

Miranda's feet leave the ground, and then she is falling, her pajama top billowing around her shoulder blades. The kittiwakes chitter as she flies past.

The tide will just be starting to come in when they find her, her plait come loose, the batter on her broken fingers clouding the water.

At home, the pancakes blacken and the smoke alarm screams.

Chapter 2

AUDREY

Dear Future Me,

OK, sooo this is pretty weird but our teacher has told us to write to ourselves (!) about the stuff we want the grown-up us to have achieved twenty years from now.

As if "us" right now and "us" then are two different people.

I know, right?

Told you this was weird.

So hello there, older, wrinklier thirty-something Audrey. How are you?

Before we get to all the achievement stuff, I want to say that I hope you're OK and, more importantly, that all the people you love are OK. These last few years...well, let's just say they've been really tough.

First there was Dad. He was ill for such a long time and losing him was the worst experience of your life. I bet you still miss him. Please tell me you haven't forgotten all the little things you loved about him... the way he'd whisper "you all right?" whenever he saw you were upset, the Dolly Parton songs he liked to sing whenever he took a shower, the way he had to leave the room before the end of "The Snowman" because he could not cope with the devastation of the boy knelt alone in the snow...

Then there was all the worry about Mum.

She says that they got it in time, but I'm guessing the fear never really leaves you.

OK, I just read back through what I've written so far and I've realized this is turning into the saddest, most depressing letter ever.

So. Moving on to the official actual stated purpose of this assignment...

Future achievements.

Hopes and dreams.

Here we go.

Buckle up, buttercup...

I know it sounds corny but I'm keeping everything crossed you've somehow managed to find your place in the world, that you're "bien dans sa peau." (You learned this phrase in French class last week.) Madame Laurent said it's hard to translate exactly, but it means that you are comfortable in your own skin. It stuck because right now you don't feel like that, you never have. I think it's because you don't quite fit here in this school, in this town. Even though you want to, REALLY REALLY BADLY.

What else?

You'll have probably moved away from home because of your job. Are you a museum curator or a teacher? At the moment you can't decide. Let me tell you...right now, sitting at this desk, writing this letter, imagining you spending your days handling ancient exhibits and being PAID for it?

GOOSEBUMPS!

It's like Mum always says. Do a job you love, you'll never work a day.

I hope you still come home. That you bring your kids to see their granny and be spoiled. How many do you have? Miranda says she's not going to have any, that she doesn't want to have do the stinky nappy changing part (she came over for tea the other day and just as you were all eating your nuggets and chips Ned did one of his famous exploding poos), but I think she'll change her mind.

Soooooo...steering this letter away from the subject of baby poo (talk about going off on a tangent!) and back to those hopes and dreams...

My main wish for you is that you got to university. To Cambridge and Corpus Christi College, and its green quads and stone staircases and punting on the water on hot summer days (sigh). Mr. Wilson, your history teacher, thinks you have what it takes, but full angst disclosure: just having applied worries you. You feel as if the mere act of putting yourself out there is a risk, like you're raising your head above the parapet and announcing to the world that you think you're clever, that you're special, when in truth you aren't convinced.

Anyways, you hope he's right and that your courage pays off.

I keep looking at the pictures in the college brochure and thinking of you in lectures and that library. It is jaw-droppingly, ridiculously beautiful. Basically it is like something out of a film. A Harry Potter film. Except REAL LIFE. What did you decide to specialize in, in the end? You're pretty intimidated by the thought of the entrance interview (translation: completely, bone-shakingly, massively terrified) and the questions they might throw your way, but you've worked so hard on your application essay and you're praying that it, more than anything, will show them how much you want this, how much you deserve to be offered a place...

Audrey lifts the toilet seat and rings the bowl with bleach; then she dunks the brush and scrubs. The loos in this house usually aren't too bad—Kitty and Jago are academics, neat, considerate people—but Kitty is away at a conference, and last night Jago had a party and left the downstairs bathroom awash with vomit.

Mopping floors. Polishing glass. Scouring sinks.

Scrubbing toilets.

Audrey usually tries not to think too hard about the fact that this is how she fills her waking hours. Over the years she has trained herself not to wonder about what could have been, to shut down even the hint of a daydream about the life she'd once thought possible. Cleaning is, and always has been, a means to an end: a job that fit around the school day. Plus, it had been one of the few things people had been willing to pay her for when she'd found herself out in the world at eighteen with only a handful of qualifications.

But the letter has messed with all that.

It had arrived this morning, her name and address in neat capitals. It had taken her a moment to understand what it was. Assuming some mistake, she'd checked the envelope, making sure she was definitely the intended recipient. But then she'd read the first paragraph again, slower this time.

Realizing this was her seventeen-year-old self had knocked her sideways.

The teenage Audrey had been so full of potential; more than that, she'd dared to believe the grown-up her might go on to *fulfill* that potential.

But teenage Audrey hadn't known what was coming down the track.

That Cambridge wouldn't think her worthy enough to grant an interview.

That her mum's cancer would spread.

That she would not sit her final exams.

Audrey had learned about her Corpus Christi rejection that November. They'd buried her mum by February. With no parents and no extended family to take in her and her two-year-old brother Ned, there had been talk of foster care. Then the social worker had posited an alternative: Audrey was about to turn eighteen. A legal adult. If she could get a job and take responsibility for Ned, they could stay together.

She could be his guardian.

Audrey hadn't hesitated.

It had been hard at first, shaping her life around her brother's needs, forgoing her studies, weekend sleep-ins, the acres of time available to lie on her bed and read and think and doze. She'd had to bend and twist like those trees that grow around an abandoned bicycle or up through a broken cottage, but then over the years it had become second nature, and like those trees, she'd seen the beauty in her contortions, the marvel. Ned never spoke about what she'd done, the choice she'd made, but every year he would give her cards and flowers on Mother's Day, and every year Audrey would keep those flowers in their vase until they went brown and crumbly.

She reaches in her jeans pocket for her phone.

Talk to Ned. As soon as you hear his voice, you'll feel better. He's doing so well. Everything you sacrificed? Worth it.

He answers after the second ring.

"You're up."

Her brother still lives with her and will continue to do so for the next few months until he leaves for university.

"Got dressed and brushed my teeth and everything."

Ned has just finished his exams and is working the summer at the surf shop on the beach. In comparison to the Saturday jobs he's had in the past, he's unusually keen—always punctual, taking on extra shifts—something Audrey attributes to his coworker, a freckled beauty called Eleanor.

"I left you a packed lunch in the fridge."

"I told you." His voice is kind but firm. "I like eating at the burrito truck with the others." He takes a breath, as if he is going to speak, but then he seems to decide against it. "I have to go."

"Will you be home for dinner?"

Don't make a big deal. Play it cool. Definitely don't mention the fact you prepped the meatball sauce before work this morning.

But her studied nonchalance is futile; he's already gone.

She switches to WhatsApp. Scrolls to her last sent message.

The first person she'd contacted after reading her "Dear Future Me" was her best friend, Miranda. They'd been in the same class at school, and she was curious to know what her own letter contained. Unlike her, she guesses the life Miranda has built exceeds anything she could have imagined as a kid. A yoga teacher with an army of devoted students, a French dermatologist husband who was as rich as he was funny, a beautiful converted barn for a home, two gorgeous kids.

The perfect life.

Two blue ticks indicate her message has been opened and read, but Miranda has yet to respond.

Strange.

She'd thought Miranda would call the second she saw it. Not because she wanted to indulge in some trip down memory lane, but because of the other thing Audrey had shared with her.

Tucked inside Audrey's letter had been a bizarre note. A cuckoo in the nest. Flimsy and pale blue, a folded scrap, it in no way matched her own lined pages.

Audrey

I need to talk to you about something important. It's too complicated to explain here. Please come meet me tonight 8pm at the Smugglers' Church and I'll tell you everything.

Ben

Benjamin Spellman. He and Miranda were together in the lower sixth. He had been her first proper boyfriend. Audrey had no idea what his note could have been about or why he had hidden it in her letter, and so she had immediately sent Miranda a screenshot.

Finished with the bathroom, Audrey picks up the caddy that holds her sprays and cloths and heads down the hall. She usually cleans here on Fridays—does the whole place top to bottom—but Jago had messaged and asked if she could do some extra hours. He wanted everything put straight before Kitty got home.

Kitty and Jago had met and married while studying for their doctorates. Once a university power match, Kitty has since vastly outpaced her husband professionally. Regularly published, she was considered the expert in her field and was about to be anointed York's youngest ever professor of history. Jago, meanwhile, was a part-time lecturer at Teesside University and a bit of a creep.

Passing by the dining room, she sees he is still passed out on the chaise longue. The right knee of his chinos is ripped, its outer edge blotted with white dust and what looks like blood. He's been this way since she let herself in at nine, the air thick with weed. She thinks of the used condom she'd found next to the puddle of puke in the loo.

It must have been quite the party.

She's seen worse.

It's a compliment, in a way. Being a good cleaner means making yourself invisible. Someone the client forgets is there. If you stay on the edges of their life, if you keep yourself small, don't take up too much space, then they never feel any embarrassment about that overdrawn bank statement on the kitchen island or that dildo in the master bed. It was a skill that had come naturally to Audrey. She'd always struggled to fit in—she was too awkward, too nerdy—but then she'd discovered that you don't need to fit in if nobody realizes you're there. These days, even when she's not at work, she tends to live her life on the periphery.

Another check of her phone. Still no response from Miranda.

You should have waited, told her about Ben's note in person. She's probably upset. Seeing his handwriting would have brought back unhappy memories.

Because that was the horrible irony of these "Dear Future Me" letters. During the period in which the class had been busy with this assignment—writing and thinking about all the possibilities that lay ahead—one of them had their life tragically cut short.

Benjamin Spellman died on a school trip to the Lake District. He'd smuggled booze from home into his luggage, got drunk, and gone for a walk during a late-night snowstorm. They'd found him the next morning, sheltering by a wall, frozen to death.

He and Miranda had split up a while before he died. Still, she, like the rest of the school, had taken it hard.

Audrey grabs the vacuum and drags it into Kitty's study.

Even on a good day, this is her least favorite room, but after this morning's letter, the jealousy stings more than usual. Packed with books, an open fireplace takes up most of one wall, and opposite it is a Georgian sash with views of the Cleveland Hills. The shelves reached capacity some time ago, and so now Kitty arranges the books on the floor in teetering cairn-like structures that Audrey has to try not to knock over. Kitty's desk, a rosewood pedestal, sits alongside the fire, and on every surface are tiny brass lamps that make the room glow on winter afternoons.

It's like something out of a film.

She, Kitty, and Miranda had been in the same class at school, and so when Kitty returned from her conference, she would no doubt be in receipt of her own "Dear Future Me" letter. Unlike Audrey, Kitty *had* been granted a Cambridge interview and had gone on to study history there. Her many accolades are documented in a wall of framed certificates, her graduation portrait at their center. In the photo, Kitty is flanked by her mum and dad, her dad's face pink with pride.

Audrey had tried to resist this cleaning job. In fact, when Jago had first sought her out, she'd turned him down flat. In truth, she'd been actively looking for new clients after a broken boiler and leaking roof had left her seriously strapped for cash. Still, she'd said no. It was already hard enough to look in the mirror, to reconcile herself to the adult she'd become. The last thing she needed was to be in the orbit of her old class-mate, a weekly reminder of what could have been.

But then Jago had told her how much he was willing to pay—well above the going rate—and so she'd caved. He said the money reflected the additional chores—dropping off and collecting dry-cleaning, iron-ing, washing windows—he expected Audrey to do on top of her regular work, and she hadn't argued. On her first day, though, it became clear Jago hadn't discussed the arrangements with Kitty, and that she was not very pleased about Audrey's inflated fee. By then, though, it was a done deal. Kitty paid her through gritted teeth.

All done, Audrey puts the rubbish out and, as she returns inside, hears the shush of the shower upstairs. Jago must have finally woken up. A quick dash to grab the dry-cleaning—suits, dresses, and shirts—from where they leave it on the bedroom chair, and after popping the lot in her car trunk, she pulls the front door shut.

She is turning onto the coast road when her phone rings. Anticipating Miranda, a grin brims. Speaking to her friend always feels like standing in the sun. But when she looks at the call display, it isn't Miranda, but Marcel, Miranda's husband.

The speaker crackles with high-pitched gasps. It sounds as if he is choking.

"Marcel?"

"Someone found her car." Marcel usually speaks in a singsong Marseillais. These words, though—he spits them out like broken teeth. "A walker. The engine was still running."

"Has something happened?" Audrey's mind fills with pictures

of Miranda and the children in a school-run collision. "Are the kids OK?"

But Marcel is too in shock to manage the back-and-forth of a conversation.

"When they saw where it was, where she'd stopped…they guessed what she'd done."

"Marcel." Audrey's voice is sharp with growing panic. "What is it?"

"The cliffs." He is incredulous. "Miranda went there this morning. She jumped."

Chapter 3

Three Weeks Later

It's bedtime, and Audrey sits sandwiched between Enid and Edward on Edward's single divan. Enid is seven. Edward is five. Today was their first full day back at school since their mum died, and they have that fidgety, overtired energy that means they could burst into sobs or laughter at any moment. They had wanted to say good night to their father, to have him read them a story, but Marcel is not yet back from work, so Audrey has told them she will have to do.

They don't mind. Neither does she. She's helped with their care-giving since they were newborns, and has always treasured their time together.

These last few weeks, though, it's been more than that. She's needed them more than they've needed her.

"When is Mummy coming home?" says Edward when she has finished reading. "I want to tell her about Russell Macintosh. At school today he showed everyone his bum."

Edward's hair is as glossy and black as his father's had once been, but is currently missing huge chunks, thanks to a game of hairdressers with Enid last week.

"She's not coming home, Eddie," says Enid, "not ever." She huffs, officious. "That's what 'dead' means."

There have been a few tears in the last few weeks, but neither child has yet to get properly upset. Their mum being gone is still too abstract, the permanence of the situation, the finality of it, impossible to comprehend. The story they'd been told—as decided upon by their father—was that Miranda had had an accident: that she'd fallen and hurt her head.

The children demand another book, and as Audrey reads, Enid nuzzles her head into her armpit. In her favorite purple and silver leotard—she had point-blank refused to wear pajamas—she lifts one leg into the air and then the other, idly stretching her hamstrings. Audrey does find it strange to be sitting here, reading aloud as though their lives haven't just been blown apart. But she is grateful for these routines. Taking care of the kids is her one and only respite from the question that otherwise consumes her every waking moment.

Why?

Why did Miranda do what she did?

They had spoken every day, shared everything, yet she could never have imagined this was coming. Realizing her best friend had been struggling with something she had no idea about was hard. Her relationship with Miranda, their closeness, was one of the parts of her life of which she had been most proud.

And yet on this, the most important of things, she was in the dark. How could she not notice Miranda was in so much distress? Had she hidden it that well? Why hadn't her friend felt as if she could confide in her?

She pulls Enid closer, cups her damp head.

In the chaos of those days after the walker had spotted Miranda's abandoned car, Audrey had gone to Marcel. She'd thought he would be able to give her a reason, or at least to offer an hypothesis, as to why Miranda had taken her own life. But Marcel had been at as much of a loss as she was.

After that conversation Audrey's grief had narrowed into a singular obsession. The question of why her friend had taken her own life rolled around her head like a loose cannonball.

At first, she'd fixated on the arrival of the "Dear Future Me" letters and the screenshot she'd sent of Ben's note.

Surely it was no coincidence that Miranda had left the house not long after she'd set eyes on them?

But when she put this theory to Marcel, he'd been adamant they'd had nothing to do with it. He said Miranda had seemed amused by the arrival of the letter, that she hadn't even mentioned the screenshot. The police had also been in touch—as a matter of course, they had contacted her and everyone Miranda had been in phone or email correspondence with in the days leading up to her death—and their lack of follow-up suggested they also deemed the screenshot of no significance.

And so Audrey had looked elsewhere, forensically combing their recent in-person conversations, WhatsApps, and voice notes for signs that something was wrong. It felt like running her fingers through bowls of sand, sifting the grains for anything she might be able to piece together into something solid, something that made sense. But every time, she came up short.

Then there were the other questions—those that existed in the shadows. Things she was ashamed to voice, even to herself.

How could she do this to the kids?

Leave them without a mother?

For Audrey, who knew firsthand what it was to lose a parent at such a tender age, what it meant for a child to be forced to carry those consequences, the deliberate nature of her death was especially painful.

She told herself that if only she could uncover the reason Miranda had done what she did—something logical and specific, a clear cause and effect—then maybe her loss would be easier to bear.

"I wonder if the baby fox will come back tonight," says Edward. "I left him one of my sausages."

Another huff from Enid.

"You're not supposed to encourage them, Daddy said."

"I want to see him on the camera again; he's funny."

"Camera?" says Audrey.

"The doorbell camera," says Enid. "Last night a fox cub came right up to the front step. But Daddy wasn't happy. He said if he poops on the mat, we'll never get rid of the stink."

As a cleaner, Audrey is acutely aware of these cameras. People install them for security, but in her experience, they're used more for everyday acts of micro-surveillance. Once, one of her clients, on checking what time she had arrived at and left the property, had complained she'd finished forty seconds early.

After one last story, she kisses the children good night and closes the door. The sun has yet to set, and its rays honey the floor. From the landing window, she glimpses the sea in the distance, oil tankers heavy on the horizon. Huntcliff, where Miranda died, is a ten-minute drive from here. Once a Roman signaling station, the cliff bookmarks a five-mile curve of beach that is home to three small towns: Saltburn, Marske, and Redcar. A popular Victorian seaside destination, Saltburn sits in Huntcliff's shadow and has a wooden pier and rusting promenade. From there the coast becomes progressively wilder, the powdery flats replaced by dunes and patches of pebble rich with ammonite fossils. Marske, the quiet middle child, sits at the apex of the curve and overlooks the most remote and isolated stretch of beach, a place locals call the Stray. Then, finally, at the opposite end of the curve, there is Redcar, famous for its concrete steps down to the sea, garish arcades, slot machines, and tangy lemon sorbet—so-called lemon tops—that crowns its ice cream.

Saltburn, where Audrey lives, is the most isolated of the three. An outpost where everyone knew everyone else's business, often before you knew it yourself, the locals had a love-hate relationship with the tourists who were the only thing keeping the place afloat. Audrey thought of the layout of roads and streets as a trawler net laid flat, one in which she and the rest of the community were flipping and flapping next to one another like cod.

Downstairs, Audrey finds Treacle, the family cavapoo, flopped on the rug. Bored and listless, she has had neither enough company nor exercise of late. Audrey makes a mental note to ask Ned if he can help out until the family finds its feet. He could take Treacle with him to the surf shop. That way, the pooch would have regular company and access to her favorite running ground, the beach.

In the kitchen she scans the open-plan living space and shudders at the mess. The flagstones resemble the bottom of a birdcage, gritty with crumbs and tiny semicircles of mud from Edward's trainers. Then there's the sofa, matted with dog hair, and the kitchen counters, spattered with desiccated baked beans and spaghetti hoops so hard they could be volcanic. Marcel and Miranda did have a regular cleaner—a robust blond called Shirley—but she was always standing them up, and even when she did turn up, Audrey had thought her work slapdash. One time, after Audrey had been especially critical of Shirley's efforts, Miranda had asked if she would like the job instead, and then in the next breath had immediately retracted the offer as they both recoiled at the idea of one friend paying another to clean the shit stains from their toilet.

But Shirley has been a no-show for the last two weeks. Telling herself that she is just helping out, that anyone would do the same, Audrey grabs a pair of rubber gloves.

Usually, at this time of night, Miranda would still be in her yoga gear, wreaking havoc on the worktops as she made dinner. The sort of person who, within hours of checking into a hotel, would know the receptionist, bellboy, and maid by name, as well as the names of their children, Miranda had been the complete opposite of Audrey in many ways: ludicrously athletic, the first to get onstage in a karaoke bar, enthusiastic about any kind of fancy dress. They'd first met in primary school and bonded, as children do, over the most arbitrary of things: the fact that they both would rather starve than eat a mouthful of custard, their mutual obsession with the film *Hocus Pocus*—and a willingness to watch it on repeat, the way each of them fell about in hysterics whenever anyone used the word "twaddle" in their presence. They were both only children, Ned having not come along until Audrey was fifteen, and within weeks of becoming pals, Miranda had suggested they pretend to be sisters. From then on, whenever a kid was mean to either of them, or if they received a scolding from a teacher, Miranda would lean in close, grab her hand, and whisper, "Sister." Gripping the table for a moment, Audrey squeezes back tears. That one word had become shorthand for so many things: it meant "Don't worry"; it meant "I'm here"; it meant "I'm on your side."

She attacks the worktops first, then vacuums and mops before grabbing a duster and polish. The barn may have been one of those wow places that gets featured in magazines, but it was not to Audrey's taste. Something about the fact that the structure had had to put aside its true nature, don a silly costume, and play a new role, made her sad. Then there was the barn's interior. The double-height ceilings, marble worktops, and exposed pine beams were too sprawling—she preferred houses with rooms and doors you could shut—but Miranda had adored every square foot of her home, had reveled in its former purpose, and her pleasure had been infectious.

Next, Audrey turns her attention to the bomb site that is the kitchen table. Before wiping it down, she sorts the piles of mail, kids' drawings, and school permission forms that have accumulated in its center. Under the fruit bowl, she unearths a pile of leaflets for Miranda's yoga classes, the timetable listing everywhere from community centers to retirement homes to a local halfway house, then squirms when she realizes they have merged with the bank and insurance admin related to her death.

She's almost finished sorting the final pile when she sees it. An envelope with the same neat capitals of her own "Dear Future Me" letter. She picks it up. Weighs it in her palm. Torn between not wanting to invade her friend's privacy and an urgent selfish need to feel close to her again.

In the weeks since Miranda died, Audrey's made all kinds of imaginary bargains about what she'd give for just five more minutes with her pal. The price she'd pay for a glimpse of her across the street, the sound of her huffing as she opened and slammed cupboards in search of some elusive utensil, the smell of her honey shampoo as she pulled you in for a goodbye hug.

The letter might be a relic, but it was something. It was more. She removes the pages carefully, spreads them flat.

Dear Miranda

Hello hello! Hi! How's it going out there in the future??

Miranda's teenage handwriting is long and thin, the looped bottoms of her y's and g's so exaggerated that they encroach on the line below and sometimes the line below that, too.

We're supposed to use this letter to "document our long-term goals" (yawn) but let's be real... you can't see or think any further than next year and... drum roll please... the REGIONAL NETBALL TRIALS (whoop whoop). If you make it onto the Northeast squad then who knows what might happen. Coach Arbor says the England scouts come and watch their matches all the time.

Audrey beams, remembering her friend's excitement. Captain of the school netball team, Miranda had been the county's star goal defense, renowned for her ability to leap in the air at just the right moment.

She thinks back to the lessons in which she, Miranda, and the rest of the class had worked on these paragraphs. They'd taken place over two weeks, an assignment set by their English teacher, Mr. Danler. Eyes twinkling, he'd handed out the lined sheets of paper while quoting Austen's advice not to underestimate the power of a well-written letter. The class had been reluctant at first, and then, as they got more into it, their pens had begun to move faster, the ink arterial as their messages spilled onto the page.

Mr. Danler had never told them that, one day when they were least expecting it, he'd return them to their older selves. But maybe that had been his plan all along.

As for the big U (university). NEWSFLASH! You're no genius. You know that, but secretly, you'd love to go. You've never told anyone this, but you've always wanted to study psychology, to understand what makes people behave in the way they do, and maybe become a counselor one day, but your teachers have made it clear there's no way José you'll have the grades (sigh).

University? Psychology? Audrey reads the first few lines again, checking that she understood them right. She'd never had any inkling that Miranda had even toyed with the notion of a degree, let alone had a particular subject she'd been interested in. It must have been a passing whim, otherwise she surely would have shared it with her.

Still, everyone says that it doesn't matter and that the real magic in life happens when you find the one thing you love that you're good at. So maybe for you netball is that one thing? Remember when you were on tour with the girls in March? In that final match, when you were out there on the court and you leaped in the air and intercepted that ball, it felt like flying. If you're reading this as a grown-up, I hope you haven't forgotten that feeling, that magic.

As it turned out, Miranda's dreams of playing competitive netball had come to naught. A bad hamstring injury just before trials had wiped her out for the rest of the season, and she hadn't made it on to the regional squad, let alone gone on to represent her country. She'd been devastated, and had spent the months after they'd left school drifting, at a loss as to what to do next. It was only when a neighbor returned from a year working as an au pair in France that Miranda found direction. She'd gotten to talking, and before long they'd helped her secure a job with a wealthy family in Cannes. To Audrey's horror, by the following summer, her friend was gone. Still plagued by her hamstring injury, Miranda eventually stumbled on an Iyengar class at a shabby little studio near where she was living in Le Cannet. The yoga had been the thing to finally heal her, and she had been so inspired by its impact that she'd decided to train as a teacher.

Down the hall, Audrey hears a key in the front door. Marcel is home.

A dermatologist with a lucrative private practice, Miranda had always liked to joke that Marcel lived his life dressed in a permanent state of smart-casual, and today is no different. He appears in the kitchen, a brown belt cinched around navy chinos, a cashmere polo shirt tucked neatly into his waist. Everything about Marcel is precise and trim—everything except his capacity to receive and show love. Audrey has always loved his easy physicality, his expansive hugs and kisses, the way the children climbed and fitted themselves onto him like marsupials.

"Sorry I'm so late." He lifts his palms to his eyes and pushes them in toward the sockets. "Thanks for holding down the fort."

"Kids are in bed. Dinner is on the side." She nods at a foil-covered plate, then holds up Miranda's letter.

"I found it on the table." She pauses. "I wanted to feel close to her again, so I started reading…"

Marcel registers the apology in her tone and holds up his hand before she can say any more.

"Audrey, it's OK."

He leaves the meal under its foil and pours a glass of Merlot. He's about to come and join her at the table, but then his phone rings. Seeing the screen, he sighs.

"I have to take this."

He heads to the study at the front of the house, turning on lights as he goes. Speaking in French, he sounds agitated. His mum had a fall and broke her hip at the start of the year. Before Miranda died, he'd been going back and forth to France regularly to make sure she was OK.

Audrey continues reading Miranda's letter. Bringing the next page to the front, she sees it is written in blue rollerball—the first part of the letter had all been black ballpoint—and starts midsentence with words that bear no relation to the previous page. She looks again, checking. There seem to be some sheets missing.

...we never know when it might be taken from us. There's a song out at the moment, it's on the radio all the time, and it talks about how we only get one shot on this earth, how it can be snatched at any time and so we need to make the most of it, to grab it with both hands. I know it's only a song, but I think there's a lot of truth to it, especially now.

It's exactly the same handwriting. Miranda's handwriting. But the second part of the letter's change in feel and content is jarring. Audrey flounders, confused. But she remembers the circumstances under which the letters were produced.

Their work on the assignment had been sandwiched around the weekend in which Ben Spellman died. Miranda would have written the first batch of pages in the days building up to the trip, and this second, more somber set after they had returned home.

She supposes her own letter would have followed the same pattern, except that she hadn't made it to the Lake District, or indeed finished the assignment. Three days into the "Dear Future Me" writing exercise she'd been hit by tonsillitis and surrendered to her bed for the next fortnight. She reads on.

I'm scared to even ask this but... do you still think of him every day? Ben. Part of me hopes you've put it behind you, another part hopes you never forget. I've realized that I wish this letter were the other way around, that you could somehow write to me from the future and tell me it was going to be OK, that one day soon I wouldn't feel like this.

Miranda had struggled to cope in the weeks and months after Ben's death. Already slim, she'd lost so much weight that her school skirt had started to evade her hips and she'd performed more atrociously than expected in her practice exams. Their romantic history meant it had hit her harder than the others.

This second part of the letter was clearly a reflection of her mindset at the time. Raw and full of pain.

But then Audrey reaches a line that makes her stop in her tracks.

I'm even more scared to ask this next question, but here goes... Has time has helped you find a way to forgive? God, I really hope so. Who knows, maybe it's come to light by now, what happened on that trip.

Audrey scrambles to make sense of the words. She reads them back, once, twice, three times.

What was she talking about? Ben's death was tragic but straightforward. He'd got caught alone in a blizzard. Hadn't he?

She reads on, hoping to find something to explain or make sense of Miranda's comments, but if anything, her words get even more bizarre.

Everyone says it was a horrible accident. That he got locked outside in the snow. But that's not true, is it?

Audrey's hand goes to her mouth.

You know. That's the hardest part. That's what makes it hard to sleep. To eat. To look people in the eye.

The cannonball that has been rolling round and round Audrey's head for weeks slows and comes to a stop. It lands with a thud against the inside of her skull. Iron against bone.

Chapter 4

It's almost midnight, and Audrey sits next to Marcel at the kitchen table, Miranda's letter spread out before them. Usually one for soft, low lighting, especially in the evenings, tonight, just as every night since Miranda died, Marcel has turned on all the available lamps and ceiling lights on the ground floor. The result is an overwhelming orangey-white glare that has them both squinting.

Audrey reaches again for the last page of Miranda's letter and traces the lines of text with her finger.

"You know." She sits back. "Is she talking about Ben? Is she saying she knows something more about how he died?"

At first, she'd puzzled over the second half of Miranda's letter by herself. But the more times she read it, the more muddled she'd become, and so she'd asked Marcel to take a look.

Marcel blinks.

"I have no idea," he says quietly. "Until now I'd only ever skim-read the first few pages. But even if I had read the whole thing, the stuff she's talking about would have meant nothing to me."

"Miranda never told you about Ben?"

He shakes his head, gets up and retrieves the plate from the countertop. As he removes the foil and sets the meal to warm in the microwave, she rereads the sections that follow.

If things had been different, he would still be alive today. You got so caught up in the fact that you needed to teach him a lesson…
But now…
I hope that when it comes to giving people a second chance, you've learned your lesson.

Was Miranda claiming Ben's death wasn't as simple as everyone thought?
Was she saying she had been involved?
"Could this be why she jumped?" says Audrey.
Because she'd been confronted by a secret she'd kept for twenty years?
Because she was overwhelmed with guilt?
"Maybe." Marcel shrugs helplessly. "I don't know."
Audrey's brain whirs.

It would be a why. Something singular and specific, and yet even thinking it jars her. It feels so unlikely.

She and Miranda had always been so open with their thoughts and feelings, right from when they were little kids, and yet, looking back, she realizes Miranda had never really talked much about Ben's death. About how it made her feel. She had tried to get her to open up, but Miranda had answered with the same platitudes bandied about by everyone at the time: that it was sad, that she couldn't believe it, that she felt bad for his parents. Audrey knows that she could have pushed her on it more—especially once Miranda started losing weight and flunking her exams—but by that point she'd been too caught up in her own glut of personal tragedy.

Another possibility occurs.

"Maybe it was just that the letter arrived at the wrong time? If

Miranda had been battling with something in her day-to-day life, then she was blindsided by this reminder of her younger self…" Her thoughts twisting in and out of one another, she trails off.

Marcel's forehead tightens, the beginning of a grimace, but then he relaxes. Offers a friendly smile.

"Maybe." The microwave pings, and he removes the plate and comes to sit with his food at the table. "It's hard to accept, believe me, I know that more than anyone. But I think the reality is, we'll never know for sure."

Audrey shakes her head. She should feel better. Reading Miranda's letter—discovering the odd things it contained—is progress, but instead she feels upended, as if she is clinging to a raft speeding downstream. She's trying to hold tight, but she is being tossed and thrown by the roaring water beneath.

She reexamines the change in ink.

The letter is definitely missing the page or pages where the handwriting transitions from black ballpoint to blue rollerball.

"You've definitely no idea where the other sheets might be?" She's already asked him this once tonight, but she can't help double-checking.

"If they aren't on the table"—he nods at the piles of stuff she's gone through meticulously—"then I think they're probably not here."

"On the morning she died," she says, "once you realized she'd driven off, where did you think she was going? What did you think was happening?"

He hesitates.

"I guess I thought she'd told me where she was off to and I hadn't heard. That maybe she'd gone out for milk, something she'd forgotten the kids needed for that day? They always remember stuff at the last minute—cupcakes for fairs, costumes, that kind of thing. Then when she wasn't back in time for the school run, I figured there must have been some issue with the traffic. So I canceled my morning appointments, took the kids myself."

"And you didn't report her missing till later?"

The police had pieced together what they could from Miranda's movements. Her car had been captured on CCTV a couple of times before she'd turned onto the more remote country lanes. The fact she'd left her phone behind meant they couldn't use that data to chart her exact route to the cliffs.

"No." He scratches at his stubble again. She sees the skin underneath is sore. "She'd only been gone a few hours when they found her, when I got the call. I hadn't reached that point."

She feels as if he's holding something back. She thinks maybe he feels guilty for not having raised the alarm sooner, that if he had, Miranda might still be here.

"What about the night before? How was she then?"

His right eyelid begins to twitch, a tiny involuntary movement he stills with his thumb.

"This last year, we've been a bit like ships in the night." He gestures to the pile of yoga leaflets. "All these extra classes. She was out late, teaching. I didn't notice her coming to bed."

"And that morning," she says, repeating yet another question she's asked him multiple times. "You're certain. When she read these," she adds, pointing to the second set of pages, "she didn't react or say anything?"

Marcel goes to reply, but then takes a breath. The air hums with the noise from the lights, and Audrey feels the buzz in the back of her teeth.

You're pushing too hard. He's exhausted. His wife's just died.

"You know what mornings are like in our house," he says eventually. His words are patient, his delivery like slow and careful footsteps. "It's chaos. No one is paying attention to anything. Everyone is just trying to get ready, get fed, and get out of the door."

You need to be more gentle. He seems OK, like he's managing to function, but he's actually fragile. You know this.

A week or so after Miranda had died, Audrey had been over, helping with the kids, and after realizing every light on the ground floor was blazing, she'd gone around turning some of them off. Marcel's face had filled with alarm; then he'd rushed over and flicked the ones she had extinguished back on. Before she'd left for the night, he'd tried to explain. "I know it sounds mad," he'd said, arms crossed tight. "But I keep thinking that maybe the police have made a mistake and that Miranda is actually out there, in the dark somewhere, lost and trying to find her way home. I need her to be able to see us, to know where to come."

"A beacon?"

He'd nodded, relieved.

"You don't think I'm crazy?"

"I do not."

Now he pokes a fork at the wrinkled sausages and crusty mashed potatoes on his plate, and Audrey remembers Edward's comment about feeding the fox. The sausage he'd left outside.

She relays this to Marcel, and he laughs, charmed by his son, then recoils at the thought of the potential mess waiting for them on the doorstep come morning.

"I'll go and get it," she says, standing up. "Just in case."

Outside, it is still warm, the night sky smeared with stars. She breathes in. In Saltburn, where she lives on the coast, the air is always rough with spray, but here inland there is only the mustardy, brassica tang of the fields of rapeseed that surround the barn. She closes her eyes. She may be a mile from the sea, but she can always feel it at her back, a black pressure against her spine, the same way the cold water pushes up against the land.

Opening her eyes, she sees the barn all lit up and, remembering

Marcel's admission, imagines Miranda stumbling through the gloom toward its orange glow, to the people waiting for her inside.

It is a comforting thought, in its own way.

She scans the ground with her phone flashlight but there is no sign of the sausage. Either Edward placed it further from the house than he'd said, or it has already been taken. She's about to come back inside when the doorbell camera catches her eye.

Marcel is scraping his meal into the waste disposal when she hurries into the kitchen.

"The morning Miranda left the house," she says. "The Ring footage. Can I see it?"

He freezes for a second, thrown by the request, then reaches for his phone. He goes to the app, looks up the date, and scrolls through the notifications until he finds it.

"The police looked at it; so did I." He goes to hand her the device, then pulls back at the last moment. "Be warned, it's more upsetting than you may think. Seeing her. Knowing what she was about to go and do."

She nods, grateful for the warning.

She hits the Play icon and the thirty-four-second recording rolls. Miranda leaving the house trips the camera's motion sensor, and so the first thing Audrey sees is a wide-angle shot of her friend's back and the sway of her long reddish-brown plait against her shoulder blades. She takes two or three steps forward, then stops. After a brief pause, she turns around and looks back at the house, as if she's forgotten something.

Or as if she's having second thoughts?

And then there she is. Gorgeous in her enormous striped pajamas and the felt Birkenstocks she likes to wear as slippers around the house. Marcel was right. Seeing her makes her feel as if she is trapped behind a pane of soundproof glass with Miranda on the other side. Audrey wants to claw at it, to shout and scream, to launch herself at it, shoulder first, in the hope the vibrating thud will catch her friend's attention, make her look up, make her think twice.

The recording is over before she knows it. Immediately, she swipes her finger across the screen, taking the video back to the beginning. Then watches it again and again.

Each time, she notices something new.

When Miranda turns toward the camera, her mouth is pressed together as if she is angry about something.

But her eyes are unfocused.

She keeps stroking her temple with the back of her palm in that way she does when she's trying not to cry.

She was definitely upset. She might have seemed OK, but she must have been putting on a front, only managing to hold it together until she was alone.

It's on her fourth viewing that Audrey clocks it.

It feels as if the raft she has been clinging to has snagged on something hidden beneath the floodwater—a branch or tree stump—and even though the deep black river continues to surge and froth around her, for a moment she is still; for a moment, she can let go.

Finally, something.

She shows the clip to Marcel.

"See?" She pauses and rewinds the footage.

He peers at the screen intently, but the clip runs through to the end, and he does not react.

She rewinds the footage again, and this time she expands the frozen image so that it zooms in on Miranda's hands.

"Look," she says, handing him the phone. The close-up shows Miranda clutching something white and rectangular. Paper. "The letter, the things she said in it. They must have been significant." She points at the screen. "The missing pages. She took them with her."

Chapter 5

The next morning, the horizon is hazy, the air in the town so muggy you can feel it in the back of your throat. As Audrey drives down the coast road, the cliff shimmers and bounces in the distance, the hunk of clay, rock, and grass like a moving, living thing crouched, ready to pounce on the still sleeping town.

She reaches Kitty's house and lets herself in to clean. A Georgian cottage with clematis around the door and a field of a back garden, the property is tucked in one of the narrow roads that lope like lugworms from the outskirts of Saltburn to the countryside beyond. It's only a few minutes from the town center, but Audrey always thinks of the cottage as a sealed-off, separate place, a vacuum in which the inhabitants do not concern themselves with the lives of others.

For once, she's looking forward to her shift. She hopes a few hours alone will help organize her thoughts, give her a chance to make sense of Miranda's letter. Before she left the barn last night, Marcel had gently pointed out that the papers Miranda had been captured with were not necessarily the missing pages—the clip was too low-res to check—and that, even if they were part of the letter, it was also very possible, given

Miranda's state of mind, that she had only been holding on to them absentmindedly, that her leaving with them in hand was not meaningful. Audrey knew he was right, that everything he said was valid, but still it didn't deter her from rising at dawn and hunching over her phone, googling everything she could about Ben Spellman and the school trip on which he'd died.

The internet had been in its infancy then, but more and more outlets were digitizing their archives, and so she'd managed to find a number of newspaper articles, some written straight after the story broke, others after the inquest had reached its conclusion. The coroner's report had also been uploaded online.

The trip had been a three-day adventure and literature program in Cumbria's Borrowdale Valley, a way for the English students to experience the beauty of Grasmere and Wordsworth country firsthand. The class had arrived at Cleasby House—a Victorian manor near Keswick that had been converted into an outdoor education center—on the Friday, and the weather had been fine.

Audrey remembered how, in the weeks building toward the trip, the teachers had talked up the manor's remote location—so inaccessible that the coach couldn't take them the whole way, and would instead drop them and their backpacks at the bottom of a track, leaving them to travel the remaining thirty minutes to the house on foot.

The cold snap had happened on the Saturday. Much worse than forecast, gale-force winds had dumped two feet of snow on the Keswick area in just three hours, and the temperature had dropped to minus ten. Plans to spend the afternoon visiting Wordsworth's cottage and ravine-scrambling had been abandoned, and the teenagers had been confined to the dining and common rooms before being sent to their sleeping quarters at 9 p.m.

Lights out was 11 p.m., at which point the two teachers and the center's leader, a Rosa McLaughlin, had testified that the house had been locked and secure. Somehow, though, Ben had gone out through a fire door with a cache of booze brought from home. He was found the next morning, frozen to death on the manor's grounds, sitting against one of the drystone walls that bordered the property. The autopsy showed his blood alcohol level was equivalent to his having consumed three-quarters of a bottle of vodka. It was thought that the fire door had blown shut in the storm, and that any of his attempts to raise help would have been drowned out by the howling winds.

One newspaper report had questioned whether Ben had been the victim of an ongoing culture of neglect at Cleasby House, and had hinted at another—unspecified—incident that had occurred at the center the day before he died. But Audrey could find no mention of this in the coroner's report or in any subsequent articles.

This aside, Ben's death had no hint of the foul play to which Miranda had alluded. What had her friend known that no one else did?

Had being confronted with those words twenty years later caused her intense distress?

Or was something else going on in her present-day life, something she kept secret from Audrey and everybody else?

Then there was the scrap from Ben she'd found hidden inside her own letter. The scrap she'd sent to Miranda the morning she killed herself.

Audrey

I need to talk to you about something important. It's too complicated to explain here. Please come meet me tonight 8pm at the Smugglers' Church and I'll tell you everything.

Ben

Had Miranda somehow understood the significance of Ben's request in a way that Audrey didn't?

The note was strange for a number of reasons—mainly because back then Audrey thought Ben, like all boys, didn't know she existed. He might have been going out with her best friend, but even before they split, he'd barely looked at her, never mind engaged her in conversation. She can at least guess as to how the note ended up in her letter. They'd composed their pieces over a number of different lessons, and after each session they'd had to fold their pages in progress inside an open envelope. Ben must have put the note there when she wasn't looking, presuming she would see it when the teacher handed back their work to continue the next day. But then tonsillitis had struck, and Audrey had not been at school then or the following week, when the assignment reached its conclusion, and so the teacher must have sealed her unfinished letter into the envelope—and with it, the note—where it had remained until now.

As for the place he'd asked to meet...

Smugglers' Church was nothing but a spire in the middle of a grave-yard overlooking the beach, the rest of the structure having been bull-dozed back in the 1950s. Audrey wonders what would have happened if she'd got the note when she was supposed to, if she'd gone to meet him. At that time she'd yet to be kissed, let alone had a boyfriend, something the other kids—boys especially—had thought freakish. She'd always thought Ben sweet and kind, but maybe she had him all wrong? Would he and his friends have been waiting behind one of the gravestones, ready to pull some awful prank they'd cooked up?

The imagined humiliation yanks her from her memories and pulls her back to the present. Even now, as a grown woman, it makes her face hot with shame.

She is hanging up her coat when she hears footsteps.

"Audrey?"

Kitty.

Pristine in one of the oversize men's shirts and pinstripe trousers she likes to wear, everything about Kitty is high fashion, from the blunt fringe that sits halfway down her forehead to the geometric blocks of silver in her ears. Once, while spring-cleaning the cupboards in her study, Audrey had stumbled upon a shelf of old copies of *Vogue*. Hidden behind a pile of textbooks, the magazines had been arranged in chronological order and stretched back years. A well-thumbed copy of fashion editor Grace Coddington's memoir had also been there. Audrey hadn't been able to make sense of it—it was only *Vogue*, after all—but the way the collection had been stored suggested Kitty felt it illicit somehow.

Seeing her, Audrey cringes. Kitty has been messaging her, clichéd words of condolence cloaked around her actual motive for getting in touch: wanting to know when Audrey is going to collect her dry-cleaning; even at the best of times, Audrey is notoriously flaky about dropping off and collecting their stuff. The truth was that the dirty clothes were still in a pile in her trunk. She had planned to keep fobbing Kitty off by text until she got her act together, but now, having to deal with her in person is going to make that a lot harder to pull off.

"Why are you…?" says Kitty. "I wasn't sure… Not after…" She stops and takes a breath. "It's good to have you back."

In the first few weeks after Miranda died, Audrey had canceled all her jobs. She hadn't been able to function, and besides, she'd wanted to be there for Marcel and the kids. But it hadn't taken long for her meager savings to run down, and so whether she felt ready for it or not, this week she'd gone back to business as usual. That was the reality of being a cleaner who worked for herself. If you don't work you don't get paid. Forget compassionate leave. Forget being ill. Miranda had always railed against her chosen work, urged her to get a job that matched her IQ, one with sick and holiday pay. But what she never really grasped—even after having had kids herself—was that the typical nine-to-five does not correspond with the school day, or the million weeks of holiday Ned used to have off every year. Not unless you can afford to pay for breakfast and after-school care, and the forty quid a day charged by most summer camps. She had tried it once, when Ned was eight. A low-level administrative role with an estate agent. After two months she was broke and Ned was miserable, and so she had returned to cleaning. Working for herself, she could earn more money than at the estate agent, and more importantly, she could choose her own hours. At half-term she took Ned along with her and plopped him in front of the telly. No one minded, as long as she got her work done.

"Come," says Kitty, beckoning her through to the kitchen. "Sit."

Audrey follows, but every other step Kitty glances back. Despite her polished, almost couture-like appearance, Kitty is painfully awkward around others. One of those people who couldn't even cross the road without second-guessing herself. Talking with her, Audrey always felt as if she was answering a phone call from abroad, Kitty's need to pre-vet every word that left her own mouth giving her utterances a slightly delayed feel.

In the kitchen she motions to a pile of bound documents on the counter, each one as thick as a novel.

"I'm on summer break," she says, "but I have so much work to do, and if I don't keep at it, I know I'll fall behind." Her hands flutter around her neck. "I'm reading through these PhDs while I still can."

Audrey nods.

There had been a point in time when she'd thought she and Kitty were one and the same—that the evenings and weekends she spent poring over her books put them on a par—but then she'd learned something that made her realize Kitty was operating on a whole other level. It had been January, the first day of term after Christmas break, and their tutor group had been cloistered inside thanks to torrential rain. Everyone had been chatting, comparing present hauls, when someone lamented how they hadn't done any of their homework and were now going to be in detention. That's when Kitty had told them how she'd been so worried about completing all her assignments that on Christmas Eve she'd found herself unable to sleep. So, after retrieving her exercise books from her bag, she had sat in bed and completed every single piece of homework the teachers had set for the holiday period. Then, when she'd realized there was still another hour to elapse before she was allowed to rouse her parents, she had written a five-hundred-word report on the last novel she'd finished—*David Copperfield*—in her reading journal.

She was thirteen years old.

Audrey, like the others, had thought it odd, but she hadn't paid it much mind, not until Kitty won a place at Cambridge and she didn't. Then that Christmas Eve anecdote had rocketed to the front of her brain, and there it had stayed.

It was that kind of thing that must have given her the edge. Set her apart from the likes of you.

She stops. Thoughts like this were disorienting. She'd lived alongside Kitty and some of her other classmates for years, and had only ever thought of them as they were in the present day. Since the letters, though, they've become hologram-like, flickering and switching so quickly between their teen and adult selves that it is as if she can see both versions of them at once.

Kitty stands by the marble-topped island and puts her hands down flat, the muscles in her forearms hitched high against the bone.

"I am sorry," she says, her voice wavering. "About Miranda. I know you and she were good friends."

Her emotion sets Audrey off-balance. Despite their having once been classmates, their conversations are usually perfunctory—functional exchanges about the fact the house is running low on polish, or a request to give the inside of the oven a once-over—and so this makes her throat tighten. She fastens her arms around herself, as if to soothe the ache at her core, the same question turning over and over like a heartbeat.

Why?

Why did she kill herself?

Kitty seems to register her distress.

"Maybe you've come back to work too soon," she says. "I'll make some tea, and then you should go."

Audrey knows she is, in her own clumsy way, trying to be kind. But she also knows Kitty almost certainly has an ulterior motive. Kitty doesn't like being there when she cleans, and if she had realized Audrey was coming today she would have made sure to be out. It wasn't unusual. Most people preferred a "The Elves and the Shoemaker" style of cleaner. Someone who pulled the clogged hair from the drain and mopped the sticky stains, then was gone by the time you got home.

"Tea would be good," says Audrey eventually.

Kitty sets the kettle to boil and searches for mugs in a cupboard.

"Jago mentioned you did some extra hours?" she says brightly. "Few weeks back." The question is most probably innocuous small talk; still, Audrey is careful with her answer. She isn't sure how much Kitty knows about the party, and while she doesn't particularly like Jago, she doesn't want to cause trouble.

"He was worried about keeping on top of things while you were away." Audrey thinks of the used condom she'd found in the downstairs bathroom. "Didn't want you to come home to a mess."

Kitty reappears from behind the cupboard door, and Audrey sees her face does not match the chirp in her voice, but if Kitty suspects Audrey is covering for her husband, she does not say it.

Audrey notices a stack of mail on the table.

"Did you get your letter—the one we wrote at school?"

The question seems to leave her mouth of its own volition. Audrey hadn't planned on talking to Kitty about the letters, now or ever—in fact, she usually goes out of her way to avoid any reference to their teenage years—but she is so out of sorts and her need to change the subject overrides all that.

Kitty fiddles with the blunt line of her fringe but doesn't answer.

"Remember Ben Spellman?" says Audrey.

"Of course." Kitty frowns, flattening the hair against her forehead, thrown by yet another change of tack.

"Miranda. In her letter, she talked about Ben…" Audrey hesitates, not sure how to phrase her next question. "The trip where he died. Did you ever hear any rumors that things weren't as they seemed?"

Kitty takes a no-nonsense breath in, pulls herself up tall.

"He got drunk and went outside in a snowstorm. Fell asleep and froze to death." Her summary is the humdrum drawl of someone who considers the whole thing ancient history. "Why?"

"Miranda. She seemed to think his death might not have happened the way everyone thought."

Kitty smiles kindly. "We wrote those things when we were kids. Everything was exaggerated, everything was a drama."

Audrey disagrees, but she has no desire to argue. She points to the bound pile of doctorates. She finds essays and dissertations in Kitty's study sometimes when she's dusting, and when she does, she has to stop herself from poring over them. She'd once lost half an hour to ten glorious pages a student had written on the connection between red lipstick and the suffragette movement.

"Any good?"

Kitty holds out her hand, tilts it this way and that. "Some show promise, but most are just trotting out the same old theories." She picks one from the top of the pile. "They're supposed to be historians, but they're allergic to primary sources. I'm like a broken record in tutorials."

She goes silent then, fiddles with her earrings. When her eyes flit to the hall, Audrey understands this is her cue to leave.

"I'll be back to normal next week for sure," says Audrey, gathering her things.

She wonders if Kitty is still going to pay her for today. She looks to the spot next to the fruit bowl, where they usually leave her cash, hoping it will act as a prompt, but Kitty is already bumbling back down the hall, ready to see her out.

When they get to the front door, she opens it, then seems to have second thoughts and pulls it shut. Audrey is touched, and readies herself for a parting hug. Maybe she's going to pay her after all?

But then.

"I hate to hassle you, with everything you've got going on…" Kitty bites her lip. "It's just…my Gieves and Hawkes suit, I need it. A guest lecture at the Victoria & Albert Museum I've got coming up."

Audrey has no idea what a Gieves and Hawkes suit looks like, and so isn't sure if it is in among the pile in her trunk.

Kitty peers out of the door, toward Audrey's ancient purple Ford Ka.

"Totally understandable if you haven't gotten around to dropping everything off at the dry cleaners yet," she says, moving toward the vehicle. "I can just take it back from you now; it's no trouble."

On reflex Audrey shoots out her arm, blocking her way.

"No need. The clothes, they're all in the shop." Audrey knows she should tell the truth. Kitty has already given her a get-out clause, and besides, under recent circumstances she has a more than valid excuse for not having gotten around to it yet, but she can't bear the look she knows will appear on Kitty's face. "Should be ready Monday."

"Wonderful." Kitty claps her hands, and Audrey knows she doesn't believe her.

"See you next week," says Kitty cheerily, then catches herself. A frown, and Audrey knows she's fretting over whether this was the right note on which to end their meeting. When she speaks again, she changes it up, thickens her voice with compassion. "Only if you feel up to it. No pressure."

Chapter 6

It's 5 p.m. on Thursday, and Audrey and Ned are walking to his school awards night: an event to recognize students that have shone in the classroom and on the sports pitch, it rewarded excellence throughout the academic year. Ned has been tipped for both the math and biology prizes, and to mark the occasion, he's rented a charcoal suit, a pale green tie, and silver cuff links that he's polished till they gleam.

Audrey had thought he'd be uncomfortable—her brother is usually happiest in salt-ringed surf shorts and the gaudy red and yellow Hawaiian shirts he buys online—but he seems to be relishing the formal wear, and holds himself with a grace and composure that is at once all she wants to look at and also something from which she feels the need to turn away. She never knew it was possible to be so proud of someone that it caused you physical pain, that its warm mass of sunshine could reach such volume, it felt as if you were going to crack in two.

"After the ceremony," says Audrey, "I thought we could go for dinner, celebrate?"

The air is brisker than it should be for the first week of July, and as they get closer to where the school sits on the coastline, the pavement clouds with a sea fog that reaches their waist.

"Already made plans," says Ned, craning to see which of his friends are milling by the gates. "I'm going out with Eleanor and the lads."

He's spent the whole journey walking one or two steps ahead, and Audrey keeps catching flashes of the pale skin behind his ears, so stark against the rest of his ruddy surfer's tan. She knew it was just that he was excited to get to the event, but to her it had felt as if he had already started the process of breaking away—from her, from here.

Whenever she thinks ahead to the end of September, when he leaves for university, she finds it hard to breathe. It's as if she's a vessel, like one of those giant whisky bottles people use as a piggy bank. The bottle had once been full, but in recent years the coins had been emptying; now, with Ned about to move out, it feels as if there is only a handful of change left in the bottom. She fears that, once the last of the pennies has gone, she will become light and unstable, that at the slightest knock, she will topple and shatter.

"No worries," she says quickly, trying to mask her hurt. She'd booked a table at The Seaview, a fancy place that served things like crab brioche and shrimp arancini that she could not really afford. "We'll have bubbles when you get home. Toast your success."

"Wouldn't wait up," he says, but seeing her expression, he stops. "But how about tomorrow? Cheeky Buck's Fizz first thing?" The fake enthusiasm in his voice breaks her heart just a little.

Ned has always been a kind boy, but these flashes of indulgence and his careful, tender way of speaking to her, are new. It started the day Miranda died. She had been too distraught to call and tell him what had happened, but that hadn't mattered. The town had done it for her, word shifting and weaving through the streets like the starlings that cloud the end of the pier. As soon as he'd heard, he'd come straight to her, scooped her up off the floor, and held her like a toddler until she fell asleep in his arms. The role reversal had happened easily, instinctively, but when Audrey had woken up she'd felt off-kilter, like a record needle dislodged from its groove.

She takes in the sea fog swirling around her stomach and wishes it would reach high enough to cover her completely, to obscure her like a snowdrift she has to fight and thrash against to make even the smallest forward progress. At least that way, she thinks, her outside experience of the world would match her inside. Because no matter how proud she is to be here with Ned tonight, how overjoyed she is for all he has achieved, none of it can cut through her grief and the question that continues to consume her.

Why?

Why did Miranda kill herself?

One month later and still, all they had were vague assumptions: that she'd been depressed, that she'd been struggling more than anyone realized. Audrey had obsessed endlessly over the things she'd read in Miranda's letter, and the reasons she might have taken some of its pages with her to her death. The facts, as she saw them, were these:

One. As far as she knew, the letter's arrival had been the single out-of-the-ordinary thing that had happened to her friend that day, or even that month.

Two. It had contained references to an incredibly tragic event—Ben's death—and hinted that Miranda seemed privy to some information.

Three. There were pages missing.

Four. Miranda was pictured leaving the house holding sheets of paper.

The letter *had* to be significant, didn't it?

But significant enough to trigger her death?

The school building rears up in front of them, all pebble-dashed concrete and flat roofs that leak when it rains. The signage over the door has not aged well, each letter elongated by rust stains that bubble and crack. There have been a few additions to the complex in the twenty years since she was a pupil—a new dining hall and science block—and the sports hall has been renovated, but apart from that, it is still very much the late-1970s comprehensive she had once inhabited.

She looks at the masses of young people arriving with their loved ones in tow, and wonders how many of them plan to wriggle free of the trawler net and leave town now that this first part of their education is complete. To go somewhere where they can walk the streets and not recognize every second person that passes by? To no longer live blinkered from the world beyond?

After the ceremony is over, the audience leaves the hall and congregates in a courtyard for drinks. Ned peels away toward a morass of friends who ruffle his hair and knock shoulders in congratulation—as predicted, he'd stolen both the math and biology prizes—and so Audrey retreats to the quiet corridor that leads off from reception.

Stay another fifteen minutes, twenty max; then say your goodbyes.

The corridor is dark, the floor battered herringbone parquet. On one side are doorways to the headmaster's and deputy head's offices; on the other are glass cabinets crammed with trophies and walls covered with framed photos of sports teams that stretch back decades. Audrey walks slowly from one end of the corridor to the other, the haircuts and collar shapes in the photos morphing and changing over time. Halfway along the wall there is a table filled with everything from sexual-health leaflets to piles of the school's most recent newsletter. She picks up a newsletter and flicks through the thin pamphlet to the alumnae "In Memoriam" section. Miranda's obituary shares a page with that of a pupil who had attended the school in the early 1980s.

Someone appears at the end of the corridor. A rod of light falls on the person's face, and Audrey sees an older woman. She looks familiar. Probably a grandparent. Peering at an enormous silver netball shield, she has her hands clasped behind her back, her finger joints bumpy with arthritis. Slowly, she sidesteps along the corridor. She seems not to have realized Audrey is there, but as she gets near, she reaches one of her gnarled hands forward and gestures at the spread of young faces.

"Would you believe I can remember most of these kids by name?" Short, stout, and wearing a powder-blue suit pinioned just above her breasts, everything about this woman screams "staid old lady," except for what looks like a Pride flag tattoo on the underside of her wrist. "Some, I can even remember what position they played."

Audrey looks at her again, trying to place her, but before she can make the leap, the woman identifies herself.

"Mrs. Arbor. PE." She pats her chest. "Susan," she says, offering her Christian name. "And you are Audrey Hawken." She taps her closed lips, thinking. "Not one for sport, not even badminton."

Audrey laughs.

"Correct."

"I'm retired now," she says, peering at the open newsletter. "Here tonight with my granddaughter. You?"

"My brother."

She nods at the photo of Miranda.

"You're not supposed to have favorites…" She quiets. When she speaks again, it's in the same jolly inflection she used to roll out at parents' evening. "She was a gifted player, but mostly she was a great kid, a pleasure to coach."

Audrey remembers a story Miranda had told her about a match they'd played against a rival school. The other umpire had consistently and unfairly called out Miranda's team for fictitious fouls. Susan Arbor had said nothing, and the other team had won the match. Afterward, they'd been in the minibus, navigating their way out of the car park, when Susan braked and pointed out a shiny red Jeep. She told them it belonged to the biased umpire; then she angled the minibus so that it scraped the Jeep's paintwork from trunk to hood—a thick silver gash—and drove them all back to school.

"She thought so highly of you." Audrey is anticipating a warm exchange of memories, but when Susan turns to face her, she is met with a hard stare.

"In situations like these, I find it hard to believe everyone was caught unawares," Susan says coolly. "That everyone thought everything was fine."

Audrey cocks her head to one side, not sure what she's talking about.

"You were supposed to be Miranda's friend. Real friends are there for each other—real friends notice when something is wrong."

Audrey is too shocked to respond.

Her silence seems to further rile the retired coach, and Audrey thinks she is going to let rip again, maybe even scream and shout, but then she seems to run out of energy.

"No one has any time for anyone anymore."

"I was there for her," Audrey says eventually. "Miranda gave no indication she was struggling." She feels like the Jeep Susan had damaged that day after the match—as if she's had a chunk gouged out of her middle—but still, she tries to remain polite. "She seemed OK. Not just to me, but to her husband, to everyone."

Susan humphs, making it clear she does not believe her, then turns to walk away. There's something about the action—the absolute disregard it shows for everything Audrey has said—that flicks a switch.

"Actually, you have no idea what you're talking about." Her vocal cords are so taut, she speaks in a whisper.

Susan stops, considering.

When she finally turns around, Audrey sees she has that studied cavalier posture all teachers adopt when they're about to dole out an especially harsh punishment.

"Your closest friend threw herself off a cliff," she says, matter-of-factly.

"You really expect me to believe there weren't any signs in the buildup to that event?"

"There weren't—"

Susan holds out a single finger, silencing her. "No one was there for her," she says. "Same way they weren't when you were kids."

Audrey's mouth falls open. "What?" she says finally.

"After that boy died. Ben. Her boyfriend or ex-boyfriend, I can't remember which. She was a mess. Such a mess she stopped playing a sport she loved. Gave up on a future that would have made her a star." The words burst from her like overripe fruit. Sour and fermented. "I tried to persuade her to change her mind, to get her to talk to her friends about what she was going through, but she said there was no one, that she was handling it on her own."

Audrey shakes her head. "Miranda dropped out because she got injured. Her hamstring."

"Injured?" The teacher says the word lightly. "Miranda was in peak physical condition when she walked away from the netball court. Scouts were circling, looking to trial her for nationals."

Audrey wants to dismiss this as she has everything else the coach has said, but there is something about the way Susan parried her story—instant and unthinking—that she knows means the woman is telling the truth.

She tries to respond, but she feels suddenly adrift, like a ship that's slipped its rope.

Miranda voluntarily stopped playing netball?

Then lied about it?

She reels, scrambling to recalibrate.

Susan nods, then before she walks away, looks at the trophy cabinet once more, eyes running over her former glories: memories of tournaments won and lost, the hundreds of kids she can remember by name, even now. Audrey thinks it extraordinary that a person who predicated her whole career on pride—instilling it in others, in the school, in the team—can also be so expert at inducing shame.

———

Audrey says goodbye to Ned, then returns home. The sea fog has bloomed while she was inside, and the town is smothered from rooftop to pavement in dense, pearlescent cloud. It makes the water seem closer than it is, its whisper and shush a stranger trailing at her back. Despite the lack of visibility, Audrey strides forward at pace. Hyper-alert, she feels as if she has been lanced with an adrenaline shot that has launched a terrible new set of questions ricocheting around her mind.

Was Susan right? Did you let Miranda down when you were kids?
And then did you let her down again?
Were you not there when she needed you the most?

She thinks about the weeks that have elapsed since she'd read Miranda's letter. Other than looking at the doorbell footage, a quick google, and a brief conversation with Kitty, she'd done nothing.

Were you still letting her down?

After Susan had gone, Audrey had stood alone in front of the wall of team photos, trying to process their exchange, and that's when the idea had started to form.

There had been a whole class of kids there in Keswick when Ben died. A patchwork of different firsthand memories and experiences, far richer and more detailed than any coroner's report. People who might be able to make sense of what Miranda had alluded to in her letter, and why being confronted with those words twenty years later had sent her to her death. If she wanted to find out what happened, she could go and talk to them, ask them what they knew.

It wasn't as if they were hard to find. She brushed shoulders with most of these people every day; the problem was, she usually went out of her way to avoid eye contact, never mind conversation. Asking them about their memories would require her to stop being invisible and leave her open to questions about who she was, what she'd done with her life.

To invite comment.

Judgment.

The real issue wasn't whether or not she *should* go and ask them questions, but whether she *could*.

At the house, she stands on the front step, key in the lock. Number 25 Brunswick Road has been home all her life. A three-bed terrace on a quiet road, five minutes' walk from the beach. When her mum died, there had still been a good chunk left on the mortgage—her parents had been more into overdrafts than savings accounts, and so the property had been her only inheritance—but over the years she has chipped away at the payments, and now she and Ned own it outright. Once crammed with people and stuff, it became even more chaotic after her parents were gone: the ancient washing machine clattering the wall as it finished its spin cycle, the windows misted with condensation, there was never any loo roll, and the counters were always awash with orange peel and knives sticky with jam.

She goes inside and launches herself up the narrow stairs to the spare room and its shoeboxes of photos and certificates. If she is going to do this, then the first thing she needs to figure out is exactly who was there on the trip. She can only remember a handful of names, but if she can find the class portrait from lower sixth, then she'll have a definitive and ready-made list of people.

She rarely comes in this room, even to clean, and the shelves are filmed with dust, the air stale. She pulls the first box down onto the floor, tips out the contents, and starts filtering the larger-format school photos, but is soon distracted by images of her parents.

Marilyn and Arthur Hawken had been a May-September romance, Marilyn having only just turned twenty-three when she met and married forty-two-year-old Arthur. Arthur had been a welder and, before he met Marilyn, had worked away on jobs that took him from Retford to Abu Dhabi. The combination of shift work and living in digs had made it impossible to settle down, but when Marilyn came along, everything changed. After they married, he made sure to only take work close to home. It was less profitable, but he didn't care. They had ten great years together before COPD reared its head. The price you pay for prolonged exposure to welding fumes. The disease was slow and cruel, and toward the end had left her father literally gasping for air.

Audrey picks out a picture from the family's first and only holiday abroad, her parents sunburnt in a Greek bar, raising a toast with comically large glasses of white wine. In another it is winter, and she is a snotty-nosed toddler, her father kneeling next to her in the slush. Audrey's favorite is the one of her parents at a fancy dress party, her mum a pirate, in gold earrings and frilled white shirt, her dad a parrot, in cardboard wings and glued-on feathers. Locked in a smooch, her dad had held up one of his wings so that it obscured the bottom half of their faces, a comic attempt at lovers' privacy.

Marilyn had fallen pregnant for the second time at forty-one. She'd told anyone who'd listen that Ned had been a late but lovely surprise. But in the morphine haze of palliative care, she'd confessed to Audrey that she'd let her contraception lapse on purpose because she'd thought a new baby would soften the impending loss of her husband, that being needed by a tiny human again would make his being gone easier to bear.

Tenderly, Audrey replaces the photos in their container, covers them with the lid.

She searches more boxes, quicker this time, and eventually finds what she's looking for sandwiched between two certificates. Bordered by a gilt-edged cardboard frame, the picture had been taken in the assembly hall and showed the pupils arranged in three rows: the tallest kids on a bench at the back, the shortest on chairs at the front.

At the time, the school had been a healthy mix of academic ability and social class. Some kids had had doctors for parents and lived in detached houses with drives and conservatories and summer holidays in Majorcan villas; others came from fishing families who expected them to help with the dawn haul, and came to class with pollock guts on the soles of their shoes. Looking back now, though, Audrey realizes the actual divide in her year group was nothing to do with how clever you were or how much your parents earned. Rather, it was about those who wanted to leave the seaside town, to move where there was more—whether that be money, opportunity, or diversity—and those who were happy to stay.

My main wish for you is that you got to university...

Cambridge had been her chance to leave. Going there would have given her the kind of life she'd always wanted. Access to a world of learning that would let her brain vault and leap and grow. Mr. Wilson, her history teacher, had told her she was bright enough, but advised that she play it safe with her admission essay. "Keep it simple and go with the one on Elizabeth the First," he'd said. "Oxford and Cambridge, these places are old. Traditional. They don't want anyone rocking the boat." But she'd wanted to impress the director of studies, to find a way to stand out from the crowd, and so she'd ignored her teacher and submitted her other, more left-field effort instead.

More fool her.

The rejection had arrived by post in a thin brown envelope.

Even now, she had no idea if they'd rejected her because of the gamble she took, if her essay's subject matter had been too bizarre, or if it was just that it wasn't good enough—if *she* wasn't good enough. Either way, she'd blown it.

Then she dropped out.

It was the first and last time she'd taken such a risk, that she'd stepped out of line.

Never again.

Her story was that she'd become a cleaner because it was the only job she could get that would accommodate her ability to care for Ned, but sometimes she wondered if that was entirely true, if the real reason she'd bailed on her ambitions was because deep down she knew she wasn't up to it—not just at Cambridge, but anywhere.

Her finger roams across the class portrait, seeking out Miranda. She finds her in the middle of the back row, her smile gummy. Athletic and long-limbed, she had such thick brown hair that whenever she tried to contain it in a ponytail, the bobble immediately flopped under the weight. Miranda had always been the kind of pretty that didn't need to try. She'd rarely worn makeup and had favored jeans and Converse over dresses and heels, even when she met Marcel and he started taking her to flashy restaurants and parties on the Côte d'Azur.

Learning Miranda had lied to her about her injury—that she'd voluntarily walked away from a sport, and maybe even a career, she'd adored—is as shocking as it is confusing. Audrey cannot understand why she would have done such a thing, and she certainly can't fathom why her friend hadn't told her the truth? Miranda's injury had been a central part of her narrative: the whole reason she'd ended up a yoga teacher. Audrey knows she should be hurt by the lie, but her resistance to Susan's reasoning, a refusal to believe that grieving for Ben would have had such a cause and effect, blocks the feeling from forming in full. Even so, it feels as if her and Miranda's bond has sustained a devastating compound fracture.

Returning to the class photo, Audrey seeks out herself. If anything, her smile is even bigger than Miranda's, her eyes shining, shoulders back. The teenage her looks eager. Ready. Excited for what she believes is coming next.

She tries to swallow, but can't. It's as if there's something blocking her throat—a lodged air bubble that's slowly muscling its way to the surface.

She thinks again about the accusations Susan had made. She knows that figuring out why Miranda died could never make up for not having been there for her, but she also knows, in the soft marrow packed in the hollows of her bones, that it may, in some private but important way, be how she stands in her friend's corner, how she makes amends.

The pressure in her throat is getting stronger. The bubble forcing its way out. She tries to squash it down, but it is too overwhelming. She holds her breath, fighting to keep it contained, and almost has it back under control when she glances at Miranda's gummy smile, at the ponytail that droops onto her shoulders the same way Enid's does.

Surrender.

She screams.

Then she screams some more.

When she is done, she sits there trembling. The sides of her mouth are sore, her eyes water, but she feels better—different, as if she has just blasted off a rough carapace.

She returns to the rows of classmates in the portrait, scans the window of student names printed in tiny calligraphy below. Some of the kids she can recognize just by looking at them, but she is surprised at how many she had forgotten completely until now. She tucks the photo under her arm and replaces the boxes on the shelves. She decides it doesn't matter if they have nothing new to add, that if after talking with them she's left in the same limbo she is in currently. The vital thing is that she asks the questions—that she tries.

On the landing, she pauses at the doorway to Ned's room. His bed is made, the curtains open. A poster of Barron Mamiya cresting a monster wave dominates the wall, his surfboard rearing up behind him. She looks at his shelves, full of the manga comics he loves and, with a smile, she realizes, his old plastic dinosaur collection.

Her phone trills with a message from Marcel. He wants to know if she can move in for a few weeks to help with the children before and after school, just until he gets his head above water at work.

She doesn't hesitate to say yes.

The message sent, she thinks of the feeding, bathing, and bedtime routine that will occupy the days and nights that follow, and for the first time since talking with Susan Arbor, the blood ricocheting around her veins steadies. She returns to the dinosaurs on the shelf. As a toddler, Ned had tended to chew their feet and tails, and even at this distance, she can see the ancient bite marks. She wishes her brother could stay here with her forever, but she also knows there is another fiercer part of her that needs to see him escape this place, to go to university and fulfill his dream of becoming a doctor, to do that which she could not.

She goes to her room and throws some things in an overnight bag. After her scream the house feels quieter than ever, the rooms pristine. Tomorrow it will be a relief to close the front door behind her, to have somewhere else she needs to be.

Chapter 7

For Audrey's first night at the barn, she makes a bolognese. She knows that neither she or Marcel are likely to have any—their appetites have shrunk to nothing, and on the rare occasion she does eat, it's at odd hours, leaning against the worktop at 11 p.m. with a bowl of dry cereal, or a slice of ham at breakfast—but the children's appetites will more than compensate.

Checking the sauce for flavor, she tastes salt on her lips. It was the wind. All day it had buffeted and whipped the surf, suffusing the air with tiny crystals that settled across the town like dust. The cliffs had seen the worst of it, the waves throwing themselves at the ocher rock face like a tantruming child, clamoring for attention. Audrey was always aware of the sea, no matter the weather—its constant encroachment and retreat—but today it had felt brazen, as if the water were doing all it could to swallow the place whole.

Marcel yawns.

"OK if I go for a nap? I'm exhausted."

"Of course."

Still struggling with sleep, he's already warned her not to worry if she hears someone wandering around after lights out tonight. That since Miranda died, he often pads about the barn till dawn.

Audrey had asked Marcel about Susan's claims—if he knew his wife had quit netball voluntarily—but the revelation had left him just as baffled. It turned out Miranda had told her husband the same story she had told everyone else, the one she had maintained for decades.

While Audrey cooks, she looks over to the kids in the kitchen's lounge area: Enid practicing the splits on the rug, Edward poring over an old Ordnance Survey map he'd found. She's glad she can help with their care, but being here without Miranda feels like a kind of trespass. Cooking in her kitchen, washing up. Being the one to decide what in the fridge to keep and what to throw away.

She remembers the day the family moved in. Enid had been six weeks old, and although her eyebrows and lashes had yet to make an appearance, her hair had been an inch long and chick soft. Miranda had given her new baby a tour. Describing each room in turn, she had showed the child where the sun would rise and set, where she would sleep, and how, if you looked hard enough, you could see a stripe of the North Sea from the master bedroom.

"Did you know there's an entire forest under Redcar beach?" says Edward to the room. He holds the map so close it touches his nose.

"What?" says Enid. "No, there isn't."

"There is. We learned about it in school last week. A ghost forest. Every few years, when there's a really bad storm, it washes all the sand away and you can see it."

Enid scoffs and shakes her head.

Audrey's phone beeps. Another message from Kitty, pointing out that she failed to deliver the dry-cleaning last week and asking that it be returned to her at the earliest opportunity. Audrey replies with a thumbs-up emoji, then burrows in the freezer in search of garlic bread, but all she can find are stacks of batch-cooked food—lasagna, shepherd's pie, and risotto—labeled and dated in Miranda's handwriting. It's bizarre: the volume of it, the organization. She holds a Tupperware container of fish pie in the air and calls to the children.

Edward is now supine and has hooked one leg over a footstool, the map in the air. Enid is using the back of the sofa as a balance beam.

"Is this the kind of stuff you normally have for tea? I mean, would you prefer this instead of spaghetti? It's OK if you do." She knows she's pandering, but as she sees it, she should do all she can to keep them on an even keel.

It had been the same with Ned when their own mother died. He had been two, much younger than Enid and Edward; still, the day after she passed he'd cried and asked for her again and again. Audrey had not known what to do or where to go. Miranda had come over to help and suggested they take him to his favorite indoor play area. Being there among the toddler din and reek of café chicken nuggets while trying to contend with the loss of her mum had been surreal and incongruous, but it had brought Ned comfort.

Edward clocks the Tupperware she's holding, pulls a face, and sticks his finger down his throat.

"Yuck."

"Mummy said she didn't have enough time to cook anymore and so she started doing all that frozen stuff," volunteers Enid. "She says it tastes the same, but it doesn't. The potato is mushy."

Audrey thinks of the yoga leaflets she'd found on the table, about how Marcel had said that before Miranda died, they'd been like ships in the night. She ferrets one out, scans the timetable. It seemed to feature the same number of classes Miranda had always taught, but then, maybe it was out of date.

She leaves the bolognese to simmer, takes a seat at the table, and gets the class photo she'd found earlier today. After propping it against a vase, she grabs a pen and paper and tries to come up with a plan. First she copies the list of names listed below the picture. Twenty-six altogether. Then she puts a line through Miranda's, Ben's, and her own name. That leaves twenty-three people.

She lets her pen roam up and down the list. After crossing out Kitty—she didn't think she would get any more out of her than she already had—she puts an asterisk against those people she still sees around town. Social media and word of mouth should help her track down the rest.

She decides to start with Ben's best friend, Leighton Walsh. In the photo he is in the first row, arms crossed against a doughy belly that strains against his school shirt. He and Ben had made an odd couple— Ben tall and lithe with a shag of caramel hair, Leighton bumbling along beside him—but they had been inseparable, and so Audrey hopes that if anyone were to know anything more about the school trip, it would be him.

She underlines his name twice. Talking to him will be a priority.

Marcel appears in the doorway, and she starts.

"It's no good." He sounds desperate. "I can't sleep."

Stubble glitters his cheeks, and she notices how his lips are flaky and cracked.

He gets a glass of water and comes and stands behind her. "What's this?"

She explains. "I'm going to look into the stuff Miranda talked about in her letter, try and figure out if or how it might be related to what she did."

He drags his fingers across his cheek. "If you think that will bring you peace?"

"I don't know, but I want to try."

He puts a hand on her shoulders, squeezes. "Then you should."

He drifts over to the sofa area and snuggles himself in next to where Edward is lying. As soon as his face touches his son's shoulder, he closes his eyes, and finally his chest begins the slow rise and fall of slumber.

Marcel and Miranda had made a beautiful couple. Audrey had always marveled at their elegant, easy way of being around each other. They could be doing the most mundane stuff—grocery shopping or emptying the dishwasher—and it would still seem as if they were performing a kind of dance to which only they could hear the music.

She returns her attention to the list of names on her sheet. After reviewing them, she creates a second list of people who weren't in the class but who she wants to talk to all the same: Rosa McLaughlin, the trip's outdoor leader; Mr. Danler, the English teacher who had sent out their "Dear Future Me" letters; and Ben's parents.

All done, she serves the food and calls the children to the table.

Enid takes one mouthful and pushes away her plate.

"Not hungry," she says quietly.

"Maybe have some of Mum's fish pie from the freezer later?"

Enid nods.

Audrey opens her cardigan, an invitation to come and sit on her lap. Enid accepts, and once she's in position, Audrey pulls the knit around the child's shoulders like a blanket, holding her close until she says she's ready to be let go.

Chapter 8

LEIGHTON

Dear Leighton

Or should I say, dear New And Improved Leighton? Because that's what you are by now, right? Someone different, someone better... someone worthy of the one you love?

I'm hoping that by the time you read this you will have confessed your true feelings...and more importantly, that those feelings will have been reciprocated, that you two are finally a couple.

It's funny. You always thought the idea of love at first sight was fake, that it only happened in films...but I guess most people think like that, until it happens to them.

The power of love.

People say that a lot, sing about it in songs.

Again, it's one of those things that seems hokey until you experience it firsthand.

But it is powerful. So powerful it has made you determined to do something you've never felt capable of till now: to lose weight, to transform. No more oversize T-shirts, no more moob jokes. Hopefully it won't take long to slim down, to beef up, but then you've got so good at waiting these past however many years, what's a few more months?

I'm trying to imagine how it might have happened, how it all played out once you declared your feelings, but for some reason the only thing I can visualize in any detail is how shocked everyone at school would have been when they finally found out about you guys. How they probably gave you shit, made fun, but how you both couldn't care less because you were finally together, how you ignored the looks and the whispers and now spend your days walking around loved up, holding hands.

I'm already proud of the person I know you're going to become, excited for all the happiness that is waiting for you, just round the corner...

The gym is tucked around the back of the Sainsbury's in one of those parts of the town to which the tourists never venture because it is too ordinary, too prosaic. An former industrial unit, the walls are a mix of corrugated iron and brick, the protein-shake-packed fridges lit with a blue glow. Audrey approaches the guy at reception. An upright slab of bone and muscle, his abs are a ridged ladder that protrude through the front of his T-shirt. On the wall behind him is a mess of framed quotes and mantras:

OUR INTENTIONS CREATE OUR REALITY

YOU HAVE BEEN ASSIGNED THIS MOUNTAIN TO
SHOW OTHERS IT CAN BE CLIMBED

YOU ARE THE ARTIST OF YOUR OWN LIFE; DON'T
HAND THE PAINTBRUSH TO ANYONE ELSE

According to Google, Ben's best friend Leighton is the owner of this place, which means he must still live locally, although Audrey can't recall the last time she saw him around town.

Before she reaches the desk, the receptionist tips his head to one side. "Audrey?"

She clocks his name badge.

"LEIGHTON."

"That's right," she says, trying to marry up the kid from the class photo with the man standing before her.

"How're you?"

Audrey falters. She's spent the morning psyching herself to come here—rehearsing her opening line—but his changed appearance has thrown her off track.

Leighton reaches for a leaflet and tries again, like a quiz show contestant guessing at an answer.

"Are you thinking of becoming a member?" He runs a pen down the price list. "We have a number of packages—"

"No," she says, cutting him off. "I'm here about Miranda, Miranda Brévart." She stops, realizing most people will remember her by her maiden name. "Miranda Mansfield."

For a moment Leighton doesn't say anything; his face is perfectly still, like a paused video. Audrey is wondering if it's possible he didn't hear her, if there's something wrong, when he finally speaks.

"I couldn't believe it. Still can't, if I'm honest." He cradles the bottom half of his face with his hands, adopting the same expression of shocked sympathy most people display when talking about Miranda's death, but unlike them, Leighton's voice is strained and shot through with emotion. She wonders if maybe he had lost someone to suicide in the past? If Miranda's death had triggered traumatic memories? "She was a special person. I wanted to come and give you my regards at the funeral, but you were obviously overwhelmed."

"You were at the church?" Audrey is surprised, but then she had been touched by just how many locals had bothered to pay their respects.

"We were classmates." He draws himself up to his full height, pops his hands on his hips, affronted. "I wanted to say a proper goodbye." He leans forward, drops his voice. "Grief is love not wanting to let go."

Audrey flounders; then she looks at the wall behind him and realizes it must be some kind of quote. That he's trying, in his own way, to offer comfort.

She asks if they can talk privately, and after he's guided them over to a gap at the side of the desk she explains about Miranda's letter—how she'd alluded to the circumstances surrounding Ben's death not having been quite as they seemed.

"Wait," he says, resetting. "You mean those 'Dear Future Me' letters? The ones from when we were kids?"

He screws up his face, trying to connect the dots. No doubt he thought Audrey was here to invite him to some memorial service. She starts again, from the beginning, giving him time to catch up. As she talks she's aware of the heat in her face—it's embarrassing, inserting herself into someone's day like this—and is hit by the urge to make her excuses and flee, but she keeps talking, squashing the impulse down as best she can, and after a little while, she feels the heat dissipate.

She doesn't tell him about her plans to track down all of their classmates—she worries that he might think her weird, or that it might put him on his guard. Instead, she positions her interest as a just-passing-by curiosity, a way for her to soothe her grief.

"Those letters." Leighton whistles, and she can't tell if he had been pleased or disappointed with what he'd read in his own pages. "Did you know only six percent of people end up in the career they dreamed about as kids?" He reaches up and, without looking, taps a framed mantra behind him that reads:

Your dreams are your life's purpose; don't give up

"I run this place, but I'm also a motivational coach." He offers this piece of information shyly.

"Impressive," she says. "Good for you."

He nods, his cheeks pinpricking red.

She waits a beat, not wanting to undermine her compliment by coming in too fast on the one thing she actually wants to talk to him about.

"You and Ben were close," she says. "I wondered if anything Miranda said in her letter chimes with your memories of the Lakes? If there was anything out of the ordinary, something that never made it into the coroner's report?"

At the mention of Ben's name, Leighton inhales sharply. Audrey frets that she's annoyed him, that he thinks she's dishonoring his friend's memory.

"Nothing comes to mind," he says quickly. "But it was so long ago."

Audrey bites her lip. She has fretted about exactly this. Has too much time elapsed for anyone to remember anything significant? Still, she waits, hoping for more. When he doesn't elaborate, she tries a different tack.

"Miranda was vague about why they broke up. Did Ben ever tell you what happened?"

He stops, thinking back, his eyes out of focus, as he scours old memories.

"Whatever it was, he must have been at fault because he was constantly trying to win her back." He laughs, fiddles with a pamphlet on the desk. "Even on that trip. A month later, he was still begging and pleading with her to even look at him."

Hearing this detail, Audrey is hit by something she had forgotten till now. One time when she was over at Miranda's house, Ben had called for her and she had refused to come to the door. She thinks of Miranda's letter.

If things had been different, he would still be alive today. You got so caught up in the fact that you needed to teach him a lesson... But now...

I hope that when it comes to giving people a second chance, you've learned your lesson.

Was that what Miranda had been referring to? That she regretted not letting him apologize? That she wished she had given their relationship a final shot?

But then Leighton volunteers something unexpected.

"Maybe they broke up because she discovered he'd been messing around."

Audrey blinks.

Unfaithful to Miranda.

Ben?

She holds this new information up to the light, compares it against what she'd thought she knew of him and their golden-couple status.

Miranda's feelings for Ben began when they were in Year 11. At first it was surface stuff. He was gorgeous and she—like many girls—nursed a furtive attraction. But then in the lower sixth, he'd won the part of Willy Loman in the school's production of *Death of a Salesman*, and Miranda's feelings had intensified. She and Audrey had been on the props team, painting and building scenery, and so Miranda had got to observe him in rehearsal for hours at a time. He'd delivered his lines in this slightly odd way that had Miranda hypnotized, soft-spoken and stilted, as if he were picking his way along a narrow path. He'd also revealed a capacity for kindness. One of the kids from Year 8 had won the role of Happy, but in the first weeks of rehearsal had been gripped by stage fright, blushing and stuttering. Ben became his friend, laughing and joking with him during breaks, never once losing his patience—unlike their increasingly frustrated drama teacher—and eventually the boy had relaxed. On the opening night, his performance had been stellar and word-perfect.

"No," says Audrey. "That can't be true. Ben was infatuated with her."

Leighton pulls a face. "You sure about that? He *said* he was desperate to get back with Miranda, but we all say a lot of things we don't mean." Again, his eyes slip out of focus. "I'm not sure Ben was truly loyal to anyone. Even those who loved him. The whole time we were away in the Lakes, he followed Kitty around like a lapdog."

"Kitty Veigh?" Audrey says, reverting to her maiden name. She cannot remember Kitty ever having any boyfriends. She was always too busy studying.

"Weren't her parents super strict?" says Leighton. "Maybe she used that trip to make the most of being unsupervised for once. Decided to let her hair down?"

Audrey cannot reconcile this scenario with the Kitty she knew from back then. Still, she resolves to ask her about it the next time she's at her house cleaning.

"When I opened my letter, there was a note inside from Ben." She explains what it said. "He must have put it there before he went to Keswick. I'm guessing it was some kind of prank?"

Leighton looks perplexed. "Who knows? Once upon a time I would have said no, absolutely not. Ben was a good guy, the best. But that last year at school…" He stops, adjusts the nap of his T-shirt. "He surprised me, the stuff he was capable of." He shakes his head. "Maybe he just wanted to get your advice on how to get through to Miranda, though. Maybe he thought that, as her best friend, you would know what to say or do."

Audrey's eyes flutter, trying to correct course. Ben and Leighton had been the best of friends. Famously close. That had always been the accepted lore. And yet here was Leighton telling her it was not the case.

It feels as if her memories are disintegrating, the broken pieces reforming into new shapes and structures that make no sense.

"What do you mean, 'the stuff he was capable of'?" she says, needing to know more. "Bad stuff?"

Leighton shrugs, but his face is blank, lost in some moment he isn't willing to share.

She thanks him and goes to leave. She's almost at the door when he calls after her.

"I forgot to say...you ever thought about leveling up? You know, a change of career?"

Normally she'd keep moving, pretend she hadn't heard, but losing Miranda has created a rupture: access to a seam of frustration she's starting to realize has probably always been there underneath, hard and mineral. It seems to insulate her, to make her less worried about whatever the world may think of her and her failures. She turns to face him head-on.

"Why'd you ask?"

"You were one of the clever ones," he says, and it's obvious that in trying to sound more confident than he is, his words have come out louder than intended. "I always thought you were the type that could do anything they wanted." He sees her face and knows he's made a mistake, but he's in too deep now; he has to keep going. "I'm offering a special coaching package at the moment, ten sessions for five hundred quid. Help bring the true you to fruition."

Audrey gives a noncommittal nod.

"I'll think about it."

———

On Saturday morning, Audrey parks on the strip of roadside gravel; then she helps the kids out of the car while Ned gets Treacle out of the back. It is a beautiful day, the sun a fat orange yolk, the air balmy. Warsett

Hill—the route to the cliff edge—stretches up in front of them, a shallow incline awash with poppies and periwinkle. The only structure for miles is a dilapidated farmhouse halfway up the slope, its windows boarded over, the roof nothing but wooden slats and the odd lonely tile. Beyond it is Huntcliff and the North Sea.

"Pretty," says Enid, surveying the flowers.

Audrey keeps her eyes low to the ground. The thought of retracing Miranda's final steps fills her with a panic she doesn't understand. But the kids. They've been asking to see the place where she fell and hurt her head for days now, and it's become clear they're struggling to imagine it— that they need something tangible, *somewhere*, to situate their mother's last moments.

Marcel had been supposed to come, too, but when it came time to leave he'd been upstairs on a call. Speaking in French, his words had been strained and pleading—presumably something to do with his mum. She felt for him. Making sure an elderly parent was being properly cared for in France while he was undone with grief mustn't be easy. They'd waited until he was finished, the kids restless and hovering by the front door, only for him to take Audrey to one side and say he wasn't going to come after all, that he thought he might break down and frighten the children.

"You OK, Aude?" says Ned, putting the dog on the lead. "Stay in the car if it's too much."

Ned wasn't supposed to be here, but he'd arrived to collect the dog just as she was leaving, and had offered to come along for moral support.

"No," she says, taking Enid's hand. Enid carries a posy of tulips, Miranda's favorite. "I can do it." *For them*, she thinks, looking at the kids.

They begin the short hike to the Cleveland Way. A popular walking route, it hugs the top of Huntcliff and the coastline either side for miles. Audrey locks her focus to the ground. She doesn't want to look up; she can't. Besides, she already knows the crescent of beach starts below to their left, and can tell how close they are getting to the drop by the noise of the kittiwakes calling to one another. Breeding season is now in full swing, and the cliff face is dotted with chicks peeping out from nests, beaks gaping.

She understands why Marcel couldn't face coming here. She didn't want to see it either, to have to think about how Miranda must have felt that morning, to worry if she had been cold in her pajamas, to look at the meadow of flowers, the farmhouse, the sea, and think about how these were the things she would have glimpsed right before she jumped. To wonder again and again if there was anything she could have done to prevent this.

But this isn't about her; this is about Enid and Edward, and finding a way to help them grieve. If her own experience of losing her parents is anything to go by, then she knows it will most likely creep up on the children in ordinary, particular moments—when Miranda isn't there to make sure they have their favorite ice cream spoon, when no one else knows which exact parts they like to sing when "We Don't Talk About Bruno" comes on in the car, when Marcel fails to fiddle with the soft, downy backs of their necks as they cuddle in bed after a bad dream— moments that build and grow until it feels as if they are being peppered with tiny missiles all day, every day.

They reach the path, and Ned tells the kids to keep back from the wire fence that separates the Cleveland Way from the edge. Audrey feels her phone buzz in her pocket and, checking it, finds a message from Kitty complaining that she urgently needs her dry-cleaning back ASAP. Audrey knows she is at fault, but still, she grimaces. She hates being nagged, but she hates Kitty's petty needs intruding on such a personal moment more.

She turns her phone on mute and, eyes still low, notices a series of painted slate disks pinned to the grass. Some give warnings to stay clear of the drop, others contain the number for the Samaritans, and one features a message: "Just in case you've forgotten today, you are special, you are loved."

"Where did it happen?" says Enid, grinding her toe into the path's chalky white surface. "Where should I put this?"

Audrey stalls. In the last few seconds, her legs have gone soft and wobbly, as if the bones inside had dissolved.

"We don't know exactly," says Ned, "but that doesn't matter. You put it somewhere you think your mum would like."

Enid surveys the grass and the pathway. Eventually she lands on a clutch of pink bell heather, and goes and lays her posy next to it. Edward pulls out a piece of paper from his pocket—a picture he's drawn of Redcar Beach's ghost forest with his mum sitting against a leafy tree— and secures it underneath the flowers. Audrey braces herself, ready for the tears she thinks are sure to follow—but no sooner have they put down their offerings than the kids race off, chasing each other through the grass. Ned lets Treacle off the lead and launches after them, screaming and whooping, his arms stretched wide.

At school pickup the other day, Enid's teacher had taken Audrey to one side and told her that Enid seemed to be coping OK in class. "This is how children grieve," the teacher had said. "We call it puddle-jumping. One minute they will be paralyzed with sadness; the next they're laughing and playing chase. The chopping and changing is a safety mechanism that stops them from being overwhelmed." Audrey had to stop herself from asking about her own sorrow: how sometimes it felt like a surging tide she couldn't turn her back on for one second; how she was scared that if she did, it would leave her engulfed, unable to rise to the surface.

She scuffs her toes in the grass and wonders if Miranda's coming here had any significance, or if it was just the spot's notoriety—the default first and most obvious local place and method that had sprung to mind.

For the thousandth time, Audrey runs through her friend's letter in her head.

You know. That's the hardest part. That's what makes it hard to sleep. To eat. To look people in the eye.

She was doing her best to approach the classmates on her list but, Leighton aside, when it came to actually talking to people her progress was frustratingly slow. She was fast discovering there weren't enough hours in the day to do this, hold down her job and look after the kids. Increasingly frazzled, she frequently skipped lunch, did the online grocery shopping while sitting on the toilet, and had discovered the joys of dry shampoo. Still, she was doing everything she could to keep her foot on the pedal and had made some inroads with her other, smaller list of names. Mr. Danler and Ben's parents had yet to bear fruit, but she was pretty confident she'd located Rosa McLaughlin, the center leader from Cleasby House, on LinkedIn. She was now a senior broker at the Kensington branch of Savills. Audrey had sent her a message asking to talk.

A man in hiking boots approaches. His beard and hair are yellowy-white, his eyes peacock blue.

He notices the posy and stops.

"My friend," says Audrey. "She died here. Few weeks ago."

He offers his hand.

"Ivan Kirby. Retired coastguard. I walk this stretch of the path every day. Keep an eye out for anyone looking like they might need a friendly ear." He motions to the Thermos in his backpack. "Or a cup of tea." He stops, distracted by something over Audrey's shoulder. "Tell them to give that place a wide berth." She turns to see that Ned and the kids have wandered close to the farmhouse and are doing cartwheels in the grass. "Coulby Farm. Whole place is rotten. Ceilings coming through, walls falling over."

He kneels down, brushes samphire from one of the slate disks.

"You make these signs?" says Audrey.

"When I was a coastguard, I used to get called to deal with what happened afterward." He waves at the cliff face. "Now, I make it my mission to not let it get to that stage." He stands up, looks from her to the children's memorial. "That morning. I'm sorry I wasn't here."

He goes on his way, and Audrey is left alone. She closes her eyes, and for a few minutes, she lets herself imagine Miranda making her way up Warsett Hill toward the cliff. When she reaches the edge, Audrey opens her eyes, and for the first time she looks out to sea.

Chapter 9

MELVYN

.

Dear future Melvyn

Our teacher has given us two weeks to complete this assignment and won't say when he's going to return these letters, but it doesn't take a genius to figure out he'll hand them over at the end of upper sixth, just before we all leave for uni or whatever. That means when you open this envelope you will have just finished your A levels and be keeping everything crossed you've done enough to get the grades to go to Newcastle, to follow in Dad's footsteps.

So I suppose that also means you'll be getting ready to leave home, to leave here...to go somewhere you can meet new people, maybe even make some friends?

Jeez, why does even just writing that down fill me with terror?

OK, look. I know you're worried about how you'll cope. You've always been shy, more comfortable in a blind on a nature reserve than in a crowded room, but (unsurprisingly) just recently it's gotten so much worse. You're self-conscious about how you look, your weight (although that's changing now, without you apparently even having to try…) but especially your skin. Please God let that new acne medication work! But I tell you something: getting away from this school and the people in it, especially certain individuals, will be good for you.

Until then, it's OK to spend all your time out at the reserve, it's OK to go back to keeping yourself at a distance, because courage, you have realized, is overrated, as is joining in, at least where this lot are concerned…

Audrey spends the morning cleaning at a bungalow in Marske, then heads to her next job, an Airbnb on the seafront. More and more of the houses and flats she works these days are holiday rentals. It's not surprising. She'd once looked up how much a two-bed cottage went for in high season and had been flabbergasted at the money involved.

Living in a tourist town was all Audrey had ever known, and yet it had always felt odd. These were the streets where she got on with the everyday—the humdrum that was grocery shopping, school runs, and smear tests—but it was also somewhere others came to as an escape. It made Audrey feel as if the front door to her house was permanently open, that the town was never really hers, a borrowed place where people saw only the things they wanted to see.

On the way to the Airbnb, she stops at the tiny bookshop behind Saltburn station. Edward has spent the last few days pining for a guide to petrified forests he found online. He'd looked for it in the school library, but to no avail, and so yesterday—after he talked about it for the thousandth time—Audrey had called the bookshop and managed to reserve a secondhand edition. She plans to surprise him with it after dinner tonight.

She's barrelling toward the door, head down, when she collides with a woman looking at her phone, coming the other way. A thump, and her phone flies out of her hand and onto the pavement.

"Shit," the woman says, retrieving it from the floor. She runs her thumb over the now cracked screen, her mouth and cheeks bunched in repressed annoyance. She's trying to work out whether it's OK to direct her anger at Audrey—she knows they're both at fault—but then she looks up. Her face goes slack as she realizes who she is, then reassembles into a tentative half smile. She shoves the damaged device into her back pocket.

"How are you holding up?" she says gently. "You OK?"

Audrey starts. This kind of thing has happened so many times in the last few weeks—strangers approaching her, often without any pre-amble, and offering the kind of concern you might expect from a close friend or neighbor—and yet it always sets her off-balance. She was well aware of how quickly word spread here; it wasn't that. It was more that she'd always thought of herself as fairly invisible, and yet these people—these strangers—knew who she was, knew who Miranda was to her, and wanted to console her.

She thanks the woman for her concern, gives her the same generic response she's developed for encounters just like these, and goes on her way.

Inside the shop, Audrey collects and pays for Edward's book, then lingers a few minutes in the nonfiction stacks. She loves this place: the ornate pilasters and corbels that frame the display window, the way the door tinkles when opened, the smattering of sand on the floor. She lands on the new Hallie Rubenhold, opens it, and speed-reads the first chapter. She doesn't *think* she knows anyone in the shop—not the bookseller at the till or any of the other browsing customers; still, she's on edge, guard up, as if what she is doing is wrong, a statement of intent that could be challenged at any moment.

And so, when the man approaches, she feels as if her worst fear has come true. She shoves the book back onto the shelf and steps back, like a shoplifter caught red-handed.

The man smiles, and Audrey goes to squeeze past him, out of the shop.

The man laughs.

"It's me, Melvyn. Melvyn Arkwright, from school."

Audrey does a double take.

The Melvyn she knew, the one in the class portrait, had been overweight and wan, with a bulb of red spots around his chin. A keen birder, he'd often arrived in class with binoculars around his neck, and was so quiet she can't remember ever having exchanged a single word with him. This guy is tanned a rich berry brown, his arms and legs dotted with insect bites. Tall and wiry, he's wearing cargo shorts and has a bottle-green fleece tied around his waist.

He grins, and she guesses he's experienced this reaction before.

"Melvyn." She cringes, newly self-conscious of the bleach-stained leggings, Crocs, and T-shirt she wears to work.

"Call me Mel," he says; then, hearing himself, he cringes. "God, that was so tacky. Sorry."

She laughs.

He'd been one of the classmates she'd been hoping to find through social media—she'd presumed he'd left town a long time ago—but looking at him now, she realizes this could be a repeat of what happened with Leighton, that he has changed so much, he could have been in Saltburn the whole time and she wouldn't have had a clue.

He seems to read her mind.

"I've been away, doing conservation in the Hebrides. I'm home for the summer. Got a project with the RSPB. The kittiwake colony."

Audrey remembers the birds' din when they'd taken the children to the cliffs, and winces.

"Where are you staying?"

"Short let in Marske." He waves vaguely in the direction of the next town along. "I was going to stay with Mum and Dad but…" He tails off. "It didn't quite work out."

He finds her gaze and holds it. After a few seconds, Audrey realizes her cheeks are burning. She looks away first, breaking the spell.

Melvyn coughs and pushes back his shoulders, changing gear. "Sorry about Miranda. She was a wonderful person."

Audrey stalls; he and Miranda hadn't been friends, but he talks as if they were.

He registers her confusion.

"I bumped into her in town a few times." He pulls a random book from a shelf, then slots it back. "We chatted in passing."

Looking closer, she realizes she can see puckered craters beneath his beard. Acne scars. If anything, they make him more attractive.

"It doesn't surprise me, seeing you here," he says, bumping his finger along a row of history spines. "I'm glad you haven't lost your love for it."

Again, Audrey blushes but, to her surprise, finds herself feeling neither uncomfortable or embarrassed. To realize someone saw her, even back then, is like being shown a beautiful photograph of herself she hadn't known existed until now.

She eyes the time. She wants to ask him about Miranda's letter and the trip, to take the opportunity to push forward and cross another name off her list. She had seen Kitty on Friday, after she'd finished cleaning, told her what Leighton had said about Ben supposedly having had a thing for her. Kitty's response had been curt. "Leighton is very much mistaken, I didn't have a boyfriend until my second year at university. Even then, Dad went nuts."

Another check of the time. If Audrey doesn't leave soon, she'll be late for her next job, and the owners need the apartment turned around before their tourists check in at 3 p.m.

"Can I get your number?"

Melvyn's mouth falls open, just a little, and now Audrey sees it is his turn to blush, the red spreading above the line of his beard. She realizes he thinks she's asking him out.

"I want to talk to you about Miranda."

"Miranda?"

The red darkens to maroon, his face an odd mix of disappointment and concern.

"I'll explain when we talk." She taps his number into her phone and starts backing toward the exit. She realizes she's already looking forward to seeing him again.

————

The next day Audrey is at Kirkleatham Museum, the local heritage center where she cleans once a week. Her only nonresidential gig, it pays ten percent less than her usual hourly rate; still, when she saw the ad for the job, she'd applied the same day. That was four years ago, and while she is under no illusion about the nature of the work—her role is the same as ever: to polish, mop, and scrub the dirt of others—she relishes every shift and often stays longer than she is supposed to, hovering by the treasures in storage at the back of the house, to which the public have no access.

Today is no different. She hasn't a second to spare at the moment—what with her work, the kids, and her inquiries into Miranda and Ben—but still, after clocking off half an hour ago, she has dawdled in the archives, peering at the objects from the museum's vast Gertrude Bell collection, only a fraction of which are on display. Bell had been an explorer, one of the first women to graduate from Lady Margaret Hall in Oxford, and had gone on to spend the rest of her life mapping the Middle East. The museum was the repository for many of her letters and diaries, as well as other prosaic—but to Audrey, more fascinating—items, like her vanity case, hat, and shoes.

This is where she is now, halfway down aisle three, in front of Gertrude Bell's brogues. She squints at the fragments of dirt still lodged in the leather, at the stains on the laces, the scuff marks on the heel, and wonders about the places Bell walked, whether she wore tights or socks, if she ever got blisters in the desert heat.

Bell fascinated Audrey. She had campaigned openly against votes for women, this despite the fact that at university, she and the other female undergraduates had been made to sit with their backs to the professor during lectures and forbidden from speaking. This despite the fact she'd had to contend with a complete lack of female toilets, other than those where she lived in college.

Public conveniences for women. It had been this niche topic that Audrey had ultimately chosen to submit for her Cambridge admission essay. In it she'd argued that having somewhere women could safely and hygienically go to the loo outside—and some distance from—the domestic space was pivotal, if not key, to the whole suffrage movement. She'd claimed that the fight for and emergence of "halting stations," as they were called then, had single-handedly done more than the vote and contraception combined to emancipate women.

She is preparing to leave when her phone beeps with a message. Looking at the screen, she sees she actually has three unread texts. This is not unusual; the signal in the archives is patchy at best. The first message is from Kitty, haranguing her yet again to pick up the dry-cleaning, the second from Ned, telling her he is going away camping with Eleanor this weekend. The third is from an unknown number. Opening it, she finds a text from Rosa McLaughlin, the outdoor leader at Cleasby House, the residential center where Ben had died.

Audrey, hi. I'm super busy closing on three sub-five-mill properties

this week and so I'll keep this brief. In short, everything I had to say about that awful weekend I said at the inquest. Contrary to some of the accusations leveled against me, I did my job and was not negligent in any way. I was scapegoated for what happened, and it caused great damage to me personally and professionally. You asked if your friend might have had something to do with Ben Spellman's death. I saw no instance of foul play involving her, but I will say that nothing about my time in the Lakes would surprise me. The one thing I learned during the three years I worked at Cleasby House, that weekend especially, is that kids are horrible, terrible human beings, especially teenagers. Their cruelty and selfishness knows no bounds. My condolences about your friend, but I have worked hard to distance myself from this incident and so I would appreciate it if you do not contact me again.

"…kids are horrible, terrible human beings."

It seemed that, even before Ben's death, Rosa had not had the best job experience.

Audrey puts the phone back in her pocket and leans against the mop, shoulders slumped. She'd been so hopeful, but Rosa had made it clear she was a dead end.

Trying to make herself feel better, she reimmerses herself in Gertrude's adventures and the explorer's brogues.

How *did* she cope during those three years at Oxford?

Did she just make sure not to drink very much? Develop an extra robust bladder? Lift her skirts and pee behind a bush when no one was looking?

Audrey had researched and written the whole thing in secret, only showing it to her teacher, Mr. Wilson. He had declared it eccentric but brilliant, then advised her to instead submit her other essay, on the safe bet that was Elizabeth I.

If only she'd listened.

She picks up her mop and bucket. The filthy water sloshes and slops against the sides. She thinks again about Rosa's brush-off. She wanted to unearth something new about Ben's death, but maybe she was kidding herself. Maybe all she was going to end up with was a collection of setbacks and people's dim, misshapen memories. She wonders if this was going to turn out like her life: stalled and unremarkable.

Slowly, she makes her way out of the stacks and toward the exit.

Chapter 10

That afternoon Marcel tells Audrey not to worry about the school run—that he's going to finish work early and pick up the kids—and so after she's finished with her last cleaning job of the day, she drives out to South Gare Lighthouse and sits on the sea wall, watching the terns. The lighthouse sits at the Redcar end of the beach, on a promontory diametrically opposite Huntcliff, the sand's other bookend. She and Miranda used to come here when they were teenagers—and sometimes even as adults—to lie in the dark and watch the light sweep again and again through the black sky. Sometimes they would talk; sometimes they would doze, lulled by the beam's constant motion. It had felt as if they were at the center of the universe, as if while they were there beneath the beacon, their problems and heartaches dissolved to nothing. Now Audrey sits in the daylight and tries to locate that same feeling, to be soothed in the same way she had once been, but within minutes she becomes overwhelmed and has to leave.

When she gets back to the barn, she discovers the table set, sunflowers in a vase, candles lit, and Marcel and the children busy in the kitchen.

"Come in, have a seat," says Edward, with all the formality of a maître'd. He takes her coat and bag and leads her to the table. Once she's sat down, he snaps out a napkin and places it on her lap with a flourish. "Relax, for tonight you are our guest."

She laughs, thankful for the light relief, and looks to Marcel for an explanation.

"We wanted to say thank you," he says, sliding a pizza out from the oven. Wearing an apron, shirtsleeves rolled up, Audrey can see floury handprints on his shoulder and the back of his thigh, and she knows it means the kids climbed up on him for a cuddle at some point when they were making the dough. "To show you how grateful we are to you for taking such good care of us these last few weeks."

"We've made your favorite," says Enid, coming over with the water jug. "Sourdough margarita!" She pours Audrey a glass, then leans in close and whispers, "It's my favorite, too."

"Wow," says Audrey. "I feel so spoiled." And she does. The gesture is lovely, but in truth, the thing she is enjoying more than the fuss and the candles is getting to see Marcel being engaged with his kids again. He's so good with them—encouraging, gentle—and they are drinking it up, bouncy and alive, like flowers turned toward the sun.

"Seriously, though," says Marcel, bringing the cooked pizzas over to the table. "We couldn't have got through this last month without you. I couldn't have got through this last month without you." He reaches for an envelope propped up against the flowers. "You spend so much time looking after all of us, we thought you deserved a bit of TLC."

"Some Pampers," says Edward, guiding a giant slice of pizza down into his mouth from above.

"Pampering, not Pampers," tuts Enid. "It's not a pack of nappies."

Edward carries on his way, unconcerned.

The envelope is stiff white card. Inside, Audrey finds a voucher for a local day spa.

"Thank you," she says, touched. "But this is unnecessary." She looks at each child in turn. "I like looking after you guys."

"Have a massage, have a facial, nap, laze around in the fluffy white bathrobe," says Marcel. "Let other people run around after you for a change."

Audrey knows the spa by reputation, but she has never been there before. Notoriously expensive, it is attached to a luxury hotel out York way. A good three-quarters of an hour by car. She knows she should feel grateful, and she does, but she also feels anxious about the thought of going there alone, as if maybe she won't know what to do, how to behave.

Marcel comes and joins them at the table. He raises his water glass in a toast.

"To Audrey." They all drink, and as he sets his glass back down, Audrey sees that his hands are shaking. He drops his head to his chest, trying to stanch the shuddering sobs now jolting his body.

"Daddy?" says Enid.

"I keep thinking it's my fault, that she wouldn't…if I hadn't…that if I didn't…"

Audrey gets up, goes and stands behind where he's sitting and wraps her arms tight around him.

"You did nothing wrong. You were a good husband. The best. Miranda adored you."

After a little while, Enid and Edward come and join her. They burrow in under Marcel's arms and rest their heads on each side of his neck. They hold him like that for a while, until the pizza has gone cold. Then, carefully, they retake their seats.

Chapter 11

BELINDA

Dear Future Belinda

The teacher has told us to imagine what we might be doing years from now, what we want to achieve. I know I shouldn't let it bother me, but the way he talked, it was like he thought wanting to leave here was a given, that none of us could write about hopes and dreams in the same breath as staying put in Saltburn. Like, who does he think he is? But, here's the thing, that's not what I think, not what I want. In fact, my main wish for you is quite the opposite. Maybe I'm a hopeless romantic (lord knows I'm a sucker for the boys who shower me with hearts and flowers), but I want you to be able to stay in this beautiful place until you are old and gray. I want you to get a job, to build a life that lets you be close to the ocean and sky and cliffs you've always known. To be able to remain close to your family. To fall in love and get married here (maybe a beach wedding, barefoot at sunset?), to raise your children here (you want at least five!). It's not just the pretty scenery (although it is gorgeous), you like living somewhere where everyone knows you and you know them, where you have roots, where you have history. It makes you feel safe and loved. Like you are part of something, like you belong. So bollocks to that teacher and bollocks to his definition of what a hope or dream should look like. As far as you're concerned, there really is no place like home...

Belinda lives in an apartment in The Zetland. A grand Italianate building, it occupies a prime seafront position on a corner overlooking the slope down to Saltburn beach. It had been one of the world's first purpose-built railway hotels, with its own private platform from which guests would disembark straight into the lobby. It had been converted to flats in the 1990s. These days, anyone wanting to get on the train has to walk a few minutes down the road.

At school Belinda had been on the netball team with Miranda, but Audrey's main memory of her is to do with boys, not sport. Belinda had never not been in a relationship. A pioneer, she had been one of the first girls to openly hold hands with a member of the opposite sex—in Year 7, to boot—and in Year 9, on Valentine's Day, an older boy she had been seeing—who drove a car—had met her at the gates with a bunch of roses.

Before the letters, Belinda had been one of those people of whom Audrey had only a dim awareness—someone she passed by all the time without registering her presence. But now…Belinda been in the queue at Sainsbury's when Audrey'd clocked her, heavily pregnant and munching a packet of Twiglets she'd yet to pay for, and it was as if she was somehow in lurid, hard-to-miss Technicolor. Audrey had waited for her at the exit and explained about the letters. Belinda had reacted with the same "you what now?" response as many of the other classmates she'd approached—a pause, followed by a slight pulling back of the head, as she tried to connect the letter's arrival with her current conversation—but Audrey was becoming practiced in her follow-up. She had developed a patter that quickly got them to a point where she could start asking useful questions.

Once Belinda understood the nature of Audrey's interest she'd been more than happy to help, and told her to come over to her flat, that it would be a rare treat to have adult conversation during the day.

As Audrey broaches the entrance to the old hotel, she passes a couple walking a trio of sausage dogs. Seeing her, they slow, and after making deliberate, prolonged eye contact, they purse their lips and blink, a silent offering of sympathy. Audrey gives a nod in thanks.

Belinda buzzes her into the communal entrance and tells her to come up to the second floor. A double buggy spattered with biscuit mush and an array of wellies litter the vast entrance hall. Audrey climbs the two flights and is welcomed on the landing by Belinda in a dressing gown and slippers. Her belly is beach-ball round, the gown's tie only just reaching across the middle, and her hair is plaited and pinned milkmaid-style up and over the top of her head.

Inside the flat, Belinda gestures at the chaos. "Welcome to the madhouse."

A TV blares, and a fetid smell, like dog food that's been too long in the dish, fills the air. Audrey scans the room and spots the source: a toddler with a swollen nappy, lumbering from sofa to sofa.

Another child, wearing a diamond tiara, tugs at Belinda's dressing gown.

"Betty won't give me a turn on the Trunki," he says, pointing at a little girl brum-brumming her way around the room on a suitcase with wheels. "It's not fair."

Belinda refuses to be drawn into the conflict and diverts the boy to a toy kitchen in the corner.

"Make me some breakfast?" she says, pointing at the wooden fruits and utensils. "I'm hungry."

Audrey takes in the room. She'd been here once as a kid, when the place was still a hotel. An overpriced lemonade in the lobby with her father—a rare bank holiday treat. The Zetland, more than anything, she thought, was a bellwether for how much the town had changed and was still changing. It had been the thing to mark Saltburn's switch from fishermen's hamlet—a place more notorious for its smuggling than the quality of its catch—to tourist destination. It had been the nucleus around which the Victorian houses were arranged, on streets named after jewels: Coral, Garnet, Ruby, Emerald, Pearl, Diamond, and Amber. It had emblematized the latest era of Airbnbs and second homes.

Audrey tries to imagine how Belinda's flat might have been configured when it was the hotel. Perhaps a four-poster where the kitchen table now stands? A stack of suitcases in place of the sofa? An armchair draped with a sable and trilby hat where a baby walker idles?

Belinda notices her looking around.

"It's less than ideal," she says, "living in a flat with small kids, but I put up with it for the view." Belinda waddles over to the side of the apartment that overlooks the parade. In the distance is Huntcliff, its steep brown shelf surrounded by the high tide. "Ever since Miranda died, though, it's the last thing I want to see." She reaches for the cord on the blinds. Drops the venetian in one dramatic whoosh. She turns to Audrey. "Miranda had kids, right?"

"Two."

"I played netball with her," Belinda says, readjusting the tie on her dressing gown, "though I only had a fraction of her talent."

She motions for Audrey to sit down, but she has counted at least four under-fives rampaging around the living room—she has no idea if they are all Belinda's or if it's some kind of playdate situation—and so she decides to make this quick and remains standing.

"After our chat in the supermarket, did you have a think? About that trip to the Lakes?"

Belinda blows out a puff of air and looks off to the side, as if she's panning her thoughts for scraps, and Audrey frets again that it was all too long ago. That she's asking people to recall memories that no longer exist.

Belinda hoists a toddler onto one hip and proceeds to feed him a banana.

"The main thing that came to mind was how they put people who wouldn't normally hang out together in pairs. It was supposed to help use make new connections." Belinda says the last word with a sneer. "Miranda and I were teammates, and so we weren't even allowed in an activity group together, never mind sharing a room."

"Who did she share a room with?" This detail has eluded her so far. She isn't sure if its lost to the annals of time or if she can't remember because Miranda had never shared it with her in the first place.

"Camille." Belinda sticks out her tongue and pulls a face.

"Camille Rea?"

A beauty pageant regular, Camille had made the local papers when, in the upper sixth, she'd made it all the way to the final of Miss Great Britain. Audrey had made contact with her, but was struggling to nail down a time for them to talk.

"Miranda said she wasn't so bad, but you know her. She liked everyone." Belinda says this with disdain, as though Miranda's affability was some kind of failing. "Who else have you spoken to—from school, I mean?"

"Melvyn Arkwright; Kitty Plaige, Veigh as she was known then…" Audrey falters, distracted by a picture on the dresser. A wedding photo.

She moves closer, wanting to be sure.

"You're married to Leighton?"

"Certainly am." She does a kind of mock curtsy. "Mrs. Belinda Walsh, that's me."

Audrey looks at the room of children through fresh eyes.

"How long have you been together?"

"Happened a few years after we left school. He'd had this massive glow-up. I hardly recognized him." She winks. "It was only a one-night thing, but I got pregnant with our eldest, and we decided to try and make a go of it." She gestures at the room, full of children and laughs. "And then I kept getting pregnant. Leighton loves babies, says he wants a football team."

"Actually," says Audrey, "he was one of the first people I spoke to about Miranda. I went by the gym."

"He didn't mention it." Belinda laughs. "Or maybe he did. I'm so tired looking after this lot, my head is like swiss cheese."

She takes the wedding photo from Audrey. Smooths her finger over her image's face and the sweep of her train, spread like a white puddle on the grass. "This feels like such a long time ago, but school feels like a bloody eternity."

"What about the residential center where you stayed? Cleasby House. There are hardly any pictures of it from back then."

"If I remember right, it had been a stately home, then converted to your standard outward-bound center," says Belinda. "That weird mix of mullioned windows and lino floors they often have. The bottom half of the house was all communal areas. A dining hall, common room, pool table, equipment room, that kind of thing. Then upstairs were the dorms. I think it was two or three to a room. Bunk beds. Communal bathrooms."

"And the gardens?" says Audrey, thinking of the place where Ben died.

"They surrounded the entire house, but we never spent any time there. Whenever we went out, it was off somewhere for a hike or a trip in the minibus."

Audrey runs through the remaining list of questions she asks everyone she talks to—Did you hear any rumors about Ben's death? Did you notice him or Miranda acting strangely that weekend? Does anything Miranda said in her letter chime with you?—but Belinda either can't remember or comes up blank. Audrey's almost done when the toddler Belinda is holding sneezes, releasing a spray of banana mush onto her dressing gown. She scrambles for a wipe.

"I'll leave you to it." Audrey gestures at her leggings and Crocs. "Work."

"There is one thing I remember about that trip to the Lakes," says Belinda, dabbing at the spattered fruit, "but it wasn't to do with Ben."

"Oh?"

"You mentioned Melvyn Arkwright." Hearing someone else say his name, Audrey is surprised to find she has to fight to keep her face neutral. "He and Miranda barely spoke at school. Well, Melvyn never spoke to anyone, full stop. But that weekend…maybe it was those new connections at work. I kept seeing them together, in the corridor or on the dorm staircase, whispering."

"Did you ask her about it—Miranda?"

"She said he was homesick, that she was making sure he was OK."

Audrey is grateful for any tidbits of information about the trip, but she's continually surprised by how much it stings to think of them all there without her, to remember how it had made her feel even more left out than she was already. She'd had tonsillitis before, and so she'd recognized the symptoms immediately. Still, she'd been so desperate to go, she'd tried to hide her illness from her mum, forcing down her toast even though her throat was raw, trying to seem bright and alert even though she'd been delirious with fever. But it had been no good. Her mum was no fool. She took one look at the yellow pustules clustered at the back of her daughter's throat and told her she wasn't going anywhere.

The toddler in the tiara tires of the toy kitchen and returns to Belinda's side.

"It's not fair," he says, eyeing the little girl on the Trunki. "Tell her to get off. It's my turn."

"Life isn't fair," says Belinda. "Know why?" The little boy shakes his head. "Some people cheat."

Audrey had planned to put the spa day voucher at the back of a drawer and then forget it was there, the thought of going alone to a hotel like that too intimidating a prospect, but Marcel was insistent she make use of it as soon as possible and had all but bullied her into booking the first available weekend.

That Saturday she turns up at the allotted time, dons a white robe, and goes to sit on one of the loungers by the pool. It's nice, in a way, but as far as she can tell, you paid a fortune to come here and yet all you really get for the privilege is to sit by or wallow in hot, bubbly water, and have to cope with complete strangers getting to see what you look like in a dressing gown. Then there is her struggle with the act of doing nothing. The last month had seen her in a state of constant forward motion—of days filled with work and the kids, and the push, push, push for answers. She'd given herself over to it completely, let it subsume her every waking thought, and so now to just…stop. She feels like a speeding car that has been plucked out of the air, not going anywhere, wheels still whirring.

She's just finished eating lunch in the spa's minimalist all-white and bamboo restaurant—a tiny slice of rye and salmon that the menu claimed was a sandwich—and is on her way to the hot stone massage Marcel had booked as part of her package, when she sees them: Kitty and Jago, and an older couple whom she quickly realizes are Kitty's parents. They must have been sitting here the whole time. Kitty, Jago, and her mum are in the same white robe and slippers as Audrey, but Kitty's dad is dressed in regular clothes. Portly in brown cords and a blue and white gingham shirt, a bald head mottled with freckles, he's aged significantly since the graduation photo in Kitty's study and has one gold incisor.

Audrey thinks of the barrage of dry-cleaning texts in her phone, the fact that she has yet to go and pick the clothes up, and wonders if she can swerve the whole situation—skulk around the edge of the room without them seeing—but before she can navigate her way through the arrangement of tables, Kitty spots her and, after a moment of bewilderment, smiles.

It would be rude not to go over.

Audrey approaches, gives a tiny wave.

Kitty and her mum and dad are all drinking beakers of sludgy green juice. Jago, on the other hand, is sipping prosecco from one of those cloudy plastic flutes they use in the spa.

"Audrey," says Kitty, her voice shrill. She grabs her dressing gown and pulls it up high to her neck. "I didn't know you came here?"

"It's my first time."

Kitty nods, and Audrey can't tell if she's glad for her or reassured her presence here is a one-off.

Two waiters appear and place a plate of salad in front of each of them.

"Jago and I are members." Kitty gestures at her parents. "It's Mum's birthday."

"I don't know what possessed you," says Kitty's dad, bringing his face in close to the meal as if checking for contaminants. "You know I don't like swimming."

"It's not swimming, Dad," says Kitty, and Audrey hears the hurt in her voice. "It's hydrotherapy."

Jago finishes his glass of prosecco and signals to the waiter for another. Kitty's dad raises his eyebrows—an almost pantomime-like signal of disapproval—and Kitty, clocking this, pulls her dressing gown even higher.

"This is my mum, Polly," says Kitty, "and my dad, Richard." She turns to her parents. "Audrey is our cleaner. Has been for the last year. We went to school together."

At this detail, Polly looks up. She's small and spindly; the toweling robe all but engulfs her childlike frame. She has a strawberry birthmark on her left cheek. It looks like a splash of blood among the white.

She considers Audrey, scans up and down, as if she's recalling some obscure fact.

"Very pleased to meet you," she says, but the words feel rote, as if they're masking some other more important thought. "You do such a beautiful job of keeping my daughter's cottage spick-and-span."

"Can she do anything to sort out that mess of a garden before your party?" says Richard. Even though the slight is clearly directed at Kitty, he makes a point of not looking at her.

"Richard," says Polly. The scold is gentle, but Audrey can feel her holding back, as if she wants to stop him from saying anything more but doesn't want to risk his ire.

Audrey knows the party he's referring to. A grand, catered affair being held to celebrate Kitty's professorship, it was scheduled for a weekend in August.

"What?" He senses an opportunity to air more grievances and takes it. "It's an embarrassment." Now he does turn to Kitty, stares her down until she looks away. "And I bet you still haven't ordered the glasses I suggested?" He lets the question hang like a threat. "If you don't give the caterers enough notice, they'll palm you off with thick-stemmed tulips." He grimaces at the imagined social faux pas. "Whole thing will be a shambles."

Kitty mouths at the air, trying to come up with a defense, when Polly puts her hand on her knee and squeezes, urging her not to bother.

"I should go," says Audrey. "My treatment."

Without looking at her, Jago raises his plastic glass in a toast.

"Enjoy."

"Happy birthday," says Audrey to Polly, before going on her way. "Hope you have a lovely day."

She beams and raises her glass, but then, as she places it back down on the table she catches her husband's eye and shrinks deeper into her giant robe.

Kitty says goodbye quietly, her face twisted into an apology for the awkward family scene Audrey has just had to witness. She looks so fragile in that robe, without her usual tailoring and blocky jewelry—a small formless thing—that Audrey has to resist the urge to grab her hand and whisk her far away from here and her father's put-downs. Instead, she offers a smile and holds Kitty's gaze, a moment of tiny solidarity. Kitty smiles back, grateful.

Chapter 12

ROBBIE

Dear Future Me

Hello big guy! How's it going? Are you smashing it? Of course you are!

I hope you're still as funny as you are now, always making jokes, always making everyone laugh, still killing it on the rugby pitch, hanging out with all your mates...yadda yadda yadda...

That's the type of thing you want me to write here, isn't it, Dad? That's the type of thing you expect me to think, to say?

You see, I know you're reading this, secretly checking it over same way you do most of the school work I hand in. One of the many special privileges that comes with being headmaster, am I right?

You're wondering how I know...

It was Mr. Knox, my Geography teacher, that let it slip. Just over a year ago now. He collected our exercise books at the end of the lesson and we went on our way, but reaching the end of the corridor I realized I'd forgotten my coat. When I came back to get it I saw the books in a pile and then I saw mine, put off to one side. He presumed I knew and when he saw me looking he winked, said something about a spot check, how he wondered what you'd make of my thoughts on soil erosion. Once I was aware of it I saw it happening all the time in every subject, realized you talked about things on our weekends together, flagged problems or achievements, that were so specific the only way you could have known about them was if you had access to the work itself. I suppose I should have been annoyed or embarrassed, that this should have been yet another thing that was part of the mind fuck that is attending the school where your Dad is the head teacher, but in truth I was happy. Chuffed that, for once, you were paying attention to me.

Truth is, I feel like you care more about this school and the kids in it than you do me. You certainly spend all your time here. Was that why you and Mum split, because you were never around? Married to the job?

Maybe that's why I act up sometimes, because I'm jealous of it, of them, of their hold over you? Because I know that if my behavior is problematic enough you will be notified, that I'll be called to your office for a chat (you call it a "talking-to"...tomato, tomato)? You see, although I make a big song and dance about me hating the fact you're the boss — whenever anyone mentions it I nod and groan the way they expect — I'm actually so so glad I'm here at this school with you, I always have been. I like seeing glimpses of you throughout the day, I like knowing you're close by. I try to make the most of our weekends — to hover at your side. I even eavesdrop on your phone calls sometimes, but they're not enough.

Truth be told, I already feel sad about leaving here, not because I'm scared of the big bad world, of where I'll end up — but because it means leaving you.

I suppose the answer is to find new ways of getting your attention, of making sure I stay on your radar. Maybe I'll get rich? Become famous? Make the papers? I'll figure it out. Until then, I like knowing *you're reading these words, combing over my mistakes, checking my marks. I think of it like a kind of long conversation, one I don't want to end...*

Audrey turns up just as Robbie's weekly "meet-the-public" session is finishing, and hangs at the back of the room, watching him in action. The headmaster's son, Robbie would smirk whenever his dad spoke in school assembly, and was one of those horrible performative bullies who'd trip someone over in the corridor in order to make his friends laugh. Now he sits at a wooden table in Saltburn's drafty Methodist Hall, opposite an old man worried about how he is going to afford his fuel bills come winter, and Audrey can tell that Robbie is not really listening. Trussed in a suit two sizes too small, his face is fixed into an expression of extreme concern.

One of the ones to leave, Robbie had made his fortune as a trader in the Square Mile before returning home to forge a career in politics. The area had always been a Labor stronghold, but in the maelstrom of Brexit, Robbie had managed to turn his seat Conservative. From what Audrey had heard on the grapevine, he was using his time in the Commons not to better the lives of his constituents, but to further his own craven ambitions.

Once the last constituent has gone, Audrey approaches and is about to introduce herself when a young woman in a navy trouser suit blocks her way.

"The session is over. You'll have to come back next week."

Ordinarily this kind of encounter would have sent Audrey scurrying for the hills, and while she feels uncomfortable and maybe even a little chastened, her need for answers is so all-consuming, she holds her ground.

"This is a personal matter," she says, trying to sound more confident than she feels. "Robbie and I were at school together."

At this, Robbie gets to his feet and comes around to her side of the table.

"It's OK," he says, dismissing the aide. He takes in Audrey's stained leggings and Crocs, and his eyes narrow. Audrey freezes, holds herself still, like a deer that senses predators nearby. At school Robbie had an uncanny—almost sharklike—ability to zero in on a person's weakness. In the blink of an eye, he could look at someone and know which bruise to press. The one thing of which they were most self-conscious or ashamed. Their fears and their secrets.

"I can guess why you're here and want to assure you I'm doing everything I can to get access to Huntcliff fenced off." There is no press around, and yet he talks as if he is giving a sound bite to a news program. "People go on about the right to roam, but it's a dangerous spot, has been since we were kids, and should be treated as such." His aide brings over something for him to sign, and he scribbles his name without breaking stride. "We've had commercial interest in redeveloping the land, replacing that rotten farmhouse, for a while." He taps his nose as if he's sharing a secret. "All TBD for now, but let's just say, if I get my way, then Saltburn might become home to a luxury private members' club."

Audrey thinks about how Huntcliff had looked when she'd set out for the school run first thing. A ruff of sea fog had clung to its middle, like a huge Tudor collar; the tide was out. On the beach, tractors had towed craft to meet the water.

"It's not about that," she says. "Well, not directly. I wanted to talk to you about those 'Dear Future Me' letters we all received." But Robbie isn't done.

"With the right investment, we could be a premium coastal destination," he continues. "The housing stock has the holy trinity—original windows, high ceilings, original features. And Huntcliff, with its views and proximity to town, it's *begging* to be gentrified."

Robbie seems to have forgotten Audrey is there. She finds his eyeline, waits for him to look at her—to see her—then tries again to explain about the letter.

"Ben's death," she says. "Miranda implies there was more to it. You ever hear or see anything about that? Did your dad ever say anything?"

At this, Robbie swallows. It's a tiny thing—nothing, really—and yet Audrey senses the mention of his father has thrown him off-balance, like a tightrope walker that has made the mistake of looking down.

"Those letters. That teacher." He tuts, full of bluster, and Audrey feels as if he's overcompensating, that this is him trying to find his footing. "I was talking to Kitty about it at a dinner party over the weekend. Surely he shouldn't have been allowed to keep them and then just spring them on us like that? Like, hello, data protection."

Robbie and Kitty were part of the same niche set. Wealthy and connected, their milieu also included a prominent local eye doctor and his wife, a famous cricketer who had spent his retirement buying up most of Staithes, and a knitwear designer who lived in London but traveled up on weekends. Like Kitty, they all lived on the outskirts of town and you never really saw any of them around—they seemed to shop and socialize elsewhere—but Audrey knew from the embossed invitations on Kitty's fridge and the notations on her desk calendar that their social life was active and involved a certain formality and type of venue entirely alien to her.

"So, Ben?" says Audrey, trying again.

Robbie reaches inside the wrist of his suit jacket and tugs each shirt-sleeve into place.

"Truth be told, I think Ben Spellman was a bit unwell." He checks to make sure no one is looking, then holds his finger against his temple and twists it this way and that. "Violent tendencies. It wasn't common knowledge, but I heard Dad talking about it on the phone once. He lashed out, hurt his best friend, of all people." He leans in, conspiratorial.

"Ran in the family, apparently." He stretches his mouth wide, baring his teeth in an expression that is part horror, part concern.

"He attacked Leighton?"

"That seemed to be the gist of it."

"I've already talked to Leighton. He never mentioned it."

Robbie shrugs. "Makes sense. It isn't really on, is it? To speak ill of the dead."

"Have you seen him recently?" she continues. "Leighton? He's changed so much. He looks like a different person."

Robbie dismisses this with a wave, as if he's batting away an insect.

"People don't change, not really. They might get better at hiding who they are, at passing themselves off as something else, but underneath they're the same. Think of everyone in our class…" He pauses, reaching for an example, then smiles when he finds one that works. "Think of Kitty. She's a chum, but my God, once a perfectionist, always a perfectionist. I remember this one time, she got her first and only ever B grade on a Classics mock. She took one look at the mark and went outside and threw up. She's the same now. That's why she's so good at her job, why she's so successful."

Audrey tries to disagree, though she knows *she* has failed to transform into a better version of herself. But before she can say anything, Robbie is looking again at her Crocs and leggings, and she realizes that he's been toying with her; he has been building up to this all along. "How about you? Is this how you thought your life was going to turn out?"

The parliamentary assistant sidles up next to him, a phone at her ear. "Your car is outside."

Robbie makes his apologies, and Audrey thanks him for his time.

"I'll get Huntcliff fenced off," he calls back on his way out of the hall. "Send in the bulldozers. You watch. I'm nothing if not a man of my word."

Chapter 13

Audrey drops the kids at school, then returns to the barn and sets about searching for a leotard Enid has only just told her she needs for a gymnastics competition tonight. She tries the obvious places first—her bedroom and the utility room—then she heads for the master suite. Enid and Edward have understandably regressed and taken to co-sleeping with their father a few times a week. As a consequence, lots of their clothes and toys have migrated there.

She walks down the hall, tidying as she goes: a rogue pair of pajama bottoms retrieved from the banister, a wet towel rescued from the bathroom floor, the LED lights around Edward's desk turned off. This, like the nine-to-three of the school day—making sure to have snacks on her at all times and hustling to have the kids first in the showers after swim class—has returned quickly, like muscle memory. It feels good to be relied on once more, soothing, like stepping into a well-worn pair of shoes.

It's not just the routine that has been a comfort. The sense of trespass she experienced that first night she came to stay has now gone. She has realized she's living a shadow version of Miranda's life. Waiting in the same car parks, small-talking with the same parents at the school gate, ironing the same uniforms. Audrey knows it's an illusion, but every time she retraces her steps or sees the world through Miranda's eyes, she feels close to her friend, and sometimes, just for a moment, she can convince herself she's still here.

Audrey has now spoken to eleven of the classmates from the picture, and it's clear that, for some, the letters have unleashed a kind of reckoning. There was Kevin Knotman, married with three kids, who on receipt of his "Dear Future Me" decided to come out and leave his wife of fifteen years. Then there was Katerina Lee, a successful barrister who, on being reminded of her childhood dreams, had quit her high-status, hard-won chambers and started applying to drama schools. There was Susan Batley, who, on reading how badly she had once wanted to travel, had promptly put the family home up for sale, bought a camper van, pulled the kids out of school, and persuaded her husband that they should spend the next year touring Europe. Talking to them, Audrey got the sense that they felt as if they had been sleepwalking through life and that the arrival of the letters had woken them. Being confronted by their forgotten selves—those parts of them that had been suffocated through necessity or pragmatism—had had a liberating effect. Despite this liberation, whenever Audrey finished her questioning, she couldn't help feeling that their newfound freedom was also tinged with sorrow: a horrible epiphany about how much time they had wasted.

In the master bedroom, she continues to tidy while she searches, harvesting a selection of Marcel's dirty shirts from the back of a chair and making the bed.

She stops to look at the framed pictures on the chest of drawers in the corner. A few show Miranda holding Enid and Edward as tiny babies in the labor ward, her hand pierced by a cannula. Two are of the kids in their most recent school pics, and another shows a much younger Marcel and a few of his fellow medical students in a bar after graduation. Marcel's arms are slung around a girl with bobbed blond hair. Audrey picks up the wedding portrait and holds it close. The couple had married at Saint-Jacques-le-Majeur in Nice, a stunning seventeenth-century baroque church, and although the weather had been unusually bad—epic rainstorms and thunder pummeling the wedding party all day—they'd taken it in their stride. Marcel had guided his bride to the reception under a huge white umbrella while she gathered her skirts up out of the deluge. In the picture they aren't looking at each other—Miranda is focused on the wet pavement, Marcel on the route ahead—but both their faces are shining, goofy, and in love. They'd met when Miranda was working as an au pair. Marcel had yet to specialize and was a junior doctor at the local hospital when Miranda came in with one of her young charges who'd broken their elbow trampolining. They'd lived in Nice for years before Miranda persuaded him to start a practice in northeast England.

Audrey was continually surprised by the hold this place had on people. Kitty, Miranda, Melvyn, Robbie: they'd all left as soon as they could, had made a success of their lives elsewhere, but eventually they'd chosen to come back. Or, she wonders, was it even a choice at all? Did being raised here mean there was something in you, a magnetic tidal pull—just like the kittiwakes—one you could only resist for so long?

Miranda had said as much, explaining her decision to come back as almost involuntary: "I know it has its problems, that not much happens, but it's the one place that makes sense to me, where I feel like I make sense." While Audrey couldn't believe Miranda wanted to leave her life in France—the beautiful gîte and pool, the weather—she wasn't going to question it. Since she'd moved away, they'd written, called, and visited each other as often as they could, but still Audrey had missed her badly. In the weeks building up to her friend's return, she'd felt happier than she had in ages.

Audrey eventually locates the leotard, sticky and stained with chocolate, under a pile of dirty washing at the foot of the bed. She decides to take it with her to work. She'll put it on an express wash and tumble-dry it while she does her shift. The client won't mind.

She's getting to her feet when she hears a trill-trill purr coming from downstairs. The landline. She sighs and heads for the living room. Until Miranda died, Audrey had been unaware the family even had this phone. Like everyone, they lived their lives on their mobiles, but Miranda's death had brought an unusual amount of activity on the relic, mainly from journalists trying to get a quote or interview from the grieving family.

Landline calls, Audrey has decided, are never good.

"Mrs. Brévart?"

"Who is this?"

"Webb Family Law." The woman is friendly. "We've been trying to contact you."

"Family law?" Audrey scrambles. Is this something to do with Miranda's will? But no, of course not. If it was about that, they'd be asking for Marcel.

"It's about the petition for divorce. The form? There are some bits of information we're missing."

Audrey notices a stray breakfast bowl on the floor by the sofa. A circle of yellow milk shallows its bottom; its sides are congealed with broken cornflakes.

"Did you say 'divorce'?"

"Yes, the petition." The woman's voice strains a little, her patience fading. "We've left you numerous messages. On your mobile?"

Audrey thinks again of how she has been experiencing a shadow version of her friend's life—how it has created the illusion of closeness in death. As she listens to the attorney breathing on the other end of the line, though, she is hit by a new and horrible thought. Had her closeness with Miranda been an illusion for much longer than she'd realized?

"Mrs. Brévart, are you there?"

Chapter 14

BEN

Stray Beach, 2003: One month before the school trip

Saturday night, a bonfire party, and instead of enjoying myself I'm running around, tending to the pile of driftwood we use for fuel and making sure everyone has a drink. I've been the same all summer, even going so far as to bring spare batteries for the music system and zip ties to connect the windbreaks people use for shelter. Miranda thinks it's a weird fad. "Next thing we know, you'll be doing canapés," she says. "Offering everyone a bit of cheese and pineapple on a stick." What she doesn't realize is how much I need this, how making sure these parties run smoothly has given me a sense of control, a fix of normality when things are anything but.

Tonight, though, any control I feel dissolves the minute I see *him* arrive.

I drop the bag of zip ties, and they scatter on the sand. Scrambling to gather them, I watch as he greets people, revealing the bottle of rum inside his coat like it's a prize. He's wearing one of those oversize T-shirts he likes, but still the fabric clings to his stomach rolls. He's reveling in the attention, but then someone presses his belly button and makes a honking sound, and he whips his coat shut.

I remind myself of his promise. Tell myself that if he was going to say anything, he would have done so by now.

But then I also know how easily things can change, how stuff can flip slowly, so slowly you hardly notice, and then, like dominoes falling, all at once.

Then there's the rum.

What if he has too much to drink, drops his guard, and tells someone what happened between us?

Miranda appears and slips her arm around my waist.

"Too many people," she groans. "So many randoms."

She's right.

The first bonfire was at the start of the school holidays, just a few friends and some beer, but word spread, and as the summer went on, more and more kids started to show. Tonight I reckon there's around thirty of us, more than ever, but the atmosphere feels forced, like people are doing daft stuff just to have a story to tell at school on Monday.

I rest my chin on the top of her head and close my eyes. Lately I've been finding it difficult to sleep. Being next to her, though, my mouth in her hair, I feel like I could drift off, like I could dream. But then I open my eyes and look at *him* wandering around with his rum, and I wonder, as I have so many times since it happened, how she'd react if he was to tell her, if she'd still want to be my girlfriend?

At the shoreline someone laughs at a joke a bit too loudly and my insides clench. Are they laughing because of me? But when I look, I see it's Robbie and some boys from the rugby team, that they're playing a game with a dead crab.

I watch as he brays and struts around the beach with his acolytes in tow. Then my gaze reverts back to *him*. He's sitting by the fire now, taking tiny sips from his bottle.

"Shall we go?" I say, taking Miranda's hand. It's too stressful being here, waiting for the other shoe to drop. "We could sit up on the dunes, or go to the Smugglers' Church; then I'll walk you home?"

She squeezes my hand, but she stays where she is, by the fire. She, like everyone, can feel the bite in the air. She knows it means we're on borrowed time, that soon it will be too wet and cold to be out here after dark. That this might be the last time we're all together. Next year we'll scatter into the diaspora of adulthood, into new lives.

"Stay a bit longer?" she says and kisses me.

We haven't talked about what will happen when we leave school, whether we'll remain together. I know she'd like to travel. I do, too, but I'm not sure I'll be able to go anywhere. Not anymore.

He catches my eye from across the bonfire. Offers a half smile and raises his bottle in a toast.

I remember the expression on his face when he realized. When the secret I have guarded so carefully crumbled. It felt like falling from some unknown height. Like you've been pushed from a building but you have no idea how long it will take for you to hit the ground.

It's after 10 p.m. when it starts with Robbie. Every time I pass by, they smirk or snicker. There is whispering. The nudging of ribs.

I tell myself I'm paranoid, that they're just being their usual dickhead selves.

But then I'm sorting one of the windbreaks, reattaching it to the iron rings that stick out of the groynes, when Robbie approaches, his minions trailing behind.

An explosion of laughter and one of the lads is pushed forward.

Jokes are made.

They say enough to make it clear they know.

They know everything.

For a moment the world seems to stop, everything is silent, frozen. I reposition my feet a little wider on the sand, to steady myself, and search the dark, checking to see if anyone has overheard.

So I was right.

He couldn't keep it to himself after all.

Robbie makes another joke.

His friends punch each other and shove their faces against their forearms, trying to muffle their laughter.

My brain feels hot, like it is pulsing against my skull. I kneel down and grab a handful of sand and throw it into Robbie's open mouth. He recoils, blinded and spluttering, just as Miranda appears.

She looks from me to Robbie and glowers.

"Psycho," says Robbie as he paws at his tongue.

Miranda drags me away to a spot near the dunes.

"What is going on with you?" she says. Miranda has an overly generous view of Robbie and his behavior. She says it must be hard to attend the school where your dad is the headmaster, that he only picks on other people because he wants to beat them to the punch. "Are you OK? Whatever it is, you can tell me."

She waits for me to reply, and when I say nothing she shakes her head and walks away.

The bonfire is almost out. I grab a piece of driftwood from the pile and am about to throw it into the dying flames when I stop. There's no point, the party is over.

My eyes droop. It would be so nice to close them, to sink into the sand, into sleep, right here, but I fight to keep them open, to watch until the last of the embers turns black, then I kick sand on the ashes, bury the thing whole.

Chapter 15

Audrey waits until the children are in bed. After pulling up a seat opposite Marcel at the kitchen table, she reaches forward and closes his laptop.

Marcel blinks, his mouth pursed, ready to object. She doesn't give him the chance.

"You were getting divorced?" She has stewed on it all day, the anger building inside her, becoming more pressurized, more dangerous. "She *kills herself* and you didn't think to mention that your marriage had broken down?"

When she'd moved in, Marcel had given her the log-in to the Ring app. After getting off the phone with the attorney, she'd once more looked up the footage of Miranda leaving the barn on the day she died. Again and again, she had paused the clip at the moment Miranda stroked her temple with the back of her palm. Had she been trying to not cry because she and Marcel had just had an argument? The stuff she'd been clutching. Were they not, in fact, pages from her letter, as she'd surmised, but divorce paperwork?

Marcel pulls back his shoulders and sits tall. Audrey thinks he is going to try and mount some kind of defense, but then at the last minute he slumps.

"How did you find out?"

"Her attorney called."

A half nod.

"I presumed she'd told you," he says in his singsong Marseillais. "That you'd never said anything before because you were being polite, but then when she died and it became clear she hadn't confided in you after all, I couldn't bring myself to say anything." He squeezes his hands into fists. "That's why I can't eat or sleep. The guilt. I feel responsible, like maybe I caused her to do what she did."

"You think?"

The words leave her mouth like a one-two punch, and she immediately regrets them.

Marcel sits there, devastated.

Audrey tempers her tone.

"Is there someone else?"

The implication annoys him and he rolls his shoulders, as if to shake it off.

"I just… We just…" He stops, resets. "It hadn't been going well for some time."

Audrey holds her silence. She doesn't believe him and he knows it.

She's angry, but it's more than that. Learning he'd kept this from her hurts deeply. Throughout the horror of the last few months, she'd been so grateful to have Marcel at her side, to know she had his back and he had hers. He had been a refuge, someone she could trust and rely on, but now it seems she'd got it all wrong.

"So letting me investigate whether it was the letter that upset her. That was what…? A helpful distraction? A decoy?" She thinks of her pursuit of her classmates. The newfound sense of purpose she's felt these last few weeks, as if she were doing something vital, something important. Has she been a fool?

"What? No, no. *Je le jure*," he says, lapsing into his native tongue. "I swear."

Audrey considers this, wary.

"I just can't believe you didn't say anything. You said yourself you feel guilty, that you think the divorce might be the reason she jumped, but you kept quiet. It feels like it was more important for you to come out of this the good guy than for people to know the truth."

Marcel doesn't respond, and they sit there in silence. Then something in him shifts.

"You can't comprehend it, can you?" he says, a new flint to his tone. "That there might have been stuff going on with Miranda, and you didn't know about it."

"What?"

"You think she told you everything? You can't even consider the possibility she might have kept some parts of her life to herself?" He shakes his head. "You obsessed over that whole netball injury thing, but there's loads you didn't know, things she didn't share."

His words are like shrapnel.

"Like what?"

"You becoming Ned's guardian, for one. She admired you greatly for everything you did to keep him out of foster care, but she also pitied you. She talked all the time about how sad she was that you missed out on a chance at a career, a family. A love life."

Hearing him talk like this is shocking. It feels as if he had been wearing a mask—a mask Audrey had thought was his face.

His voice trembles, as if he knows he's about to hurt her.

"But she also thought you used your situation as an excuse. She said that you taking on Ned wasn't the thing that took away your big chance at life. That you gave up *before* your mum died." It feels as if he has kicked her to the floor. Sinking his boot into the soft fleshy part of her stomach. "Miranda said that after Cambridge turned you down, you withdrew your UCAS form and didn't even try and get in anywhere else. You let one setback, one rejection, determine everything."

Audrey isn't sure how long she has been sitting there when Marcel reopens his laptop. His hands are shaking, his eyes wet. He takes a breath, as if to speak, but then thinks again, and after roughing his elbow against his tears he starts to tap and click at the keys.

Audrey knows she should get up, to go to bed, but the pressure that had built and grown inside her all day is gone. She feels like a deflated balloon. Limp and useless.

After their set-to, Marcel gives her a wide berth. More often than not, he leaves her to look after the children, gone from the barn at 7 a.m., not to return till eight or nine at night. She hopes it's because he regrets the things he shared—that he's ashamed—but on the rare occasions she sees him, he seems more distracted than embarrassed, as if he's forgotten their argument ever happened.

A week goes by, then another. Without him around to lean on, Audrey's grief becomes harder to keep at bay, and so she tries to lose herself in work, in the routine of caring for Enid and Edward.

She realizes the information about Miranda and Marcel's divorce is significant—that it's highly plausible it was somehow to blame for Miranda's suicide—and yet she finds she's unable to let go of her quest to get to the bottom of what had happened in the Lakes. Partly because she genuinely still thinks it a credible motivating factor—the timing was too significant; the letter arrived, and minutes later she walked of out the door—and partly because having a reason to talk to people about her friend, to ask them about her, was a way to stay connected to her, to make sense of their history, their friendship. Audrey might have to rebuild what she'd thought about Miranda—about them—from the ground up to understand her friend anew, but if she didn't, she'd be left with nothing more than a pile of ruins.

Still, her momentum has stalled. Other than Melvyn, who has agreed to meet her for brunch on Monday, and Camille, who was still proving impossible to tie down, the outstanding names were all people who no longer lived locally and who had little to zero internet presence. A boy called Ricky Larkin was the trickiest. The school eco-warrior, when it came to climate change and pollution he'd been way ahead of the game and an active member of the local branch of Surfers Against Sewage, but she could find no trace of him on any social media platform or website. As for the remaining people from her other list: she'd posted a note through the door of Ben's old cottage in Marske in the hope his mum and dad still lived there and had asked the school if they might pass on a message to Mr. Danler, the now retired English teacher, but had yet to get a response from either.

Those were her days.

As for her nights…

Sleep was more and more elusive.

The process of falling asleep was fine—she was usually unconscious within minutes—but after a few hours she would wake and that would be her till dawn: lying there thinking about Miranda and the things Marcel had said. Learning Miranda had thought of her in that way was as humiliating as it was hurtful. Worse than that, though, Marcel's revelations had compounded Audrey's already deep pain. Now, as well as being heartbroken by the loss of her friend, she also felt as if she was mourning the relationship she *thought* they'd had. The bond of which she'd always been so proud, that one thing she had valued and nurtured above all else.

After another night of insomnia Audrey gets up early, sorts out the kids, then heads over to Brunswick Road. She needs to stock up on fresh clothes and check that Ned has been keeping on top of things.

Getting out of her car, she's hit by the seaweed tang that proliferates on particularly hot summer days. Brunswick Road always gets the smell worse than anywhere else—something about the arrangement of streets—and while most of her neighbors wrinkle their nose and close windows, Audrey has no problem with it, probably because she associates it with home and the years in which she still had both parents. What it must be like, she wonders, to have grown up inland, without these constant incursions from the sea into your nose, onto your skin, into your lungs? For her, home was a literal terminus—there was her town, and then the cliffs, and then the sea—with one way in and one way out. How must it feel to live somewhere in the middle of the country, somewhere without that kind of finality? Somewhere that, when you closed your eyes and imagined the world around you, it was possible to travel outwards in any direction.

She knows her brother will still be in bed—his shift at the surf shop doesn't start till ten—and so she lets herself in quietly and creeps up the stairs. In the bathroom she's pleased to see the towels are fresh, the floor clean and loo roll stocked. Looking at herself in the mirror, she allows herself a moment of pride. Taking on the care of a two-year-old when she was only a kid herself had been overwhelming, but Audrey thinks she's done a pretty good job of raising Ned; that he is the honest, responsible person he is today in some part because of her.

She grabs some toiletries and is on her way out when she sees it: a makeup bag on the window sill, bloated with mascara and lipstick. A selection of brushes and face wipes clutter the space nearby.

Ned has company.

It's a surprise. Not that he's sexually active, but that he brought someone here without discussing it with her first.

She decides to leave before they can wake—she'll talk to him later—but as she backs on to the landing, she collides with a girl on her way out of Ned's room. Eleanor, wearing nothing but a T-shirt emblazoned with the logo of a local coffee bar—Ned had told her that as well as working at the surf shop, Eleanor is a barista. Her hair is mussed, and her face so flushed, it's hard to make out the freckles beneath.

"Hi." Eleanor tugs at the T-shirt, trying to cover her bare bottom. It would seem the pair were now far more than coworkers.

"Hello." They've never met properly; Audrey's only ever seen her in passing when she's picked up Ned from work. "I'm Audrey, Ned's sister."

Eleanor steps forward toward the bathroom.

"Sorry, I just…"

Audrey moves to let her inside, and once she hears the *shunk* of the lock being slid into place she goes to Ned's room.

He is lying on the bed in his boxers, looking at his phone.

"Audrey." He sits upright. "You didn't say you were coming over."

She clocks the various dresses and cutoff shorts on the floor, and realizes last night wasn't a one-off.

"You could have asked," she says.

Ned pushes himself upright.

"Asked?" He crosses his arms, matter-of-fact. "Aside from the fact that I'm eighteen and this is my house too, you're not my mum. You don't get to tell me what to do."

She tries to respond, but it feels as if she has been slapped. A single brutal strike.

Ned clocks her hurt and his face starts to fall, but he fights it, determined to stand his ground. This, Audrey discovers, is more hurtful—a moment she will struggle to forget.

Her phone rings and she reaches for it immediately, grateful for an excuse to remove herself from the situation.

Her gratitude fades the second she sees the caller ID.

Marcel.

After a brief hello, he gets straight to the point.

"I'm going to ask you something, and I don't want you to get offended," he says quickly. He takes a breath. "Had Miranda been helping you out? Financially, I mean?" He follows up with a quick-fire tumble of caveats. "It's OK if she was, don't worry; I'm not going to ask for the money back. I'm glad she could help. I just need to know."

"*What*?" Audrey is too insulted to play nice. "No, of course not."

"Oh." Marcel seems both relieved and disappointed. In the background, she hears the click and tap of a keyboard. "Our joint account. Something's not right." More clicking. "In the six months before she died, Miranda authorized a number of cash transfers. I didn't register them at first, because of the reference she used, but the amounts involved… There was no way they were to pay for yoga equipment."

"How much money are we talking about?"

"Ten grand."

Audrey speaks coolly. "Maybe it was something to do with the split? She could have been worried about how she'd be for money afterward." She knows this is a low blow, but she hates that Marcel's first assumption was that she'd needed a handout. She thinks of the times she scrabbled around for money to replace the boiler and fix the roof. Things might have been tight over the years, but she'd never asked Miranda for a penny.

"She would have kept the barn," says Marcel. "I would have paid maintenance. I would never have left her and the kids high and dry."

Audrey says nothing.

"I've asked the bank to look into it, but they're so hard to deal with. Even getting them to stop her debit and credit cards has been a struggle."

"I can't help you, I'm sorry."

As she hangs up, Audrey hears Eleanor turning on the shower and thinks of how Ned had spoken to her just now. His words were defiant but his delivery was deliberate, as if he was trying his best to be nice. It was the way you spoke to someone you were angry at, but who you also felt sorry for.

You let one setback, one rejection, determine everything.

She heads downstairs. In the hall she sees the mirror above the shoe rack and, remembering her earlier moment of pride at how well she'd raised her brother, feels stupid. This time she scuttles past her reflection with her head down and shoulders low.

Chapter 16

Later that day, Audrey uses her fifteen-minute window between jobs to stop at the dry cleaners. She's never seen the girl behind the counter before—she's only ever been served by an ex-hippie called Leonard with Joni Mitchell lyrics tattooed on his forearm—but whoever this is, she's struggling to locate things on the racks, and as a result a large queue has formed. Audrey feels a pinch of disappointment that Leonard isn't here. A wry, quiet man, he has a generous nature and always finds a way to make her giggle. Once, six months or so ago, unbeknown to her, Jago had left weed and a baggie of white powder in the inside pocket of a jacket she'd taken in to be cleaned. When she'd gone to collect the clothes, Leonard had taken her to one side. "I don't care what people do for fun," he said as he handed her the drugs in a separate bag. "Live and let live. But these people you work for—they need to be more careful. *You* need to be more careful. Not everyone is like me, you understand?" Audrey had been mortified, but she hadn't known how to bring it up with either Jago or Kitty. In the end, she had simply returned the jacket to Jago's wardrobe and hooked the offending bag over the coat hanger. The following week the bag was gone. Jago had never said a word.

Ten minutes later, the new girl behind the counter is still dealing with the same customer as when Audrey first walked in. Audrey thinks about leaving and coming back another day, but Kitty is already furious at the delay, and this is Audrey's only chance to collect her and Jago's things before she cleans there on Friday. She dreads to think what Kitty'll say if she turns up empty-handed again.

She hears whispering and turns around to see two young girls with goth black hair and impeccable eyeliner. One wears a delicate silver nose ring. They freeze, then look away. Audrey goes to turn back, but then one of them pipes up.

"She was your friend, wasn't she? The woman that died."

Audrey nods, touched that these young girls are about to offer their sympathies, but then the one with the nose ring leans close, whispers.

"Is it true she left a note?"

"Excuse me?" says Audrey, taken aback. She knew people gossiped about Miranda's death—that speculation was inevitable—but until now it's only ever happened out of her earshot.

Audrey tells herself they're just kids, stupid teenagers. Still, she wants to swear, to shout and rant until they understand that spouting this kind of crap is very much not OK. She settles for a glare. Holds it till they look away.

As she turns back around, she spots Belinda through the shop window, pushing a pram with a toddler inside, another child riding on a buggy board. Seeing Audrey, she slows and, after offering a smiled hello, carries on her way. Audrey watches the day-trippers and locals go by—the tourists in a quick march, on their way to bag a prime position on the beach, the locals meandering through mundane tasks—and is wondering how much longer she is going to have to wait when she sees Belinda again, coming back the other way. This time she zeros in on where Audrey stands and directs the buggy toward the door of the dry cleaners. Audrey thinks she's going to come inside, but Belinda hesitates—maybe because of the size of the queue—and after another glance at Audrey, disappears from view. It's very odd, but then, Audrey knows what it is to run errands with small children in tow—how their whims, tantrums, and sudden needs mean you march to the beat of their drum, leaving restaurants before you've eaten, abandoning the cinema halfway through a movie, waiting ages to get to the front of a queue for the merry-go-round, only to walk away at the last minute toward some other attraction.

Bored, Audrey sifts through the piles of leaflets on the counter. It's the usual stuff—an advertisement for doggy day care, Chinese takeaway menus, a bus timetable—but at the bottom she finds a stack of flyers for Miranda's yoga classes, the timetable printed on the back. It feels as if someone has taken a fist to her diaphragm. *Thump.* It's just a flyer, a small thing, but like so many small things these days, it hits Audrey harder than usual, and she swallows, trying not to cry.

She'd passed the lifeboat station on the way here, and it had set off a terrible chain of thoughts about how exactly the authorities had gone about recovering Miranda's body from the rocks. She'd presumed it was a coastguard boat, but maybe she was wrong. It's unbearable, imagining the scene. Whoever it was, she hopes they were gentle, that they cradled her friend's head as they laid her on the deck.

The queue shifts. Finally, the girl behind the counter seems to have found her groove.

Audrey looks again at the yoga flyer. Ordinarily the locations and times would mean little to her, but these days she sees the world through the filter of Miranda's death, measures things against it, past, present and future, especially the day she jumped. Marcel had said that the night before she died, Miranda had been out late teaching, but there is no class listed for that day or time. Audrey remembers what the kids had said about their mum batch-cooking so as to cope with all her extra classes, and figures the flyers must just be out of date.

Finally, she reaches the front of the line and hands over her ticket. When the girl returns promptly with the clothes sheathed in plastic, Audrey breathes a sigh of relief. But instead of disposing of the finished ticket, the girl hands it back.

"Two of the suits aren't ready."

"I handed them in ages ago."

The girl smiles blankly.

"I can only bring you what's there."

"Have they been lost?" Audrey thinks of Kitty's face when she has to tell her the news. What was it she'd said she needed for her lecture? She looks at the pile of clothes, suits and shirts in front of her. Kitty's love of masculine tailoring means Audrey can never tell which stuff is Kitty's and which is Jago's.

"I'm sure they're fine, everything's just a bit"—the girl motions to the line now snaking out of the door"—at the moment. Leonard is back in a fortnight; he should be able to help you then."

Audrey goes to protest, but the girl has already moved on. Audrey has to lean to one side as she reaches to grab the ticket from the next customer.

Chapter 17

The Stray Café is a small single-story structure named after Stray Beach, the area it presides over. The most dangerous and desolate part of the coast—a spot where the rising tide comes all the way to the dark pebbles that mark the foot of the dunes—is a dull mustardy color, and sectioned by a series of wooden groynes that stretch like fingers down to the water's edge. The groynes are there to prevent longshore drift, a type of wave that, unchecked, would slowly erode the sand, but they also act as a bizarre form of goalpost, the Stray being the spot where the sea currents prefer to toss their wares onto land. Giant clusters of jellyfish, translucent crab skeletons, and sometimes even the bloated corpses of porpoises appear there every day.

Inside the café, Audrey sits opposite Melvyn and prepares to quiz him on what he remembers about the school trip to the Lakes. She has a cleaning job to go to straight after this, but she wants him to take her seriously, to give her questions the import they deserve, and so she has come dressed in a white linen shirt, jeans and gold sandals, and has worn her hair loose. Even sitting down, she's aware of how differently she's starting to carry herself when talking to her old classmates—spine erect, chin up, gaze level—that for the first time since she was a kid, she feels full of pluck, galvanized by her need for answers.

Melvyn has been telling her about Sam, his young son from a previous relationship.

"I don't see him as much as I'd like; they live in Stoke."

"Does he come and stay with you?"

"I tend to go to them at the moment. My accommodation…" He grimaces. "It's pretty basic. But then I'm out most of the day anyway, at the colony. We're studying the impact of climate change on their breeding habits."

In cargo shorts and a navy jumper bobbled with fluff, his calves and wrists are pocked with even more insect bites than the first time she saw him. As he talks, Audrey finds herself seeking out the constellations of tiny half-moon acne scars in among his beard, and thinks of what Robbie had said—about people being the same person they were at school underneath, no matter how much they may seem to have changed in the intervening years.

Through the window she spots Ned and Eleanor walking hand in hand along the top of the dunes, Treacle tugging on the lead. Ned still takes the dog to work with him at the surf shop whenever he can. They must be on break. She knocks on the glass and waves, and in that same moment, she clocks their pinched faces, the fast, jerky way Ned is gesticulating. She realizes they are having a fight.

"My little brother," she says. "He leaves for uni in a few months. He's going to study medicine at UCL. All being well." She crosses her fingers, the way she always does when she talks about Ned's impending A level results. Melvyn's face changes, and she worries he thinks she's bragging. "I don't know what I'm going to do without him. I feel like a train that has run out of track."

Melvyn sets down his knife and fork.

"Or," he says, his features back to normal, "it's a chance to start a new journey."

He places a paper bag on the table and pushes it toward her.

She looks at it, confused.

"You seemed pretty engrossed." A tiny smile. "I thought you might want to finish it, in your own time."

She opens the bag. Inside is the Hallie Rubenhold he'd caught her reading in the bookshop.

"You got this for me?" she says. She's touched that he was paying attention, that he still recognizes this part of her. "Thank you."

He nods, and they watch each other for a moment.

Audrey is the first to speak again.

"The morning Miranda died. Were you there at the cliffs? Did you see anything?"

Melvyn's eyes widen, and he sits back, trying to adjust to the abrupt change of subject.

"The colony stretches three miles," he says, doing his best to roll with it. "I wasn't at Huntcliff that day."

He looks out of the window, toward that section of coast, and it's then that Audrey realizes she has deliberately sat facing the opposite way, that, like Belinda, she is trying to avoid seeing it. Before Miranda's suicide, she'd thought Huntcliff majestic, the constant glimpses of rock jutting up into the sky as you moved through town a gift, the squares of yellow and green that carpet its incline a welcome banner as you approached from afar. Now it was more like a specter, a constant and unavoidable reminder of the manner in which she'd lost her friend.

Audrey explains about Miranda's letter—how it seemed to have made her confront something she kept secret for twenty years—then tells Melvyn what Belinda said about seeing him and Miranda talking together on the trip.

"You weren't friends, and so she thought it odd."

Melvyn laughs.

"If you're asking whether or not I can remember if I had a

conversation with Miranda on a staircase at some point on a school trip that happened two decades ago, then I have no idea. Maybe she did see us chatting. Maybe I was just asking her the way to the loo."

Audrey laughs. She knows he's right—she's had this exact thought so many times herself—and yet, she keeps asking the questions because she also knows how fickle memory can be, how surprising. That sometimes our minds cling on to the tiniest of things—a color, a smell, a passing comment—and refuse to let them go.

Outside the wind is up, the sea pleated white. A black circle blots a section of beach next to one of the wooden groynes that punctuate the sand, the remnants of a bonfire.

"In truth," says Melvyn, "I think that whole letter-writing exercise was a crock of shit." He scratches at a large bite on his wrist. "Write about your hopes and dreams," he says in a breathy earnest voice, aping a teacher at the front of the class. "Following your dream in our society is like a bloody religion. The consensus is that if you achieve your dreams, they'll make you happy. But will they? The whole thing is nonsense, like something an ad man dreamed up. We're told that if we deviate from our dreams, it's a betrayal of our true selves, our one shot at a happy and fulfilled life. If we fall short, then we're somehow a failure." He scratches too hard at the bite, and it starts to bleed. "I don't buy it."

Audrey picks at her fingernails, ashamed to admit that this is *exactly* how she's always thought about her life, why she categorizes herself a failure.

"People make mistakes. There are bumps in the road. You decide to change jobs, or you're forced to." Melvyn goes quiet and looks at his lap, lost in some private memory. "I subscribe more to the Churchill way of looking at things," he says. "You know, that line about success not being final and failure not being fatal? How in the end, it's the courage to continue that counts."

Marcel's words boomerang around Audrey's head again.

You let one setback, one rejection, determine everything.

She looks at the hem of her linen shirt resting on her jeans, and thinks of her Crocs and leggings waiting for her to change into in the trunk, of the toilets waiting to be scrubbed.

Had *she* lacked the courage to continue?

There are so many more things Audrey wants to ask Melvyn, but she's been derailed by the turn in their conversation. She tries to reassemble her thoughts, but it's too much.

"I should go," she says, getting to her feet. "Work."

"Sure. Of course." He stands too quickly and almost upends the table. He fumbles, trying to rearrange the menu and bowl of sugar packets.

———————————

Outside, in the car, Audrey's inadequacies press down on her like gravity, pushing her lower and lower, until she feels as if she might disappear into the ground itself.

She's wondering if she should try and change in the back seat, or wait until she arrives at the client's house, when Melvyn appears.

She lowers her window.

"Sorry about the rant. I can be a bit much." He grins shyly, and for a brief moment, the boy he used to be rises to the surface. Audrey remembers what Robbie said. *People don't change… They might get better at hiding…* "Are you free this weekend? If I promise not to go off on one again, we could meet up?"

…you missed out on a chance at a career, a family. A love life.

Audrey musters her best and biggest smile.

"I am free, yes," she says, trying to steady the wobble in her speech, "and I would like that very much."

Chapter 18

Early morning, and Audrey is in the kitchen making the kids' packed lunches. She butters the bread on autopilot, her mind consumed by thoughts of the classmates she had yet to speak with, of the questions she still wants answered. This feeling—of being there but not actually being there—was fast becoming her default. It was as if there was no longer enough room in her skull for the everyday, as if the only reason she was able to do the school run, cook dinner, brush her teeth, was thanks to the muscle memory and the fact these things were largely rote.

She blunders through, almost in a trance, and is almost done when Marcel appears and, after greeting her with a curt nod, sets to work making himself an espresso. She wraps the last of the sandwiches in foil and pauses, watching as he tamps a scoop of coffee into the steel filter. She still hoped he might apologize, that he'd take back some of the things he'd said, but the more time passes, the more unlikely she realizes this is. Still, at least her humiliation has dissipated. In its place have come flashes of anger that ambush her when she is least expecting it.

She goes to the wall calendar and tries to work out when the current school term ends.

"I keep meaning to ask," she says, circling the last Friday in July. "Which summer camp have you signed the kids up for this year?"

Marcel turns, looking perplexed.

"It's on my to-do list. I just haven't gotten around to it yet." He switches on the coffee machine. "How far in advance do people tend to book?"

"Far," she says, having to shout a little over the machine's rattle and clank. "The summer holidays are the Gobi Desert of childcare."

She waits for him to respond, to start panic googling potential options on his phone.

"Sign them up wherever you think best," he says eventually. He leans in close to the coffee machine, carefully overseeing the trajectory of black liquid into his cup. "Don't worry about the cost."

Audrey looks at the packed lunches on the counter, and the bowls and cereal she has set out, ready for when the kids wake. She thinks of the clean uniforms waiting for them on their beds, the forms she has filled in for upcoming trips, the gifts she has procured for the friend's birthday party they are attending this weekend. She knew Marcel was grateful for her help, but surely he didn't think one day at a spa meant he was absolved from his duties for the rest of time?

"They're quite easy to look up," she says, working hard to keep her tone even. "You could do it yourself now."

Marcel reaches in his back pocket for his wallet.

"I'm so clueless when it comes to stuff like this. Here." He tries to offer her his debit card. "Book whatever you think works best."

This time Audrey gives in to the rage.

"Do you think I'm the help?" she says, gesturing to the clean kitchen. "That I'm your nanny?" She takes a breath, trying to calm down, but it does nothing to abate her anger. "I know you see me as some loser nobody who cleans houses for money, but that's not what I'm here for. Enid and Edward are like family to me, and I love them and want to take care of them, but I'm not staff. They're *your* children."

Carefully, Marcel replaces his debit card in the wallet.

"Of course I don't think you're the help. I tell you all the time how much I appreciate everything you do for them—for us. It's just..." He pauses, and Audrey feels as if she can hear his mind whirring, searching for excuses. "The clinic. I'm trying to hold down a job."

Audrey bristles.

"And I'm not trying to hold down a job? Or is it just that you don't think of my job as important?"

Marcel blinks, disoriented.

"Maybe you're right about me being rejected from Cambridge," she says finally. She realizes she started this argument because she wanted to return to the stuff he'd said previously—that she wants her chance to reply. "Maybe I gave up on my studies too soon. But I made a choice, and that was *not* to give up on my family. I chose *not* to give up on Ned."

She's rehearsed these lines, this comeback, so many times in her head. She had thought it would make her feel better. That it would even the score somehow. But, she discovers, it has done neither of those things. And so now she lets rip with something she hasn't rehearsed but feels deeply all the same.

"Quite honestly, it feels like *you* have given up on the most important thing of all—your kids. This is the worst and most vulnerable time of their lives, a time when they need you the most. What you do or don't do now is going to stay with them forever, shape them forever, and yet you don't seem willing to be there, even in the smallest of ways." Marcel scowls, a warning, but she pays it no heed. "Was that why you and Miranda were getting divorced? Because you weren't there for *her*?"

Silence.

"Marriages break down all the time. If you weren't to blame, then why not just tell me why you were splitting up?" Still he says nothing, but she continues, undeterred. "Every time I ask you to explain, you fudge, you dodge, you evade."

Marcel's espresso is steaming hot, but he tosses it to the back of his throat in one.

"You're a coward," he says, refusing to engage with her criticism. "Ned's almost a grown man. You're free to do something different, to try again, but you continue to hide behind him." He talks as if they are trains on different tracks, but it's clear she's hurt him, that he wants to retaliate and that this is the best way he knows how. "You talk about the choices you made in the past, and they were admirable. But now you have new choices, you've had them for some time, and yet you act like they don't exist. And what you don't seem to realize, Audrey, is that doing that is also a choice. *Your* choice."

Audrey can feel the terrible words she wants to say blooming inside her like spores. Things she can never take back. Things that would sever her from Marcel, from the kids, forever. She leaves before the words have a chance to escape.

Chapter 19

Friday, and Audrey is at Kitty's house. After leaving the half of the dry-cleaning she *had* managed to collect on the back of the chair, she zips the vacuum around the master bedroom, changes the bedsheets, dusts, and heads downstairs. Still wound up from her argument with Marcel, she works faster than usual, her movements jerky and rough. She knows she wouldn't feel like this if what he'd said to her was untrue, but admitting that is hard.

In Kitty's study she zooms the vacuum around the teetering towers of books that populate the floor. A stack of invitations sit on the blotter, waiting to be addressed. Thick white card printed with black copperplate, they are for the party to celebrate Kitty's professorship in August, the one her dad had spoken about.

She whizzes the vacuum back out into the hall, but in her haste she clips one of the book stacks and it topples to the floor.

"Shit."

She gets on her hands and knees and starts rearranging the books. Some have slipped under a gap beneath the desk, and so she lies low and bats her hand around in the dark until it lands on the rogue hardbacks.

Dragging them out into the light, she sees she's brought some papers and old mail with them. She balances the books on the pile, and is about to put the paperwork on Kitty's desk when she stops. In among the post is an envelope addressed to Kitty in the same neat capitals as had been on the outside of her and Miranda's "Dear Future Me" letters.

Mr. Danler's handwriting.

Kitty has folded and slotted her pages back into the envelope at the wrong angle, and Audrey can't help but make out a few sentences.

Certain words jump out at her.

Cambridge.

Exams.

Proud.

University.

The exact things Audrey herself had so desperately wanted.

It's not surprising. Back then, it was all many of them had thought about.

Unlike her, though, Kitty had made the grade. She'd been better, cleverer.

Audrey knows it's wrong—that reading it is bordering on self-harm—but she can't help herself. She edges the rest of the letter out from its envelope.

Dearest Kitty,

We're supposed to write our hopes and dreams for the future—where we want to live, the job we want to do, the places in the world we want to visit—but I have only one wish and it's this. I hope, more than anything, that you have made Mum and Dad proud.

This is all that matters, this is all that has ever mattered.

Right now you are sick with fear. There are so many hurdles to clear before the end of sixth form, so many chances to come unstuck. First, you need Cambridge to grant you an interview, then, if they do that, they need to offer you a place, then if they do that you need to get the required grades.

If you don't get in you will have let everyone down, you will have failed. And if that happens I don't think you will be able to live with yourself...

Audrey looks from the letter to Kitty's graduation picture on the wall. She must have walked past it a hundred times, but now she realizes she'd misunderstood the expression on Kitty's face. She'd always thought her smile proud—arrogant, even—but now she sees it for what it actually is: relief. She thinks of the day she bumped into Kitty and her family in the spa, looks at the way her dad seems to be clutching at his daughter's elbow in the photo, as if it is the handle on a prize cup he is about to lift into the air. For the first time, Audrey gets it. Kitty had spent a lifetime desperately striving—even when she was a kid—and so it was no wonder she second-guessed herself all the time, how she rarely took any time off.

Dad always says it's not enough to just do your best, that you have to do whatever it takes, and so you've decided that until you have written your admission essay, until you have been granted an interview, you will study every single night and every weekend, and that if you are tempted, even for a second, to deviate from this plan, all you have to do is imagine having to tell them you have been rejected, that all they have done for you has gone to waste. You know how they'll be, how they'll punish you. They won't speak to you, won't even look at you. Never forget that Dad spent his childhood dreaming of opportunities like this, that all he ever wanted was to be allowed to study, to reach his full potential. But he wasn't as lucky as you, he had to sacrifice those dreams, to get a job he didn't want. He says you need to do this for him, that your success will make everything he missed out on worthwhile...

A slam.

The front door closing.

"Hello?" says Jago.

Audrey hears him stomping down the hallway and quickly fumbles the pages back into the envelope. She drops it on the desk and turns around to see him standing in the doorway. He eyes her warily. Audrey can't make sense of it, but he looks almost afraid, as if braced for some onslaught.

Had he seen her with the letter?

She finishes balancing the remaining books onto the pile.

"Had a bit of a collision."

"Right."

His voice is strained. Because he doesn't believe her?

She notices he has a prerolled joint tucked behind his ear.

He stands there for a few moments more. The air between them is charged, as if there is a question he wants to ask but can't.

"I'll leave you to it," he says finally, then backs out into the hall.

Audrey waits for her breathing to slow; then she unplugs the vacuum and winds the cord. On her way out, she glances again at the graduation picture amid Kitty's wall of accolades. It is bigger than all the other frames and has been positioned center stage. The smaller certificates orbit it like cold gray moons.

Chapter 20

CAMILLE

Dear Camille

Wherever you are in the future, whatever you're doing, please know that I am incredibly proud of you. You're only seventeen and yet you've already achieved so much, provided so much, for your Mum, Dad and little sister.

I know you're feeling the pressure, that what once brought you so much joy now means you find it hard to sleep sometimes, hard to eat, but it's a price you're willing to pay. The level you're at now with these pageants, the kinds of prize money involved, it's made your family so happy, has given them things and taken them places they never thought possible. Dad doesn't have to work nearly so many hours, the fridge is full, the heating on.

And yet, I also know you wish it could go back to how it was. To the silly little beauty queen comps in village halls and leisure centers, to the dance shows and the tutus, to where the top prize was a rosette or a sash or a plastic tiara. It was so much fun and it didn't matter where you placed or if you messed up.

You know everyone at school thinks you're stupid but you don't care because you know you're smart in all the right ways. You've figured out how to make the most out of what you've got, not only that, you're willing to work hard, to keep going, even if it doesn't give you the same buzz it once did, even if it makes you cry sometimes and that's because these days you're not doing it for you, you're doing it for them and that weirdly makes it so much easier.

Audrey has now arranged to speak on the phone with Camille on six different occasions, but every time she has bailed at the last minute. In the end, Audrey suggests she drive out to see Camille in person. She figures that if Camille knows she has arranged her work commitments around the visit, then it will make her more likely to follow through. Still, Audrey spends the hour's journey to Hurworth, a gorgeous spot of a village on the river Tees, praying for her phone not to beep with a message saying she has to cancel.

An ex-beauty queen, Camille has always been the same. She'd regularly turned up late for class, had missed one of her exams completely because she got the day wrong, and famously, had once raised her hand during a science lesson and asked the teacher if other countries also had moons. She'd thought the moon belonged to the UK, that only Brits saw it at night.

Audrey pulls up outside the neat bungalow, fearful of yet another WhatsApp asking to rearrange, but as it happens, Camille is already stepping out onto the path to greet her.

Wearing white jeans and a checked shirt knotted above her belly button, Camille has made more effort for a Monday morning than Audrey does for even the most special of Saturday nights. At school her beauty had been cartoonish—false tan, fake eyelashes, hair extensions and acrylic nails—but now Audrey sees that even though her hair still looks professionally blow-dried and her face is made up in one of those perfect no-makeup makeup looks, Camille has ditched the disguise and embraced her actual features. Compared to the class photo, this Camille actually looks like herself.

She gives Audrey a wave, then disappears inside. Classic Camille.

Audrey imagines her running to save a pot that is about to bubble over, or to retrieve a renegade infant who has made a break for it up the stairs. But as Audrey makes her way toward the open front door, she notices that the path is actually a wide concrete ramp, and that in the hall she can see a wheelchair complete with head and neck support.

She pulls the door shut, and Camille calls to her.

"In here."

Audrey follows her voice, and as she gets closer, she becomes aware of a rhythmic noise overlaid with what sounds like Camille, murmuring and giggling.

The room she turns in to is ordinary. A sofa and TV hug one wall, a sideboard crammed with framed photos fills another. But against the third wall is a hospital bed, and in it a teenage boy, an oxygen tube tucked into his nostrils.

"Jackson, this is Audrey," says Camille from her chair at the boy's bedside. "We went to school together."

Jackson raises his hand. "Hello, Audrey from school."

Pale with curly brown hair, he is wearing a Sam Fender T-shirt and has a smattering of dark fuzz on his upper lip. The wall behind his bed is a wash of Spider-Man posters and beautiful black-and-white pictures of Zendaya. Tubes snake in and under his bedcovers and connect to a stack of machines on the floor.

"Respiratory failure," says Jackson, once Audrey's finished looking. He rolls his eyes. "It's a bitch."

"Jackson," says Camille, but her scold is halfhearted and punctuated with a smile.

She motions for Audrey to sit down.

"Sorry this has been so difficult to arrange. I make all these plans, but we never know if it's going to be a good day or a bad day." She yawns, and up close Audrey can see that, even though her foundation is thick and expertly applied, there are shadows under her eyes. "I seem to spend my life letting people down." Another yawn, louder this time, and Camille blinks. "Sorry. We get enough from the government to fund a carer two nights a week, and so I do the rest."

"Nights?"

"I stay up with Jackson till five, then my other half takes over for a few hours before he has to go to work. Jackson needs to be on the ventilator when he's asleep"—she points to a large face mask hanging from a hook—"and when he's on the ventilator, he needs to be monitored."

"Watching me while I sleep." Jackson does a comedic shudder. "Creepy."

Camille pretends to biff him in the ribs. "It's either this or a hospital ward."

"And we didn't like that," says Jackson. "We did not like it one bit."

"He lost a lot of weight," says Camille, "and he was miserable. We both were." She smooths a section of hair between her fingers, as if examining it for split ends. "I try to have a nap during the day, but it doesn't always happen."

She sets a Marvel movie playing and guides Audrey toward the kitchen.

Once they're out of earshot, Camille turns and hugs Audrey tightly. "About Miranda. I'm sorry."

She smells of figs and is surprisingly strong, her arms ribbed with muscle. Audrey realizes this must be because of Jackson—helping him in and out of the shower or wheelchair.

"You said you think she did it because of her letter?" Camille says as they come apart. "The ones we wrote as kids?" Audrey registers the lightness in her tone. Maybe Camille didn't let the letter hold much weight; maybe she saw it and laughed at this relic of her younger self.

"That morning. She might have taken some of the pages with her, but in the ones she left behind she says some odd things, about the class trip to the Lakes."

She waits for Camille to respond, but her earlier breeziness is now gone. She holds her silence, her face watchful.

"Someone said you two shared a room?"

Camille nods slowly.

Audrey holds her nerve until finally Camille relents.

"We didn't know each other before the trip, not really."

Audrey waits for more, and when Camille doesn't elaborate, she tries another prompt.

"In her letter, she seems to be alluding to something bad that happened?"

Camille fiddles with the ends of her hair again.

"Those letters. Back then we all just assumed everything would be straightforward, didn't we? Everything was based on a best-case scenario. We were so naive, about life and its many curveballs." She looks toward the living room. "I was so naive."

"Please," says Audrey, trying again, "if you know anything, however small, tell me. Not knowing why she did it—why she jumped. It's unbearable."

Camille taps the base of her thumb against her lips, as if she's biding time, and Audrey starts to give up. She can't tell if Camille knows anything or not. She's clearly had a different life path from most; maybe the mental load of caring for a sick child means any memories from back then have been long relegated to the dump. But then she exhales, a long slow surrender.

"I guess it doesn't really matter anymore. Not now."

"Please, if you know something. .."

The counter is lined with blister packs of medication and pill capsules. Camille sets to work dispensing tablets into a clear plastic container.

"The whole way to Keswick. I was sitting in a different part of the coach, but I could see Ben trying to get Miranda's attention, everyone could. Any time the teacher was distracted, he would get out of his seat and go stand by hers. She wouldn't even look at him."

Audrey knows this—it chimes with what Leighton had told her about Ben doing everything he could to win her back that weekend—but she doesn't want to rush her. Camille's decision to speak feels precarious, like a branch placed across a swollen river.

"I didn't think much of it, but then on the second night at the center, the night Ben died, something happened." She counts out the last of the pills and starts making notes on a clipboard. "I woke up, just after midnight. I'd wet the bed." Camille relays this information without embarrassment. "It happened all the time back then. The doctors said it was a stress response to all the competitions, all the pageants. It was mortifying, but at least it usually happened at home. Now here I was in this place with this classmate who I barely knew, and I had no way of hiding the mess." She shakes her head. "I couldn't lie there all night in it, so I got up and quietly tried to sort myself out, but I ended up waking Miranda."

She turns away from the counter, and Audrey sees she is smiling, but also sad.

"She didn't once laugh or make fun or ask why this was happening to a seventeen-year-old. She just sorted it out. While I cleaned myself up, she went to the laundry room and snuck some clean sheets so we didn't have to tell any of the grown-ups. She dumped the soiled ones in the laundry room; then we remade the bed together and went back to sleep. Just as I was drifting off, I heard something hitting the window. Pebbles. I stayed where I was. We'd been hiking all morning and I was exhausted, but Miranda, she got up. No sooner did she peer out than she huffed and closed the curtains. As she got back into bed, she muttered something. It was very quiet, but I heard."

Audrey feels as if she is almost to the other side of the river, but still she cannot afford to misstep. The slow thrum that has been inside her, driving her forward, starts to speed up, an urgent, almost painful whir. This was it: she was finally going to get her answer, her why.

She keeps her voice quiet, almost a whisper. "What did she say?"

Camille can't meet her eye. She directs her words to the floor. "She said she wished he would get the message."

Audrey's mouth falls open. Her thoughts spin faster and faster. "She knew Ben was outside in the snow?"

Camille nods. "And she left him there."

Chapter 21

The day after she meets Camille, Audrey gets a reply from Ben's mum. Laura Spellman explains she has been away on holiday and has only just got Audrey's note, but that she'd be more than happy to get together. At first Audrey has no intention of accepting the invitation. Since leaving Camille's she's been churned up, ricocheting between dismay—at what Miranda had done—and the urge to mount a fierce defense in her friend's honor. Miranda wouldn't have known Ben would die that night. Her actions had been tragic, but she could not and should not be held responsible for his loss. Still, Miranda's culpability aside, Audrey's knowing what she knew had meant looking Ben's mum in the eye was going to be a struggle. But then she'd started to wonder. Maybe being made to bear witness to the impact of Laura's loss up close could be a kind of penance for the part—albeit inadvertent—that Miranda had played in Ben's death?

Audrey arranges to meet Laura Spellman on Tuesday afternoon, and spends the days in between convincing herself of this argument. She thinks she's all set, that she has her head straight, but after she pulls up outside the house, she finds she lacks the courage to knock on the door.

Five minutes pass. Audrey is late for their meeting, but still she doesn't move.

Ben had grown up on this street and had lived here until he died. Slap-bang on the Marske coast, the top of the road was ordinary, all double-glazed houses, front gardens, and wheeled trash cans. Halfway down, boat tractors and cobles—the flat-bottomed, high-bowed fishing vessels particular to the northeast—start to replace the parked cars, and further on, sand smatters the tarmac, a gradual creep that soon turns into packed beach that consumes the pavement and leads to the sea. Audrey wonders what would happen if the tide ever reached the houses. If Ben had paused to take in this view before he left for the coach that would deliver him to the Lakes, and ultimately, his death.

According to Camille, when Miranda saw Ben at her window that night she'd assumed it was just yet another of his attempts to win her back. She'd had no idea he'd been locked out. When they found his body the next morning, she was horrified. Threw up her breakfast right there at the table.

Everyone says it was a horrible accident. That he got locked outside in the snow. But that's not true, is it?

This was the memory Miranda had been confronted with on the morning she died. Until that moment she must have struggled with the guilt, but somehow compartmentalized her secret. Then the letter had smacked her in the face out of nowhere.

Audrey had asked Camille why she hadn't told the police what she knew.

"What difference would it have made?" she'd said, heading back to check on her son. "Ben was dead. There was no malice in what she did. It would only have gotten her into trouble. I swore to myself not to say a word to anyone, including her, and I didn't." At the threshold to Jackson's room, she saw that he'd fallen asleep and had stood there watching him, her face serene and full of love. "Knowing what she'd done, having to live with that. It was punishment enough."

Audrey thinks of the grace with which Camille tended to her child's needs, and how she'd kept Miranda's secret for decades, protected her without her knowing. She realizes that—probably like most people—she had got Camille all wrong, that she had an inner steel, a resilience and integrity that Audrey couldn't help but admire.

As for herself, she supposes she now has her answer—her "why." Her theory about the letter having been the thing to send Miranda to her death had been correct. The knowledge has yet to give her any peace, any closure, but she hopes that might come in time.

Her phone beeps with a message. Another angry text from Kitty, demanding to know where the other half of her dry-cleaning is. In Ben's cottage, a woman pulls the nets aside and peers out of the window. Laura Spellman. Audrey can't put her visit off any longer.

At the front door, Laura greets her with a hug.

In her late fifties, Laura is bone-thin and has the same faded blue denim eyes as Ben. It's a fine summer day—Audrey has not bothered with a coat—but Laura wears tights and a ribbed polo made of coarse wool.

"It's all so sad about Miranda." Laura is a wisp of a woman, but she holds Audrey the same way her own mother used to: strong and sure, with her arms crisscrossed against her back. "She was a lovely kid."

For the first time since Miranda died, Audrey feels safe, protected, and when Laura goes to pull away, she resists, wanting to prolong the moment.

"Come in," Laura says, guiding her into the living room. "In your note you said you had some questions about Ben?"

Her hair is as fine as a baby's, her face papery and mottled with sun spots. She reminds Audrey of a tree that has long ago perished but is still standing.

"Before Miranda died, we received these letters we wrote at school. In hers she mentions Ben..." Audrey falters. Her plan had been to ask if Laura or her husband had ever heard anything—either from the police or the teachers—that didn't sit right about the weekend their son lost his life, something that bothered them, but perhaps hadn't made it into the official verdict. After talking with Camille, though, such questions feel pointless, and she can't bring herself to ask them anyway.

It was on the drive back from Hurworth that she'd made the decision never to tell anyone about the role Miranda had played in Ben's death. Not even Marcel. She didn't want to tarnish her friend's memory, but it was more than that. Talking to Camille had given her what she'd wanted—a reason for what Miranda had done, an answer—but now that she has it, Audrey realizes that sometimes the reason might be more hurtful than the not knowing. And if she was struggling to accept why Miranda had left Enid and Edward to grow up without their mother, then she knew that once they got older and learned the truth, they would almost certainly feel the same way.

It was simple.

When it comes to being left behind, no reason will ever be enough.

Now Laura smiles kindly. "I know about the letters."

"You do?"

"Mr. Danler. He gave us Ben's a few months after he died. He felt we should have it. Explained his plan for the others." She looks down at her lap, adjusts the way her tights gather around her knees. "Though I didn't get to read it until I was out of the hospital."

Audrey frowns.

"I had a breakdown," Laura explains. "Six months before Ben died. It had happened once before, when I was postpartum, but this time I found myself in a really bad way. Psychosis. I was hospitalized, put on some fairly intense drugs."

Audrey remembers what Robbie had said about Ben's mental health issues: that it had run in the family. She'd thought he was just being mean, and is surprised to learn there was some truth to it.

"And Ben's dad?" Audrey's been wondering about him since she got here, trying to read the room for signs of another person.

"We stayed together awhile after I got better, but we couldn't make it work." A tiny shrug. "He lives abroad now. Verona." Laura gets to her feet. "Would you like to see it—the letter?"

"Oh, no, it's OK." Suddenly Audrey realizes that being around Laura and her fragility is too much. She cannot go through with her penance after all.

"Please," says Laura. "I hardly ever get to talk about Ben these days." She motions for Audrey to follow her into the hall and heads upstairs. "Especially with those who knew him."

Ben's bedroom looks untouched: a single bed under a bay window with a view of the sea, a desk, a PlayStation, a noticeboard packed with photos and programs for the different school plays he'd once starred in, a pair of black-and-white Vans tucked against the skirting board. Laura goes to a cardboard box in the corner and starts searching through the papers inside.

Audrey peers at the collage of photos on the noticeboard. Most are of Ben and Leighton messing around at parties or on the beach. Ben is skinnier than she remembers, his hair thicker and more unkempt, but his beauty—a smile that felt like a secret only you knew, his eyes—is faithful to her memory. There are a few of him and Miranda, but her favorite is one of Miranda alone, in her netball uniform. She seems unaware of the camera and is sitting in the grass of the sand dunes, a dog curled in her lap. Her hand smooths the nap of the dog's ears; her head is bowed close to its fur.

Laura comes and stands next to her.

"Ben's death hit him hard," she says, motioning to a picture of her son and Leighton together. "They'd had some kind of teenage spat beforehand—about what, I have no idea—and at the time Ben died, they weren't speaking. Leighton didn't come to the funeral. I think he felt too full of regret that they hadn't made up sooner."

She hands Audrey an envelope.

"Ben never got to finish it, obviously. It's not an easy read—not for me, anyway."

"Are you sure?" Audrey tries to hand it back. "It's so personal."

"Please." Laura is insistent.

Reluctantly, Audrey pulls out the pages and reads.

Dear Ben

I'm not exactly sure when the teacher will give you back this letter—whether it will be in a few months or at the end of the year—but whenever it is that you come to read this, I hope that things have got better, that you are no longer so confused, so sad.

Right now all you can think about is Miranda. You miss being with her so much it hurts. You know you need to explain. To try and find a way to show her how sorry you are, how much you regret what you did. And you will. Right now, though, your head is a mess. There's no way you can deal with her until you get your own thoughts straight.

There is one thing you don't regret and that's what happened with you and Leighton. No matter what he might say to the contrary, you know you're in the right, that you had good reason (some might say the best reason) for betraying him in the way you did, and even now, despite knowing how badly he's hurting, how messed up he is, you're still in no doubt that, given the chance, you'd do the same again.

What Leighton doesn't seem to realize is that you had no choice.

No control.

But then maybe by the time you are reading this letter he will have experienced what you have, and he'll get it, he'll understand. And maybe even find himself able to forgive.

Seeing his handwriting reminds Audrey of the note she'd found in her own letter: Ben's request that she come and meet him at the Smugglers' Church. He'd written it. The note, with his need to talk to her privately, has taken a back seat in recent weeks; all her focus has been on the other classmates and making sense of the things to which Miranda had alluded. Now Audrey takes the various bits of information she has amassed and tests them against the note like jigsaw pieces, searching for a fit. The most likely reason—the thing that has come up most often—is that Ben wanted her advice on how to get back in Miranda's favor, but then the things he'd said here about holding off until he had his own thoughts straight would seem to contradict that theory. Maybe she'd never get to the bottom of what he'd wanted from her; maybe it was unconnected. Either way, after Camille's revelation, it—like everything now—seemed done and dusted.

Laura sits on Ben's bed. She smooths her palm across the duvet.

"Having to see me in the hospital like that, not having his mum around for nearly a year…it hit him hard. That was why he smuggled that booze on the trip, why he was drinking alone."

Audrey looks at the noticeboard of pictures.

"The things he says about Leighton." She thinks of her conversation in the gym. Leighton hadn't alluded to anything that came even close to making sense of the things Ben had said. "What is he talking about?"

Laura tugs at the crumpled tights around her knees.

"I know very little about the last year of my son's life." She speaks quietly, but her tone is practical and no-nonsense. "People tell me not to blame myself, that the breakdown wasn't my fault, but it's futile."

Audrey looks out of the bay window, to the sea at the end of the road, and thinks again about what would happen if the tide were ever to encroach the street—of all the things that would be damaged or washed away. The more people she talked to the more she realized how so many of the kids in her class had endured their own encroaching tides. Ben, Miranda, and even Kitty—permanently under the gun thanks to her dad's ambitions—had all suffered silently, carrying burdens that no teen-ager ever should.

"I am sorry," says Audrey. She adds, "For everything," and even though she knows Laura understands her words as condolence, her apology is wholehearted and full of regret.

Chapter 22

After everything that's happened, it feels weird to be getting ready to go on a date, but when it came to Miranda there was nothing more to do; thanks to Camille, the case was now closed. And so, with Marcel's comment about her lack of a love life still ringing in her ears, come Saturday night, that is exactly what Audrey does.

Defuzzes her legs.

Moisturizes the rough skin on her hands.

Makes sure her mouth is lip-balm soft.

Melvyn has told her to meet him outside the entrance to the Valley Gardens. A local attraction, it consists of a maze of paths, tracks, and flower beds, as well as a tea room and miniature railway. Walking there, Audrey feels lighter and happier than she has in a long while. Saltburn is chaotic, with sunburned day-trippers herding bedraggled children toward the station after a day on the beach. Every street is double-parked, the bins overflowing with fish and chip wrappers and half-drunk bottles of pop. Still, she finds herself weaving effortlessly through the throng. Melvyn has been cagey about this evening, and so—not sure if the gardens are a meeting point or the place he plans for them to spend the entire evening—she has hedged her bets with a red tea dress and a pair of tennis shoes that can handle most terrain, be it pub, beach, or field.

Her last date was over a year ago. Someone she'd met online. She'd always been terrified of the cutthroat world of apps, but Miranda had begged her to give it a try. The guy, a quietly spoken osteopath called Seb, had been lovely and she'd thought the night perfect. Conversation had come easily, they'd laughed, they'd had chemistry. At the end of the evening they'd shared a taxi to his place, and she'd left the next morning. But then she'd messaged asking to meet up again and had no response. Eventually, he'd replied and said that although he'd had fun and thought her pretty, he wanted someone with more ambition, someone who was going somewhere in the world. And that was that.

Audrey arrives at the gardens ten minutes early, but Melvyn is already waiting for her, a bulging backpack at his feet.

"Well," he says as she approaches. He puts his hands on his hips and beams as if he can't believe his luck.

"Well," she repeats, and then she has to clamp her lips because otherwise she worries her grin will be too big.

He nods at the backpack.

"I've made us a picnic." He sucks in his breath and puffs out his chest, feigning pride. "Packed a bottle of wine and everything."

She widens her eyes, mock impressed. "Fancy."

He motions for her to enter the gardens, then settles into step alongside her. The evening light through the trees is peachy, the air mild, and as they descend the path, her blood seems to fizz beneath her skin.

"How's it going with the list?" he says after a while. "The people you wanted to talk to from our class."

She tries to keep her voice blithe, to offer no hint as to the secret she now carries.

"I'm waiting on replies from one or two," she says, trotting out the line she's decided to use from now on. In reality, she plans to let it all fade away. "The only person I haven't been able to contact is Ricky Larkin. Remember him?"

Melvyn tightens his jaw. Ricky's name seems to anger him. "Last I heard he was working abroad, for BP."

That explains it. Melvyn has devoted his life to conservation work. He probably has little time for those who make their living from fossil fuels.

"An oil company? No way."

Melvyn bats a fly from his arm, distracted. "People change."

"In truth, I kind of need this whole thing to be over," says Audrey, and this time it isn't a line. "Trying to track everyone down, to figure out what happened, all while I've been grieving…it's taken its toll." She hasn't dropped her guard like this with anyone, shared the mental and physical cost of her investigation, and at first it feels scary, like stepping out into thin air. "I'm strung out, exhausted," she continues, and there is something about the way Melvyn listens to what she is describing—carefully, intently—that makes her feel as if the ground has appeared to meet her.

Halfway down the woodland trail, the path steepens, and as they take a bend, Melvyn stumbles. Audrey grabs his hand to steady him, and after he recovers neither of them lets go.

They pass an old man, and he and Melvyn nod in greeting to each other.

The man is familiar but Audrey can't work out where she recognizes him from.

"Rambler," says Melvyn by way of explanation once they've passed by. "I see him out at the colony all the time." Audrey realizes it's the retired coastguard, the one who makes the slate disks.

They're almost at the opening that leads down to the beach when he guides her to the left and up a scree bank. At the top they pick their way through brambles, Melvyn apologizing every time Audrey's leg or arm gets scratched. Then suddenly they're out the other side, at the edge of a tiny meadow studded with poppies and buttercups. They are the only people here.

"Found it when I was observing the nesting sites," he explains. "I overshot with the drone and stumbled on this place. Took me a while to figure out how to get here on foot."

She takes in the ring of trees that borders the edges and the view of the North Sea, spread out before them like a bolt of navy velvet. She's flattered at the amount of thought he has put into tonight. The care. It's a gift she doesn't know how to accept.

She'd only had one long-term relationship—a nine-month thing with an attorney called Noah—and it had never involved anything like this. They'd met when he hired her to clean his house. Fifteen years her senior, Noah was divorced and said he wanted to keep things casual. It took her a while to understand that what this actually meant was that he would never put any time, thought, or effort into her or the things they did together. She'd continued to work for him the whole time they were an item—three hours every week at a rate of £10 an hour. At the time she'd been so focused on Ned, on paying the bills, on keeping their heads above water, it had never occurred to her to ask for more. When she broke things off, Noah hadn't been able to understand why this also meant she no longer wanted to be his cleaner.

Melvyn lays down a blanket and starts removing food from his backpack. It's a feast: antipasti, cheese, a baguette, hummus, olives, and a bottle of cold sauvignon blanc wrapped in newspaper.

While Audrey kicks off her tennis shoes and settles cross-legged, he pours her a glass of wine.

She sips. It is delicious, cold, and tart.

"So...birds," she says playfully but also genuinely interested. "I remember you being really into them as a kid." She thinks of the conversation they'd had last time. He'd railed against the notion of fulfilling your dreams, and yet that was the exact thing he seemed to have achieved: a job that was also his passion.

"They fascinate me, always have." He looks down, smooths a blade of grass through his finger and thumb, then snaps it at the root. "But there were a few twists and turns before I got to study them full-time."

"What is it about them that interests you?"

"Oh, God." He laughs and tosses the grass to one side. "Everything." He nods toward the cliffs. "One focus of our study this summer is how the kittiwakes raise their young. They're one of the few species where the chicks keep returning to the nest, even once they can fly. Their parents are fierce and keep feeding them until they're old enough to fend for themselves. We've found that each kittiwake parent knows exactly what their fledgling sounds like, that they can identify it amongst all the other calls, and if a bird or a chick who isn't theirs tries to come into their nest, they can get quite violent. They just kick them out onto the rocks. And don't get me started on how they defend their young from predators— they are terrifying."

"So a lot like some human parents," she says and laughs.

"Worse." His eyes widen. "I've seen them take on birds three times their size and win. When it comes to protecting their young, they do whatever it takes."

His description of these birds reminds Audrey of what Kitty had said in her letter about her dad. She had never liked Kitty much—in truth, she'd always thought her a bit of a snob—but now, knowing the pressure she'd been under back then, how her going to Cambridge had seemed to be more about fulfilling his thwarted dreams than anything she wanted for herself, Audrey finds herself feeling strangely protective toward her old classmate. Receiving her own "Dear Future Me" letter has forced her to confront the fact that she failed to fulfill her own hopes, and the sadness that brings. Now she wonders if it might be sadder if you didn't even get to choose those hopes and dreams in the first place, if you had to try and achieve those foisted on you by someone else.

"How about your parents?" she says. "What's it like being back around them after so long?"

"Weird. Good. Uncomfortable." His eyes drop to the ground and he fiddles with the edge of the blanket. "You know the Maya Angelou quote about home, that you can never go back, but you also can never leave? I think there's a lot of truth to that." He shivers, as if to rid himself of the thought.

Audrey's phone rings. Not wanting to be rude, she leaves it where it is in her bag and lets it go through to voicemail.

"When does your stint on the colony finish?" She hates that she's already worrying about the end of the summer—that she feels upset at the prospect of his leaving.

"September. I've applied for a few different projects after this. There's one in London I really want. Walthamstow Wetlands."

Her phone rings again.

"You want to get that?" He smiles. "Seems important."

"Sorry."

When she gets out her phone, she sees Ned's name on the caller ID.

She answers. "Marcel asked me to call you," Ned says. "He says you need to come and meet him at the police station."

"What? Why?"

Melvyn registers her concern and starts to pack away the picnic.

"We were at the barn dropping off the dog when Marcel got a call. He asked if Eleanor and I could stay and watch the kids and if we could phone you, tell you what was happening." He stops, and she can hear him issuing muffled instructions to someone. A crackle, and he's back. "The police have recovered dashcam footage from an unrelated incident. The van in question drove past Warsett Hill on the morning Miranda died. It captured her on the cliffside."

Audrey's hand flies to her mouth.

Ned takes a breath and she braces herself. He's going to tell her the recording captured the moment Miranda jumped. The chance to see her friend one last time feels like a ruby in a drawer, a precious treasure she had no idea was there. Only this morning she had buried her face inside the folds of Miranda's camel hair coat, hanging where she'd left it on the rack by the door, and had closed her eyes and breathed deeply, scavenging any trace of her. The need is ferocious, the want for even just one last glimpse. Still, these are her friend's final moments, and the thought of it having been documented on film makes her stomach heave.

But that's not it.

"In the footage," says Ned, "the police say there's a second figure. A person stood next to Miranda on the cliffs." He is incredulous. "She wasn't alone."

Chapter 23

Audrey and Marcel sit across from the police officer in a small room at the station. Detective Sergeant Peter Reese has a narrow face, with not quite enough room for his features, and every time he smiles, it seems as though his eyes, nose, and mouth are vying for space. But he actually seems to care; his manner is kind and courteous, and after a few minutes in his company, Audrey is glad he's the one who's been assigned Miranda's case.

She looks to Marcel. Seated in a chair next to her, he has his coat collar turned up and his arms crossed. She reaches for his hand, squeezes it, and for the first time since their argument, he looks at her dead-on.

"Thank you," he says quietly, "for coming."

The detective opens a laptop and cues the dashcam footage. Then he turns the machine around so they can all see the screen.

The clip had been recovered in a separate investigation into a road traffic collision. The crash had happened in Hambleton, in the next county over, on the same day Miranda died. One of the officers who'd been tasked with reviewing the dashcam from the vehicles involved had read an online article about Miranda's suicide, and when he'd spotted her on the cliff he'd flagged it immediately.

"She comes into view at eight ten a.m.," says Reese. "We need to study the footage properly, to try and improve the resolution, but hopefully it should be enough as it stands for a positive ID."

Audrey feels the tremor in her hands and curls them into fists.

Miranda was not alone when she died.

The revelation is still too shocking for her to compute. She has spent so many hours trying to imagine her friend at the edge of that cliff, torturing herself with guesses at the thoughts that must have been running through her head, desperate to rewind the clock so she can comfort her and beg her to step back, and now she has been told this wasn't how it was at all, that somehow the truth is more horrifying than the nightmare she's been picturing this whole time.

The footage is silent, the POV from the car broader and more expansive than she would expect. She soon recognizes the road the van is on. It seems to be heading south, inland toward Brotton. She always forgets how flat the coastline is until you get to Huntcliff. Nothing for miles and then— rupture—a giant promontory that pushes up and out toward the sky, as if it is trying to escape from the beach that goes before it. On the dashcam there is a speck of coast, the sea a splash of blue and white, and then the vehicle broaches the bend that overlooks Huntcliff. The detective hits the Pause button.

"There, see?"

Audrey's heart stutters. She is both frantic, desperate to look, and gripped by an almost visceral need to turn away.

Caught in this push-pull, she and Marcel lean toward the screen. The two figures in the distance are small and grainy, but still Audrey easily recognizes one of them as Miranda. The length and reddish-brown color of her hair, and the billowing fabric of her pajamas, are unmistakable. Standing at an angle to the cliff, she seems to be in dialogue with the other person and is clutching something in her hands.

The same thing she'd been clutching when she was caught on the doorbell camera leaving the house?

The missing pages from her letter?

"It's her," says Marcel quietly and slumps back in his seat.

Audrey nods her concurrence. There's no doubt.

She knows it's macabre, but she wants to ask the detective to send her the clip so that she can watch it alone again and again, to leave it playing on a loop by her bedside table, the glow from the screen watching over her while she sleeps.

She grips the sides of her seat, her fingernails digging into the springy gray fabric.

The detective taps the screen.

"How about the person stood next to her? Recognize them?"

Audrey and Marcel take turns playing and rewinding the clip multiple times, freeze-framing on the second figure at different moments, but it's impossible to tell if it's a man or a woman, let alone identify their face.

"Sorry," says Marcel eventually, conceding defeat. Audrey does the same.

"What now?" asks Marcel after a moment.

"From what we can see on the dashcam, there is no second car in the Warsett Hill shoulder," Reese says, pointing to a spot in the bottom right-hand corner of the screen, "which isn't to say they weren't parked somewhere nearby, or that the dashcam failed to clock it." He slides his hand forward, shuts the laptop. "Going forward, our priority is to find out what that second person was doing there and why they didn't come forward. If they were trying to persuade Miranda not to jump, then it's odd that they didn't call an ambulance or report what had happened. So we have to ask ourselves…if they weren't there to help her, then what were they doing?"

The detective's question makes Audrey sit straight.

She uncurls her fists and lays her hands flat on the table.

"What are you saying?"

Reese tells them the news quietly, as if he's sharing a secret.

"We have more inquiries to make, but I think it's very likely this will soon turn into a murder investigation."

Chapter 24

The next morning, Audrey is standing outside the sports hall where Enid has her gymnastics training. Marcel had promised his daughter he would take her to class this Sunday, but after they got back from the police station, he'd stayed up most of the night, pacing. When Audrey had found him asleep first thing, she'd decided to let him get some much needed rest and brought a reluctant Edward and the dog along for the ride. Now she has one hour in which to try and keep him entertained and, having forgotten the iPad, has resorted to a game of hopscotch.

She uses a stone to scratch numbers on the pavement, then tosses it onto the number seven and hop-jumps over to it.

"Can we go to Redcar after?" Edward asks as she hands him the stone. "Get a lemon top?"

It's almost lunchtime, and the sun is fierce. This means the ice cream parlor will already have a queue around the block, and that he'll eat a fraction of the roast she has in the oven. But then, he asks for so little these days. He used to always be on Miranda for extra screen time, to stay up half an hour later, for Treacle to be allowed to sleep at the foot of his bed.

Not anymore. She worries that he's denying himself pleasure on purpose, that maybe he thinks it's wrong to want to feel good, to enjoy things even though his mother has gone. It's not just Edward. The months of grief have left them all flattened. It feels as if they've been trapped inside one of those wildflower presses, the screws at each corner twisted tight. With every day that passes, they become a little more desiccated, fragile, and gossamer thin.

She takes Edward's lemon top request as a small but positive sign.

"OK, but only a single scoop."

"Yes." He punches the air in triumph. "Maybe we could go to the beach there, too, look for the forest?" He'd been thrilled with the book on petrified woodland she'd got him, and had pored over the pictures for hours. "Please?"

"Remember what I told you? It only shows itself after a bad storm." She gestures at the sun and clear blue sky. "The weather is fine."

Edward huffs, then throws his stone. It lands on the number eight and he hop-jumps forward.

Audrey yawns. She might have gone to bed after they got back from the station last night, but that didn't mean she'd slept. As soon as she got under the duvet, she'd turned on her lamp and lain there for hours rereading Miranda's letter, studying the things she'd said for anything that might explain why someone would want to do her harm in the present day.

In the interview room, Detective Sergeant Reese had again asked Marcel about the morning his wife died, but he'd stuck to his story, insistent that she'd left the house spontaneously and, as far as he knew, hadn't planned to meet anyone.

The biggest question was why the person standing next to her had not come forward.

Had they watched her jump? Had they encouraged her somehow? Had they tried to stop her?

Or had they been the one to send Miranda hurtling over the edge?

You know. That's the hardest part. That's what makes it hard to sleep. To eat. To look people in the eye.

And if Audrey's initial theory was correct, and the letter had been the thing to send Miranda rushing from the house that morning, then how did it link to that person? Had they also been privy to what really happened to Ben that weekend?

Her first thought was that Camille hadn't been telling the truth when she said she'd kept Miranda's secret to herself all these years. If someone else knew Miranda had been responsible for Ben's death, then maybe they had met on the cliffs for some kind of confrontation. Had they wanted revenge?

Audrey had reminded Reese about Miranda's letter, and although he had thanked her and said they would take the PDF she promised to email him into consideration, the detective had been more preoccupied with the lack of evidence involved in Miranda's journey to Huntcliff that morning. There was no CCTV, no phone data, no witnesses. But, he'd said, thanks to red tape delays, they still had Miranda's car in custody, and so they planned to swab it for DNA. He also said they were going to expand their review of her phone, combing her SIM card for messages, calls, and location data in the months leading up to her death, to see if it revealed anything of note.

Audrey has already decided that she will resume trying to speak to the remaining classmates from the school trip, and maybe even revisit a few she has already talked to. Now, though, her questions will have a new focus: about whether what happened back then might make someone want to hurt Miranda in the present day. Before, her questions had been aimed at finding out whether she'd jumped because she'd been confronted by a secret she'd kept for twenty years. Now the question was: *did* she jump? Did she fall? Or was she pushed?

Edward returns to where she stands, and this time he aims the stone at the number ten square. He misjudges, and it bounces clear of the hopscotch.

A man in hiking boots and shorts approaches. Ivan. The coastguard from the cliffs.

Audrey thinks again, how she's noticing people in a way she never did before Miranda died. She'd moved among these same faces—brushed shoulders, queued in shops, waited at traffic crossings—for most of her life, but had never looked at them. She feels like a radar that has been plugged into the mains for the first time, the display screen bleeping constantly.

Ivan retrieves the pebble, hands it to Edward.

"How are you holding up?" he says once Edward is back to playing the game.

Audrey thinks of the moment she opened her eyes this morning, about how, for a few seconds in the cruel hinterland between sleep and consciousness, she had forgotten that Miranda was gone and had thought about what she might get her for a birthday gift. It wasn't until November, but she'd seen a chunky gray mug and milk jug in the boutique by the station she knew Miranda would love. Gray ceramic, they each had a tiny Dalmatian on the side, their spots bumpy to the touch.

There is so much she could say, so much she could try to articulate, but ultimately it boils down to three words.

"I miss her."

Ivan nods. "They say losing someone to suicide is like grieving with the volume turned up."

Audrey wants to correct him, but she doesn't know him well enough to explain about the potential murder investigation.

Sweaty children and their parents start filtering through the sports hall doors. Training is finished.

"Better go," she says, taking Edward's hand and moving to head inside.

"That guy I saw you with," says Ivan, calling after her.

Remembering how and why she'd had to cut short her date with Melvyn last night, she blenches.

"Tell him I saw surveyors sniffing around Coulby Farm this morning," he says.

Surveyors?

She thinks back to her conversation with Robbie, about his political ambitions for developing the area. It seemed he was going to get his way with Huntcliff after all. Still, Audrey can't understand why Melvyn needs to know this. Are there kittiwake nests in the ruins, or will the surveyors being there disturb the colony somehow?

"If they find him squatting there, he'll be in trouble."

Squatting?

Audrey wants to ask Ivan what he means, but he is already on his way, and she can see Enid waiting for her through the swing doors. The last child to be collected, she stands next to her coach, scanning the crowd, her face crimped with worry. Audrey shouts across the racket.

"Here." She waves madly, desperate to put her out of her misery. "Enid."

The little girl's shoulders collapse, the tension leaving her body, and Audrey realizes how, even though it has only been a few minutes, Enid had been genuinely frightened, that she had thought nobody was coming for her, that she had been forgotten.

Audrey gathers her up into her arms, and once Enid's breathing has slowed, she pulls away, just a little. It's quiet in the hall, but Audrey puts her hands over the child's ears, as if she is trying to protect her from the noise.

"I'm here," she says, over and over. "I'm here."

Chapter 25

On the last day of term, Audrey is in the playground, waiting for Enid and Edward to finish school for the summer. Their classrooms are relatively close to each other, and over the last month, she has adopted a waiting technique that involves standing equidistant between the two, then swiveling her head left and right, left and right, until one of them appears. It's worked well so far, but her chosen spot is exposed, at the outer edge, and today is hot—so hot that even at this hour, the sun blazes, a spread of blinding white light that has everyone else hiding in the shade.

She had called Camille last night, asked if there was any way someone other than her could have known about Miranda ignoring Ben in the snow. Someone who might have had motive to exact revenge or blackmail. But Camille had been certain. No one else had a clue. She swore that, other than Audrey, she'd never told a soul.

Audrey finds the thought that someone may have killed her friend horrifying, and yet, to her absolute shame, in the days since the dashcam footage emerged, she has found that the discovery of the second person has given her some relief. If Miranda was murdered, then it means she didn't leave them alone on purpose, that she hadn't deliberately left her children without a mother.

Audrey pulls at her T-shirt, trying to waft air onto her back and stomach, and has just risen up on her tiptoes, trying to see inside Edward's classroom, when she senses someone looking at her. Turning around, she sees Belinda, standing on the other side of the fence that separates the primary school from the preschool. Audrey wonders if she's seen her here before, but just hadn't registered it—if this is another instance of her new radar at work.

Belinda offers a tentative wave, which Audrey returns.

Finally, Enid and Edward emerge. She hurries them out of the playground, toward the car. She is desperate to get inside, to blast herself with air-con, but no sooner has she made sure the kids are strapped in than Belinda approaches, pushing a buggy. Up close Audrey sees her ankles and fingers have ballooned; the ridge underneath her breasts is damp with sweat.

She gestures at Enid and Edward. "They Miranda's two?"

Audrey nods. "I've been helping out, just until their dad gets his head above water."

Audrey goes to get into the car. The heat emanating from inside is searing, and she doesn't want the children sitting in it for too long. But Belinda blocks her way with the buggy.

"The other day, after you came by, you got me thinking." She adjusts the sunshade on the pram. "I spent the kids' nap time combing the photo stream for old pictures. Fancied a trip down memory lane."

Inside the car Enid complains about the temperature, and Edward scalds his hand on the metal seat belt clasp.

"The photo stream," says Belinda. "We share it. Leighton and me."

Audrey looks to the car, torn between wanting to hear what Belinda has to say and the increasingly grizzly children.

"There were a few pics from when we were at school." Belinda is whispering now. "Just random snaps at the disco or sports day or whatever. I clicked on one and it did that thing where it recognizes common faces in your collection. It offered up all these other photos." She stops, glances at the kids to make sure they aren't listening. "Photos and videos."

Audrey realizes the import of what she's trying to tell her, and stills.

"The majority of the photos and videos…" says Belinda. "They were saved in this one album, on a separate drive." She pauses. "The drive Leighton uses for all his gym paperwork."

Audrey's pulse skitters in her wrist. The sun beats down on her shoulders, her scalp.

"In the days before those 'Dear Future Me' letters arrived," says Belinda, "he was so excited, happier than I've seen him in ages." She cups her bump, and when she speaks again it's as if she's forgotten Audrey is there. "I thought it was because he knew the baby was going to be here soon."

She quiets, hijacked by the things now swirling round her skull. Audrey worries she's having second thoughts, that she's about to pull back from whatever it was she was about to say.

"Belinda," she says gently. "What were they—the photos and videos?"

"They went back years," says Belinda in a detached monotone. "Decades, even. They'd all been taken at a distance, and just show boring everyday stuff, like her walking to her car or buying groceries." Again, she retreats within herself, as if she's realizing something for the first time. "She didn't seem to know she was being photographed." She teeters, not sure she wants to say the things she'd been planning to say after all, but then she smooths her hands over her giant cupola of a belly. Audrey doesn't know if the baby kicks or if it's just that she's made her decision, but Belinda pulls herself up tall.

"I've been going back and forth for weeks, wondering whether or not to say anything." She gestures at the pram and now her words speed up. "He's their dad. He provides. I mean, what would I do without him? But then I saw you just now, and all I could think about was the reason she's no longer around."

"Who was it?" says Audrey, no longer able to keep quiet. "Who was in the photos?"

Belinda takes one last look at Enid and Edward bickering in the back seat of the car. Her decision is made.

"Miranda," she says eventually. "All of the pictures are of her, their mum."

Chapter 26

As soon as Audrey has the kids fed and settled in front of the TV, she goes to Marcel's study at the other end of the barn, closes the door and calls Detective Sergeant Reese. She had urged Belinda to contact the police herself, to share what she'd found, and Belinda had promised to do exactly that, but Audrey is worried she might hold off until she has confronted Leighton, giving him the chance to delete everything. Or that she'd just have second thoughts.

It takes a while to get through the switchboard. While she waits on hold, she listens with one ear to the kids, suddenly raucous down the hall, and wonders what will win out—her need to go and make sure they aren't destroying the barn, or her need to speak to the detective.

But then, just as she hears crockery smash against flagstone, Reese appears on the other end of the line.

He explains he's in a hurry, about to leave for the day—"My wife's birthday"—and asks if he can call her back on his mobile.

She worries he won't, that he'll get caught up with something else, but he's true to his word and a few seconds later, her phone rings.

She can hear him walking, the roar of background office noise.

She explains she has some new information regarding Miranda's case.

"It's about an old classmate of ours. Leighton—Leighton Walsh."

She expects Reese to be all ears—eager to know more, grateful for a lead—but instead he takes a breath, and when he speaks, his words are rote, his tone one of forced patience.

"As you know, even before the dashcam footage emerged, we spoke to you and every other individual that messaged or called Miranda that morning, and indeed the day before she died." She hears a swish of a door opening and the high-pitched chirp of a car being unlocked. "Like you, Mr. Walsh had an innocuous reason for being in touch." He huffs and grunts, and she hears what sounds like the click of a seat belt being fastened.

"Wait...what? Leighton was in contact with Miranda before she died?" Thoughts clatter through Audrey's mind. Could Miranda and Leighton have been having an affair? Was that why he had so many photos of her? Why she and Marcel had been getting divorced? But no, no way. She thinks of Leighton in his clingy T-shirt and tinted eyebrows. Miranda would never go for someone like him, would she?

"They weren't friends. What was his reason for being in touch?"

"I can't tell you that." She hears the growl of the car engine starting up. "But I can assure you it was nothing suspicious."

Another crash of crockery from the direction of the kitchen. Audrey dips her head out into the hallway for a moment, listening for cries of pain, but there are only whispers and stifled giggling. She closes the door again.

"I think you might need to take a second look at him."

"Why is that?" The detective is on speakerphone now, his words tinny.

She recounts what Belinda had told her about the cache of photos and videos.

Reese does not respond, and for a moment Audrey thinks he has not heard her or that maybe the signal has cut out, but then he speaks. Slowly, carefully.

"How many pictures are we talking here?"

"She said there were hundreds, if not thousands."

He whistles.

"So, will you?" she says. "Take a second look at him, I mean."

She can hear the sound of him breathing, the car's speaker amplifying and distorting the noise.

"I think that's the least we'll do."

The wait to hear what—if anything—had come from her call to the police is agonizing. Audrey has been stuck in a horrible limbo for days when she finally hears back from Mr. Danler, the teacher who set the "Dear Future Me" assignment. She arranges to visit him at his house—an old vicarage an hour away in Osmotherley—and gets there late morning. It's warm, the moors on the other side of the vicarage garden wall purpled with heather, but instead of sitting outside, Mr. Danler brings her into the tiny living room with its closed windows and peat fire.

"So," he says, once his wife has sorted them out with coffee and biscuits, "tell me, what did you end up doing with your life?" The former teacher is thinner and also somehow shorter than he was at school, but his eyes twinkle the same. "If I remember rightly, you were one of the clever ones—very bright."

The last few months have inured Audrey to this question.

"I applied for Cambridge, but I didn't get an interview," she says without missing a beat. "Then my mum died, and I took on the care of my brother. I clean houses for a living."

Mr. Danler cringes at his faux pas.

"You became his guardian; you found a way to provide," he says, and it feels as if he's correcting her. "I remember now. Admirable."

Audrey tries to focus, but the room is too hot. "You heard what happened to Miranda?"

He nods. "Sorry for your loss."

"Remember Ben Spellman?" she says. "I discovered recently that Miranda blamed herself for his death. She wrote about it in her 'Dear Future Me' letter." She feels herself sweat. Mr. Danler is content in his jumper and thick cords, but for her the fire is too much.

"Miranda was in no way to blame. Ben was very troubled before he died. Things at home..." He falters, not wanting to betray a confidence.

"His mum," says Audrey. "I know."

"Ah." He nods. "Then you understand. His behavior that year changed. His grades deteriorated."

"His behavior? You mean like in class?"

He nods.

"There was all the garden variety stuff. Back-talking teachers, being late, missing homework, but there was other more serious stuff, too. There was one incident I remember, with his best friend, of all people."

"Leighton?"

Mr. Danler nods.

"It happened a while before he died. I don't know the details, just that whatever he did was bad enough to merit a discussion about his being suspended. His father argued mitigating circumstances, that Ben was struggling with his mum being ill, and in the end they settled on a few weeks of detention."

Audrey thinks about what Laura Spellman had said about Leighton not coming to the funeral. She'd thought it was because of some silly fight, that Leighton had felt guilty for not having made up with his friend before his death. But maybe it had been more than that.

"Whatever happened between them, I suspect Ben wouldn't let it lie."

"What do you mean?"

"I attended the coroner's inquest into Ben's death, as did a number of teachers from school. I remember they interviewed a young woman, one of the people who worked at the outdoor center, asked her about something that had happened the day *before* Ben died."

Rosa McLaughlin, thinks Audrey. The center's leader.

"They were trying to establish the center's track record with pupil safety—if his death was an isolated incident. This woman talked about how they'd gone rappelling, and that she was absolutely certain she'd done all the proper checks, but that just before someone was about to ascend she'd noticed something wrong. She said someone had clearly tampered with the belay, that it was nothing too serious, just teenage high jinks, one kid trying to rattle another, and the line of questioning fizzled to nothing."

Audrey tries to match this up with Rosa's response to her request for information. Rosa had refused to engage in specifics, but the way she'd talked about teenagers—their capacity for cruelty—implied something far more than your average tomfoolery.

"You think it was Ben?"

Mr. Danler hesitates, as if he's worried they are being watched, then gives the tiniest of nods.

"The woman said she couldn't be sure who had tampered with the belay. Or who it was intended for. All I know is that when I heard that story, his was the first name that came to mind."

Mr. Danler's theory seems to chime with what Robbie said he'd overheard his father talking about on the phone. Ben had done something bad to Leighton, and then in the Lakes he had tried to hurt him again? Why? Was it in any way connected with what was going on with Leighton in the present day—to his stash of Miranda photos?

Audrey lets the questions pinwheel and retreats into memories of Miranda: of them hibernating on the sofa in the double slanket Miranda had bought them as a joke one Christmas, eating cinnamon buns in the car after a farmers' market, sending each other endless iterations of the same Pedro Pascal sandwich meme.

It seemed like such a simple, inadequate thing to say you missed someone—after all, you could miss the bus, miss a point, miss a target—but Audrey thought it perfectly embodied the daily, if not hourly, experience of the fact her friend was gone.

She missed her.

"It wasn't easy," he says, "figuring out where to reach you all. Social media only gets you so far; after that it came down to word of mouth. Calling up friends of friends." He smiles indulgently. "It took time to get everyone's address, but I'm glad I kept at it."

"Did you even consider the impact they would have?" She is surprised to hear the change in her voice. She realizes she is angry at Mr. Danler's thoughtlessness, at how he had just sent these things out to amuse himself. The letters had been an earthquake for the recipients, exacting and unasked for, and yet for him they had been nothing more than the culmination of a pet project.

Mr. Danler watches her carefully.

"I know it must have been a huge knock to your confidence when Cambridge turned you down. We were all as surprised as you were. But the thing about life is we all get setbacks. It's how we deal with them that counts. Have you ever thought about trying again? Further education, I mean?"

"I'm a bit old for all that." Audrey goes to reel off the usual excuses, but she struggles to find the words. *Admirable*—that's the only word she can think of. The way he had described her a few moments earlier, when she'd told him she'd become a cleaner. Was he right? Was what she'd done not a sign of weakness, but of strength?

Mr. Danler adds another brick of peat to the fire and embers spit onto the hearth.

"You have the same brain. It might be a bit rusty, but with a little practice it will be as brilliant as it ever was. You could go to night school, finish your A levels, then a degree." He nudges the brick toward the back of hearth and orange sparks scoot up toward the chimney. "It's never too late."

Chapter 27

BEN

Stray Beach, 2003: One month before the school trip

idnight. Most people have gone, and the ones that remain are getting ready to leave. Miranda asks if I want to walk home with her and some of the others, but I'm still furious about Robbie, and I know that it doesn't matter how exhausted I am; if I go now, I'll lie awake all night.

I tell Miranda to go on without me, make a joke about needing to tidy up after the guests, and as she walks away, I set to work gathering the empty cans and bottles into a bin bag. Miranda has left her denim jacket behind, so I pick it up and place it on a rock. I'll take it with me, give it back to her tomorrow.

I place the rubbish bag next to the bins on the dunes and return to the shore. The tide is on the turn, and even in the dark, I can see the film of water slide its way across the sand.

I'm on my way down to the waves when I see him. Sitting against the groyne closest the sea, he's looking into the dark, a silly grin on his face. He waves, and the gesture is the sloppy exaggerated movement of a drunk.

"Ben." He's happy to see me and seems to have zero worries about his earlier indiscretion.

I come and stand in front of him, but he's having trouble focusing and he rubs at his eyes, trying to sober up.

"You said you were going to keep it between us."

When he doesn't reply, I hold my silence, wait for him to understand.

"Wait." He sits up a little straighter against the groyne. "You think I told?"

I hold my silence and his face tenses.

"I didn't say anything, I swear." He is so earnest that for a moment I doubt myself. But then he reaches out, touches the side of my calf, says something more, his words slurred.

I bite the inside of my cheek until it bleeds.

———————

I walk the length of the beach and back again, kicking at shells.

Back at the bonfire, I'm about to hook a right, toward the dunes and home, when I see he's still there, sitting against the groyne. He's fallen asleep, his arms limp at his sides.

The tide has a good while to go before it reaches him. Still, if he doesn't wake up he'll get soaked. I head over, and as I reach down to give him a nudge, one of the zip tie packs falls out of my pocket. I pick them up, my fingers digging into the sand as I try to get a purchase on the thin hard plastic.

I look at his sleeping face, his features slack, mouth gaping, then I shove the zip ties into my pocket but keep one out. As I loop it round his wrists and through the groyne's barnacled iron ring I keep expecting him to wake and push me away, but the rum he was drinking has knocked him out.

Once it's done, I retreat and wait for the water to come. Fixed to the wood like this, he reminds me of something from a Greek myth, an offering to the gods.

I'll let the water come so far, no higher than his waist, then I'll cut him free.

Give him a scare. Teach him a lesson.

I retreat back to the dunes. It's dark and quiet, the sloped sand like a comfortable seat. Then I watch and wait.

Chapter 28

The investigation into the identity of the second figure on the cliffs rumbled on. Though tight-lipped about where they were with Leighton and his photos, the police had updated Marcel and Audrey on the DNA swabs they'd taken from Miranda's car. The tests had turned up a number of traces they couldn't attribute to friends or family; the problem was that there was no way of knowing if the people to whom the samples belonged had been with Miranda in the car that morning, or weeks—or even years—earlier. Still, they were running them through the system all the same. Combing through the messages, emails, and location data from Miranda's phone, they'd discovered that in the months before her death, she had visited certain places on the same time and day every week. Some were predictable—the kids' school, the halfway house, community center, studio, and Teesside University, where she taught her yoga classes twice a week—but she'd also visited Huntcliff on numerous occasions. Detective Sergeant Reese had said that, if it weren't for the second figure, they would assume these had been scouting trips, her sussing it out as a potential suicide location, or that she had kept going there intending to kill herself, only to not follow through.

On Redcar Beach this morning, Audrey trails an intrepid Edward as he kicks and peers at patches of sand in search of the petrified forest geologists said was still there, buried deep below. She's trying her best to be present, to listen. To respond to the things he says, but since the discovery of the dashcam footage, she's found herself even more obsessed with the need to know what happened to Miranda than before. She goes through the motions of regular life—looking after the kids, working, cooking, shopping—but she is continually distracted, her thoughts elsewhere. After leaving Mr. Danler's yesterday, she'd made a second approach to the outdoor education leader, Rosa McLaughlin, asking about the things she'd said at the inquest. She knows Rosa had requested she not contact her again, but Audrey's reached a point where she no longer cares for such niceties, where *all* that matters are answers, the truth, the clarity she believes will bring her some kind of peace.

She looks at the cliffs in the distance, imagining her friend there in the months before she'd died. The cliff face is reddish brown, its clay surface marked by a series of lines that run from one side to the other. Audrey knows it's the strata—the layers of ironstone poking through—but whenever she looks at it, she cannot help but think of it as a giant claw mark, made by some leviathan when the earth was still taking shape.

Miranda had never been a hiker—Audrey had never really heard her mention the spot—so why the repeat visits?

"The book says there were oak and fir trees," says Edward.

Audrey tries to give him the focus he deserves. She makes herself look at him, rather than through him, and sees his hair has almost grown out, the chunks Enid had hacked from the back and sides blending in with the regular length. Another few weeks, Audrey thinks, and she'll take him to the barber's.

Edward stoops to inspect an area of rock protruding from the shoreline. "It says that sometimes, if enough sand is washed away, you can find acorns and branches. Once, someone even found some leaves." He bashes his wellies against the edges of the rock, trying to clear the sand, then gasps, excited, and reaches for a small blackened lump. Rinsing it in the sea, though, it soon becomes clear it is nothing more than a mussel shell, and disappointed, he windmills his arm and dispatches it into the ocean.

"I told you. There needs to be a really big storm before we can see the forest." She gestures at the sky. "Heavy seas."

Edward scowls and moves on to another patch of rock.

"The book says we used to be able to walk from here to Denmark without getting our feet wet, that the forest was part of Doggerland." He squints at the horizon. "Do you think they called it that because it had dogs living in it?"

Audrey smiles. "Maybe."

She had always wanted children of her own. To know what it was to be pregnant. To give birth. Her own flesh and blood. She'd once wondered if looking after Ned had been enough to make up for it. And now she wonders the same about helping to care for Enid and Edward. Was it the same? Was it enough?

Ordinarily, around now Audrey would be on her shift at Kirkleatham Museum, but whereas Enid had gone to spend the day at her friend's house as planned, the tandem play date she'd organized for Edward had fallen through at the last minute. Marcel couldn't help, said he had a day of back-to-back appointments, and so she'd decided to call in sick. She hated lying and worried about inconveniencing the museum—if she becomes unreliable, they'd ditch her for someone else in a heartbeat—but it was the one job she couldn't bring him along on. Besides, hanging out with Edward was fun. It would do both of them good to noodle around together for the day.

She finds a chunk of driftwood, kicks it onto its side, and sits down to watch Edward dig.

Frustrated by his lack of success with the rock formations, he has decided to take the reveal of the ancient forest into his own hands, and set to work excavating a hole with a plastic spade Audrey realizes he must have secreted in his raincoat on their way out of the barn. He's hip-deep inside the beach hole when she hears a buzzing from above. It sounds like a swarm of wasps, but when she looks up, she sees a drone, swooping and dipping through the air. She scans the sand for its owner and soon spots a figure holding the remote control a short distance away.

Melvyn.

Seeing Audrey, he waves, and after guiding the device to the sand, he collects it and walks over to greet them.

Audrey cringes inwardly. She hasn't seen him since their aborted picnic in Valley Gardens and has yet to reply to any of his messages asking if she wants to arrange another date. She'd told herself she didn't have the time or headspace to start a relationship, but looking at him now she feels giddy and realizes how much she likes him—how she hasn't liked anyone this much in a very long time.

She braces herself for the awkwardness she is sure will be there, or worse, his offense or hurt at being ghosted.

He displays none of those things.

"What a treat." Melvyn beams. "I'm so happy to see you."

"Sorry for not being in touch," she says. "After that night—"

"I get it," he says, cutting her off. "You've got a lot going on. It's OK."

He seems to mean it, and Audrey relaxes.

"I was going to message you, actually. Let you know I'm going to be away for a few days. I'm going out on the study boat to observe the birds' fishing grounds. But once I'm back, or once you're out the other side—whatever comes first—give me a call, OK?"

Audrey grins. All her resolutions fading fast. Maybe she should try and make a go of it with him long distance? Maybe it could work?

He nods at the drone in his hand.

"Had it out over Coatham Turbines," he says, motioning toward the giant windmills that populate this part of the sea. "The kittiwakes like to hunt there."

He nods at Edward's now sizable ditch. A question.

"He's looking for the petrified forest," she says. "I've told him we have to wait for a storm, but the heart wants what the heart wants."

She realizes the significance of the phrase as soon as it leaves her mouth. So does Melvyn. He smiles.

Edward spots the drone and, abandoning his spade, scrambles up from his trench. He reaches out his hand to touch one of the propellers, but then draws back at the last moment, worried he might cause damage.

"This can fly all the way out to the turbines?"

Melvyn kneels down next to him and holds the device so the boy can examine it better. "It could go further if I wanted it to. Up to four miles."

Edward's eyes widen, his mind churning through the possibilities, and then, as it lands on mischief, they narrow.

"Could you fly it over our barn? Could we see it from here?"

Melvyn looks to Audrey for the answer.

"It's a mile inland," she says, turning toward the esplanade. "I guess so."

Given the green light from Audrey, Edward focuses his attention on Melvyn.

"Can we?" the boy says, hands clasped to a beg. "Please?"

Melvyn laughs.

"OK, but only for a little while. I need to save the battery for the birds." He checks the drone, then sets it down on the sand a meter or so away. He looks to Audrey. "Come and stand next to me." He taps the screen. "Be my guide."

Audrey does as he says and Edward flanks the other side.

She's surprised to find that the image is in color; the cars and spots of people beneath are crystal clear. They watch as it soars over the parade of shops and amusement arcades that line the seafront, and moves toward the roofs and chimneys of the terraced houses behind.

It takes Audrey a moment to get her bearings, but before long she starts offering directions.

"Follow Grewgrass Lane, then bank left." She watches as the machine leaves the houses behind. "Head east toward Upleatham and Saint Andrew old church," she says, marveling at the pasture and wheat fields below. "The barn is on the village outskirts."

Melvyn does as she says, and once it's on course, he offers the controller to Edward.

"You want to hold it for a bit?"

Edward hesitates, torn between not believing his luck and fear.

"It's easy," says Melvyn, placing the controller in his hands. He stays behind him for a moment and then, once he is sure he's OK, takes a step back.

Speaking quietly so Edward can't hear, Audrey updates Melvyn on the latest developments in Miranda's case: the second figure in the dash-cam footage, the things Belinda had told her about Leighton.

Once again, she finds she's able to let her guard down, to give Melvyn the unvarnished truth about the toll these new developments had taken on her state of mind.

"So now the big question is whether or not the second figure being there with Miranda on the cliffs could have been connected to the letter, and what happened to Ben in the Lakes?"

Or if that person was Leighton.

"What do the police say?"

"That they're investigating all possible leads," she says, putting on the detective's placatory tone. "In truth, I don't have much faith."

"I hear you," he says. "They're not the easiest folk to deal with."

He stops, distracted, writhes at a cluster of insect bites on his arm.

"So itchy. Every time I'm at the cliffs I get eaten alive."

Audrey remembers her conversation with the former coastguard outside Enid's gymnastics class.

"I saw that rambler the other day," she says. "The one from Valley Gardens. He seemed to think you were squatting at the farm. He wanted to warn you he'd seen surveyors about."

Melvyn tugs his sleeve low, covering the bites.

"Are you?" she says when he doesn't answer.

"Am I what?"

"Squatting."

"Of course not."

He peers over Edward's shoulder, tweaks the drone's course ever so slightly.

"I camp there occasionally when I'm doing night observations," he says after a moment. "If the weather gets bad, or I need to get my head down for a few hours."

Melvyn goes to look over Edward's shoulder again, but Audrey pulls him back.

"You've been camping a hundred meters away from where Miranda died," she whispers. "You need to talk to the police." She reaches for the card in her bag with the detective's number. "You might have seen something useful. You might recognize the second person."

Melvyn holds up his hand, trying to slow her down.

"I wasn't there that night—the night before she died. Otherwise, of course I would have said something."

Audrey sags. Of course it was too good to be true.

"I'm almost at the barn," says Edward, getting excited, "I can see it. I can see Daddy's car."

"Well done," says Melvyn, coming to help.

"His car?" says Audrey, trying to get a clear view of the screen. She thinks of the day of back-to-back appointments Marcel had described. "You must have the wrong place."

But when she looks, she sees the swaying fields of oilseed rape and the barn's distinctive apex roof. Marcel's silver Audi is parked out front.

"There's Daddy," says Edward. He puts his mouth close to the screen. "Helloooooo."

Marcel stands outside the front of the house. He leans toward the door and then steps back, as if he's calling to someone inside.

Audrey struggles to make sense of what she is seeing. Maybe Marcel has fallen ill, or forgotten something important and has returned home to retrieve it?

She's reaching for her phone, about to call him and check that everything is OK, when another person emerges from the barn. A woman.

At this distance Audrey cannot make out her facial features, only her bobbed blond hair.

While Marcel locks up, she goes to wait by the car; then he comes to join her. He heads for the driver's side door, but then he seems to have second thoughts, and circles back to where the woman stands and wraps her in his arms.

At first Audrey puts what she's seeing down to Marcel's easy physicality, but then he pulls back slightly. Audrey only realizes what is about to happen at the last minute and whips the screen up, out of Edward's hands, just in time to see Marcel cradling the woman's face with his hands. Then he leans in and they kiss.

Chapter 29

MIRANDA

Saltburn, 2023: The morning of...

The day starts with an argument. Whispers that snip at the dawn air. It's been like this for weeks, a horrible back-and-forth that feels like we are throwing the same rock at each other, over and over again. After last night, though, our words have a new intensity, an urgency, like everything is about to come to a head.

Marcel wants to tell the kids we're splitting up, to get them used to the idea that we won't be living in the same house. For the last few weeks we have been bombarding each other with the terrible admin that comes with extricating one life from another—legal paperwork and attorneys' emails—but now he wants to step up the pace. He insists we need to tell the kids today. I disagree. He says it's because I'm in denial, that I'm still hoping to change his mind, and he's right, but that's not the reason I'm so against it. In truth, it's because I cannot bear the idea of the actual moment the words leave our mouths. Their faces and questions. Their upset. Their fear.

Downstairs, I worry he might decide to tell them anyway, that he'll just go ahead and do it before we leave for school, and so I try to make the most of the time we have left and conjure the best possible mirage of a happy home. After rolling up my pajama sleeves, I plait my hair to keep it clear of the batter, tuck it into my top, and set to work making pancakes.

The kids play with the dog on the rug, and as I crack eggs into a bowl, I catch Marcel eyeing me from across the kitchen. He's been like this since last night—watchful, as if I'm a lit firework that has yet to go off.

I feel like a fool. All those years earlier I'd believed him when he told me it was over. I'd thought that moving hundreds of miles away from her, back to England, would mean it stayed over, that the passing of time meant we were out of the woods, that the years had made us safe again, good as new.

Turns out we've both had secrets in our marriage. That we've been nurturing them in tandem, like gardeners fussing with sunflowers on either side of a high brick wall. But whereas I now know about this, that leaving France didn't put an end to his affair after all, he still has no clue about mine. Nor does anyone.

His phone rings, and seeing the number, he retreats to the hall and starts talking in French.

I whisk the batter. Pour oil into the pan. Having a family, being married—being happily married? They'd never really been on my wish list. I'd dreamed of other things, a different kind of life, but I'd grown into it, been proud of it, let it become part of my identity, and now it seems like even that is going to be taken from me. In the mornings, when I walk Treacle on the beach, I torture myself with the same question. Is it better to have had this life, this marriage, even for a short while, or would it be less painful to have never experienced it at all?

Marcel is still on the phone, but now his tone changes. He sounds apologetic, frightened. Like he is trying to soothe the woman on the other end of the line. I leave the pancakes for a moment and go to where he's pacing in the hall. I take the phone from him, hold it to my ear.

"Hello," I say. "Hello?"

Chapter 30

The afternoon that follows Audrey seeing Marcel on the drone is uneventful. Between leaving him numerous voicemails, she hangs out with Edward, collects Enid from her playdate, makes tea, and drives the children and Ned to Enid's gymnastics competition. Her brother had dropped Treacle back at the barn while they were eating, and to Enid's delight, had asked her if she'd like him to come and watch her perform.

Now on the journey home, despite the back seat being too cramped for his lanky frame, Ned is sitting with the kids, again to their absolute delight. Audrey glances in the rearview mirror, clocks the way his knees are folded against his chest, and smiles. She knows he's wedged himself there to try and cheer up Enid, to distract her from that fact that she finished second from last.

It's been hours, but Marcel has yet to engage with any of Audrey's messages. She hadn't asked outright what he'd been doing at the barn, who he was with—trying to explain about the drone felt too difficult. Instead she'd said she was checking in and asked him to call as soon as he was free. In return, he fired back a curt WhatsApp and said all was fine, that he wished Enid luck in her competition, and that he'd be home around ten o'clock.

In the meantime, Audrey has been revisiting all the things Marcel had told her that don't quite add up. Whether it be his plausible but odd account of Miranda's leaving the house on the morning she died, keeping the divorce secret, or telling Audrey he was going to work, only to be caught in a romantic clinch with a stranger, the lies and omissions were starting to pile high. Sitting atop the pile is a new thought, ugly and newly formed, one she's struggling to acknowledge.

Could she trust him? Should she?

Another thought presents itself.

One she hardly dare acknowledge.

Eventually she comes at it furtively, glances at it side-on.

Could it be that Marcel was the second figure on the cliffs? That he killed Miranda?

"Aud-reeeey," says Edward not long after they've pulled out of the car park. "I'm hungry. Can we stop for chips on the way home?"

"Chips! Yes!" says Ned, and claps. "We want chips!" he chants. "We want chips!"

Edward and Enid join in.

"That guy me and El saw you with in the Stray Café a few weeks back," says Ned once the chanting has died down. "Is that who you're dating?"

The question catches Audrey off guard, and as she pulls away from the traffic lights, she stalls.

"I wouldn't say we were dating." She restarts the car and tries to ignore the beeps from the queue of traffic behind her. She doesn't want to get into it with Ned right now, and so she fudges. "It's early days."

Ned nods. "He friends with Miranda?"

He starts to tickle Edward under the arms.

"Not really." She avoids his gaze in the rearview; she knows they're both grown-ups, but she finds this awkward. "He was in our class at school."

Edward is now laughing so much he can't catch his breath, but Ned doesn't let up.

"El recognized him. She said she'd seen them hanging out together, at the coffee bar?"

Audrey rolls her eyes. This place. There was no such thing as blending in. It didn't matter what you were doing, someone would *always* notice.

Ned holds his hands in the air briefly, giving Edward a moment of respite, then goes in for one final tickle.

"They might have said hello to each other in passing," says Audrey, "but I don't think they were friends."

Ned nods, then nods again.

"That must be it."

Done with the tickling, he and Edward launch into a game of thumb wars.

"So listen," he says, after Edward has beaten him twice in a row. "I've got something to tell you and I don't want you to be mad." His voice is light—playful, almost. "Eleanor is pregnant."

Audrey's hands fall loose against the steering wheel. She tries to speak but nothing comes out.

Edward grins.

Enid is the first to find the words.

"Eleanor is having a baby?" she says. "You're going to be a daddy?"

Ned takes a breath, unexpectedly moved at hearing her say his new title out loud.

"Yep," he says, his voice thick with emotion, "and you two are going to be chief babysitters."

"Yes," says Edward, fist-pumping. "I've always wanted to be a babysitter."

And now Audrey is furious because she's realized this is the real reason Ned wanted to come along to the competition tonight, and why he has told her something so important here, while she is driving—so she cannot properly react. He might as well have tied her to a chair, then made sure to be a safe distance; at least there would have been some honesty in that.

"I've talked to Mack at the surf shop, and he said there's a job for me there full-time if I want it. I've done the math. If El moves into Brunswick Road, then we should be OK for money."

Audrey digs her nails into the steering wheel.

"What about UCL?"

"I'm going to call them tomorrow, tell them I no longer want the place."

She wants to hit the brakes, to get out of the car and come round to the back and drag him out onto the pavement. To shake him and make him see that he cannot do this.

"I don't care if Eleanor is having triplets." Audrey tries not to escalate to a shout, but she can't stop herself. She will not let this happen again; she will not let history repeat itself. "You are not calling anyone. You've wanted to be a doctor your whole life."

Edward wails, and Audrey feels a stab of guilt that she didn't wait till they got home to have this argument, that she has upset him by raising her voice. But then he presses his face up against the glass.

"The chip shop," he says, putting his hand to the window as if he is saying farewell to a lover. "You just drove right past."

————

Audrey waits up for Marcel, but when there is still no sign of him at midnight, she decides to call it a day. Usually, her insomnia strikes after she has been asleep for a few hours, but thanks to Ned's earlier bombshell, tonight she cannot even manage that. The thought of him giving up his place at UCL makes her feel sick. The urge to shout and bully and cajole until he sees sense is overwhelming. At the same time, she cannot bear the thought of Eleanor being left alone to raise their baby. Of him missing out on that. How could they have been so stupid? How can he be so naive? She wonders if, were she to push hard enough, she could get him to defer for a year instead of withdrawing completely, but she knows this is not the answer. Once Ned is on the parental treadmill of caring and providing for a family, it will be impossible to get off, especially to go and spend five years studying and not earning any money. She tries to imagine how things will play out if Ned has it his way—to work through the practicalities of their situation. If Eleanor moved into Brunswick Road, where would that leave Audrey? She was staying at the barn now, but she was itching to return to her own home, her own space. Did she really want to share her house with a young family, even if that family were her blood? Did she really want to live cheek by jowl with a couple who were young and in love, averting her eyes every time she walked in on them mid-smooch, wearing earplugs so she didn't have to hear them fight or fuck at night—or worse, becoming her niece or nephew's babysitter by default, juggling a baby and her life all over again?

She eventually drifts off around 3 a.m., but at dawn she wakes with a start, disturbed by Marcel coming home.

She gets out of bed and creeps downstairs, where he is taking off his shoes in the hall. She decides to get straight to it, to disarm him with her bluntness.

To make sure he has no time to come up with a lie.

"Were you having an affair?" She keeps her voice hushed so as not to wake the kids. "Are you *still* having an affair?"

He continues unlacing his shoes.

"I saw you with a woman. At the barn yesterday."

At this, Marcel looks up.

"You were here?"

His right eye is bloodshot, the iris speared by fat red lines.

"Was that her? The woman you've been seeing?"

He stands up. His shirt is creased and hangs loose over his chinos. "Can we talk about this after I've had some sleep? I'm exhausted."

"Is she the reason you and Miranda were getting divorced?"

He tries to head upstairs, but she blocks his way.

He takes a step back and she thinks he is going to protest, that they are going to row, but his shoulders wilt.

"Her name is Cecile." He sighs. "We were at medical school together."

Audrey thinks of the graduation photo in the master bedroom: Marcel's arm slung around a blond girl.

"We had a thing a few years ago, when Miranda and I were still living in France, but Miranda found out and I broke it off. We moved away. I promised Miranda it was over, and it was—but then when I was home looking after Maman at the start of the year, we bumped into each other."

"And so what?" Audrey says, not even trying to hide her contempt. "You picked up where you left off?"

She thinks Marcel is going to bite, but he thinks better of it.

"Once upon a time Cecile was my dream woman, someone I'd hoped to spend the rest of my life with. Being with her was like stepping into a time machine. I felt young, happy. Full of possibilities."

A flight of fancy, thinks Audrey. Temporary. Meringue light. How could he not have realized he'd eventually have to come back to reality?

"Did Miranda know?" She tries to figure out how this piece of information might fit with the lies and omissions she has already encountered: to see how or why they might have led to her friend's death. "That you'd started back up with her again?"

"Only once it had ended." The side of his mouth twitches. "But even now, after everything that's happened, Cecile won't accept it's over.

She's here, in North Yorkshire, staying in a hotel. I spent most of tonight trying to make her see sense."

Audrey thinks of how they'd embraced by the car. Marcel's easy physicality aside, it hadn't looked over—far from it.

"I don't understand why you don't think this had something to do with her death? How you're so sure?"

His mouth starts to twitch again, and this time the movement is more pronounced, as if his body is fighting to voice something he wants to keep to himself. He goes to move past her up the stairs, but Audrey isn't finished.

"I know you're grieving, and clearly you've had all this going on, too, but you've got to step up. With the kids. You're never around, and even when you are, you're not present. I'm taking the best care of them I can, but they need *you*; they want *you*. Take some time off, reduce your hours. I don't care how you do it, just that you do."

Marcel nods, and the gesture is a mix of acceptance and defeat. Finally, she lets him pass.

He makes his way toward the master bedroom, his socked tread a soft slow thump.

Chapter 31

In Kitty and Jago's house, Audrey loads the dishwasher, then sets about spritzing the kitchen worktops with Cif. The party to celebrate Kitty's professorship is in ten days' time, and it seems as if she has started to prep in earnest, with cases of wine and champagne stacked in the larder, bulk-bought napkins on the counter, and new garden furniture. Judging by the volume of booze, it's going to be a large gathering. Audrey is already dreading the cleaning aftermath.

Once the worktops are wiped down, she grabs the vacuum. She pauses before turning it on, cocks her ear toward the living room.

Today is the second week of the summer holidays, and—in theory—Edward and Enid's second week at forest camp. However, this morning, when it had come time to leave, they had retreated to the top of the stairs and tied themselves to the banister with Enid's dressing gown cord in protest. Audrey had tried to talk to them about why they didn't want to go, but they wouldn't be drawn out. Marcel had stepped in, hoping to jolly them out of whatever was bothering them with jokes and tickles, but that only made things worse, and eventually both children had erupted into tears.

In the end Audrey had caved—Marcel was scheduled to be in surgery all day, so he couldn't exactly call in sick—and told them she would take them along on her cleaning jobs, that she'd done the same with Ned when he was small. But in the last few hours, she has discovered this pair are a whole different kettle of fish.

At her first job of the day, a holiday rental in Marske, Edward had spilt juice all over himself, and then Enid had flooded the bathroom sink while trying to clean him with dampened and rapidly disintegrating toilet paper. Now they keep disappearing off into other parts of Kitty and Jago's house, even though she has expressly told them not to.

She vacuums the kitchen, then works her way down the hall. The machine is loud, but still, as she nears Kitty's study, she can hear thuds and shrieks. She leaves the vacuum going and marches into the room, ready to tell them off, but the mess renders her speechless.

Books lie in lines across the floor like toppled dominoes, and sheets of paper are splayed across every surface. As for the children: Edward is standing on Kitty's desk chair, holding a book on the Irish potato famine like a bat; Enid is on the other side of the room, arm raised, a cricketer about to bowl, a ball of scrunched-up paper in hand.

"What?" Audrey is too aghast to be angry. "This is someone's house. These are someone's things." She surveys the room and is surprised to find that she feels more disappointed than furious. "I am so upset with you both right now," she says flatly, and then she has to stop herself from invoking their mother, asking them what Miranda would think of this behavior.

Enid seems dazed, her eyes unfocused, as if in some kind of trance. But then she comes to and drops her paper ball.

"Sorry," she says. Her lip wobbles and she folds her hands together the way she does when she is frightened. As she takes in the results of her destruction, Audrey realizes she's not scared of any punishment that might ensue, but by her loss of control.

"They were going to take us on a field trip."

"What?" Audrey shakes her head, confused.

"Today, at forest camp. They said they were going to take us out to see the kittiwakes. At Huntcliff."

The moment of understanding hits Audrey like a brick. She goes to them, brings them to her, and then, for the first time since Miranda died, she starts to cry. The children pull away a little, shocked but also curious. They have never seen her in tears. Then they close around her even tighter and pat her back with small hands.

"Living room," she says after a while. Her voice is strict, but she punctuates her words with kisses on the tops of their heads. "If either of you so much as move an inch before I say it's time to leave, then there is no screen time for a month."

She tidies the books first, rearranging them into their various teetering piles, before moving on to the mosaic of notes, bills, academic papers and student essays that blanket the carpet. Eventually, her tears stop and her breathing steadies. She does her best to group the relevant sheets back together, and is making good progress when she sees it.

A line of cramped writing, looped and cursive, it encroaches on the line below and sometimes the line below that.

Audrey's studied it so often over the past few months, she's reached the stage where she'd know it anywhere.

Miranda's handwriting.

Chapter 32

At first Audrey falters, confused. It feels like that moment when you recognize someone you know out of context. Then she tugs the paper out from the underneath the mosaic. The writing is in among other pages, half-encased in an envelope she has seen once before.

Kitty's "Dear Future Me" letter.

She shuffles through the paper and separates Kitty's part from the four sheets in Miranda's handwriting.

Phrases and words jump out at her.

You left him there to die... He would still be alive today if you hadn't ignored him... You keep thinking about his Mum and Dad, how they must feel.

Audrey can't be certain, but she's pretty confident these are the missing pages from Miranda's letter. A skim-read seems to confirm Camille's account of what had happened on the school trip: how Miranda had ignored Ben's plea for help, and so had held herself responsible for his death.

They'd been inside Kitty's pages all along. Audrey thinks for a moment. Had they been here the first time she'd looked at Kitty's letter? She'd only read the first page; then she'd been interrupted by Jago arriving home. Had she just not seen them?

And if these weren't the sheets of paper Miranda had been pictured leaving the house with on the doorbell camera the morning she died, then what were they?

She doesn't hear the front door.

It's only when the vacuum gets switched off, and its roar fades to a wheeze that she looks up.

Kitty stands in the doorway, eyes wide at the chaos before her. Finally, she zeros in on Audrey, pages in hand.

"An explanation?" says Kitty solemnly. "Now."

Chapter 33

Kitty stands in the doorway, eyes darting around the room. At first glance her posture is relaxed, but on closer inspection the tendons in her neck are pulled taut, her jaw set.

Audrey gets to her feet, defiant.

"You had Miranda's missing pages, and you didn't think to say anything?" She shoves the letter in Kitty's face.

"What?" Kitty blusters, but the tendons in her neck soften, as if she'd been anticipating something far worse.

"The bit of Miranda's letter that was missing, the part we thought she'd taken with her to the cliffs." Audrey snaps the paper flat. "All this time, it's been here."

Kitty tugs at the silver cubes in her earlobes, trying to catch up. She takes a breath and exhales. When she speaks again, she keeps her words slow and steady.

"I had no idea they were there, truly."

Audrey harrumphs, unconvinced.

"Don't you think I would have said something?" says Kitty. "Why would I keep it to myself? It makes no sense."

But Audrey isn't going to back down that easily.

"How can you possibly not have known? Even if you couldn't remember the things you wrote in that class, as soon as you saw the handwriting, read the things she talks about, it should have been immediately obvious those pages didn't come from you."

At this, Kitty appears to relax a little.

"My letter." She smiles sadly. "I'm guessing you've read it."

Audrey nods. She has been too shocked to feel any embarrassment at having been caught snooping, but she now feels it start to creep in.

"Some."

"Then you'll know." Kitty grimaces. "It documents a part of my life, my mental health, that I thought was long behind me. The pressure I was under…" She glances at the graduation picture on the wall and shudders. "It was brutal. I read the first page and a half and decided not to continue. I shoved the pages back in the envelope and put it to one side."

"You honestly had no idea those pages were there?"

"Not until this moment."

Audrey shrinks to the ground. She sets Miranda's pages on the floor, arranging and rearranging them like a damaged picture she is trying to piece back together.

"Then how did they get there?"

Chapter 34

The storm hits just before midnight. Rain and wind lash so hard against the windows, it sounds as if the barn is being pelted with stones. Edward wakes, confused, and comes into Audrey's room. She manages to settle him back into his divan, but no sooner has she returned to bed than she hears footsteps on the landing.

"Can I sleep with you?" Edward says, one pajama leg rucked up around his knee. "The noise, it's scaring me."

Audrey hesitates. She knows from past experience that sharing a bed with him is like trying to sleep alongside a hyperactive puppy, but then, after finding Miranda's missing pages today, she senses true rest is going to be elusive anyway.

When she'd got home from Kitty's, she'd returned the sheets to Miranda's letter and assembled them in order. For hours she'd read and reread the now complete text from start to finish, hoping to find some new clue or hint as to why her friend might have gone to those cliffs, and perhaps the identity of the person who had stood next to her, but to no avail.

She thinks about what Mr. Danler had said about what he suspected had happened between Ben and Leighton in the Lakes. The new pages might confirm what Camille had told her, but maybe that wasn't the end of the story; maybe there was more to it, another part she couldn't yet see.

As for how or why the missing pages had come to be inside Kitty's letter, neither she nor Kitty had been able to make sense of it. She'd told Kitty about the dashcam footage—how they now knew Miranda was not alone on the morning she'd died—and Kitty had been as shocked and as full of the same questions as Audrey still was. It had provided a strange feeling of solidarity, in a way, to know that, even for a short time, some-one else was experiencing the same need for answers that now dominated her every waking thought.

Audrey thinks again of Kitty's reaction once she'd realized what it was Audrey had found. She'd seemed almost relieved. Had she been worried about something, some other secret she hadn't wanted Audrey to know about—something to do with Jago, perhaps? Their finances? Audrey has always thought Kitty and Jago were like everyone else—that her invisibility meant they didn't care if she saw the period stains on the bedsheets, the Valium in the bathroom cabinet, the used condom on the downstairs toilet floor after a party—but maybe she was wrong. Clearly there were things in Kitty's house, in her life, in her marriage, she'd prefer to keep private.

One thing she had been open about was the difficulties of her teen-age years. The strain she'd been under. It has been weeks since Audrey first stumbled on Kitty's letter, but there are some lines she can recall in heartbreaking detail.

I have only one wish and it's this. I hope, more than anything, that you have made Mum and Dad proud.

This is all that matters, this is all that has ever mattered.

Audrey's thoughts return to the part of Miranda's letter she'd found in

Kitty's study. The discovery begged another question. If the sheets of paper Miranda had been captured with on the doorbell camera weren't from her letter, then what were they, and why had she taken them with her?

She lifts one side of the duvet, and Edward leaps forward and hops in. Immediately he turns on his side and presses the freezing soles of his feet against her calf.

"Who will die next?" he says quietly.

Audrey is too blindsided by the question to respond straightaway.

"I hope it's not you. Or Enid. Or Daddy."

"We'll all die one day." Audrey wants to soothe him, but she knows she cannot fudge, cannot escape the fact of death. "But when we do, you will be a very old man with gray hair and wrinkles."

"Promise?"

Audrey wants badly to do as he says and guarantee the impossible. To comfort him with certainties out of her control. But it's too much like a lie, and so instead she strokes his hair and lets his request sit in silence.

"Is it a very powerful storm?" says Edward after a while, his words slow and slurry.

"Very," she says, still stroking his hair, but he is already breathing deeply, his pillow rippling with snores.

Eventually, she, too, falls asleep. In the morning, when she wakes, Edward is gone—she presumes back to his own bed, or to the kitchen in search of breakfast.

Outside the storm has cleared and the sky is pale gray, the air still.

Showered and dressed, Audrey heads downstairs, but only Enid is lying on the rug watching TV.

"Is your brother still asleep?"

"He wasn't in his room," Enid says, her eyes still glued to the screen.

Audrey looks out of the window. Marcel's car isn't there. Usually by this time he's left for work, but maybe he's taken Edward somewhere—to an appointment?

"Has he gone somewhere with your daddy?" says Audrey, checking each of the downstairs rooms in turn.

"Don't know."

Audrey returns upstairs, calling Edward's name as she goes. She tries to ignore the panic nipping at her heels, but as she checks each room and finds each one empty, it starts to gain on her. She checks again, this time crawling under beds and opening cupboards to be sure, but when there is still no sign of him, she gets out her phone and calls Marcel.

He picks up after two rings, and her phone fills with the hollow roar that comes from talking to someone through a car speaker.

"Is Edward with you?" she says.

"I'm on my way to the clinic. Why would he be with me?"

Audrey's chest buckles. "Was he here when you got up?" She speaks fast. "Before you left, did you see him?"

"No. Audrey, what's going on?"

"He's not here." She stops trying to fight the panic and lets it engulf her. "I've searched the whole barn but I can't find him."

"OK…" He pauses and she hears the *click-click-click* of the indicator. "I'm turning off, I'll be back as soon as I can."

"Should I call the police?"

"Yes. I'll be home soon."

Audrey dials 999 and, wanting to be sure, sets about searching the barn again, top to bottom, but there is still no sign of him. The operator puts her through to the police and she tells them what has happened. They take down some information, a description of Edward, and promise to get someone out to her immediately.

She's outside, walking the garden perimeter, when her eye lands on the front door. The doorbell camera. If Edward went out that way, there'd be a record. She'd be able to see what time he left the barn, the direction he was heading.

If he was alone.

She opens the app on her phone and, with fumbling fingers, loads the activity from this morning, but the stress makes her clumsy and she clicks on the wrong link. A string of deleted files going back months zooms up the screen. She swipes at the files, trying to return to the home page, but the app is slow to respond and instead it inches through pages of old notifications. Audrey watches it reach the date of Miranda's death, and shudders. She's scrutinized the footage of her leaving the house that final morning too many times to count. But then the app inches back even further, to the night before. There are loads of notifications, many of them after 9 p.m. Marcel had said Miranda had been out teaching and that he'd been asleep in bed when she'd returned home, so why were there so many comings and goings? Audrey clicks on the first one. It shows a blond woman at the door. Agitated, she's arguing with whoever is on the threshold. Audrey is certain she has seen her once before, on the drone camera. Marcel's old flame. Cecile.

Marcel had said nothing about her coming to the barn that night.

Her stomach falls away, like a lift that has had its cables cut.

More lies.

She wants to scroll through the other notifications that follow this one. To open and study each one, but there is no time for this now.

She navigates the app back to today and clicks on the first logged activity at 5:45 a.m.

Edward.

Wearing wellies over his pajamas and holding what looks like his red spade, he emerges from the house, looks around, then carefully pulls the door closed behind him.

Audrey scoops a bewildered Enid up from the rug and carries her to the car. The dog follows. Before setting off, she calls Marcel.

"I know where he is," she says, trying not to think of all the roads Edward must have navigated alone, all the strangers he must have passed, to get where he is going. She tells Marcel where to meet her.

"How can you be so sure?" he says.

She thinks of the way Edward's cold feet had pressed against her calf last night. How she knew the precise moment he'd fallen asleep by the sound of his breath. How in these past few months, her ability to read his and Enid's smells and noises and tics has become second nature, instinctive.

As if he is part of her.

"I'll explain later," she says, starting the car. "But trust me, I'm right."

"OK," he says eventually. He keeps the line open and Audrey thinks he's going to say something more—that he's going to tell her something important—but there is only the roar of his driving, an interminable white noise. Finally, he hangs up.

Chapter 35

MIRANDA

Saltburn, 2023: The morning of...

At first the woman on the other end of the phone says nothing. Her breathing is quick and panicky, staccato, like she has just finished crying. Eventually she starts to talk, first in French, then in frantic broken English that goes from pleading to accusatory and back again.

Cecile.

She came to the barn last night, looking for Marcel.

That was the first I knew of it, that they'd restarted their affair. And that it had ended.

The kids were in bed, but still he let her in, and she stood there in the hall, begging him to change his mind.

This was it, I thought. This was the reason he wants to split. Because of her.

Because of an affair that has now ended.

But after she'd gone Marcel told me that it wasn't his relationship with Cecile that had soured things between us, that he found it hard to explain, that his unhappiness ran deeper and more complicated than a simple infidelity.

And so, sad and humiliated, I decided to tend to my own secret.

To go and see him.

Now, more than ever, I knew I had to pull out all the stops. To do everything I could to make sure it would work out in my favor.

I stand there in my pajamas and Birkenstocks. On the phone, Cecile continues to talk. She has started to cry again, and her sentences are wild and hysterical. I can hear gulls in the background, the buffet and slap of wind in the receiver. She tells me where she is, and says she is going to do something stupid, says that Marcel needs to come now or he'll regret it. I tell him what she's planning, try to hand back the phone, but he refuses to take it. He says they are empty threats, that she is crying wolf, that she has done this before. But I tell him that if he won't go to her, I will.

"Go," he says. "More fool you."

Chapter 36

Redcar Beach has been swept clean by the storm. The sand smoothed flat. Audrey and Enid stand on the esplanade and scan the coast from left to right. The tide is out and clusters of people walk dogs at the shoreline, but there is no sign of Edward. Her panic had abated a little; now, though, it ramps back up, her heart banging against her chest. She was so sure he would be here, so certain she knew where he was going. She is torturing herself with thoughts of all the hazards he might have encountered on his journey here—a collision with a car, an abduction—when Enid spots him.

"There," she says, pointing toward Marske. "Near the rocks."

Audrey squints, and then she sees him, too: a tiny figure hunched over on his knees. Digging.

She messages Marcel, telling him his son is safe; then she and Enid launch themselves down the concrete boat ramp and into a sprint.

"Edward," she shouts as they get close. "Edward."

He doesn't look up. Focused completely on the job at hand, he is leaning over a hole, jabbing at the sides with the red spade.

By the time they reach him, they are both panting. Audrey wants to scoop him up into her arms, to crush him to her and check for injuries, but as she approaches he recoils.

"You are in big trouble, Eddie," says Enid once she's caught her breath. She puts her hands on her hips. "Big. Trouble."

Edward pays her no mind.

"It's not *here*," he says, angry. His eyes are swollen from crying, his nose snotty. He glares at Audrey. "You said it would appear after a big storm, that the sand would be all washed away." He returns to his dig and she realizes the spade has splintered. As he drives it back into the ground, the cracked plastic warps and bends.

Audrey crouches to his level.

"I'm sorry it hasn't shown itself this time, but I wasn't lying. The forest is there right beneath our feet and always will be." His digging slows, but he still won't look at her. "It might be in a few months, or it might be years, but there will be another storm, a really massive one, and then the forest will appear, I promise."

He keeps his head low and looks at her through his grown-out fringe. He seems to be examining her, checking for something.

"Mum always said you were the person she most admired in the whole world. That you were like a superhero, but better."

Audrey is astonished. Miranda had never said anything like this to her. The contrast between it and the things Marcel had said Miranda thought about her is startling. She's still trying to process the words when Edward abandons his spade and comes to her. Pulling him close, she sees his tiny hands are blistered and sore, the knees of his pajamas sopping.

"I want to see her again," he sobs. "To talk to her. Just once."

Marcel appears in the distance and waves.

Audrey thinks of the doorbell footage—of Cecile at the house the night before Miranda died.

Liar, thinks Audrey. *Cheat*.

And then…

Murderer?

Enid runs to greet him, and Audrey stays with Edward.

"Me, too," she says and presses the flat of her palm against the sand, trying to imagine the trunks and branches below.

––––––––

They get Edward home, bathed and changed, and after Marcel calls his practice to say he won't be coming in after all, father and son settle cross-legged in front of the TV and embark on a game of *Super Mario*. Now that Edward is safe, all Audrey can think about is the footage of Cecile at the barn the night before Miranda died. She's desperate to access the app, to study the clips properly, and so after making sure Enid is OK—as soon as they'd got back, she had retreated to bed with a Jacqueline Wilson—Audrey goes to the bathroom, locks the door, and, with jittery hands, gets out her phone.

Opening the Ring app, she goes to the deleted files she'd stumbled across this morning. This time she is methodical, taking her time opening and watching each clip in turn. There is limited audio, but rewatching the clip of Cecile's arrival at the house at 9:05 p.m., Audrey's pretty sure it was Marcel who had answered the door. She studies the expression on Cecile's face for clues. She seems upset and keeps brushing her hands through her hair. After a few minutes, she comes inside the barn, and the clip ends.

The next notification is fifteen minutes later. It shows Cecile leaving. And she's in a hurry.

Two minutes after that, there is another notification—this time, of Miranda leaving.

In this clip Marcel can be heard shouting after her, asking her where she is going. Miranda does not respond.

So much for her being out at a yoga class.

The next time the app is activated is after midnight, when Miranda returns to the barn. She looks tired. Defeated. Had she been angry about Cecile, gone out somewhere for a walk to blow off steam?

Audrey closes the app, unlocks the bathroom door, and heads for her car. She's not going to bother confronting Marcel with her discovery. She doesn't want to give him the advantage, the chance to formulate a story, to prepare. Clearly, something had transpired between the three of them that night, and yet he continues to lie about Cecile and her presence in his and Miranda's life in the buildup to his wife's death.

What did he have to hide?

The drive to the police station takes ten minutes. On the way there, she sees the steeple of Smugglers' Church, peeping over the rooftops, and thinks of the note Ben had hidden inside her letter asking her to meet him there. It had once been the only church in the area, and the congregation would walk for miles to get to service. Funerals would see people carry the coffin along the dunes to be buried. Did Ben's asking to meet her there have any significance, or was the churchyard just somewhere quiet, somewhere he knew they weren't likely to see anyone from school? Again she wonders if there was more to his death than Miranda's letter seemed to describe. Mr. Danler had thought the inquest suggested there had been other things at play that weekend—things which might have contributed to Ben's demise.

Inside reception, Audrey asks for Detective Sergeant Reese and goes to wait on a bench. Coming here—reporting Marcel—feels like a betrayal, and yet she doesn't think she has any choice.

Half an hour later, Audrey is sitting opposite Reese in the same interview room he'd used to show her and Marcel the dashcam footage.

He listens to her politely, then watches the doorbell clips on her phone.

"We know about Cecile," he says once she's done.

"You do?"

"We're looking into it." He stops and corrects himself. "We've been looking into it."

"Oh." She sits a little taller in her chair. "How about Marcel? Is he under suspicion, too? Do you think they had some involvement in Miranda's death?"

Reese grimaces.

"Cecile is a person of interest," he says eventually. Audrey waits for him to elaborate on Marcel, and when he doesn't she tries a different tack.

"And you still can't tell me anything about Leighton? Why he had all those photos of Miranda?"

The detective tenses, then holds out his hands as if he's asking for mercy.

"Sorry."

She thinks back to the one other occasion she'd had reason to be in this room.

"Can I look at the dashcam footage? Of Miranda?"

The first time she'd seen it, she'd had no one with whom to compare the figure standing alongside her friend. Maybe if she took another look, she'd be able to get a sense of whether or not the other figure's height and build could be a match to Cecile or Leighton—if it was possible one of them had been the second person on the cliffs that morning.

Reese nods, leaves, and returns with a laptop.

The clip appears on the screen, and he sets it playing.

The road appears, the mica in the tarmac twinkling in the early summer sun. A glimpse of sea, and then the van broaches the bend above Huntcliff. Audrey braces herself, ready for what's coming, and then there they are in the distance: Miranda and some other unnamed person, the sea spread out behind them. Audrey hits the space bar, pausing the clip, and leans in toward the screen. She scrutinizes the second figure for a few moments, then hits the space bar again and again, hoping to glean more detail from the second-by-second progress of the tape. The figure is slim and tall, that's for sure. She's not sure of Cecile's height or build, but it could be Leighton.

After rewinding and playing the clip back for the tenth time, she shakes her head. "It could be anyone," she says.

"We tried to enhance the image." The detective spins the computer to face him and taps at the keyboard. "Still, the resolution isn't great. The person looks like they're wearing a cap or hat of some kind, so we can't see their hair. They have their back to the camera the whole time, and so their gender is also still unclear." He turns the laptop back toward her, and she sees a grainy still on the screen.

Reese is right: it offers nothing new.

"What's that?" Audrey says, noticing a second JPEG behind the still's right-hand corner.

"The jacket the person is wearing," says the detective, motioning for her to enlarge the pic. "It looks tailored, or like a uniform of some kind. There's a design printed on or woven into the material. We're searching for matches to brands, but it's a bit like looking for a needle in a haystack."

Audrey studies the design. The jacket's material is a dark color—it could be blue, black, or brown; it's impossible to tell—and a series of light-colored arrows in the center of the jacket follow the trajectory of the person's spine until they reach the shoulder blades, then branch off to either side. It's unusual. If the detective hadn't said it was tailored, she'd think it sportswear of some kind. The kind of thing someone who works in a gym would own?

Audrey slumps. She's clutching at straws, and she knows it. Coming here has achieved nothing except to make her feel bad. Marcel has lied, and continues to lie, and yet she is the one who feels like a snitch.

She thanks Reese for his time and leaves. She's getting into her car when her phone rings.

Rosa McLaughlin, the outdoor leader from Cleasby House.

Audrey had thought her follow-up request such a long shot that she'd mentally tabled it the moment she'd pressed Send.

"Are you a journalist?"

Rosa's voice is as gruff as her initial text had been abrupt. Audrey stalls, too thrown by the question to respond.

"Because if you are, you need to tell me now."

"I'm not a journalist," Audrey manages finally. "I swear."

Rosa exhales. "I'll tell you what I know, and then please, leave me the fuck alone." She stops, as if registering her own rudeness. When she speaks again, it's clear she's trying hard to be polite. "You asked about the inquest. After Ben's death, the people who ran the center were freaking out. They lost so many bookings and were facing bankruptcy. Ben was an anomaly, and they needed it to stay that way. If anything else had come out, any other hint of negligence at Cleasby House, then that would have been it. They'd have gone under for sure."

"So what you said in your last message, about the incident that happened the day before Ben died, about it being teenage high jinks... That wasn't true?"

"They told me to play it down, said that I would be prosecuted, not them. That it would damage my future prospects." A bitter laugh. "I was young and didn't know any better, so I did what I was told."

"What happened at the rappelling?"

"Like I told you before—kids are horrible, terrible human beings."

Audrey holds her silence. Is Rosa about to confirm what Mr. Danler had surmised? That Ben had messed around with Leighton's climbing gear? That he'd tried to do his best friend harm?

A huff, and then Rosa's tone changes. There is a new seriousness to it, a careful way with words that suggests she's remembering the day in real time.

"Someone deliberately tampered with Ben's carabiner. I told the coroner it was only enough to give him a little fright as he descended the cliff, but the truth was that if I hadn't noticed, he would almost certainly have fallen a hundred feet to his death."

"*Ben's* carabiner?" Audrey says, trying to grapple with this revelation. "You're sure?"

"Yes. I'm also pretty certain who did it. I'd caught him taking food from the backpacks earlier that day. Whined the whole way during the walk. At the cliffs I found him going through the packs again, and thought he was searching for more food. But I remember the look on his face when I did a last-minute check before Ben's descent and realized the belay was unsafe. He was freaked out, but he was also disappointed— very much so."

"Can you remember his name?"

Rosa laughs.

"My dad's a lifelong season ticket holder for The O's. It's spelled differently; still, every time I dealt with him that weekend, I thought of the club."

"The O's."

"Leyton Orient. The football team." She pauses, wanting to make sure Audrey understands. "Leyton, Leighton. They sound exactly the same, said out loud."

Chapter 37

RICKY

Dear Ricky

This letter is supposed to be all about the things we are looking forward to in the future, but when I think about the decades ahead I'm more frightened than hopeful.

I am genuinely scared about what kind of world you will be living in when you read these words.

Rising sea levels.

Melted icecaps.

Rainforest gone.

Species extinct.

Sweltering temperatures.

Floods.

Water wars.

Right now you're playing your part, trying to make a difference, however small, and I hope with all my heart that it has helped, that the governments and the corporations have all seen sense and changed their ways, that the Earth is no longer in jeopardy.

The next morning, Audrey is at Kirkleatham Museum, mopping the entrance hall. After the last few days, she's glad to be here. The constancy of the old house and its artifacts is a comfort, the contained order of its glass cases a reminder that some things can be relied upon to stay the same.

She'd called Detective Sergeant Reese last night, told him what Rosa had said about Leighton. After she was done, she waited, hoping for some reaction, some tell on his part, but the detective was his usual implacable self, and after taking down Rosa's details, he'd thanked her for her time and hung up.

Mr. Danler and Robbie had been right about someone tampering with the climbing gear, but had mixed up who had been trying to injure whom. Mr. Danler had said that there had been some incident with Leighton way before the Lakes—something for which Ben had been formally punished. So maybe Leighton had wanted to exact his own punishment on Ben? Had the incident with the climbing gear been his way of trying to seek revenge? And then, when that failed, had he tried to hurt him again the next day? Ensured he was locked out? Spiked his drink, maybe? Had Ben passed out and frozen to death because he'd been drugged?

But surely if that had happened, there would have been traces in the autopsy.

It feels as if there is a puzzle spread out before her and that the pieces on each side have been assembled, but in the middle there is a giant gap—a gap she has no idea how to fill.

She drags her bucket over to the stairs and is about to head up to the first landing when her phone alerts her to a FaceTime. She doesn't recognize the number and so she declines, but then a few seconds later, she receives a text from the same person.

Audrey, it's Ricky Larkin. I just got your messages. I wasn't ignoring

you. The rig I'm on at the mo doesn't have wifi. I'm free for the next hour or so then I'll be out of range again for another three weeks. R

Ricky. The last classmate on her list. She'd thought he was a lost cause.

Audrey looks through the double doors to the car park beyond. The museum is due to open in five minutes, and visitors are already pulling up, but maybe Ricky knows more detail about what happened between Leighton and Ben. Maybe he could contribute something, however small, that might help her understand how or why the arrival of the letters had led to Miranda's death?

The landing will have to wait until next week.

She drags the mop and bucket into the walk-in cupboard to the right of the entrance; then she calls him back. Ordinarily she avoids communicating like this—it makes her self-conscious—but it feels more polite to stick with Ricky's preference.

For the first few seconds, all she can see is the whip blur of a ceiling fan, then the phone tips.

"Audrey Hawken. As I live and breathe." Ricky moves through what looks like a hotel room—beige walls, mirrored wardrobe, anodyne watercolors—then flops on the bed. His smile is a brilliant white, the bridge of his nose is striped with sunburn.

At school he'd worn his hair long and had always been a bit smelly. Like damp clothes left too long in the washing machine. She remembers his backpack. Made out of rough green canvas, it was covered in hand-drawn CND logos and tiny circular badges pledging affiliation to everything from Greenpeace to PETA.

"Thanks for coming back to me." The closet Audrey's in had once been the house cloakroom, and she has always liked its dark cloistered quiet. She runs her foot back and forth over the rungs of the scraper still fixed to the wall by the door.

"I would have replied sooner, but this job..." He pushes his head back into a mound of pillows and whistles. "I was only supposed to be out here three months. It's already been six. Having a few issues out here with the pipework. The wife and kids are going mental. Still, it's good money."

"Melvyn said you work for BP?"

Audrey tries to maneuver herself into a better light, to frame the shot without the cleaning products stacked on the shelf behind her.

"Melvyn...Melvyn Arkwright?" He laughs. "That's a blast from the past."

"He's in town for the summer. That's how I got your number."

Ricky nods, but she can tell that he's not really listening and is more focused on adjusting the collar of his polo shirt.

"Your messages," he says. "You asked about the school trip. About Ben. Sorry to disappoint, but I don't have anything useful to tell you. Apart from Ben dying, my main memory of that weekend is of hunger. I was a full-on vegan at the time, and the kitchen had no idea what to feed me. I lived on lettuce and bread for three days straight."

"How about things between him and Leighton?" she says. "Remember anything unusual?"

"Weren't they best mates?"

"They'd had a falling-out. Did you see them argue or fight at all?"

"I wasn't part of their crowd. I had no idea they weren't friends anymore, then or after."

Audrey hears the curator unbolting the main door and greeting the first visitors. She knew talking to Ricky was a shot in the dark, that it was unlikely he would know something that would help her make sense of it all. Still, now that she's ticked all the classmates off her list, she's surprised at how crushed she feels. The prospect of resorting to her regular life—the aimlessness of it—feels like trying to remember a bad dream from the night before. It fills her with a muted dread.

"I know this is a terrible thing to say, but when they found Ben dead that morning, I just figured it was karma." Ricky gets up from the bed and reaches for a bottle of water. "Remember how popular he was? Everyone thought he was great, but he had a dark side. Then I'm sure Melvyn already told you that."

Audrey thinks of the less than complimentary things she's learned about Ben over the last few weeks: his possible infidelity with Kitty, the fact he'd done something to Leighton that was so heinous it had almost got him suspended from school. But she can't recall anything negative Melvyn might have said.

"Back then I was a proper eco-warrior." He laughs at his own naivety. "Surfers Against Sewage. Before I had mouths to feed, and when I had no idea how the world actually worked. We used to pull all this activist vigilante shit. Thought we were going to change the world. This one night, about a month or so before Ben died, I was on the beach. In the dunes. The water company had been illegally pumping a load of crap—literally—into the sea at night, and so we took it in turn to do shifts, take pictures and samples, that kind of thing. Trying to catch them at it. I was monitoring the pipe that comes out on Stray Beach. There'd been a party on the sand; the bonfire was almost out. I'm watching and waiting with my night-vision camera, and then I see Melvyn in the viewfinder. Someone had tied him to one of the groynes and the tide was coming in. Some kind of sick joke." Audrey remembers Ben's letter.

You know you need to explain. To try and find a way to show her how sorry you are, how much you regret what you did.

She feels as if someone has taken a hammer to her skull. *Crack.* In the aftermath, her thoughts crash and rattle against one another, trying to rearrange themselves anew.

Has she gotten it all wrong?

Is this what Ben had been talking about? Not something awful he did to Miranda, but to Melvyn?

She feels the closet walls pressing in on her, the lemon bleach smell from the cleaning chemicals clustered at the back of her throat.

"Melvyn was hysterical. He genuinely thought he was going to drown. If I hadn't seen it with my own eyes, I wouldn't have believed it."

Audrey thinks of all the times she has talked to Melvyn about Miranda and Ben. He, more than anyone, knows the lengths she has gone to in order to figure out what happened to her friend. What it had cost her emotionally. Even if this incident had happened a while before the trip, she can't understand why he didn't say anything to her about it—why he didn't think it was relevant.

Was he embarrassed? Even after all this time?

"Are you saying Ben was the one who tied him up?"

"Yes, and then he fell asleep. He did try to help, when he came around, but by then he wasn't needed." Ricky stops, thinking. "I'm pretty sure that was why they split—Ben and Miranda."

"Wait…Miranda knew about this? About the prank?"

"Ben was just waking up in the dunes, and so I went to the shoreline. I was taking off my shoes, getting ready to go in the water and cut him free myself, but then she appeared from nowhere." Even now, Ricky is breathless with admiration. "Miranda was the one who swam out and rescued him."

Chapter 38

MELVYN

Stray Beach, 2003: One month before the school trip

The sea froths at my waist. A spring tide, it will be higher than usual, enough to cover me twice over. I pull against the tie cinched around my wrists, but it's fixed fast to the groyne, and struggling only makes the plastic cut deeper. I stopped screaming for help some time ago, but now, as the brine stings my torn flesh, I twist back toward the dunes and shout.

It had all been going so well. After weeks of watching the parties from afar, I'd finally plucked up enough courage to come and join the crowd. I'd thought people would ignore me or make fun, but they were all so different from how they are at school and seemed to consider my presence a quirk, a novelty that made them smile. Usually, when people talk to me, there is a point where their eyes dart across the red bumps and lumps that crater my skin, and they react, a blink or a twist of the mouth in revulsion, but here in the dark, you can't see anyone's face clearly, and even though I keep waiting for it, that moment, it never happened.

I drank a little before I got here, and then more as the night went on. It helped me relax, to chat with people I wouldn't normally, to laugh, to feel part of things. But then someone said something to Ben, and he got angry, made accusations.

The moon appears from behind the clouds, and I think I see somebody on the coast road, their arm pulled forward by a dog on a leash. I yell louder, but my cries are lost in the roar of surf, and I realize that even if someone glanced in this direction, they wouldn't see me, that shackled to the sea side of the timber, I'm invisible.

I know why this is happening, why Ben thinks I deserve this. He's angry. But no matter what he might think, I never said a word, not to anyone.

The water sloshes at my armpits, the cold like a spreading bruise.

Is he really going to leave me here to drown?

I don't want to believe it, I can't, but the water keeps getting higher.

The groynes disappear completely at high tide, and so some, like the one I'm attached to, have a tall pole reaching toward the sky with what looks like the skeleton of a red lampshade attached. The shade is there to warn swimmers and small craft of the hidden obstacles beneath. Sitting here, I feel like if only I could reach up and flick a switch, I could light the bay. Summon a rescuer to cut me free.

A car revs in the distance. Or maybe it's something else.

I realize he's not coming back. That this is it. A mewl escapes from my mouth, and then I am crying and whimpering and begging for my mum, the way I used to when I was small.

The tide is getting stronger. My ribs buckle against the surge, and I snap at the air for breath. I think of the other creatures in the surrounding mass of water: the seals, crabs, and brown jellyfish you see jeweled into the shoreline. I imagine them circling beneath the surface, slinking against my sodden jeans and nipping at my shoelaces, intrigued by this new addition to their world.

As the next wave hits, I close my mouth and arc my face toward the sky. The lampshade on the pole above clangs and wobbles in the breeze.

A splash.

Then a shout.

My name.

I think it's him, that he's come back for me after all.

But then they shout again, and I realize it's not Ben, but a girl.

She swims close, feels for my wrists under the water, starts to hack at the ties with something small and sharp.

"What is wrong with you?" she shouts toward the shore. Her face is next to mine and I can feel her breath. She grunts in frustration.

And then a voice from far away, back toward the dunes. Ben.

"I fell asleep." His words are groggy. "Is he OK? Oh my God. Is he dead?"

Whatever she's using against the ties isn't working. She brings it to the surface and I see a bunch of keys. She chooses a different one, inhales, then dives again.

"What's happening?" screams Ben. Sloshing. It sounds like he's coming into the water, too. "Where are you?"

I feel her working away at the ties with the key, a sawing motion that hurts my wrists, but then they're free. Her head breaks through the waves. She pushes a thick mass of hair out of her eyes and gulps for air.

Miranda.

I try to bring my arms back round to the front, to swim, but my muscles are numb and they sway limply in the current.

"He's OK," she shouts to Ben, and floats me on my back against her hip. With one hand hooked underneath my arms, she uses the other to swim to shore. "You're OK."

She plows us back through the waves.

"I owe you," I think. "I owe you."

Chapter 39

In Guisborough Forest, Audrey waits to collect Enid and Edward after a day at summer camp. The other parents and carers mill around the huts that form the camp's base, but Audrey hangs back, too focused on her phone to make small talk. Since her conversation with Ricky, she's called and called Melvyn, to no avail. She knows he's out at sea, on the study boat, that the signal will be unreliable; still, she keeps trying. She's desperate to ask him about the prank Ben had pulled—to find out why he never said anything. He knew what she'd been trying to unravel, how she'd struggled to unlock the sequence of events before Ben had died, and yet he'd chosen to keep a key part of the puzzle from her. Why?

Had it been so traumatic, so embarrassing, that he still hadn't felt able to talk about it? She remembers what Belinda had said about seeing Miranda and Melvyn whispering in corridors on the school trip. Ricky said it had happened a month or so before the Lakes. Was this what they'd been talking about—how Miranda had cut him free from the groyne that night?

Once more, her phone connects to his, and while it rings she takes a breath, willing him to pick up, only for it to go through to voicemail yet again. This time she doesn't bother leaving a message, and after putting her phone away, she moves toward the other adults. She's almost at the huts when she stops, distracted by a lone figure off to the right. Sitting on one of the stumps that circle the adventure playground, he is wearing a T-shirt that grips his biceps.

Leighton.

His kids must also attend this camp.

A person of interest.

Someone who had tampered with Ben's climbing gear.

Someone who had messaged Miranda on the morning she died.

Someone who, according to Belinda, had been taking pictures of Miranda for years.

Stalking her?

Audrey marches over to where he sits, but he's got ear pods in, his eyes closed, and she has to tap him on the shoulder to get his attention.

Seeing her, he swears under his breath.

"Was it you?" she says loudly. "Was it you with her on the cliffs?"

His mouth goes slack with panic, but then he snaps to and hustles her away from the others, out of earshot.

"It's a misunderstanding."

"Really?" she says. "Is it also a misunderstanding that you have all those photos of her? Videos?"

He cups his face with his hands, brings his elbows in close to his chest. She realizes he is shaking.

"The police confirmed my alibi this morning." His voice trembles. "Call the detective if you don't believe me."

Audrey studies his posture, the way he's rocking slightly, back and forward on his heels. She has no idea if he's telling the truth, but when she can verify what he's saying so easily, lying seems futile.

"Were you stalking her?" She pauses, trying to reconcile the wildly different explanations that have been running through her head for weeks. "In a relationship with her?"

"I wish." He drops his arms to his sides and smiles sadly, full of longing. "I loved her. Always have."

"Loved her?"

"Very much. Since school. She had no idea."

"Did Ben know?"

He winces at the mention of his name and goes to reply, but then stops himself.

"He knew how I felt, but he went out with her anyway. He said he had no choice, that he couldn't help his feelings." He shakes his head. "Snake. I never forgave him."

He runs a finger down the ladder of abs protruding through his T-shirt.

"I suppose I should be grateful." He flexes his forearm, assessing the musculature, but he seems separate from his own physicality, as if he's checking the workings of some machine. "He's the reason I'm the man I am today. Why I started taking care of myself, why I do the job I do. Wanted to make sure I was never overlooked again." He drops his arm back to his side. "To help others who are also tired of being overlooked."

Audrey thinks about her conversation with Rosa McLaughlin, and decides to ask him straight.

"At the Lakes, did you try to kill Ben?"

She watches him carefully, waits for some flash of fear or guilt, but instead the question seems to give him a boost, and he lifts his chin, defiant.

"Before that trip, he'd been trying to win Miranda back for weeks. He'd profess his love for her to anyone that would listen, go on and on about how devoted he was to her, how she was the only one for him. But it was all rubbish. He didn't care about her, not like I did. She was just one of many. At the Lakes I kept seeing him sniffing around Kitty. It felt like he was dishonoring Miranda somehow."

"So you tampered with his climbing gear?"

Again, he checks the forest track, making sure there is no one around.

"I just wanted to frighten him, maybe humiliate him a little."

"It was a hundred-foot drop," says Audrey. "What did you think was going to happen?"

Leighton flinches.

"My plan was just for him to descend the rock face faster then expected, to make him scream or cry in front of the others." He sags. "But I didn't know what I was doing. The equipment was new to me." He looks Audrey in the eye, his face creased with regret. "I realized my mistake when the instructor found the harness. Somehow she knew I was responsible. She looked straight at me, terrified. She was incredulous at what I'd done, at what would have happened." An eruption of children's laughter spills from somewhere in the camp. He waits for it to die down before continuing. "I was so relieved she'd found it, but then I got scared. The instructor didn't take me to task in front of the others, but I was sure that once we got back to the center she'd haul me in front of the teachers—that I might be suspended, or even expelled. But no one said a thing. That night, before dinner, she came up to me. Told me I was going to get away with it, but that she knew what I was, what I'd done."

"What about the night Ben died?" Audrey says. "Were you with him then? Did you get him drunk? Lock him out?"

Leighton holds up his hands, a gesture that is part protest, part plea. "I had nothing to do with that, I swear."

Once more, Audrey realizes there's no way to know if Leighton's telling the truth, except in this instance, she doesn't know how to verify his account.

Yet, she thinks to herself. Yet.

He thinks they're done and goes to retreat. Audrey is on him in an instant.

"As well as taking pictures of Miranda, following her around, you were harassing her, messaging her?"

He stiffens. She senses that he does not accept this version of events. This version of himself.

"Actually, it was Miranda who got in touch with me. A few weeks before she died, she came to see me at the gym. She was interested in signing up for my coaching course. Said she'd been trying to turn her life around, to better herself, but that she was having a crisis of confidence. She thought maybe I could help." He beams. "I couldn't believe it. I was so happy. This is it, I thought. Invisible string. You've waited for her, wanted her your whole life, and now this is going to bring you together." He stops for a second, enjoying the memory of that feeling. "She said she was going to think about it, but then she went quiet. So I followed up. When she didn't respond, I followed up again." He throws his hands out into the air. "The morning she died, I sent her another email asking to see her urgently."

"And these were the messages the police found on her phone?"

A nod.

"They looked into it, realized it was legitimate, but then Belinda found my photos." He looks to his lap. "She thought the worst. Called the police." He looks back up at Audrey. "I was hurt she did that, that she didn't come to me first, but also I get it, I do." His gaze falls back to his lap, lost in some thought he can't or won't share. "After that they kept accusing me, asking if I was the person out there with her on the cliff. I told them no. I wouldn't let anyone else touch a hair on her head, let alone hurt her myself."

Audrey hears the pride in his voice and recoils. Leighton had stalked Miranda for years, and yet he really thought of himself as noble—her secret protector.

"They didn't believe me, clearly, but then yesterday they finally managed to get the CCTV for the barre class I go to, confirmed I was there that morning, *not* out at Huntcliff."

Audrey says nothing, still trying to take it all in. Miranda had sought out coaching? Marcel's affair and the impending divorce had obviously knocked her for a loop.

"Look, I know the photos thing seems weird, but I didn't intend for it to be that way. It was a gradual thing."

Audrey side-eyes him, full of contempt.

"Remember when she left for France?" he says, scrambling to explain. "You were devastated, I'm sure. She was your best friend, after all. So was I. But her leaving town was really good for me. I had no choice but to forget her, to try and get on with my life." He has been speaking quickly, eager to make his case, but now he slows. "Then," he says, taking a breath, "she came back." He stops. "I was married with kids. Still, I was giddy every time I saw Miranda around town. Happy. Alive in a way I hadn't felt in ages." Again, he goes quiet. "But then I found I wanted more, needed more." His eyes dart left and right, as if he's trying to navigate his way out of a maze. "I was trapped in this tiny flat full of babies and toddlers, and Miranda was like this emblem of a more carefree time, when there was still everything to play for. She never realized, I don't think. Saltburn is such a small place, it's par for the course that you see the same people around. Sometimes she would see me, and she'd stop and chat, ask how I was."

His eyes still.

"I really did love her," he says after a little while, and Audrey realizes he thinks this explanation, combined with her silence and the fact his alibi has been verified, means everything is OK. Water under the bridge.

She looks at him, disgusted.

"You obsessively took pictures of her without her consent. You stalked her. You tried to murder her ex-boyfriend. At best it's fucked up, at worst it's criminal. What it most definitely is not, is love."

Leighton shakes his head—no—but his eyes are wet. He knows what Audrey says is true. Behind him, a line of kids emerge from the trees near the huts, finished for the day. Audrey leaves him there and goes to greet Enid and Edward.

Chapter 40

I t's early evening at the barn, and Audrey has a shepherd's pie in the oven. She's invited Ned and Eleanor for dinner in the hope that she can talk to them about the baby, to persuade them that it's in all their best interests for Ned to keep his place at UCL.

Marcel is late, and so while an exhausted Eleanor lies on the sofa eating crackers and Ned tries to keep the increasingly hangry Edward and Enid from having a meltdown, Audrey covers the pie and veggies with foil to stop them from drying out and reaches for her phone.

She is still trying to reach Melvyn on the boat, to ask him about the things Ricky had said, but yet again the call goes through to voicemail, and so she busies herself with setting the table.

Since talking to Leighton this afternoon, she's spent the day trying to recalibrate what she does and doesn't know about Miranda's death. Leighton wasn't entirely innocent, but he hadn't killed her. Marcel and Cecile, on the other hand... Audrey's paranoid that Marcel knows she showed those doorbell clips to the detective, that he's going to confront her, to accuse her of betraying him and the kids, that her actions are going to take their only remaining parent away from them. And yet, as far she can tell, it is he that has done all the betraying.

On the sofa, Eleanor yawns and closes her eyes. Almost immediately she falls asleep. Ned watches her for a second, and then his eyes go to her belly. He smiles.

Despite her misgivings, Audrey had offered her congratulations as soon as the pair had walked through the door, fussing around Eleanor with water and cushions for her back.

Ned leaves the kids somersaulting across the floor and comes to the sink to help Audrey with the washing-up. Halfway through, he leans his head on her shoulder. "Thank you," he says, quietly. "For not making this weird."

"Have you called them yet?" she says. "The university?"

"I have." He takes a breath. "They said I can defer. And they said that when I do start there, they have special accommodation for undergrads with infants, that Eleanor and the baby could come and live there with me while I study."

"Really?" Audrey turns to face him. While this should come as good news, Ned's whole plan seems so naive. She worries that once he realizes how hard it is to look after and provide for a child, he'll back out. "Isn't London expensive? What will you live on? And isn't studying medicine full on? How will you manage? What about money?"

"It won't be easy, I know that, but I'll figure it out." He looks to Eleanor again. "*We'll* figure it out." He dries the last of the dishes and sets the tea towel on the side. "Life is never simple. But that's the joy of it, right?"

It's an hour later, and the kids are using bolster cushions on each other like pugil sticks when Marcel finally walks through the door. Audrey gets the food out of the oven and calls everyone to the table.

"I'd have been home sooner," he says as he hugs the kids hello. "But the police called, asked me to stop by the station on the way home." He ushers Audrey over to the other side of the kitchen, out of earshot of the children. "They've made some progress with Miranda's phone and wanted to cross-check a few things."

Audrey tenses. Had the police decided there was merit to the doorbell footage she'd brought them? Had they questioned Marcel about Cecile? Is the house of cards he'd built about to come tumbling down? But no, he seems more perplexed than worried. "Those twice weekly visits to Teesside University? It wasn't a yoga class."

Behind them, Ned calls the kids to the table and serves them helpings of pie. Eleanor is still asleep on the sofa.

"Since the start of the year she has been enrolled in an access course there," says Marcel. "She was hoping to do a degree. Psychology."

Audrey thinks of the first part of Miranda's "Dear Future Me" letter, the batch-cooked food in the freezer, the coaching sessions she'd considered with Leighton. It wasn't just a whim. All this time she'd wanted to go to university, had harbored that dream, and she'd been trying to finally make it happen.

"I don't know why she would keep something like that secret," says Marcel. "If that's what she'd wanted to do, I would have supported her."

Audrey watches as Ned covers Eleanor with a blanket.

"They also looked into those bank transfers I asked you about," Marcel continues.

"University fees?" says Audrey. "That would make sense." After her conversation with Mr. Danler, she'd googled "night school." She had been shocked at the expense.

"The money was going into a personal account. They wouldn't tell me the person's name."

Eleanor wakes and rears upright. A cough, and then she leans over the side of the sofa and vomits.

Ned grabs some paper towels and goes to her aid.

No one bats an eyelid, except for Marcel, who looks around, baffled.

"We've got something to tell you," says Ned as he dabs at the rug.

Chapter 41

It's Friday night, and—against her better judgment—Audrey has agreed to a few hours' work serving drinks at Kitty's big party to celebrate her professorship. It was all very last minute—three of the undergrads they'd hired to waitress had dropped out—and so Jago had called Audrey in a panic around 5 p.m. As he'd begged her to come and help out, all she could think about was the day she'd bumped into Kitty and her parents in the spa; Kitty's father's certainty about his daughter's supposed incompetence. And so even though Audrey knows she'll hate every second, she also knows the only thing she'd hate more is for the party to be a disaster because it is so woefully understaffed. To give Richard Veigh that satisfaction. Besides, she figures it's better than sitting around at the barn and fretting about when Melvyn might get all her messages and call her back. About why he's kept so many things to himself.

She's navigating the car along streets full of sunburned day-trippers on their way to the station, their calves spattered with drying sand, when she passes the dry cleaners and clocks a tanned Leonard behind the counter.

Finally. He's back.

She pulls in and parks on a double yellow. Stopping will make her late, but she doesn't care. If Leonard can locate Kitty's missing items, then Audrey won't have to endure any more of her nagging.

Inside the shop, she scrabbles for the ticket in her purse.

"The girl you had covering," says Audrey. "She could only find half of the stuff?"

"Let me see," says Leonard, and disappears out the back. He's not gone long, and when he returns he has the missing items folded over his arm. Audrey claps her hands, delighted.

"You found them."

"It wasn't her fault," he says, removing the ticket stubs from the plastic sheaths. "I put them aside on purpose. Didn't want her coming across it by accident, getting you in trouble." He leans in. "Your boss. They did it again—left some stuff they shouldn't have in the pockets." He shows her a small plastic bag he's hooked over one of the hangers. "But this time there was a *lot*. Like I'm talking intent to supply a lot. Tell them to be more careful in future. And watch your back."

Audrey groans. *Bloody Jago.*

She thanks Leonard for his discretion and heads back to the car.

She's winding her way down Marine Parade when she sees the entrance to The Zetland hotel is open, and a very pregnant Belinda is struggling to carry a cardboard box down to the pavement. She wonders how many times before now—when her radar was turned off—that she drove past the flat conversion and failed to clock Belinda outside. It's startling how full Audrey's world has now become, how rich with familiar faces, how much more there is to see, only now that she thinks to look for it.

She pulls in and lowers her window.

"Need help?"

Belinda releases the box from her grip, and it crashes to the floor.

A purple resistance band, a pair of jeans, and the wedding photo she'd seen that time she visited the apartment, spill over the side onto the pavement. Belinda tosses her hair over her shoulder, adjusts her bra strap.

"Thanks, but that was the last of it."

Audrey looks and sees there are already a number of other boxes dumped in front of the railings.

"I've kicked him out," says Belinda. "Going to try going it alone." She taps out a rhythm on the apex of her belly. "The timing isn't ideal, but then, it never is."

"I'm sorry," says Audrey.

Belinda surveys Leighton's things.

"All these years," she says, her voice brittle, "he wanted something else. *Someone* else. I was just his way of making do, and I didn't even know it."

————————

Audrey continues on her way to Kitty's cottage. As she draws near to the turn-off, she slows. Jago had requested that Audrey and the other catering staff keep the drive free for guests, and so she parks a short walk away, at the top of the rough track that leads into the property. But the track is more rugged than she realized, and as she pulls in she hears her tires grind and crunch against the rocks.

Inside, the house is buzzing with activity. Champagne flutes rattle in cases stacked ten high, ice clatters into vast plastic buckets, and in the garden, she can hear the scrape of metal as the final marquee posts are slotted into place. It is a beautiful late summer evening, the light buttery, the air warm.

As with almost everything in Kitty's life, Audrey knows tonight will be a success, that afterward people will remember the party and feel proud they were invited, privileged to know someone so bursting with accomplishment, so special.

She looks down at the white apron Jago handed her to put on when she'd arrived, at her cheap black lace-ups, the way the sole is starting to come away a little at the front.

She's used to feeling jealous of Kitty, of her life and her achievements, and ordinarily she'd expect tonight to be a rainbow of other ugly emotions—shame and regret, to name a couple—but, she realizes, she feels happy for her, and even though she would never be in her employer's league, she was starting to own and feel pride in who she was, cheap lace-ups and all, that the last few months have left her changed. That, little by little, she could feel this new sense of herself starting to show. She thinks of a rescue cat her dad had once brought home from a shelter. Skittish and terrified, the creature had spent the first few weeks hiding, but gradually it had started to appear, tiny flashes of whisker, ear and tail that vanished no sooner had you glimpsed them, until one day it had padded into the kitchen, and for the first time, they saw the animal whole.

"Audrey?" Kitty appears from nowhere. Wearing an oversized man's tux and white silk shirt, her fringe and bob are held in place by hair clips designed to keep them from curling until the last minute. The collar of the suit jacket is edged with black satin, and a white handkerchief sits upright in the breast pocket. "What are you doing here?"

Audrey realizes she's left the dry-cleaning in the car, and is about to offer to run and get it when Jago appears, disheveled in a seersucker suit, his eyes bloodshot.

"It was me," he says. "I called her, asked her to help out." He motions to the chef at the counter behind him, frantically blobbing mounds of black caviar onto row upon row of tiny round blinis, the champagne flutes beside him yet to be unpacked. "You told me to sort it, and so I did," he adds gruffly.

He eyes Audrey the same way he did that day he'd found her in the study with Kitty's letter—warily—but, just like that time in the study, his expression is loaded, the air charged with something she doesn't understand.

Kitty frowns, but then seems to snap to.

"Fine. Audrey, I need you to make sure all the loos are spick and span, enough toilet roll, fresh hand towels, Aesop candles lit; then, when guests start arriving, if you could be the one to wait by the door, take their coats, offer them a welcome drink—"

She's cut off midflow by Richard, barrelling in from the garden.

"The flower beds are a *mess*. Thick with weeds."

His wife, Polly, follows him like a tiny shadow, shimmering in a maroon sequin shift dress.

"No one cares, Dad." Kitty's voice is jolly, but Audrey can tell she's working at it, that her smile is a little more forced than before. "They're not coming to look at the garden, they're here for me."

He stops, appraises her tux. Looks to his wife, eyebrow raised.

A moment of understanding passes between them.

"Let's get you upstairs," Polly says to Kitty. "Finish getting ready?" She ushers her daughter away and beckons for her husband to follow. "Maybe see what else you have to wear?"

Audrey grabs some rubber gloves and bleach, and is heading to make a start on the downstairs loo when the doorbell goes. Thinking it an early guest, she abandons the gloves and goes to answer it, only to be confronted by a giant arrangement of orchids and lilies. A woman peers around the edge of the flowers.

"Delivery." She staggers forward, and Audrey moves to let her through. Three more giant vases wait on the gravel. "Where do you want them?"

Audrey cranes her neck toward the kitchen in search of Jago, but he has disappeared.

"Let me go and ask." She takes the stairs two at a time and heads for Kitty's bedroom. She's about to knock when she hears voices from within.

Richard.

"Any news?"

A pause. "I decided not to go for it in the end." Kitty's voice is small. "I want to build up some experience as a professor first, make my mark on the department."

"But we're talking Harvard. Ivy League."

"York is an excellent and respected institution," Kitty says, her voice getting even smaller.

"You probably wouldn't have gotten it anyway," he says. "They want the elite."

Audrey balls her hands into fists, mortified. Kitty is so proud; hearing her being spoken to like this is as shocking as it is embarrassing. She cannot bear to hear any more and sneaks back downstairs.

How must it feel to know your own father thought you weren't good enough and probably never would be?

How it must it feel to have him say those things to her on this, of all nights?

The doorbell goes again. Audrey decides not to bother Kitty with questions about the flowers and runs back down the stairs to discover the florist has gone, apparently having already made her way out to the back garden.

She opens the front door, and as she and the person stand there, clocking each other, there is a moment of pause. Audrey is the first to come to.

"Sergeant Reese?"

Her first thought—that he's tracked her down here because he has urgent news about Miranda's death—is one that she will later realize makes no sense.

Reese steps back and glances up at the house, as if to check he hasn't made a mistake.

"Is this the residence of Dr. Jago Plaige?"

Audrey nods.

"I'd like to ask him a few questions."

Chapter 42

Before Audrey can do as the detective says, Kitty thunders down the stairs. She muscles past Audrey so fast that she stumbles, and has to right herself.

"Is there a problem?" Kitty says in a high, bright voice. She's changed out of her smoking suit into a dressing gown, and while she talks she knots the belt tight around her middle.

Reese explains that he's here to talk to Jago. Audrey thinks of the dry-cleaning still in her car and the drugs Leonard had alluded to in the pocket. How he seemed to think the amount he'd found was enough to suggest Jago had a serious problem.

"Jago," shouts Kitty without taking her eyes off the detective. "I need you."

It takes a while for her husband to emerge and when he does, he moves slowly, sullen, like a child who's been called to the table for dinner. Once he understands who the person standing on the doorstep is, though, he straightens up and offers his best, most charming smile.

"Everything OK?"

"Could we talk?" Reese's eyes flit to Audrey, lurking in the hallway. "Somewhere private?"

Audrey rarely sees Kitty and Jago together as a couple, but when she thinks of them—of their marriage dynamic—she always sees Kitty as the dominant one in charge of her hapless husband. Now, though, seeing how the pair stand in relation to each other—Kitty simpering behind Jago's shoulder, head bowed in deference—for the first time it strikes Audrey that it's actually the other way around. That perhaps Jago is the one in control.

Jago leads Kitty and the detective into the living room.

They haven't closed the door properly, and so Audrey decides to hover for as long as she can. She knows it's wrong to eavesdrop, but she's worried about the drugs in her car.

"Dr. Plaige," says Reese, "tell me about your relationship with Miranda Brévart."

Chapter 43

On hearing her friend's name, Audrey's breath catches in her throat. She wants to barge in and demand the detective tells her what is going on, but she knows that if she does, he'll just go ask and Jago his questions elsewhere. She might never learn why the police are interested in him.

"Miranda?" says Jago calmly.

"My old classmate," says Kitty. "The one who died." A pause. "Why are you asking my husband about her?"

"You don't know anyone called Miranda?" says Reese. "Our investigation shows that for the last six months you were her tutor. Is that not correct?"

"Oh, *Miranda*." A tiny laugh. Jago sounds relieved. "I have so many students, I don't know all their names."

Silence.

Audrey may not be able to see the scene on the other side of the door, to register the expression on the detective's face, but she can feel it. The quiet is dangerous. Something bad is coming, and Jago is too arrogant to realize.

"The night before Miranda Brévart died," says the detective, "she came here, to this house."

"What?" Jago's voice rises an octave.

Audrey has to stop herself from blurting out the same question. The hall seems to pitch and shift like a boat on the swell. She palms the wall, steadying herself. She cannot believe what she is hearing.

"Why would she have done that?"

"There must be some mistake," says Jago.

"No mistake," says Reese. "We've been through her phone data."

Back toward the kitchen, Audrey hears a metallic clatter: someone dumping cutlery on the counter and the rattle of plates stacked on top of one another.

"Were you friends at school with her?" says Jago to Kitty. His voice is high and inflected with hope, as if he's just remembered the answer to a question at a pub quiz. Audrey guesses he's smiling, as if he's figured it all out. "Maybe she was coming to see you?"

"We were more acquaintances than friends," says Kitty carefully. Audrey hears the docility in her voice and knows she's not responding to her husband; rather, she is addressing her answer toward the detective. "Besides, I wasn't here that night. I was away in Sheffield, at a conference."

"And how about you?" says the detective. "Were you here?"

It takes Jago a few moments to reply, and when he does he speaks slowly, as if he's choosing his words carefully.

"I had a party."

Audrey thinks of the used condom she'd found in the bathroom the next day. Jago passed out on the chaise longue with a cut knee and trousers covered in chalky white dust.

The same white dust that packed the path by the cliffs?

"This party. Could Miranda Brévart have been in attendance and you didn't realize? How many guests are we talking?"

Jago says nothing. Audrey can't work out if it's because he doesn't know, or if he thinks the answer is somehow incriminating.

The detective grips on to the silence like a door that until now has only been open a crack. He reaches his fingers through the gap and pulls.

"You're known for having inappropriate relationships with your students. Isn't that right, Dr. Plaige?"

The question seems to suck all the air out of the room. Even on the other side of the door, Audrey can feel it.

Had Jago been there with Miranda on the cliffs? Was he the person in the dashcam footage?

She thinks of the light-colored darts arrowing up the back of the jacket, and tries to remember if she's ever seen a formal suit of his with that design.

A cork pops in the garden, followed by a swell of laughter. A few bars of music blare from a speaker, then come to an abrupt stop.

"Miranda Brévart," says Reese, circling back. Audrey feels as if he's jumping from topic to topic on purpose, to disorient them. "There were messages on her phone, from a year ago. Exchanges between the two of you." The detective pauses. "Dr. Plaige, was Miranda Brévart blackmailing you?"

Audrey jolts, shocked but also insulted by the accusation. Miranda would never.

"I think we need to end this here," says Kitty firmly. She sounds confident, in control, but she can't maintain the facade, and in the next sentence her voice cracks. "If you want to ask more questions, you can do so with an attorney present."

"Word at the university is you've been under investigation," says Reese. "That you've had numerous affairs with your undergraduates."

"I was cleared," says Jago, his voice strained. "It was a misunderstanding."

"Was Miranda Brévart one of those students? Were you having an affair?"

Another jolt. Audrey huffs, outraged at the suggestion. Miranda wouldn't give a creep like Jago the time of day.

A prickle of doubt.

Would she?

"Enough," says Kitty, and Audrey hears footsteps approach. She retreats down the hall toward the kitchen.

Kitty opens the front door and stands there, spine erect, waiting for the detective to leave. He takes his time, hands her his card, and then at last he's gone. Kitty slams the door shut and, as she turns around, locks eyes with Audrey. Audrey knows Kitty realizes she's been listening in; that she'd heard everything.

Audrey expects Kitty to be embarrassed, readies herself for the explanation she is sure will come, but instead Kitty pulls her dressing gown even tighter.

"Terrible what the police will do when they have no real leads," she says with a shake of her head. "They start blaming anyone and everyone. So desperate." Then she stomps back upstairs.

Chapter 44

MIRANDA

Saltburn, 2023: The night before...

Since Cecile is gone, I get in the car and drive to Jago's house. Learning Marcel had restarted his affair was devastating, but knowing I have a secret of my own fortifies me. It's like wearing a talisman that no one else can see, a charm that protects me against anyone who might wish me ill.

I know Jago won't like my turning up unannounced, but after tonight I need to see him more than ever. As far as I'm concerned, my problem is as much his as it is mine. He needs to step up and take responsibility, to help me figure out a way through. Whatever happens when I knock on the door, I decide I won't take no for an answer, that I won't leave until he gives me what I need.

Chapter 45

Audrey launches herself out of the front door in pursuit of Reese. He's at the end of the drive, about to get in his car.

"Wait!"

He turns and then, seeing her, raises his eyebrows. She rushes over to him, worried he might flee.

"Miranda came to the cottage?" she says. "Is Jago a suspect?"

He presses his lips together. "I can't talk to you about this. It would jeopardize the case. You understand?" Audrey nods, begrudging, and he relaxes a little. "What are you doing here anyway?"

"Work." She lifts the corner of her apron. "I usually clean their house, but tonight I'm helping with the party." She takes a breath. "You really think there's a possibility that Jago is the second figure on the cliffs?"

"We need to look at his phone data, and for that we need a warrant. We're not there yet, but give us a few days, and we will be."

"What about Cecile and Marcel?" she says, thinking of the doorbell footage.

Reese shifts his weight from foot to foot, directs his gaze somewhere off to her right.

"Cecile is troubled," he says carefully, "but she has a solid alibi for the morning Miranda died."

Audrey considers this.

"Jago isn't Miranda's type," she says with more confidence than she feels. In truth, when it comes to what her friend wanted or thought about this world, she's no longer sure of anything.

Reese smiles kindly. "But you already know she and Marcel were in the process of getting a divorce."

"Yes, but that doesn't mean she was having an affair…"

The front door opens and Jago emerges, pulling one of the other waitresses by the hand. He searches the drive, frantic. Seeing the detective, he makes a beeline for him, dragging the young woman in his wake.

"Tell him," he says, once they come to a stop.

The waitress looks to the ground.

"Miranda," she says quietly. "The night of the party. She came to the door. I answered it."

"Who are you?" says the detective gently.

"Cordelia." She lifts her chin, meets his eyes. "I'm one of Jago's grad students."

"*And?*" says Jago impatiently. Cordelia flinches.

"She wanted to speak to Jago. I told her he was busy. It was pretty obvious there was a party happening, but she wouldn't go, said she was worried about her exams, that she was convinced she was going to fail. I told her to come back another time or to talk to him about it when he was at work, at the university."

Reese nods, and Audrey can't tell if he believes her or not. Everything Cordelia said is plausible, but none of it explains why there was someone there with Miranda at the cliffs.

"Are you both willing to come down to the station and make a statement to that effect?" says Reese.

"Of course." Jago breathes out, relieved. He thinks he is off the hook. But Audrey notices Cordelia seems subdued, her hands folded underneath her apron.

The detective gets in his car and as he pulls away, Jago turns to Audrey.

"Everything I told him is true. I had nothing to do with her death." He sighs, and Audrey thinks he is about to get wistful, but when she sees his face—eyes and mouth set firm—she sees something more like pragmatic surrender. "Though he's right about Miranda blackmailing me. But not in the way you think."

Audrey looks back in the direction in which the detective had left.

"Last year, Miranda got wind I'd been playing about. She saw me with one of her yoga students." He speaks quietly, but his shame is barely there, faded over time. "She told me to hire you as our cleaner. Told me how much to pay."

Audrey's mouth falls open. A year ago.

She thinks of her leaking roof back then, her ancient boiler. How strapped she'd been for cash. She'd been so worried, but then had been blessed by a sudden influx of work. Well-paid work, at that.

Had Miranda been behind all those new jobs?

Her throat tightens and her vision blurs. It had been such a kindness—not just the help, but the fact that Miranda had understood this was the only way Audrey could accept such help.

"So, if you hadn't hired me…what? Miranda would have told Kitty?"

Jago stretches his mouth into an awkward smile, baring all his teeth. "I hate her for putting me in that situation, but I was also a bit jealous."

"Of me?"

"Having a friend like that. Someone willing to go out to bat. I thought you were lucky."

An hour later, it is as if the visit from the detective had never happened. The lawn is crammed with people in linen suits and floral dresses, laughing and talking and lurching for canapés whenever they pass by.

Audrey performs her role in a daze, greeting guests and taking coats on autopilot, too in shock to leave. Again and again, she runs through the morning of Miranda's death in her head. She'd arrived at work at 9 a.m., and Jago had been passed out on the chaise longue. Miranda had last been seen alive on the dashcam footage at 8:10 a.m. That would leave more than enough time for Jago to get back here from Huntcliff. She thinks again of the cut on his knee, the white dust on his trousers. Was it the same kind of chalk you found on the Cleveland Way?

Audrey knows how slippery he is—how expert at lying to his wife. Of course he was going to claim he had nothing to do with it; of course he was going to have some story for the police. He'd rolled out that waitress like a grand exoneration, but in reality, her account meant nothing. It makes Audrey sick to her stomach to think it, but what if he and Miranda *had* been in a relationship? It was so easy to imagine a scenario in which that could have provided the seed for her death: Miranda comes to the house to see him the night of the party—just as the waitress said—but she's not there to ask for help with her exams; instead, she is hoping to make the most of Kitty being away. She discovers him messing around with some other undergrad. Miranda is distressed; she threatens to tell Kitty everything. Jago begs her to meet him at the cliffs the next morning, Miranda refuses to back down. They argue. He loses his temper, or wants to ensure her silence...

Audrey's thoughts spin and twist, playing out different versions of the same story, and while she thinks, she works. Time seems to speed up; the party chatter and music is a cacophony she has to shout over to be heard. She weaves in and out of the throng, offering trays of mini beef Wellingtons and smoked salmon, pausing every now and then to right a toppled champagne flute or to give directions to the loo, and all the while, the same questions relay around her head about Jago and Miranda.

Were they?

Was she?

Did he?

The din and kaleidoscope of faces are dizzying, and after a while Audrey switches to manning the drinks station that has been set up outside, at the back of the house. Here the table is stacked with flutes and metal buckets jammed with ice and open bottles of champagne, but it is much calmer. The bottom of the garden is marked by an ivy-smothered wall, and beyond it are fields and the Cleveland Hills, their bumps and peaks glowing pink under the setting sun.

When Kitty emerges from her room, Audrey sees she has changed out of her dressing gown into an emerald-green Ossie Clark maxi—it seems her parents got their way—and while she and the dress are beautiful, she is clearly uncomfortable, fiddling with the neckline and stumbling on the train as she works the crowd.

Robbie Rooke and his wife appear, champagne flutes held out for a refill, and Audrey remembers going to see the MP in the Methodist Hall that day.

Seeing Audrey, he squirms, embarrassed, then smiles thinly, making it clear they are not going to engage in conversation. Right now she is the waitress, he the guest. His wife is oblivious to the whole exchange, and as Audrey empties the end of a bottle into her glass, she grins at her with caviar-stained teeth.

Once they've gone, Audrey stands back to watch Kitty continue to move through the crowd. Holding the bottom of her dress clear of her feet, Kitty heads for the decking at the side of the garden, on which a microphone and small PA have been arranged. A man with shoulder-length gray hair waits for her there, and when she gets close, he offers her his hand and helps her up onto the platform.

While Kitty stands to one side, the man grabs the mic. The machine beeps and crackles, and the crowd stops talking and turns to face them.

"Good evening, everyone." He drops the mic to his hip and surveys the garden, taking it all in. "My name is Dr. Ralph Didion. I'm retired now, but back in the day, I was lucky enough to be Kitty's director of studies at Cambridge." He is wearing a navy blazer with a white handkerchief and glasses tucked in the breast pocket, and as he speaks he pushes them this way and that, as if to make sure they are properly positioned. "She was an exceptional student and a passionate historian, and I am so proud and not at all surprised to see her made a professor."

Audrey searches the crowd for Kitty's parents, and wonders if Richard will make any kind of speech. Finally, she sees him, standing with Polly close to the decking. Instead of watching Didion, like everyone else, he has angled himself toward the crowd, and whenever people applaud or whoop he shares a congratulatory grin, as if the achievements being spoken about are his.

"I knew as soon as she appeared in that interview room that she was special." Didion pulls out the handkerchief and blots the sides of his neck. "Actually, I knew even before then."

While the professor speaks, Kitty catches Audrey's eye, her face pained. It's supposed to be her moment of glory, but no doubt all she can think about is the visit from the police.

"For those who don't know, to even be granted an interview at Cambridge, you have to write a bespoke essay on your subject. Something outside of your usual A level work. The topic can be anything; it's completely up to you. I have interviewed hundreds of potential students over the decades, and so it says a lot that not only can I vividly remember Kitty's admission piece"—he reaches inside his suit jacket pocket and pulls out some folded sheets of paper—"but that I kept it." He brandishes the pages in the air, triumphant.

Kitty's face hangs loose in shock, and for the first time since she got up onstage, she stops looking at Audrey.

"They don't want to know about that," she says and goes toward him, but Didion has anticipated this. Before she can snatch the sheets away, he clutches them to his chest and leans forward as though sharing a secret with the crowd.

"She's modest," he says in a faux whisper, "but she has no reason to be, for even at the age of seventeen, Kitty Veigh, as she was known then…" He coughs. "Professor Kitty Plaige, as she's known now, was quite brilliant."

Kitty continues to stand a bit too close to him, coiled and ready to capture the pages from his hand at any opportunity.

Didion clears his throat and reads.

"Ask anyone about the history of female equality in this country, and they'll talk about Emmeline Pankhurst and her suffragettes, of the contraceptive pill, or of education for all. In fact, as I am about to prove, the single most significant and transformative thing in the fight for women's rights has been the humble public toilet."

Didion continues. "In this essay, I am going to show how the ability to spend a penny while out and about, at work or at leisure, gave rise to the biggest social change our sex has ever seen, how breaking free from the urinary leash allowed women to work, shop, travel and organize politically in a way they had never been able to before."

Audrey looks up, as if someone has called her name.

The sentences Didion reads are old but so familiar. Audrey tries to settle the glass she had been in the middle of filling onto the table, but her hands are juddering, her grip tight, and as she sets it down, the stem breaks in two. The yellow liquid bubbles and seeps into the white cloth.

It's been twenty years, but she read and reread that essay so many times before handing it in that it became like a prayer of which she remembers every word.

Didion continues to read, and as he does Audrey finds herself mouthing along with him.

She looks to Kitty for an explanation. She cannot understand what is happening—cannot compute how her words are coming out of this academic's mouth. Audrey expects Kitty to be as flummoxed as she is, but her eyes are on the ground, her arms at her side, a clutch of green silk in each fist.

That's when she realizes.

The truth of it hits her like a brick.

Kitty knew these weren't her words before her director of studies even started speaking. She is ashamed but not surprised that he attributes these thoughts, these arguments and sentences to her, because she has passed them off as her own for years.

Audrey stares at Kitty, willing her to look up. If she can get her to acknowledge her in this moment, then she'll be able to breathe.

When Kitty finally raises her head, Audrey is light-headed, her lungs shriveled from lack of air. She can see people's mouths moving, glasses clinking, but to Audrey the garden is silent. Kitty releases her dress, and Audrey sees how the silk has creased into ugly lines around her hips. She meets Audrey's eye, and her face is red with guilt, but her eyes are unblinking, defiant, like those of a dog with a stolen bone.

Chapter 46

BEN

The final bell goes, and everyone grabs their coats and bags, and hurries into the corridor. I do the same, but where others rush and chatter, I dawdle, letting myself be carried along with the current until the crowd thins. At the swing doors, I stop and squint at the friends grouping together to walk home. Everyone is buzzing about the trip to the Lakes this weekend. They speculate about who they hope to share a room with, if they're scared about the rappelling, how their older brother has told them the residential center is haunted by the ghost of some revengeful Victorian maid.

I stand there as long as I dare; then I turn around and head back down the corridor to room 303, where Mr. Platt will be waiting to oversee my detention. I'm being made to stay back every night this week, just as I was last week and the week before that. Punishment, for what happened with Leighton.

Looking back, I think it was all inevitable in a way. A question of when, not if...

It was lunchtime, and I was by the netball courts, watching Miranda train, hoping for a chance to talk with her once she was finished, to try (as I have so many times since that night at the beach) to explain, to say how sorry I was, to maybe find the courage to tell her about what was going on with Mum. They'd just finished playing and were collecting the bibs when I saw Leighton at the other end of the court, also watching the team train. Or should I say, watching Miranda train.

He's been obsessed with her for years, since the start of high school. Way more than your average crush, he's often told me he loved her, that she was the only one for him. But the thing was, the thing that Leighton and I both knew but never said out loud, was that she was way out of his league, that most girls were.

Then in lower sixth Miranda and I were put in the same class, A level English. I'd always thought she was pretty, but that year something changed. It was like we noticed each other properly for the first time. We'd share jokes. I'd catch her looking at me. She'd catch me looking at her. Soon she was all I could think about. There were a few drunken kisses at parties. Some secret hand-holding at break. Then I asked her out.

I didn't start the relationship lightly. Leighton was my best friend, and I knew how much it would hurt him, how jealous he would be, but when it came to Miranda, it was like I had no choice, no control. I didn't want to upset Leighton, and I very much wanted to remain friends, but I wanted her more.

Of course, when Leighton found out, he was furious. I was "Mr. Popular," could have any girl I wanted, so of all of them, why did I have to choose this particular one? I tried to explain, but he didn't want to hear it. He stopped speaking to me, told me he hated my guts, that I was a terrible person. That he would never forgive me.

Then, after what happened at the beach, Miranda broke up with me.

Leighton could not have been more delighted. He clearly saw it as his opportunity and started tailing her around school, pining after her.

Watching her.

That day, when I noticed him at netball training, I went over to where he stood, but as soon as he clocked me, he'd scuttled away, inside the school. I followed.

"Some friendly advice," I'd said, coming up to him in the corridor. "Stop following her around; it's creepy."

He stopped, turned to face me.

"That's none of your business, not anymore. Miranda is a free agent."

I laughed then. I don't know why. Maybe because I knew what he said was true?

He punched me. A sharp slug underneath the ribs. I doubled over, and then he hit me again and again. It was like all the rage and jealousy he'd been storing up since I first got with Miranda was coming out. I refused to hit him back, I didn't want to fight, but this only made him more angry. He started slapping me around the head, sharp little smacks that were as humiliating as they were painful. I realized he was goading me, that he wasn't going to stop, that he wanted me to react, that he *needed* me to react. And so, after a blow that left my ear hot and red, I drew back my fist and punched him once in the face. My knuckles landed with a crack against his jaw.

It was at that moment the teacher appeared.

I know I could have told them that I didn't start it, revealed the bruises already forming on my middle, explained how I was acting in self-defense, but I decided not to say a word. To take all the blame. I kept to this even when there was talk of suspension, even when they compromised on three weeks' detention. I suppose I figured Leighton's lashing out had been a long time coming, that I deserved it. We might not have been friends anymore, but the years we'd hung out still mattered, to me, at least.

I arrive at room 303 to find Mr. Platt waiting.

"Detention started five minutes ago," he says, nodding at the clock. "So you'll stay an additional ten minutes on top of the hour for being late."

I nod. I've discovered that having to be home less than usual is actu-ally a blessing of sorts. Mum used to make us all sit down for tea together when Dad got in from work. She did the same meal on the same night. Shepherd's pie on Mondays, lasagna on Tuesdays… I liked the regularity of it, the shape it gave to the week. But since she's been gone, all that has stopped. Dad never cooks or seems to eat at all, for that matter. Most nights he works late or goes to the pub, and so I eat standing up, from a plate on the counter.

I take my seat at the desk at the front of the class, and while Mr. Platt marks essays, I sit and look at the same names carved into the wood I look at every night. This is the worst part of detention. The boredom. Endless minutes to sit and relive that night on the beach, the way Melvyn's voice had cracked as he begged for his mum. To imagine what might have happened if Miranda hadn't come back for her coat. Sometimes, though, I get lucky, and Mr. Platt leaves the classroom to go and do other stuff. The first time this happened, I stayed put, scared that if I got out of my seat for even a second he'd come back and catch me, but then after the third or fourth time he left me alone in this way I'd realized he was down the corridor, chatting football with the woodworking teacher, Mr. Pew, and that he had a pattern, always returning five minutes before my detention was up.

There was no way I could leave the actual classroom without him noticing, but with him gone I could at least wander around, stretch my legs, look out of the window. That got boring fast. But then I discovered the stationery closet. Situated behind his desk, it was more like a tiny room and, critically, it had a connecting door to the classroom opposite.

Now when Mr. Platt leaves to go and gossip with Mr. Pew, I go into the closet, peer through the keyhole to make sure the coast is clear; then I head on through and exit out of that classroom door. Sometimes I wander the corridors; sometimes I go to the library; sometimes I lie flat on the playing field where no one can see me. Then a few minutes before I know Mr. Platt is due to return, I head back in via the closet and retake my seat.

When I peer through the keyhole today, though, I discover I'm out of luck. The classroom is occupied by Mr. Wilson, the history teacher, and Kitty Veigh. It's not unusual to see Kitty; I often seen her on my library wanders, doing extra studying after school, but tonight she's working on something at a desk while Mr. Wilson marks papers. I know most people don't like her, that they think she's a nerd, but I feel sorry for her. She's one of the cleverest people in our year, but she never seems to have any fun—you never see her at parties or out with friends—and whenever I've seen her studying in the library, she always looks tense, her face pushed close to the book, like she's trying to physically cram the information inside her skull.

I watch them for a while. They might not be doing much, but it's more entertaining than spending another forty-five minutes doing laps of the classroom.

Mr. Wilson has his back to me, but every now and again he twists to his right and a spread of brown envelopes he's filling with assorted paperwork. The whole thing is very precise, and he keeps checking and cross-checking the paper in his hands before paper-clipping it together and putting it inside. Once he's done, he gathers the envelopes into a pile and leaves them in a wire tray on his desk. Then he grabs his coat and bag, tells Kitty not to stay too late, and leaves.

I'm debating whether or not to open the door and breeze on through—Kitty's a nerd, but I don't think she would tell—when she stops writing and looks around. I think she's seen me, that somehow she knows I'm watching her. But instead of coming toward the stationery closet door, she goes over to the exit to her classroom and peers out. Satisfied by what she sees, she closes the door and goes over to Mr. Wilson's desk. It feels like she's coming straight toward me, and again, I think she's going to open the door and laugh, that she's going to tell me she knows I've been here the whole time, but at the desk she stops. Another glance at the classroom door, and she makes her way around to Mr. Wilson's chair and removes the envelopes from the tray. Then, taking each one in turn, she slides out the top half of the paper inside and scans what's written there. Three envelopes later, and it seems she's found what she's looking for.

Another check of the doorway, and she slides the contents of the envelope onto the desk and starts poring over the pages. After a few moments, her face reddens. I realize her breathing has quickened, that whatever she's reading seems to be causing some kind of panic. When she gets to the end, she goes back to the beginning and reads through the first few pages again, slower this time.

I can't work out what it is she's looking at. Her school report? But no, it's the wrong time of year for that.

She puts the pages down slowly. Looks from them to the doorway. Something has changed. Her shoulders are back, her eyes focused, her breathing slow. She chews at her knuckle, thinking, then goes and peers into the corridor, checking left and right.

Whatever she's doing or about to do, it's clear she doesn't want a teacher to see.

I smile to myself, pleased to discover that Kitty Veigh isn't the goody-two-shoes everyone thinks.

Back at the desk, she searches out another envelope, removes some pages from it and replaces them with the ones she was just reading. After putting the envelopes back in the tray, she scuttles back to her desk, packs up her stuff, and flees.

The whole thing is bizarre. I'm desperate to know what she's done, and so as soon as she's gone, I come out through the closet and over to the envelopes I just watched her tamper with. Looking inside, I see she's paper-clipped the pages to the other documents in there. I slide the whole thing out on the desk and see an application form for Cambridge

University. Small print at the top reminds the student that this is supplementary to the UCAS form, and that they must remember to attach their admission essay. The name on the form is Audrey Hawken. Miranda's friend. The other envelope contains Kitty's application.

She switched Audrey's essay for her own.

I can't believe it at first. There's no reason for her to do this, she's so clever, so brilliant.

Unless she thought Audrey's essay was better, that it would give her a better chance?

I'm wondering if I should switch them back, to put right what Kitty has done, when I hear footsteps. I retreat back inside the closet and squint through the keyhole. It's Mr. Wilson, huffing and puffing, like he's in a hurry. I watch as he gathers up the envelopes from the tray and a few other things from his desk; then he turns out the light and leaves.

———

That night, my insomnia is about something altogether different.

What Kitty did and why.

And more importantly, what I should do about it.

Miranda has always talked about how hard Audrey works, how going to Cambridge is her dream. I've always thought of her and Kitty as on a par academically, but maybe Kitty isn't so sure.

I decide to confront Kitty the next day at school. To tell her what I saw, that I know what she did. I know what it is to make a terrible mistake, to do something you later regret. With Melvyn there was no one to stop me in my tracks, but maybe I can help Kitty, get her to put things right, before any real damage is done.

Every time I try to approach her, though, someone else appears. It's impossible. In the end, I decide to go to her house after school, to talk to her there.

Her dad answers the door, looks me up and down, eyes narrowed.

"I'm Ben, a friend of Kitty's from school."

He pulls the door closed a little, as if he's worried I'm going to charge my way inside. Then, without taking his eyes off me, he calls to her upstairs.

She appears quickly, but when she spots me, she slows, confused. Her dad stays where he is, and she peers round him and over my shoulders, as if looking for others.

"I wanted to talk to you about the Keats project," I say, "I'm having trouble with how best to lay out his letters alongside the poems." I look at her dad. Offer my best smile. "We're study partners. Project is due Friday."

The lie reassures him, and he steps aside to let Kitty forward. I expect him to leave us to it, but he lingers, like a sentry unwilling to relinquish his post; then finally he goes.

"Study partners?" she says once he's gone.

I spent the walk here debating how best to broach it, whether to tread carefully with my accusations. Now, though, I decide the best thing to do is to just come right out with it.

"I saw you."

"Saw what?"

"Yesterday, in Mr. Wilson's classroom. I saw you switch the essays."

The change in her is instant. Her face goes gray. She checks behind her in the corridor, then turns back to me.

"I don't know what you're talking about."

I give it a beat. Hold her gaze.

When I speak next, I keep my voice low and matter-of-fact.

"Tomorrow morning you're going to go and see Mr. Wilson, tell him what you did."

Her lip trembles and she bites it, as if to stop herself from crying. I can see how scared she is, but I've already figured out a way for her to come clean without admitting to being a cheat.

"You can tell him you were curious to know what others had written for their admission essay, and so, even though you knew it was wrong, when he left the other applications on his desk that night, you had a look. Ever since, you've been worried you might have put the wrong papers back inside the wrong envelopes, and so could he please check then before he sends them off."

Her eyes lower and flit from left to right as she considers this. I breathe out, relieved. She's going to do it. But then her face hardens and when she speaks next, her voice is cold.

"I don't know what you're talking about."

I frown. "Look, I get it. You wouldn't have done something like this unless you really wanted it, but Kitty, it's wrong. More than that, it's not fair."

Her dad reappears.

"Dinner will be ready soon," he says, "and you've still got twenty minutes of French revision to do."

Kitty nods and puts her hand on the door to close it.

"Tell Mr. Wilson," I say before she disappears. "Or I will."

Her face is blank.

"I have to study now," she says, then she closes the door.

––––––––

At school the next day, I fall in beside her on the way to lunch.

"Did you talk to Mr. Wilson?"

She pulls her backpack straps close across her chest. "Leave me alone."

"You need to tell him."

She keeps her eyes ahead and picks up her pace.

"Kitty?"

I slow to a stop and she powers away, half running, half walking into the dining hall.

I don't want to report Kitty to a teacher, not yet, anyway. If I do that, she's screwed. Her Cambridge application will be thrown out, and she might get suspended, expelled, even. I'm still hoping to persuade her to make it right some other way, and so after school I go by Miranda's house. Audrey is her best friend. I'm going to tell her what I know, ask her advice.

Her mum comes to the door. Seeing me, she sighs.

"She doesn't want to talk to you, you know that."

"Please, it's important. It's about her friend Audrey."

She purses her lips, then goes inside and shouts upstairs to Miranda. Miranda calls something back.

Her mum returns.

"She doesn't want to see you," she says, then she closes the door.

The next day I decide to go to Audrey, to tell her what I know. But she trails Miranda like a shadow, and every time I come near, Miranda thinks I'm trying to get *her* attention and guides her away. In the end, I decide to write her a note and slip it inside her work at the end of English. When the teacher gives it back tomorrow, she'll find it. I've asked her to meet me outside school. I'll tell her what I know, and then I figure it's up to her what happens next. Maybe if *she* confronts Kitty, it will have more impact, or maybe she'll just go straight to Mr. Wilson.

But Audrey isn't at school the next day. Or the day after that. Someone says she has tonsillitis, that she's going to miss the trip to the Lakes and be off until at least next week, if not longer.

I consider going straight to Mr. Wilson. But no. I think of Kitty's dad, the way she tensed when he came near. If he found it what she'd done, if she was expelled, then her life wouldn't be worth living. I *have* to change her mind. Persuade her to come forward. It will be better that way.

Give her one last chance to make things right.

Chapter 47

Ralph Didion continues to speak, but Audrey has heard enough. She staggers into the house, through the kitchen, where the chefs are clearing up, and into the hall, where she collapses onto the bottom stair. It feels as if the world is falling in, her life and her understanding of it in ruins.

Kitty stole her work. Passed off Audrey's essay as her own and cheated her way into Cambridge.

But how? And why?

She hears Kitty's voice through the microphone. A cursory speech, and then footsteps.

Kitty appears and stands in front of Audrey. Her makeup is smudged but her eyes show no remorse.

"All this time," says Audrey eventually, and then, more to herself than Kitty, "I thought I wasn't good enough."

Kitty's face crumples—a mixture of guilt and horrified understanding. She knows what it is to feel less than; she hates that she has passed this particular hell on to someone else.

"You read my letter," she says, matter-of-fact. "I *had* to get in."

Audrey is aghast. "So, what...? I was just collateral damage?"

"You don't understand." Kitty tries to come and sit next to Audrey on the stairs, but Audrey refuses to budge. "The pressure I was under. I was desperate."

"How?" says Audrey. "I can't figure it out."

"I swapped them." Kitty winces at the admission. "You'd been so secretive about your admission essay—do you remember? This one day, I'd stayed behind after school as usual, and Mr. Wilson left the applications on his desk. I wanted to know what you'd written about, and so I took a look." She rubs at the corner of her eye, making the black smudge there worse. "I could tell within the first few paragraphs how good your work was compared to mine, how original. I knew there was no doubt you'd be called for interview."

"You stole my essay—my chance." Audrey's brain whirs. She wants to cry, to shout, to scream. "My whole life would have been different."

One of the caterers calls to Kitty from the kitchen.

"Just a second," she calls. She scans Audrey's face, and Audrey realizes she's assessing her for risk, that she's trying to figure out if she's going to tell, if her precious evening is about to be blown apart. "Your whole life?" she says eventually. Her tone reminds her of the way Mr. Danler had spoken to her when she'd gone to see him on the moors: firm but gentle. "It was one misstep—a big misstep, I'll give you that—but still, you never did anything to try and correct it. You never even made so much as a shuffle in another direction."

Audrey grabs her bag and coat from the living room, and Kitty repositions herself in the hall, likely ready to block her should she decide to head back to the garden. But Audrey has no desire to talk to anyone. She needs to be away from here, to be alone with her thoughts.

She looks at her white apron and cheap black lace-ups, and then at Kitty in her green silk dress.

"Enjoy the rest of your evening," she says bitterly, determined not to let Kitty see her cry. "After all, you've worked so hard for it."

Audrey walks up to the rocky track where she's parked, torturing herself with thoughts about what could have been. Had she been granted an interview, if she'd been offered a place, it would have been one of those things that was impossible to turn down, something she wouldn't have been able to let pass by, no matter the change in her circumstances. Maybe she'd have deferred for a year; maybe the college would have somehow helped her study *and* take care of Ned. Whatever happened, she knows she would have found a way, that she would have gone to university, to Corpus Christi College and its library of ancient oak desks.

But then, as she gets behind the wheel, another thought surfaces. Is she right to blame her life, her lack of achievement, on Kitty's deceit? Was not getting into that particular university really the crux, or had it been something she'd used to hide behind?

She's trying to make sense of it all, her brain pulsing and spinning, when her phone rings.

Ned.

There is no way she can hold a coherent conversation with him—or anyone—right now, and so she sends it to voicemail. But then he tries again. And follows up with a text.

PICK UP! THIS IS IMPORTANT

Reluctantly, she calls him back.

"Are you alone?" he says very fast. "Who are you with?"

"I'm at Kitty's. Just leaving."

"Good…that's good." He puffs, as if relieved, then holds the phone away from his mouth, reporting this fact to whoever he's with. "You need to come to the barn now, straightaway."

"What is it? What's happened?"

"The police. They called Marcel. They got a hit from Miranda's car. A DNA match. This person…they have a criminal record, for ABH. Actual bodily harm."

Audrey peers back down the track to Kitty and Jago's house. Was Detective Sergeant Reese right? Is Ned about to tell her the DNA was a match to Jago?

"There's no way they can say whether this person was in the car with Miranda on the morning she died or at some other time, but they think the fact that she was transferring money to them and they have a history of violence is significant."

Audrey has never thought of Jago as a violent person, and she finds it hard to believe he has a record. As for the cash…how much was it Marcel had said was missing from their joint account? Ten grand? Aren't Jago and Kitty loaded?

"I'm so glad you're OK," he says, choked. "When we heard…" He pauses, trying to compose himself. "It being Friday night and all, I worried you might be out with him."

"Him?"

For the first time since hearing Ralph Didion read her essay to the crowd, Audrey's mind stills.

"The DNA match," says Ned. "It's for that guy you've been seeing. Melvyn—Melvyn Arkwright."

Chapter 48

MIRANDA

Keswick, the Lake District, 2003

After a day of hiking, Miranda's feet are covered in blisters. She tries to ignore them, but halfway through dinner the pain becomes too much, and she goes in search of plasters and more forgiving footwear. She's roaming the corridor at the back of the house—the one leading to the walled garden—when she comes across Melvyn. He's sitting on the floor next to an ancient radiator, his knees pulled in to his chest.

"Melvyn?"

She hobbles closer, and he lifts his head. He's wearing a T-shirt and khaki cargo pants; his face is studded with painful red acne, his cheekbones sharp. Seeing him out of the baggy hulk of his school uniform, she can see how thin his arms have become in the last month, how his trousers gape at the waist.

"Why aren't you at dinner? Go quick, or there'll be nothing left."

"Not hungry." He reaches for the radiator and starts picking at the layers of brown paint.

She tenses. "What did he do? I told him to leave you alone."

"He hasn't done anything." Melvyn slumps. "Not since that night, anyway."

He manages to dislodge a big section of paint and crumbles it between his thumb and finger.

"They put me in his group. It's bad enough having to see him in school every day, but here…"

She puts her hand on his shoulder, squeezes.

"More and more, I think the only way I'm going to feel better is if I take back some control."

"What does that mean?"

"I need him to experience what I did—to make him understand."

Miranda hears the pain in his voice, and her insides twist. "Revenge? Never a good idea."

"Not that. More of a lesson. I want him to know what it is to fear for your life, to understand how it changes you, how it changes everything."

"You really think it will help?"

Melvyn sits up a little straighter, checks the corridor before he speaks again.

"I was thinking of doing something here, while we're away from home, but if I try anything, he'll be on his guard straightaway. I need someone he trusts."

Miranda looks at the hollows in his collarbones, his nails, bitten to the quick.

"Will you help?" he says. "Please?"

Chapter 49

Audrey sets off toward Huntcliff. As she drives, she keeps hitting Redial on Melvyn's number. He's supposed to be back from his boat trip today, but still it goes through to voicemail every time. She'd promised Ned she would come straight home, but even as she said the words, she knew she didn't mean them. She needs to find Melvyn. To look him in the eye and ask if he killed her friend. If he pushed her to her death. Audrey knows that what she is doing is reckless, but learning about Kitty's cheating has unlocked something in her, and she feels untethered, as if she has nothing to lose.

She tries to process the things Ned had told her. To match them against the person she thought she knew.

Melvyn has a record.

A history of violence.

The kind of person who is comfortable—experienced, even—in hurting others.

The kind of person who is capable of murder?

As she clears the bend that leads to Warsett Hill, Audrey's mind brims and races against itself, reviewing all her conversations with Melvyn so far.

It's only as she tries to hunt him down that it occurs to her how careful he has been not to tell her where he is staying. How skillful he is at keeping things vague. But that doesn't matter. If he's back in town, she knows there's one place he might be, where he spends all his time. The kittiwake colony.

At the nature reserve, she parks and trudges up the hill, past the dilapidated farmhouse, now surrounded by metal security fences and signs warning that the building is marked for demolition, toward Huntcliff. As she walks, Audrey runs through her various encounters with Melvyn, examining them through the lens of what she now knows. He'd told her he had only bumped into Miranda on the odd occasion in town, but he seemed to know so much about her; then there was the fact Eleanor thought she'd seen them together at the coffee bar. Not to mention his failure to tell her about the terrible prank Ben had pulled on him as a teenager, and how pivotal that had been in Miranda's decision to end their relationship.

Was his DNA in Miranda's car because they'd been meeting up socially, or was it something more sinister?

One thing was clear: when it came to his connection to Miranda, both now and when they were at school, he'd evaded the truth at every turn. But why?

Audrey reaches the path and looks left and right up the coast, but the cliffs are deserted. Gulls still wheel and dive, but the kittiwakes are quiet, settled in their nests for the evening.

She thinks of Miranda, that morning, standing here in her pajamas. Had the figure next to her been Melvyn?

He didn't seem like the guy to own a suit, never mind wear it first thing in the morning—she'd only ever seen him in fleeces, T-shirts and cargo shorts—but then, there was so much about him she didn't know.

Defeated, Audrey heads back to the car. She'll return to the barn as Ned requested, let the police do their thing. But then she looks again at the cordoned-off farmhouse. The coastguard she'd bumped into seemed to think Melvyn was squatting there. Melvyn had said he only camped at the property every now and again, but maybe that was another lie.

It's easy to squeeze through the metal fencing, but finding a way inside the building itself is harder than it looks. Most of the openings are boarded up or blocked by piles of smashed lintels and bricks. A set of stone steps leads down to a cellar, but the door is metal and rusted shut. Eventually she finds a bloated wooden door around the back, hanging by its top hinge. After a few shoves, it opens into what looks like a dim larder.

Looking ahead, Audrey can see holes everywhere: in the floorboards, in the ceiling, in the walls. She takes a single step forward, testing. The boards underfoot are spongy, the wood rotten and spattered with moss, but they hold. Carefully, she picks her way down the hall and calls Melvyn's name. Silence. She starts to wonder if he has, in fact, returned from his trip. If he'd gotten wind that the police were on to him. If this is the reason he still has his phone turned off.

She's heading back outside when sees it: a flash of color, brighter and newer than anything else in the place. She retraces her steps and stands in the doorway of the room where the item had caught her attention.

A purple and green sleeping bag sits rolled up in the far corner. Next to it is a pallet stacked with folded clothes and toiletries. She takes in the organization, the amount of stuff. This is not the kind of setup someone would have if they just camped here occasionally. This is a place where someone sleeps and lives full-time.

Audrey's heart quickens.

The police had said that Miranda's phone data showed she'd been out to Huntcliff on numerous occasions in the weeks and months before her death. Until the appearance of the second figure, they'd theorized that she'd been scouting the cliffs as a potential suicide location, or that she was trying to find the courage to go through with it, but now Audrey has another thought.

What if Miranda had been coming to the farm to see Melvyn?

Chapter 50

MIRANDA

Keswick, the Lake District, 2003

After they discover the body, everyone is told to go back to their rooms and stay there until further notice.

At first, they do as they are told. Some sit on their bunks and cry; others perch by the window, squinting at the drifts of blinding snow. Hours pass before the ambulance arrives, and even then the paramedics have to abandon their vehicle at the same point from which the class had disembarked and drag their backpacks and stretcher half an hour up the track.

Another hour passes. Kids begin leaking into the main corridor on the first floor, clumping together by the mullioned picture window in groups that whisper and hug and speculate. Every radiator is cranked to the max, the dry air parching throats, but the house's thick walls are cold to the touch, the window's curtains swaying in the draft.

Melvyn and Miranda are huddled halfway down the stairs leading down to the ground floor, whispering, when someone looking out of the picture window clocks the paramedics trudging through the snow to the bottom of the garden. They call to the others and everyone crowds at the glass, watching as they approach Ben's frozen corpse.

Some whimper; some hold their breath; others revel in the drama.

It is gripping and terrifying, and demands their absolute focus, and so no one notices when Melvyn and Miranda peel away to one of the nearby dorm rooms.

"What happened to just teaching him a lesson?"

The recriminations fly from their mouths like knives.

"What we did—it's not a crime."

The back and forth gets quicker and sharper, building and growing in volume until finally all their fear and anger seems to expire, and they quiet.

They look at each other. A moment of acceptance.

"No one has to know," says Miranda gently. "We weren't there. It never happened."

Melvyn folds his arms and tucks his trembling hands in tight against his chest.

"OK?" says Miranda.

"OK," he says.

Chapter 51

Inside the room, Audrey searches the plastic crate that sits next to Melvyn's sleeping bag. There isn't much: a form detailing the contact details for his probation officer, a picture of a young boy she presumes is his son, a printout of his contract with the Royal Society for the Protection of Birds. It seemed his work at the colony was a government scheme, created to help prisoners transition to regular life upon release. She recognizes the address on the envelope: a halfway house in Marske. The same one listed in Miranda's leaflets. She had taught a yoga class there.

She's about to put everything back where she found it when she notices another envelope, addressed in the now familiar handwriting of Mr. Danler. Melvyn's "Dear Future Me" letter.

The first part of the letter is unremarkable and talks about Melvyn's love of birds and his worries about going to university, but the second page gives her pause.

You've had a rough time of it lately. I'm sure even now, you haven't forgotten.

How could anyone forget something like that?

Are you still scared of water? Of the sea, and the way the tide rushes in? You used to love the beach so much, being there in the quiet with the terns, but not anymore. He's ruined that for you.

Still, you have plans for redress, to make him feel what you felt...scared for his life. Alone. If you can find some way to even the score, then maybe you'll ensure that what happened to you never happens to anyone else. You'll have peace.

Melvyn was planning to exact revenge on Ben. To do something that would make him fear for his life. But what?

Three pages in, Audrey gets her answer.

Just as with Miranda's letter, there is a change of ink and tone in the second part, written when the class had returned from the Lake District.

When we started this assignment I'd imagined you, the future Melvyn, reading these words as a separate person, different in every way to the 'me' writing them. I'd thought that all that elapsed time would change you, turn you into someone new. In reality, that process has taken only a few short days.

Now, reading back over the first pages of this letter feels like passing a mirrored building and startling at the realization someone is echoing your every move, only to understand a moment later that it's a reflection. That it's you.

I don't need to ask if you remember the moment you realized Ben was dead. The horror will be etched on your brain forever. So will the fear that followed.

The terror that someone will find out.

As for Miranda. She was OK at first, as OK as anyone could be, but as the reality of what happened set in, she's struggled to so much as look you in the eye. She can't believe you made her a part of this.

Audrey tries to marry up what she has just read with the lines from Miranda's letter, lines she now knows by heart.

If things had been different, he would still be alive today. You got so caught up in the fact that you needed to teach him a lesson.

You needed to teach him a lesson.

Was Camille wrong? Had Miranda's guilt been about more than just ignoring Ben at her window that night? Had she done something else— something far more calculated and deliberate? Melvyn's letter seemed to imply that he'd recruited Miranda's help in a prank designed to pay Ben back for tying him to the groyne, only for it to go horribly wrong. That his death had been their fault.

For twenty years they'd shared a terrible secret. A secret that, were it to get out, would ruin Miranda's life, and might even see her facing criminal charges.

Was that why she'd been transferring Melvyn money? Had he been short of cash when he was released from prison, and so resorted to blackmail?

Then the "Dear Future Me" letters had arrived.

Miranda could have come out to the farm that morning because she was worried he would increase his demands, or perhaps this message from her past self had somehow emboldened her into saying, "Enough is enough"—that she wasn't willing to part with any more cash? Either way, they would have argued. Had Melvyn then got physical? Lashed out?

Pushed her?

Audrey picks her way out of his squat and back down the corridor and door through which she came. After squeezing through the metal fencing, she heads for the shoulder. She'll call Detective Sergeant Reese as soon as she gets back to the barn. Tell him her theory.

Returning to her car, she sees another vehicle has parked across the exit, blocking her in.

Melvyn?

She approaches slowly, suddenly aware of how fast the light is fading, trying to see what kind of car it is and who is sitting behind the wheel.

A crunch of gravel.

She turns. A figure emerges from the gloom.

"Hello, Audrey."

Chapter 52

Audrey tenses, but then she sees a flash of green silk. Kitty.

"Thank God you're OK." Kitty's eyes flit up Warsett Hill, to the cliff edge. "You left in such a hurry." She looks to the ground, as though ashamed to admit her next thought. "I was worried you might do something silly."

"So you followed me?"

"You've had a big shock," says Kitty gently. "Learning about the essays... what I did." She's put one of her suit jackets over her dress, and she tugs at the collar. "I feared the worst, so I told Jago to hold the fort, came after you."

Audrey is not sure if she believes her. More likely, she thinks, Kitty wanted to make sure she wasn't about to blab her secret to all and sundry.

Audrey studies her. "Why do you stay with him?" she says.

"Jago?" Kitty blinks, confused.

"You didn't seem surprised when you learned he'd been fooling around with his students. So why? Why do you put up with it?"

Kitty is thrown by the question. Ordinarily, she would tell Audrey to mind her own business, but she seems to understand that after tonight— for now, at least—none of the usual rules apply.

She smiles thinly. "I knew he was the one for me the moment I met him. I fell hard and fast. But my parents…they weren't convinced. They thought he wasn't good enough, that he wasn't going places. When we got engaged, they tried to persuade me to break it off, told me I was making a huge mistake. For the first time, I stood up to them, told them they were wrong. And they were wrong—for a while, anyway. He was a great husband. Faithful. But now, I have to make it work with him. I *have* to, do you understand? There's no way I can let my parents know they were right, that I made the wrong choice."

Kitty fiddles with her fringe, pats her earlobes, feeling for the studs. Her muscles are so tense, they don't work as they should; her movements are jerky.

"I truly am sorry," she says, "for what I did. It was unforgivable, I know that. I was a child. I was also desperate." She stops, and Audrey realizes she is remembering her younger self, that she's trying to think of the kid version of her with compassion but can't quite get there. "There was another reason I followed you here, and that was because I wanted to make peace. To make sure you know how churned up I am about all this, how ashamed. I don't take any of this lightly; I never have. I know what I did to you—the measure of it—and I'm sorry."

They stand and look at each other, as if for the first time, the shush and crash of the sea in their ears. At the other end of the beach, a constellation of orange, purple, and yellow flashing lights mark Redcar and its arcades, but here, where they are, the night is inky, the coast beyond the jut of the cliffs unseeable, unknowable.

Audrey thinks of Ned, of Enid and Edward. Of the many stupid things they'd done in their short lives. She could see it. How easy it would be—how possible—for them to also make some terrible mistake. And how, if they did, she would forgive them, because they were just children. Kids, the way she and Kitty had been kids.

"OK," she says eventually.

"OK?" says Kitty. "You forgive me?"

Audrey gives a half shrug, unwilling to commit.

"Where were you?" says Kitty eventually.

"What?"

"When I got here, I couldn't find you. I went up to the Cleveland Way. You were nowhere to be seen."

"The farmhouse," says Audrey, gesturing toward the broken building.

Kitty squints at the metal fences, confused.

"Melvyn Arkwright," says Audrey. "From school. He's been squatting there. I think he could be the second figure—that he's why Miranda came here to the cliffs that morning. To see him."

Kitty frowns, trying to absorb the revelation.

"He's not there?"

"He's been out at sea, on a study trip, but he should've been back earlier today." Audrey puts her hand on the driver's door. "I need to go, to talk to the police."

When Kitty doesn't move, Audrey gestures at her car.

"You're blocking me in."

"Ah." Kitty stares to attention. "Of course. Sorry."

That's when Audrey notices it: a tear, just above the rim of her front right tire. The wheel is flat. She thinks of the rocky track she'd parked on for the party.

"Shit."

Kitty backtracks and comes to stand next to her.

"Good thing I'm here," she says brightly. "I'll give you a lift."

"No thanks." Audrey laughs, and the sound is brittle against the soft evening air. She may have accepted Kitty's apology, but after everything she's learned, Audrey cannot bear to be near her—not tonight; not ever.

"Don't be ridiculous," says Kitty. A new waver in her voice now, like a guitar string about to snap. "This time on a Friday? You'll wait forever for roadside assistance."

Audrey realizes Kitty is still worried about leaving her here alone, that she thinks Audrey might hurt herself.

"I'll fix it myself," says Audrey. "I have a spare."

Opening the trunk, she sees the pile of dry-cleaning she picked up earlier, and is hit by a pang of worry that Kitty will see it, too, and tell her off for the delay. Then she realizes Kitty is never going to make her feel bad again, that she is never going to clean for her again, that after tonight, Audrey hopes never to have to lay eyes on her again.

She turns on her phone light and props it in the inner corner of the trunk. It is increasingly dim—the sun has almost disappeared from the horizon—but if she works quickly, she should have the new tire on before it gets completely dark. After locating the jack, she roughs the plastic dry-cleaning sheaths to one side and feels around the felt lip for the gap that will let her lift up the trunk's false bottom and reveal the spare underneath. Try as she might, though, she can't find it.

Kitty's phone rings, and as she walks away to take the call, Audrey stands up and takes a breath, trying to reset. Her nerves are shot, her fingers not working the way she wants them to, but after a few deep breaths she feels calmer and tries again.

Once more she feels around the edge of the felt lip, but the pile of dry-cleaning keeps slipping back and blocking her way. All patience gone, she shoves the clothes hard to one side, and in her temper loosens the small plastic bag Leonard had hooked over one of the coat hangers. Two joints and a large baggie of white powder fall out.

She weighs the baggie in her hand. Leonard was right. There's way more here than you might expect someone to have for personal use.

Was that why Jago had been so odd with her since that morning after the party? Because he thought she'd seen the baggie in the dry-cleaning and that she'd kept it for herself? Or that she was planning to report him?

Was this what Kitty had been so on edge about whenever Audrey was around, too?

She's about to chuck the whole lot on the floor and leave them for Kitty to take with her when she notices a second bag hooked over one of the coat hangers. This one doesn't contain any drugs; instead, there is what looks like a wedge of folded paper inside. She pays it no mind, but then something about the pages makes her stop.

At the top of one of the pages is her name.

Kitty is still talking on the phone when Audrey removes the sheets from the bag. Carefully, she opens them.

Dear Mr. Danler

Sorry to ambush you while you're marking our schoolwork, but I've been building up the courage to come and speak to you for days now, and I can't do it, not face to face. Instead, I've decided I'm going to put everything down here, on paper, to put into words what I've done and why.

I know that once you have finished reading you will need to take action, that a response will be set in motion with the police and the university, and I expect that.

I need that.

Punishment. Truth. Consequence.

It seems to be some kind of confession.

I have done two terrible things.

I cheated on my Cambridge admission essay, passed off Audrey Hawken's work as my own.

I'm responsible for the death of Ben Spellman. I left him out in the snowstorm.

I don't want to go into the exact details just now. All that will come out in the next few days, I suppose, when the police ask their questions.

Again, I am so sorry. For everything.

Yours truly,
Kitty Veigh

Audrey reads the pages through again, twice, three times, her understanding of what happened to Ben twisting and turning like a sun catcher bending and refracting the light.

She's trying to figure out what it all means when she hears the shush of silk against gravel.

Kitty.

Slowly, she turns to face her.

Kitty looks from the pages to the dry-cleaning.

"Finally," says Kitty, a new flint to her voice. "You've found it."

Chapter 53

KITTY

Keswick, the Lake District, 2003

He will not leave me alone. It doesn't matter where I am or what I'm doing—I could be in the dinner queue, putting on my climbing harness, on a hike—and he'll try to corner me, to talk again about what he saw, what he knows.

I know it's a losing strategy, that this will only protect me in the short term, but I've been trying to figure out what to do ever since he confronted me at home, and the problem is I can't think straight. I'm too much of a mess, too terrified about what might happen next. And so I keep evading him at every turn, dodging his looks and questions, and it's been working OK.

Until now.

Thanks to the surprise cold snap, we've been locked inside the center since early afternoon, the teachers prowling the corridors for anyone who dares try and wander off upstairs. I keep looping the room and going to the toilet, as it's the one place where he can't follow me inside, but he's becoming harder and harder to dodge.

When the teacher orders everyone to bed, I'm the first to go upstairs. I'm in a room with Jane Wyatt, and on the first night, she fell into a deep sleep before I'd even finished brushing my teeth. I'm hoping she'll do the same tonight, give me some time alone with my thoughts. I'm almost there, but as I turn onto the landing, I barrel into Ben.

Somehow he was already up here.

His eyes are glazed, his cheeks pink. "Thought any more about what I said?"

I try to slink past him, but he blocks my way. Up close I can smell his breath. He's been drinking.

"You have until Monday lunchtime," he says loudly. "Then I'm going to Mr. Wilson."

I berate myself for the thousandth time, ask myself how I could do something so stupid. But the question is pointless. I know why. As soon as I read the first few pages of Audrey's essay, I was frightened. Her idea, her writing, her thesis, were an altogether different caliber from my own plodding submission. I want to be able to write something like that, and I did try, but it's like I've pushed myself so hard and for so long, my brain won't work properly anymore. Within the first few paragraphs, I knew she would almost certainly be granted an interview, whereas I, even after all the work I'd put in, wasn't sure I would pass muster.

Ben wants me to put it right. To make up some lie about how the applications got muddled. I know I could pull it off, that the teacher would believe me and I would be able to carry on with my reputation untarnished, but then what? I would be back where I started.

Two classmates pass by and I tense, worried they might overhear.

"So?" says Ben, still a bit too loud. He's been discreet until now, but whatever he's been drinking has changed all that.

Another classmate dawdles, eavesdropping.

I panic and say the first thing that comes to mind.

"Why don't we go outside, to the garden?" I need to get him away from here, from other people. "I'm not ready for bed."

He smiles, tickled by my disobedience. I've surprised him. "You heard the teacher—all the doors are locked."

"They can't lock the fire escapes."

He studies me, interested. "What if they're alarmed?"

I wiggle my head, trying to make him laugh. "What if they're not?"

His smile broadens to a grin, but I'm already losing my nerve. What if we get caught? I've never been in trouble before—not so much as a detention. I tell myself it's worth the risk, that if I had to choose between this or having my secret revealed, there's no contest.

We sneak down to the cloakroom and put on our coats; then Ben takes my hand and leads me through a corridor to the back of the house. The reason this is happening, the reason I'm alone with him, is terrible, and yet I feel a tiny thrill. I've never held a boy's hand before, and Ben is so fit, the most sought-after boy in my year.

We go past the equipment room and through some double doors into a part of the manor I've not seen before.

"Miss Whitehouse had me help carry in the milk this morning," he says by way of explanation. "Had to bring it all the way up that track. Pints and pints of the stuff."

We turn a corner, and in front of us is a door with a square window in its top half and a silver push bar across the middle.

"Bingo," says Ben, and I smirk.

I find myself wanting to make him smile again, to keep surprising him, and so I make sure I'm the one that crosses the line, not him. I push down on the bar and close my eyes, braced for an alarm, but there is only the muffled quiet created by a deep, sudden fall of snow.

The freezing air takes our breath away.

"Ha!" says Ben. He leaps across the threshold and into the snow. "Freedom."

I want to join him, but the fire door is heavier than it looks and will fall shut as soon as I let go.

"We need something to prop it open."

Ben looks up from the snowball he is shaping.

"And this is why you are the brains of the operation," he says. After tossing the snowball at a tree, he comes back and goes to the storage closet. He reappears with an empty milk crate, wedging it up against the door. I release my grip, testing. It holds.

"Bingo," he says again, and this time I laugh.

"All right, Nancy Drew."

"What?" he says, not bothered in the least. "It's how I talk."

I wonder what it must be like to go through life this at ease with yourself, this confident.

Outside it's a waxing moon, and it lights the snow-smothered lawns and hedges with a dull glow.

Again, he takes my hand.

"Let's go to the raised beds, at the bottom near the wall. That way, even if someone looks out, we won't be seen."

We pick our way through the drifts, lifting our knees high like marching soldiers and then plunging our boots back down into the powder. We giggle and shush each other, and I feel happier and freer than I have all year. For a few minutes I let myself pretend that we're out here for some other reason.

At the bottom of the garden, Ben finds a bench and uses the flat of his arm to sweep the snow from it with a flourish.

"Madame." He takes a mock bow, and I sit all fancy, as if taking my place on a throne.

A clink, and he produces a handful of miniatures from the inside of his coat.

"Thirsty?"

Aside from the odd glass of champagne at Christmas, I've never drunk before. Certainly not spirits. And I need to keep my wits about me. He holds my future in his hands. I should have a clear head when we talk.

He smiles, then smiles again, goofier this time, trying to make me laugh.

I want to make sure he keeps looking at me in this same way, that he keeps thinking of me as someone fun. Someone whose hand he wants to hold.

I take a bottle of whisky, unscrew the cap.

"Bottoms up." I down it in one. It is disgusting. I cough and he laughs, but not in a mean way.

"I need this after today," he says, swigging from his own tiny bottle.

I tilt my head—a question.

"Rappelling." He finishes his drink. "There was something wrong with my climbing gear. I almost went down the side of that rock face a lot quicker than intended, if you get my meaning."

"Seriously?" This was the first I'd heard of this.

"Some kind of prank." He laughs, but it feels forced. "I don't think they realized quite how much they'd loosened things up."

"They?"

"I've got a pretty good idea who it was."

He nods toward Cleasby House, as if he's imagining the person responsible inside.

"So, have you thought about what I said?" he says as we move on to another miniature. Vodka for me, gin for him. "About talking to the teacher, telling him it was a mix-up." His tone has been light, but now he pauses, and in the gap in between words, a threat forms. "It will be so much better coming from you."

I hate that the spell has been broken, that I can no longer pretend we're out here for some other reason.

He sees the expression on my face and softens.

"I've heard all the things you say in class. You're so clever. Special. How do you know those Cambridge geniuses won't think your essay is just as good as Audrey's, if not better?"

But I do know. Audrey's essay was exceptional.

"Besides," he says, "Cambridge isn't the be-all and end-all. There are loads of amazing universities."

"Tell that to my parents," I say. "Forget earthquakes or floods; they would consider my going somewhere like Edinburgh or Durham a national disaster." And even though the crushing truth of that statement stings, for the first time since forever, I giggle and guffaw in such way that I snort. Usually I'd feel embarrassed by this, but hearing myself I laugh even more. Ben, too.

Is this how everyone else feels most of the time? Is this what it's like not to constantly worry and strive?

"OK," I say once I've recovered. "Monday. I'll put it right."

Agreeing to this feels like surrender. Like failure. But it's also a relief.

I start to get excited. If I don't get in, then maybe Dad will let me torpedo the idea of doing a history degree altogether. I can apply to Central Saint Martins and do what I really want to do—study fashion and textiles. I've been reading up on it in the careers library. My A levels aren't a great match, so I might need to do a foundation course first, but that's OK. Right now, Dad won't even discuss the possibility.

"Good for you," says Ben, slurping at the dregs of another bottle. His stomach rumbles and he looks down in mock horror, as if that part of his body is separate from him, a rogue agent with a mind of its own.

"All the miles they make you walk up and down mountains, and then they give you the tiniest dinner portions I've ever seen. Last night I was so hungry I woke up."

I think of the large bar of chocolate smuggled inside my suitcase. I caught Dad secreting it inside my hiking socks the morning I left.

"Just in case you need a treat," he'd said with a wink, and I'd been so touched because he never does stuff like that, especially when it means breaking the rules.

I hand Ben my empty bottle.

"You're not the only one with contraband," I say, getting to my feet. "I've got chocolate in my room."

"What?" He laughs. "I like you more and more, Kitty Veigh." He shoos me off with both hands. "What are you waiting for? Go and get it."

I do as he says, but as I walk away, I realize my feet are numb and that the wind is starting to get up.

"Maybe we should go back in?" I stamp, trying to get the blood flowing. "It's getting colder."

"Not yet." He spreads his arms wide and looks up at the black sky. "It's so lovely out here." He lowers his voice. "Come on, Kitty Veigh, live a little."

My stomach flutters, then tightens the same way it does in that moment before I get a test result or essay grade. But this fear, this anticipation of what is about to happen, is different—nicer. As I head back inside, I'm smiling.

BEN

I start, and a pile of snow avalanches from my hood into my lap. I must have nodded off, and now my legs are buried in a drift that reaches my shins. I get up and stamp my feet, trying to get my blood going. I'm so cold, I'd like to call it a night, go back inside, but Kitty has gone off in search of chocolate, and if she comes back and finds me gone, she'll think I ditched her.

Usually I wouldn't give going back to my room a second thought. I'd let Kitty figure it out for herself, catch up with her in the morning and explain, but I've spent most of this weekend churned up, feeling bad about the fact that being here means I won't get to visit Mum tomorrow, and so I'm loath to make that feeling worse by leaving someone else high and dry.

I have asked Dad to explain my absence, to make sure Mum knows I haven't forgotten—or worse, that I couldn't be bothered—but I have a horrible feeling he won't even be there to do that. He doesn't like going to the hospital at the best of times, but he hates having to go alone more.

They call it a hospital; it looks more like a posh hotel. A stately home with sloping rose-filled gardens and benches everywhere. The last time Dad had refused to come inside, I'd been on edge. You never know how Mum is going to be week to week. But after a few minutes, I realized she was having a good day, and I relaxed. We went out into the garden, and she told me my hair was too long, asked if the neighbors were still feeding our cat, even though we'd told them not to—"You tell them. Molly is a first-rate actress. Oscar-winning. You tell them that"—and regaled me with a story about a fellow patient whose first, second, and current wives came to visit him as a trio and wore different, complementary shades of pastel.

When our time was up, I walked her inside and we headed for the TV room. She linked her arm through mine, and I felt happy, hopeful that what they were doing to her here was working, that she would soon be home and we could go back to how things were before.

But then, as we were walking down the corridor, we passed a row of doctors' offices and a man had emerged. In Bermuda shorts and a white linen shirt, he was in a hurry, stuffing papers into a briefcase, when a nurse stopped him.

"Doctor."

"Not on shift," he said, waving her on. "Just collecting a few bits." Then he looked back, called to someone in his office. "Chop-chop."

Mum guided me in his direction.

"Doctor," she said proudly, "this is who I was telling you about. My son, Ben."

He tensed, offered a polite grin, then called again to the person in his office.

"Let's go," I said to Mum, trying to encourage her on, but she wouldn't move.

"Doctor?" she said again, louder this time.

He exhaled and turned to face her properly. It was clear that, though he had surrendered to the delay, he wasn't happy about it.

"Ben," he said. "Your mum speaks very highly of you."

Mum looked from him to me, mouth pursed. At first, I thought it was because she was annoyed by his lack of sincerity, that she expected more of him, but then, as her gaze settled on me I realized what was happening and my stomach tightened.

She released my arm and backed away toward the doctor.

"What have you done with my son?" she said to me. "Where is my son?"

"Mum," I said, "it's me, Ben."

"Who is he?" she said, turning the doctor. "Are you in on this?"

The doctor signaled to a nurse for help, but they were busy with a patient.

"Mum," I said, going toward her. I knew what happened when she got too upset. How rough they could be. "We were just talking about Molly, remember?"

But this only made her more scared.

"Stay away," she said and pushed me hard.

I landed on the floor with a thump, and that's when I saw him, in the doctor's office. Sitting on a chair, a book in his lap.

Melvyn Arkwright.

I hadn't known his father was a doctor.

We locked eyes and he frowned, confused. My being here—the context—bewildered him. Then he looked at Mum, in the gray joggers and jumper she has to wear, and understanding dawned.

His dad was busy trying to placate Mum, but as I got to my feet, she grabbed a pen from the side of his briefcase and started waving it around.

"You're all in on it; don't say you're not."

"Mum," I said, gently, trying to bring her back to herself. I could see the orderlies approaching, a pincer movement from behind. I knew she would be restrained. Her wrists trussed tight like the legs on a supermarket chicken.

She went for the doctor, her hand arcing through the air, but before she could make contact, the orderlies had pounced. One of them gripped her wrist until she let go of the pen. The other forced her arms behind her back.

"No," I said, "you're hurting her."

But she was already being hustled down the corridor, toward some other part of the unit.

I put my hands over my ears, trying to drown out her cries, and turned away to see Melvyn standing in the doorway, the book he was reading tucked under one arm. He watched her go until she disappeared through the double doors, then he looked at me. Blinked. It felt like he was making sure to take in every detail, storing it for future use.

But I was wrong. So very, very wrong.

The day after he saw me at the hospital with Mum, he cornered me at school. I'd spent the night before trying to figure out who he might tell first—how long it would take for the news to spread.

"I wanted to say sorry," he murmured, once we were finished with morning registration. "About your mum." He adjusted his backpack, his fingers fluttering against the straps. "I wanted to tell you not to worry. I won't say a word."

He seemed genuine. But I'd been so suspicious. Gossip like that is valuable currency. Hard to resist.

It's difficult to think about that night on the beach. What I did to him. What almost happened.

I'd refused to believe his denials.

Because if he'd kept his word, then how did Robbie know? The jokes he made hadn't got the details exactly right, but they were pretty close.

I'd looked at Melvyn asleep there against the groyne, and wondered if he'd exaggerated my mum's condition for effect? If he'd embellished her distress to make sure they didn't lose interest in his story?

Turns out I was wrong on every count. When he'd promised not to tell anyone what he saw—that Mum was in the hospital—he was telling the truth. A week or so after that horrific night on the beach, I found out Robbie had actually learned about my situation through his dad. Another teacher had grown concerned about my behavior and called him at home to discuss the next steps, and the headmaster had told him what he knew. Robbie had eavesdropped on the whole thing.

I try not to think about what would have happened if Miranda hadn't come back in search of her coat, if she hadn't swum out to cut him free. She hasn't spoken to me since, and though I have tried to apologize to Melvyn, every time I come near him, he moves away, like he cannot bear to be in my presence, like he's frightened of me.

The blizzard is getting worse. The snow is falling in thick sheets that make it hard to see even a short way ahead. I stamp my feet even harder. I want to go in, to go to bed, but I'm determined to wait—determined not to abandon her, or anyone, ever again. I wait for Kitty to return.

KITTY

Back inside the center, the hallways are quiet and dark.

In my room, I creep past a snoring Jane and over to my pack. I slip my hand inside and retrieve the Dairy Milk from the hidden pocket; then I return downstairs, half skipping, half walking. On the final stair, I stumble, and as my hands fly out to steady myself, I drop the chocolate.

Retrieving it from the floor, I see there is a piece of paper tucked inside the wrapper. The fall has dislodged it. Pulling it free, I realize it's a note from home. I beam. Some of the others had also found surprise notes hidden in their things when we got here. Messages from their parents telling them to have fun, or that they miss them, or a simple "I love you." I didn't bother to look for one because it's not the sort of thing my parents do, or have ever done.

Realizing I was wrong is lovely. I feel special, warm, the same as everyone else.

I go stand by a window, angle it toward the moonlight.

But then I read what is written there.

Kitty

I worry the food might be terrible, and so I have enclosed the attached sweet treat in case you get peckish.

Have a great time and remember, when you get back it will only be four weeks till December! Four weeks till you show them what you're made of!

Dad xxx

PS. I know you've been struggling with some of the more obscure dates around the Renaissance, and so I've taken the liberty of listing them on the back of this note…I figured you could use the time on the coach on the way home to finally memorize them. You know what I say: don't do your best—do WHATEVER it takes!

I go still, my arms rag-doll limp.

Even now, while I'm hundreds of miles away, they've found a way to keep the pressure up.

To remind me about December.

The Cambridge entrance interview.

That's all they care about. All they've ever cared about.

I read the note through one more time; then I try to shake it off and head back downstairs. On the way there, I try to summon the feeling I had when I was out there before—that magic buzz—but my feet are heavy, and my jaw is set so hard my teeth ache.

Why did Ben have to be on detention that night? Why did he have to see me? I'd do anything to keep him quiet, but I know there's no persuading him.

At the end of the corridor, I discover the fire door has fallen shut. Either the storm is getting worse and blew it in, or when I edged past on my way back inside, I knocked the milk crate without realizing. I'll tell Ben we need to be more careful. If the crate were to get dislodged again, we could be stuck out there all night. Looking through the glass, I half expect to see him hovering nearby, waiting to be let in, but he's oblivious to the danger. Sunk low on the bench, he has put up his hood and tucked his chin in to his chest.

Asleep.

Another blizzard is building, the wind whipping fat snowflakes through the air.

He needs to be careful, I think. The plunging temperature combined with the amount he's had to drink…

He'll catch his death.

I realize I'm still holding Dad's note.

don't do your best—do WHATEVER it takes!

I go to press on the silver bar to open the door, but then I stop. Scan the note again. I try to imagine Mum and Dad's faces if I'm not granted an interview. They'll refuse to look at me, to talk to me.

The wind howls and batters the glass with a mixture of snow and hail as large as ping-pong balls.

I don't let the thought formulate—not completely. What I'm doing, what it means, what might happen. Instead, I keep it out of focus, a speck at the corner of my vision.

If anything, it's *not* doing something that is significant.

I remove my hand from the door. Look again at Ben asleep. Think of the way he said my name.

Kitty Veigh.

A singsong merging of the two words that made it sound like he was speaking in some beautiful foreign language.

I tell myself that leaving him out there is no guarantee that he might wake and find another way in, or he might find somewhere to shelter and survive the night.

But if he doesn't…

I watch him for a few moments more. He is very still, and snow has started to collect on his hood, a thick white stack. Then I turn around, go back to my room, and wait for morning.

Chapter 54

"You killed Ben?" says Audrey.

Kitty pulls the sides of her suit jacket close.

"When I switched our essays," she says, matter-of-fact, "he saw me do it."

Audrey thinks of the note Ben had left inside her letter, asking to meet. He'd wanted to tell her what he knew.

"On the school trip, we sneaked outside, into the snow. He was trying to persuade me to come clean, to tell the teachers what I did, pretend it had been a mistake. I went inside to get something, and when I came back downstairs, I saw the door had fallen shut."

"You left him out there? In the blizzard?"

Kitty closes her eyes for a moment, as if trying to blot out the memory.

"I knew there was a chance he might find another way back inside…"

"But you hoped that wouldn't be the case? That if he were to die, your secret would die with him?"

Kitty nods. "Afterward, I was horrified. The guilt. I couldn't eat, couldn't sleep. I decided to confess." She motions to the pages in Audrey's hand. "So I wrote that, handed it in inside my assignment, and waited for Mr. Danler to find it."

"But he didn't mark the work?"

Even now, Kitty can't hide her disgust. It was as if she couldn't tolerate the fact he'd had his students do this, that he'd felt the letters had some value other than that which contributed to her final subject grade.

"All that guff about returning them to us at some unspecified future date. I didn't believe him. And so I spent the days after I handed it in on edge, waiting for the knock on the door, jumpy every time I heard a police siren, but then the days turned into weeks, and I started to realize that maybe he'd been telling the truth. That my confession was still hidden inside my letter, and that there it would stay."

"You could still have come forward," says Audrey. "Admitted what you did."

"I lost my nerve," says Kitty. "The more time that went by, the harder it became. In the end I had this huge sense of relief that it hadn't worked, that my life could continue as normal." She laughs. "I was worried about it still being out there, of course—my confession. I asked Mr. Danler if I could have it back on a number of occasions, but he was always very coy. I didn't like it, but I figured he'd thrown them away, that the whole 'returning them at some future date' thing was a lie."

Audrey thinks of Laura Spellman's fragility, of the guilt Miranda had carried her whole life, of her own stolen opportunity.

Kitty steps closer, and when she speaks her tone is pleading, almost babyish. "Are you going to report me?"

"Which part?" says Audrey. "The fact you left Ben to die, or the fact you got into Cambridge under false pretenses?"

Kitty's face crumples.

Audrey returns her attention to the trunk of her car.

"I don't know whether I'm going to report you or not." She searches for the tire iron. "It's been quite the evening, and I just want to get this fixed and go home."

Kitty hovers, hoping for more, but Audrey is more focused on trying to expose the spare tire, to shift the bloody dry-cleaning out of the way. She gathers it up, intending to dump the lot in Kitty's arms, but then she stops. The suit jacket with the bag containing Kitty's confession. It's a man's jacket, tailored, but that's not what's strange. Kitty wore Jago's stuff all the time. It's the back of the jacket.

The pattern.

A series of light-colored arrows in its center.

Audrey's heartbeat surges: a warning knell against her ribs. She is not safe.

She decides to leave the tire for the moment and sets to work attaching the jack. She has an urgent, primal need to get out of here as soon as possible, but she also knows that, for the moment, she needs to act as if everything is fine. She pumps the lever once, twice, three times, grateful for how physical the work is—how she can mask her fear and speeding breath behind her exertions—but when she goes to grab the iron, she fumbles.

Still oblivious, Kitty picks it up and returns it to her, but as she goes to pass it over she stops and frowns. Audrey looks down and sees her own hand trembling.

Kitty hesitates. Still holding the iron, she scans Audrey's face, then the cliff edge, before finally her gaze lands on the boot and the jacket.

Her grip on the iron tightens.

She knows.

Audrey doesn't wait.

She runs.

Chapter 55

MIRANDA

Saltburn, 2023: The morning of...

I abandon the pancake batter and take the phone from Marcel. Keeping my voice low so the kids can't hear, I ask Cecile to leave us alone and tell her never to come to the barn again. That last night was unacceptable. She rails at me in French, and I hang up. When I hand the phone back to Marcel, he refuses to meet my eye. I feel sad, but also embarrassed, for him and his stupid infidelity. I buy what Marcel said about his wanting to break up being more than just the affair. It's insulting to have your life destroyed by a cliché, to have a man you thought was special—someone you've loved nearly all your adult life, the father of your children—turn out to be as basic and fallible as all the rest.

I'm back to tending the pancakes when Marcel hands me an envelope. Thinking it more divorce correspondence, I flinch, but opening it, I find something else entirely.

It takes me a few seconds to understand what it is, but when I do I giggle. Coming face-to-face with a lost version of myself is startling. Especially now. Those wants and dreams were formed twenty years ago, then pushed aside. Seeing them in print again, at the point at which I'm finally getting around to them, feels like serendipity.

As for the big U (university). NEWSFLASH! You're no genius. You know that, but secretly, you'd love to go. You've never told anyone this, but you've always wanted to study psychology...

It was only once I got older that I started to think the teachers might have been wrong, that maybe, if I worked hard, applied myself, I might have what it takes. And so, last year I went back to college. Enrolled in an access course that, if I pass, will allow me to a apply for a place for a psychology degree. Keeping the whole thing secret has been difficult, but worth it. If Marcel knew what I was doing, he would try to talk me out of it. Make gentle noises of discouragement accompanied by reassurances that he was only trying to ensure I didn't make a fool of myself. Reassurances that translated to, "I don't think you've got the brains for this." As for Audrey, I want to surprise her. I know how much she values learning, and I want to make her proud, to make her see me in a different light.

The course hasn't been easy, but I've found it much less intimidating than I imagined and often enjoyable, fulfilling in a way that school never was. But then in the last month or so, the work has started to ramp up, and I've struggled. With the exam in just a few weeks, last night the panic started to set in. Then Cecile had turned up on our doorstep. As devastating as it was to learn that Marcel had taken back up with her, it also put some much needed fire in my belly. So after Cecile had gone, I decided to do all I could to make my dream of studying for a degree a reality and went to see Jago, one of my lecturers. I knew it was outside of office hours, but when it comes to Dr. Jago Plaige, I have leverage. I've used it once already—to give Audrey a helping hand—but I'm sure I can use it again. My plan was to ask if he could give me some extra tutoring to help nail the exam.

I return to the letter.

In that final match, when you were out there on the court and

you leaped in the air and intercepted that ball, it felt like flying.
If you're reading this as a grown-up, I hope you haven't forgotten
that feeling, that magic.

Remembering the way I used to feel and talk about playing netball is hard. I loved it so much and still miss it. I brace myself, ready for what I know is coming next. This assignment straddled the school trip where Ben died, and even now I can remember how I used the remaining pages as a kind of confidant, somewhere I could document my guilt.

I still think of him often…what I did. The way I misunderstood his plea for help at the window. After I ignored him, he must have gone to try and wait out the night, to shelter against that wall, but then he fell asleep.

Those first weeks after he died were the hardest. I couldn't sleep. Couldn't play netball. Didn't want to play netball. I needed to punish myself, to feel some consequence for what I'd done, and so I walked away, told Coach Arbor I was done. I lied about why to others. To Audrey. Made up an injury. Because how could I tell them? How else could I explain?

At the time, it felt like the end of my world, but I can see now how it changed me for both good and bad. Afterward I vowed to always try and see the positive in others, to give them a second chance, even if that chance was something that on the face of it they absolutely did not deserve. Still, the burden hasn't gotten any smaller; instead, it has become part of me, absorbed like shrapnel lodged in bone.

Three pages in, the tone and content of the letter does change.

But these words are not mine.

Dear Mr. Danler…

I flick ahead, confused. My handwriting, my letter, resumes eventually, but a chunk of it is missing.

These pages belong to someone else.

...I know that once you have finished reading you will need to take action, that a response will be set in motion with the police and the university, and I expect that...

At first, it doesn't make sense. It's not like a letter at all—more like some kind of confession?

I stop.

How and why did these pages come to be mixed up with my own?

I think again of how I was so ravaged by guilt, I wondered if I should confess. Tell someone, maybe Coach Arbor, what had happened. I'd be in the middle of class, and I'd find myself overwhelmed, gripped by the need to go and spill the truth, right there and then, how I'd lie to the teacher, feigning illness, then rush from the room, speeding to reach her office by the sports hall, only to lose momentum halfway and realize I couldn't go through with it after all. In the lesson in which we finished writing our letters, the urge to go and tell her was the worst it had ever been. Probably because of the nature of the class: the things I'd written down about what happened, the memories it had forced me to relive. It was coming toward the end of the session, and the teacher had given us all an envelope in which to seal our pages. Reading back over the things I'd written about Ben, what I'd done, I got to my feet, told the teacher a lie about not feeling well, and was on my way out of the classroom when Kitty also lurched for the door, her face gray. In her haste she knocked her pages to the floor, then collided with the desk next door and sent its contents flying. My desk. The teacher recoiled from us, worried about catching the tummy bug he presumed we both had, shooed us on our way, and got down to gather our respective pages back together.

Yet again, I stalled halfway to Coach Arbor's office. Decided I couldn't tell her after all. That I couldn't bear the shame. When I returned to the classroom, I found my and Kitty's letters were neatly back inside our envelopes, ready for us to seal and hand in, along with the rest of the class.

He must have muddled the pages.

Was Kitty sick that day because she was also about to confess? Because she was terrified of what would happen next?

I read the final part again, trying to understand.

I have done two terrible things...

Kitty switched essays with Audrey. Stole her opportunity.

Then, to protect her secret, did she leave Ben there to die?

I stagger back from the stove, pancakes forgotten.

For twenty years, I thought I was the one responsible.

For twenty years, I've told myself that, were it not for me, Ben would still be alive.

And what about Audrey?

Not being granted an interview ravaged her confidence and set her on a course from which she would never recover. Never mind the fact that if she *had* been given an interview, she might have been offered a place.

Who knows where she would be in life now—what she would have achieved?

My phone pings. A message from Audrey.

She has just opened her own "Dear Future Me" letter. Inside is a note from Ben. I glance at the screenshot. He must have been planning to tell her what he knew, to alert her to Kitty's cheating.

He'd tried to do the right thing.

I close one fist around the pages and grab my car keys.

I need to see Kitty, to confront her.

On the doorstep, I pause and look at the fields and sky that surround my home. In the last few minutes, it feels like someone has turned a dial and thrown everything wildly out of focus. I close my eyes and take a breath, and when I open them again, the image is sharp, but everything looks different, an altered version of the world I used to live in.

I get in the car and drive.

People talk about the paths not taken. The "what-ifs" that shape our destiny.

Kitty, Audrey.

Me.

Everyone is about to get back on the right track.

Chapter 56

It's too dark to attempt the path down to Saltburn beach, and based on what she now suspects about Kitty—what she is capable of—there is no way Audrey is going anywhere near those cliffs. She realizes it's impossible to run away from her, to escape her completely, and so she decides to hide in the only nearby structure: the farmhouse. As she sprints toward its metal fences, she reaches for her phone to call for help. If she can alert the police, then she only needs to stay hidden until they get here, but as she pats at her empty pockets, she remembers. Her phone is still balanced where she left it, flashlight on, against the inside of the trunk.

Her insides turn.

She is out here on her own.

Just like Miranda was.

Heart hammering, she pushes through the gap in the fence, a new idea forming. She's been inside the house once already tonight, so that should give her the advantage. She'll find somewhere in one of the rooms to conceal herself, and then, when Kitty is looking for her in some other part of the building, she'll sneak back out and return down the hill to the cars and the road.

It's only once she's on the other side of the fence that she realizes the flaw in her plan. The moon is nothing more than a meager crescent, and in the dim light, it's impossible to move forward without tripping over the chunks of masonry and glass that litter the farm's perimeter. She can hardly see well enough to get inside, let alone be nimble about it.

After turning her ankle, she slows her pace and picks her way around the back, toward the scullery door. Once inside, she shoves the door back into position as best she can in a bid to make her entrance point less obvious, but the force loosens the door from its hinges, and as it pushes against the stone floor, it makes a groaning sound. Audrey cringes, worried it will lead Kitty to her, but she can't look back; she needs to keep going.

She feels her way toward the hall, wincing as her shins knock against broken chairs and splinters from the exposed lath and plaster snags against her palms. She passes the opening to the room containing Melvyn's stuff and continues on to the end of the hall. She thinks of the months he'd spent sleeping here. Did he not have an alternative? Or was the alternative somehow worse than this? He would have had a flashlight, but still, the air is cold and dank, every surface sticky with dust and mold. No wonder he was riddled with bites.

She's always thought herself a good judge of character, but she'd had no sense he was a violent person. That he'd spent time in prison. Clearly he was skilled at putting on whatever version of himself he wanted people to see. Audrey shudders; if she'd kept dating him, maybe she would have gotten to see that side of him emerge firsthand.

At the end of the hall, she stops at a doorway to a large room. It has a bay window, and some of the boards outside have fallen away, letting in a sliver of moonlight. In the corner she can make out what seems to be a dresser, toppled forward in a heap, a pile of chairs, and, incongruously, a rusting plow with huge wheels. The plow's row of curved fins stands aloft, soil caked into the metal grooves. Audrey makes her way toward the dresser, wincing each time her already bruised shins collide with the metal junk that litters the floor. After crawling in underneath the gap left between the dresser and the floor, she tries to reach the void between it and the wall, but the gap is tight. As she pulls her body across the ground a nail rips into her knee, tearing her flesh. Still she keeps going, only stopping once she reaches the tiny space at the back. There, she crouches, and resting her hands against tights already wet with blood, she tries to still her breathing and listens for Kitty's approach.

Silence.

Seconds pass, then minutes. Audrey can hear nothing except the shush of the sea and the pops and creaks of the house around her. The muscles in her thighs start to burn from holding herself in the same crouched position, but still she dares not move.

Another minute passes.

She starts to consider the possibility that maybe Kitty hadn't made pursuit after all, that she hadn't realized Audrey had recognized the suit jacket as hers, and had no clue Audrey had figured out she was the person standing next to Miranda in the dashcam footage of the cliffs. Audrey had taken off at a sprint and hadn't once looked back. For all she knew, Kitty could still be waiting by the cars, wondering what on earth was going on.

She tries to piece together how or why the two women might have ended up at Huntcliff that morning—how Miranda had wound up dead.

If she'd jumped, then why had Kitty not come forward? Why, if she was an innocent bystander, would she have kept it a secret?

Audrey isn't sure how much time has passed when she decides Kitty has not followed her after all. She prepares to crawl out from underneath the dresser, and after placing the flat of her hands on the board, she braces herself, ready for the moment her injured knees make contact with the wood. But then she hears it: the groan of the scullery door being pushed open. A moaning, scraping sound.

Kitty.

She'd followed her after all.

Audrey stays crouched, her heart beating against her chest.

Hidden. Ready.

Chapter 57

KITTY

It's dark when I leave the conference hotel in Sheffield, the roads empty. I don't have time to do my hair, and so I scrape it back under a baseball cap. If the traffic stays like this, then I should make it home just as the sun is coming up—early enough to ensure Jago and whoever he had stay over last night are still in bed.

I've known about his indiscretions for some time. I never did anything about it because I honestly didn't see any need. I was never going to act on it, to ask for a divorce, because that would require telling my parents. Would involve telling them they'd been right. Besides, what he was doing was harmless, an unfortunate predilection for flirting with giggly, long-haired undergrads that helped boost his ego. But in the last year or so, things have escalated. Someone reported him to the university after seeing him kissing a student on campus—a claim he denied—and I've seen a few explicit messages on his phone. There have been investigations, noises of suspension and other nonspecific disciplinary action.

I have tried to talk to him about it, but every time I do, he turns it into an argument packed with accusations about my paranoia that are as cruel as they are vehement. I've started to question myself. Maybe I've been making more of this than I needed to, maybe I should believe him, and not the nasty rumormongers in the faculty.

Then last night happened.

I phoned him from my hotel late, and in the background, I could hear music and a woman's voice, calling to him from some other room. Instead of calling him out on it, I decided to see this as what it was: an opportunity.

I'm hoping that coming home unannounced, catching him in the act, will bring things to a head. Privately.

I park in the garage and let myself in the back door. The place is a mess. Glasses everywhere, food ground into the carpet, a stink of cigarettes, weed, and booze. I approach the stairs, more scared than I am angry. If I catch him red-handed, what should I do?

I'm wearing my Gieves and Hawkes suit for courage, the tweed shot through with arrows of pink thread. Usually the cut makes me feel strong, armored against whatever the world decides to throw at me, but today it's not working. I'd imagined storming into the bedroom, shouting, Jago apologizing and begging for forgiveness, but now that I'm actually here, I flounder.

Part of me wishes I'd stayed at the conference, that I was still there now, listening to a talk on the importance of primary sources, blinkers on.

I tug my jacket until it sits flush against my shirt, smooth the nap of my trousers, and make my way upstairs. Halfway up I stop. I can hear snoring, fluttery and shrill, but the closer I get to the bedroom, the quieter it becomes. I retreat to the hall and trace it to its source. Jago asleep on the chaise longue. Alone.

I watch him from the doorway, relieved but also disappointed. It seems our fiction is going to limp on for another day.

A shadow at the front door, and the post slips through the letter box: circulars, a bank statement, and a hand-addressed envelope for me.

I open this first.

It takes me a few moments to understand, to realize what it is, and when I do I slump onto the bottom stair.

Finally.

After all these years.

I am safe.

My job, my reputation, the life that I have built...all safe.

The intensity of relief is shocking. It's not like I've thought about my confession every day. In fact, some months I haven't thought of it at all, but still having it out there, out of my control has been a specter that has overshadowed my entire adult life. Over the years I've come to think of it as an unexploded grenade—one that, if the pin were ever removed, would explode everything I hold dear.

Bang.

I don't bother with the first few pages. The part I need is inserted somewhere in the middle.

A stupid teenage mistake written in the heat of the moment. A way to try and alleviate the suffocating guilt.

A car pulls up outside.

I fumble at the letter, searching for the confession I'd folded inside.

But there is no sign of it.

I search again, slower this time.

There are other pages, not in my handwriting, but my confession is definitely not here. I pull the paper closer, confused, scanning the words for clues, something—anything—that can explain what these pages are, and where my confession might have gone..

A knock at the front door, and then a face appears at the window.

Miranda.

When she sees me, her eyes grow large. Her nostrils flare, shock and anger rippling across her face.

"You killed him," she says, her breath fogging the glass. "You left Ben in the snow to die."

Before she can say any more, I lurch for the door. Jago mustn't wake and hear. Outside, I usher her away from the house.

"And Audrey?" she says, shouting now. "You ruined her life!"

She holds a collection of pages in her hand.

My confession. Somehow she has it.

The ground seems to quake. I brace myself, half expecting to see my house wobble, for the bricks to shift and crumble and crash to the ground.

"I can explain." I put a hand on her shoulder, trying to calm her, but it just enrages her even more.

"Get in the car," she says, opening the door to her Mini.

"What?"

"I'm taking you to the police station. You're going to tell them what you did. Now, today."

I glance back at the door, terrified Jago will appear and nod. I don't care where we go; my priority right now is to get her away from the house and quick, before he comes round.

"My best friend barely scrapes by because of you," she says, speeding down the country lanes that lead toward town. "She's a bloody genius and she scrubs toilets—*your* toilet."

I dig my nails into my thighs and try to slow my breathing. Miranda is delivering me to the police station. She is going to tell them that I killed someone. I will be interviewed, maybe arrested. My crime will become officially documented, investigated, prosecuted. This is going to happen in the next twenty, thirty minutes, and yet my terror is located elsewhere, in that moment when my parents find out what I've done. In their shame, their disgust. Their disappointment. I've spent a lifetime trying to make them proud, to make them happy. To make them like me. Once they realize I'm a fraud, that will be it.

It feels like I've been clinging on to a sheer rock face by my fingernails and that now I can just…let go. And even though I know I won't survive the fall, to give in to it is a wonderful sweet relief.

But then vomit rises in my throat. Bile and coffee coat my tongue, sour and hot.

"Pull over," I say. "I'm going to be sick."

But Miranda keeps going, and I think I am going to have to puke right here into my lap when she glances over. Seeing my expression, she changes her mind and pulls into the small car park that foots Warsett Hill. I stumble out and crawl on all fours to a patch of grass, where I retch and vomit.

Once I am done, I sit back on my knees, hands trembling.

Miranda waits for me inside the car, engine running, but when I still haven't gotten up a few minutes later, she gets out.

"You done?"

I squint toward the crest of the hill and tune in to the churn of the sea below. It sounds like radio static, blank and constant.

Finally, I push myself up to standing, and Miranda, thinking I'm coming to join her, goes to get back in the car. I close my eyes and listen to the sea and think of my father's face. The way his smile curdles whenever I don't quite come up to snuff.

I could go to trial, be found guilty, sentenced. None of that will compare to his shame—to the realization I can no longer carry his dreams on my back. In the same way that my success has always belonged to him, my failure will be his failure.

I break into a run, toward the top of the hill and the sky and the sound of the sea.

It takes Miranda a few seconds to realize what's happening. "Kitty?" She launches into pursuit. "No."

The grass is springy, the hill steep. I can hear Miranda shouting at me to stop, but I keep going, and when I reach the top, I climb the fence and onto the cliff edge. It's higher than I thought, and looking down, I instinctively take a step back.

Miranda joins me.

"Kitty," she says, out of breath, "please come back to the car."

I realize she's still in her pajamas, that her feet are now bare.

I think of my professorship, of the party I have planned, of the people my parents have invited.

Miranda puts her arm around me, and as my face blots her shoulder, I realize I am crying.

"Come back to the car." Her voice is gentle. "Come on, I'll take you home."

Dad's mantra starts to play on repeat in my head. I try to tune back in to the sea, to let its white noise drown him out, but he's too loud, too insistent.

Don't do your best; do whatever it takes.

Whatever it takes.

Whatever it takes.

Miranda turns to go, and as she lifts her back heel in the air, I reach out, and with the flat of my hands, I shove her hard against the collarbone.

She doesn't understand what's happening at first, but then, as she loses her footing, her expression ripples from shock to understanding, to anger. The last thing I see on her face before she falls out of sight is fear. Her eyes still and wide.

I'm grateful for the sea's roar. It masks her scream, the thud as she hits the rocks below.

I don't look. I can't.

Staggering back down the hill, I go to her car, remove my pages from where she left them on the passenger seat, and leaving the engine running, I stuff them into my inside jacket pocket.

I scan the road, left and right. Soon it will be busy with cars, the Cleveland Way full of hikers. I need to get home, away from the scene, but my brain is already whirring, calculating how best to protect myself from any consequences. The most important thing is that I'm not seen by anyone, and so I'll need to pick my way through the fields, go as the crow flies.

I cross the road and launch myself into the rape. The crop is dense and shoulder-high. Pushing through it is exhausting. My eyes soon begin to itch, and my hands fill with tiny scratches, but I welcome the discomfort, the physical effort, because it keeps at bay the horror of what I have just done.

Eventually I hit the square of barley that slopes down to our garden wall.

Home.

My shirt is soaked through with sweat, my suit flecked with twigs, mud, and leaves.

I go in through the back door and creep toward the dining room. Relief. Jago is where I left him, asleep on the chaise longue. I move quietly up the stairs to the en suite. I need to shower, to collect my thoughts, to scrub any trace of Miranda from my skin and hair.

I dump my clothes on the back of a chair, close the bathroom door, and step under the water. It's hot, but I turn the dial, then turn it again. I want it scalding, for it to hurt to stand there, for my skin to sear and redden.

Did Miranda tell anyone where she was going?

Did she tell anyone what she'd found? That she was coming to see me?

Is there about to be a knock at the door?

From now on, I decide it's all about damage limitation, on insulating myself as much as possible. As soon as I'm out of the shower, I'll take the suit I was wearing and those fucking pages out to the barbecue and incinerate them. Destroy them once and for all.

Out of the shower, my skin is tender from the heat, and I have to carefully pat myself dry. I put on a robe and come out into the bedroom. I'll get the barbecue going now, before Jago wakes up.

But when I return to the chair, the suit and the pages inside it are gone. As are the other things that were there.

I step out on to the landing. Has Jago been up and taken them? Why would he do that? Does he know?

Then I smell it—the lemon bleach Audrey uses to clean the toilets and kitchen floors.

Audrey.

Miranda's best friend.

I run to the picture window at the front of the house and see her car pulling away. Looking down at the hall, I realize all the dirty glasses are gone, the carpet clean.

Jago must have asked her to do an extra shift. To make sure everything was put straight before I got back from the conference.

I return to the bedroom and look again at the empty chair. I dumped my suit on top of the stuff we leave for her to take to the dry cleaners. She's taken it, and the pages inside.

The realization leaves me statue-still. My breath stops in my throat, my skin suddenly cold.

The grenade is back out in the world. Rusty and unstable.

A groan and a cough from the dining room.

Jago is awake.

I pull my dressing gown closed, arrange my face into a smile and prepare to greet him, to lie about why I'm here. To lie about everything.

Chapter 58

A udrey?" A thump, followed by a gasp. "Audrey, this is silly," says Kitty, placatory. "Come out, and we can talk about this."

Audrey isn't falling for any of it. She now knows what Kitty is capable of—the lengths she'll go to to protect her interests, her reputation.

"Look, I know it doesn't mean much, but I am sorry." Footsteps and a dragging sound. The accumulation of dirt and debris being swept together in the train of her green silk dress. Her voice is getting closer. Audrey peers through the tiny gap in the dresser and sees a pair of feet appear on the threshold. "Miranda caught me off guard. I panicked."

Audrey holds her silence.

She can't tell if Kitty knows she's inside this room, or if she's calling her bluff.

A pause, and Audrey thinks she is going to turn around, to go back the way she came, but then she takes a step forward.

"That bloody confession," she says, and Audrey realizes she is pretending not to be looking, but that she is listening acutely, hunting her down. "The pages must have got switched before we put them in the envelopes in class. I was so worked up that day. I knew once the teacher read what I'd written, that would be it. I was so scared, I had to rush out to be sick, but Miranda got up just before me. In all the confusion I knocked everything everywhere."

Kitty seems to know Audrey's hiding in here, but how? Did she disturb something on her way over to the dresser? Can she hear her breathing?

"I've been trying to get it back ever since you took it. I went to the dry cleaners, but they wouldn't let me have it without a ticket."

Audrey's muscles begin to shudder with fatigue; her feet are numb. She wonders how long she can stay like this—if her body will give out on her, give her away. Kitty shuffles around in the dark. A ripping sound: her dress has caught on something. If she finds Audrey, what will she do? Beat her to death with the tire iron? Throw her body over the cliffs?

No one knows Audrey is out here, and Kitty has nothing to lose.

"I just wanted to talk, genuinely." Kitty sounds exhausted, beaten. "To explain." Audrey peers through the gap and sees she's come to a halt. Slumped in defeat, her head is hanging low, her beautiful dress ruined. This was supposed to have been the night that she was celebrated and admired. Audrey thinks how success is not always what it seems—neither is failure. That sometimes, hopes and dreams can actually be a trap, a weight around your neck from which you can never wriggle free.

Kitty stays like that for a few moments, and then she turns toward the doorway and returns to the hall. Audrey realizes she doesn't know where she is hiding after all.

"If you're here somewhere and can hear this, then I'm going to go now. Do whatever you need to. I've spent my entire life striving to be a certain kind of person, doing whatever it takes to keep being that person, but I'm so tired." Her voice is small. "I think I'm finally done."

Kitty sounds as if she means it, but even after the footsteps have long gone, Audrey dares not come out. She fears it's a trick—that Kitty is hiding behind a door, waiting for her to make one false move. But then Audrey hears an engine fire up in the distance and a car pull away.

Still not sure she can trust it, she waits a while longer before crawling out of her hiding place. She peers through a gap in the window boards, looks down at the car park below. Only one vehicle remains. Hers.

For once, it seems Kitty has been true to her word. She has gone and Audrey is alone. Safe.

———

Crawling out from underneath the toppled dresser is not easy. Audrey cannot get her body to work properly—her thigh muscles are too cramped, her feet too numb—and she has to heave herself across the floor like a worm before her lower limbs start to wake up. Gritting her teeth at the pins and needles in her calves, she pats her thigh, feeling for the earlier wound. The bleeding seems to have stopped.

Shaky with adrenaline, she tries to think, to work through the simple next steps.

She'll go back to the car. She'll call Ned, then the police. Then she'll drive home.

That's it—that's all she has to focus on for now.

She's heading toward the hall when she hears it: a moaning, scraping sound.

The door.

Someone is here.

Her heart batters against her ribs.

Kitty.

She tricked her, although Audrey can't fathom how.

She's too far down the hall to return to her hiding place under the dresser, and so she rushes toward the scullery. Bracing her upper body, she gets ready to strike, to scratch, to kick. She can't believe she has been so stupid. Had she learned nothing from tonight? She shouldn't have trusted anything Kitty said or did; she should have stayed hidden until morning, waited her out. She thinks she's free and clear, but as she gets close to the scullery door, she sees Kitty, there in the shadows. She holds still, remembering the tire iron. Is that what Kitty went to retrieve? Is she going to bludgeon her with it? To bash her skull like an egg? Her skin prickles. How close is she? Four, maybe five feet away? She can hear her breathing, can feel the grit in the disturbed air on her tongue.

Audrey decides her best chance of getting out of here is to backtrack, and swerves to the left, toward the broken staircase and the front door, hoping to find another way out. She soon discovers the front door is covered by a thick velvet curtain, and starts to tug it aside. She'll heave and push against the wood till it breaks, force her way back out into the open, but once the curtain has gone, she sees the doorway has been bricked up, a crude arrangement of breeze blocks and cement.

Footsteps. Kitty approaches slowly in the dark, her pace deliberate. She is taking her time. Audrey thinks she is enjoying this.

Audrey considers her options. She could go upstairs, but no, the steps are too rotten, too broken. She could try and bolt past Kitty in the hallway, but no—the tire iron. One swing toward her head, and that would be it.

She is trapped.

She looks again, searching left and right, up and down for an escape, and then she sees it. In the sitting room to her left, a thin stripe of moonlight at the window. She could climb up to the sill, kick at the boards until they break.

It's her only choice.

She feints right, then left; then Kitty spurs herself into action. As Audrey scrambles across the room, she can feel Kitty close behind her. Her body tenses, ready for the blow of the steel against her skull, but as she picks her way up and over the scattered furniture, she realizes she is losing Kitty, and that the window she's headed toward has a much bigger gap then she'd first realized.

A surge of hope. She can make it. She's going to be OK.

She pulls herself up and over a sofa piled with dining chairs, the gap in the window less than two feet away, and leaps to the other side.

It feels like falling through wet cardboard. The wood is so rotten, it disintegrates at the first touch. Audrey flails, trying to grab the back of the sofa as she flies past it, but she is moving too quickly, the ground beneath her feet dissolving.

Her body meets the cellar floor with a thump, her head boomeranging up and off the damp stone floor. At first the shock is a gift. It insulates her from the cold and the pain. She blinks, debris in her eyes, in her nostrils. Lying on her back, she can feel that one of her legs is straight and that the other stretches out to the side at an impossible angle. She blinks again, wondering why her eyes have yet to adjust, why she cannot see, but then she realizes she is in darkness.

Once she's caught her breath she tries to move, to sit up. A white-hot pain in her shoulder relegates her back to the floor. Whimpering in agony, she pats herself gingerly in the dark. Her hand soon lands on a length of something that feels like rusted iron emerging just above the slant of her left collarbone. Another farming tool? She realizes she must have landed on it, that she is pinioned to the floor. Her teeth start to chatter. She is cold and wet. She moves her hand from the iron pole, down to her blouse. The material is sopping and stuck to her skin. Blood.

Panting, she squints up toward the hole she'd created. The cellar must be six feet deep, and it is even darker down here—too dark to see what surrounds her. Using her other—uninjured—side, she reaches back and around, exploring the space around her. As she stretches a hand up toward her head, it collides with something large and metal. She goes back to it, feels the curvature of the material, the way it feeds down into the floor. A pipe.

A creak of sofa springs and the clash of wood against wood, and the space above her is splashed with the blue light of a phone.

Kitty.

The urge to ask for help, to shout, to beg, is overwhelming. But Audrey refuses to give her that pleasure, that power.

A head-and-shoulders silhouette peers over the edge and directs the light directly in Audrey's face. She blinks and tries to turn away. Will Kitty try and climb down? Finish her off while she's at her most helpless?

But then, as her eyes start to adjust, Audrey realizes something isn't right. The figure doesn't have Kitty's bob, and their build seems smaller—childlike, even.

"I need an ambulance," she says, and it's then she realizes how breathy her voice is, how slight. Has she broken a rib, punctured a lung? "Please."

The figure lets out a tiny huff of contempt, and as they do they move their head slightly. The light catches their face for the first time, and she sees it's not a child but a woman, her frame spindle thin.

She angles the phone to Audrey's apron, still tied around her waist, and tuts as if disgusted by this symbol of her servitude. Then she moves the light up toward the iron pole protruding from her body. Seeing it, she inhales sharply. The light jumps and bounces, revealing a tiny birthmark, like a strawberry under the woman's left eye.

Polly.

Kitty's mum.

Chapter 59

Audrey is in too much pain to ask what she's doing here. She's just relieved it's not Kitty, that it's someone who will actually call for help, who can make sure she is OK.

"Polly, it's me, Audrey. Kitty's friend…" She stops, self-corrects. "Her cleaner."

The other woman doesn't move.

"Polly?" Audrey says, trying to find the breath. "Did you hear me? I'm hurt. Please call for help."

Still nothing. Audrey can feel the blood pooling under her back, spreading upward and soaking her hair.

Finally the woman shifts, shines the phone light around where Audrey lies, surveying the ground. Audrey thinks she's trying to figure out if there's space for her to climb down and help her—if there's anything dangerous in the way. Then she speaks.

"I call an ambulance, and then what?"

"Sorry?"

"What will you do? If you survive? Tell everyone about my daughter, about what she did?" Another huff. "Ruin her life?"

Audrey's brain scrambles to make sense of what she's hearing.

"You knew?"

A laugh, smug and quick, as if she's just fudged a punchline to a joke she knows well. She pulls back her bony shoulders, and Audrey gets a glimpse of maroon sequins.

"I knew about the essays. Ben—that boy that died. He came to our house, asked Kitty to admit to what she'd done." She lowers her voice, conspiratorial. "Richard bought the lie he told him about them being study partners, took his eye off the ball the way he always does, but I was hovering in the back kitchen, listening. I've always kept a close eye on her. That's what mothers are for."

Audrey thinks about Kitty's letter; about her graduation portrait. The way Polly had inhabited her robe that day at the spa as if she was being swallowed up, too frail for the size and weight of it. She'd got it all wrong. Richard wasn't the master, but the puppet. Polly was the one in control.

"And did you know she killed him? That she killed Miranda?" Audrey tries to shout, to rage, but she can't summon enough air, and words come out as barely a whisper.

Another tut.

"What's the thing they say nowadays? What they call people like me? Helicopter parents—is that it? But it's not that. It's just about doing your job. Looking out for Kitty, making sure she's OK, making sure she makes the most of the chances she's given, chances I never had. After the party, she followed you and so I followed her."

"Did you know?" says Audrey, but it's becoming harder to focus. She feels light-headed, thoughts and questions slipping through her mind like sand.

"The first I heard of it was tonight, when I heard you two talking. It is regrettable, of course, and I admit I was a little shocked, but I'm also proud. She did what we always told her to do. She did what she needed to in order to succeed."

Regrettable. Miranda. Her wonderful friend.

Audrey thinks of the kittiwakes on the cliff face: how Melvyn had described their willingness to do anything to protect their young.

"You're not going to call for help, are you?" she croaks.

Polly directs her flashlight onto her pierced collarbone and follows the pool of blood spread across the floor. She taps her teeth together, thinking.

"Even if an ambulance came right now, it's too late."

"Please."

Audrey wants to close her eyes—to rest, to sleep—but she fights it.

Polly swings the flashlight back to her face and holds it there, as if committing Audrey to memory; then she turns it off.

A creak, and Audrey can hear her clambering back on the sofa, then footsteps as she retreats from the room.

"Please..." She tries to shout after her, but she can only muster enough air for a croak. "Please..."

Audrey lies alone in the dark. She keeps blacking out, then coming to. It takes all her effort to blink, to breathe.

She wonders when Ned or Marcel will report her missing. Marcel will realize first. When there's no one there to help with the kids. But then maybe he'll think she's finally had enough, that she's gone back to Brunswick Road in a sulk.

Scenes spool through her head. She doesn't know if they are dreams, memories or hallucinations, but she doesn't care because they take her away from here, from the dark and the chill. She is with her mum and dad. Her dad is smiling. She is with Miranda: they are walking home from school together; they are playing in the snow; they are watching TV in damp pajamas after a bath. She is with Ned on the beach. They pass a man walking a parrot on a leash and try to hold their laughter. She is looking at the holiday snapshot of her parents, her mum a pirate, her dad a parrot in cardboard wings. Briefly lucid, she realizes she now has her answer—that she knows why her friend died. The reason. The cause and effect. But it turns out that knowing is worse than not knowing. To be aware of the waste, the unfairness, the needlessness. And then she is with Edward and Enid when they were babies, toddling, blowing kisses. Blowing out birthday candles. She is with Mr. Danler in his too-warm living room, and he's telling her it's never too late. She likes the peat fire, moves toward its heat, its comfort. She pats the ground on the floor as if for a poker to stir the flames, and then she is lucid again, but still she keeps patting, Mr. Danler's words on repeat, feeling for something—anything—that could make a noise. Her fingers skim what feels like a newspaper, its edges damp and crumbling, the ridge of a broken tile, a plastic bag, and then they hit upon something metal with a wooden handle. A trowel?

She grabs hold of it and bangs it once against the metal pipe above her head. It clangs dully, the noise not even enough to carry up through the house, let alone the walls, to the ears of any passersby. She does it again, harder this time. And again, and again. She knows what she is doing is probably futile, that the effort is making her sweat and shake, but she keeps going. Clang. Clang. *Clang*. As hard and as often as she can. She is determined to continue for as long as she is conscious, to try and draw attention to herself for the first time, the banging a kind of Morse code that says, "I am here," "I am here," "I am here."

It's the courage to continue that counts. She knows that now.

Someone is talking, but they sound muffled, far away, as if Audrey is underwater and they are above the surface. They reach around her waist and untie the apron. There is pressure around her pinioned side, a tightening, painful pressure. She realizes they're tying the straps, creating a tourniquet. They cover her with something warm and fleecy, tuck it right up to her neck. She tries to open her eyes, but she is too tired, deep at the bottom of the ocean.

"She's lost blood," they say. "I think it might have nicked the subclavian, but it seems to be stemming the leak for now." A pause. "Tell them they need to come quick."

Audrey tries to surface. She realizes they are not talking to her but to someone else—that they are on the phone.

"Her pulse is bradycardic." They pause, frustrated by whatever questions are being asked on the other end of the line. "Look, I know what I'm talking about, OK. Just please, get an ambulance immediately."

A doctor...a doctor has found her. They know what they're doing.

"I'm going to stay on the line until they get here."

The doctor's voice is familiar, comforting. Once more, Audrey tries her hardest to breach the surface.

She opens her eyes and recoils, unable to cope with the way the blue glow of the phone illuminates the cellar. Slowly, she adjusts.

The doctor tending to her has curly hair. She reaches out to touch his arm and her fingers roam across skin bumpy with insect bites.

Melvyn.

"Help is on its way," he says. "Until then, we'll wait here. Together."

Chapter 60

Keswick, the Lake District, 2003

W hat happened to just teaching him a lesson?"

The recriminations fly from their mouths like knives.

"I told you it was a bad idea." Miranda swallows a sob. "That no good would come of it. But you went ahead and did it anyway, without me."

Melvyn has told her how he wanted to tamper with Ben's orienteering coordinates, to doctor his map so that he got lost and couldn't find his way back to the meeting point. He'd fantasized about Ben frightened and alone in the dark, waiting for Mountain Rescue.

He guides her away from the crowds of kids gathered at the window.

"This wasn't me," he says, his face white. "I had nothing to do with this. I promise."

Miranda scans his face, trying to work out if he's telling the truth.

"First do no harm," he says. "Dad says that's the first thing they'll teach me at medical school. After we talked last night, it was all I could think about. I decided you were right. Revenge would only make me feel worse."

Her breathing slows.

Melvyn presses the heels of his hands into his eyes.

"I know I didn't do anything, but I feel guilty." He gestures at the paramedics. "Like I'm responsible, like I wished this on him."

Miranda realizes he is crying.

"You *thought* about hurting him," she says. "That's not a crime."

"It feels like it."

They look at each other. A moment of acceptance. "No one has to know," says Miranda gently. "We weren't there. It never happened."

Melvyn folds his arms and tucks his trembling hands in tight against his chest.

"OK?" says Miranda.

"OK," he says.

Chapter 61

Hughes Hall
Cambridge
CB1 2EW
October 18th, 2025

Dear Kitty

I have debated for some time about whether to reply to your letter. Indeed, as soon as the trial was over, I made a vow to never think about you ever again. But Melvyn, I guess having experienced prison himself, has a more forgiving nature and thinks your apology should be acknowledged, that it will be good for me, will give me closure.

I'm writing this in the college library. Hughes Hall doesn't have the ancient oak desks you got to experience at Corpus Christi, but it is always filled with sunshine (and apparently has better heating), and I think it is just as magnificent and beautiful. It was scary, applying again and then, when I got offered a place, leaving the town I'd lived in my whole life to come here. But watching how my younger brother Ned has dealt with his own bumps in the road made me think differently about what is and isn't possible. Still, I worried I was too old, that I wouldn't be able to keep up, but the admissions tutor loved my essay on Gertrude Bell (turns out all those hours mopping museum floors were actually useful), and my fellow mature students are a wonderful bunch. Being here is a second chance for all of us in different ways. More and more, I realize that we get more than one shot at things, that there is no expiry date on hopes and dreams, and that twenty-five years from now even you will be granted a second chance of your own, another shot at life.

Still, I take comfort in the knowledge that any second, third or fourth chances you may have will be tempered by your time served at His Majesty's pleasure. Melvyn says that having a criminal conviction, a record, defines the rest of your life: the jobs you get, the places you are allowed to travel, the family that will still claim you as theirs. This, even though his crime was nothing like yours.

I know we are not supposed to differentiate between these things, that the law is the law. Black and white. Right and wrong. But I don't care what anyone says; there is light and shade, there is a difference. On paper Melvyn has a "history of violence"; on paper he committed ABH, was considered no longer fit to be a doctor and had his license stripped, his entire life ruined. In reality, he lashed out at a man who had brought his seven-year-old son into A & E badly injured, a son he had hurt and who he tried to hurt again when he thought the doctors and nurses weren't around. Still, once you have a record the details become irrelevant, and so when the police found his DNA in Miranda's car, they assumed it must be him who had hurt her. I guess when you eventually get out you'll experience far worse.

A murder conviction casts a long shadow. One you'll never shake off, no matter how hard you try. I take some comfort in that.

Do you ever think of her? Of my friend? What you did?

In your letter you told me you wanted to say sorry, but you never mentioned her name, not once, so let me write it for you here.

Miranda.

In recent months I've taken to saying her name again and again under my breath, enjoying the way my mouth presses together, then widens to shape the second syllable, then widens again to releases the final vowel into the air.

She believed in giving people a second chance.

In this she was devout.

Melvyn said that when she first bumped into him at the halfway house where he was staying, she didn't hesitate. She just rolled up her yoga mat, said goodbye to her class and took him for coffee. That all she cared about was trying to help him get back on his feet, whether that was by giving him money or moral support.

Then there's the names of her children—Enid and Edward—something you also chose to omit. Children who, thanks to you, no longer have a mum. Their father has now taken them back to France. Away from Saltburn and its sand-flecked streets. Away from its cliffs. Their barn was inland, but still, even there, Huntcliff was inescapable. You can't help but see glimpses of it all day every day. Marcel couldn't bear it, but it was the prospect of his kids having to constantly contend with that looming jut of rock and clay that was the real driving force behind the move. He knows that one day they'll be old enough to learn the truth about how their mum died, and he decided that, when that happens, he wants them nowhere near this curve of beach. It's not that he wants them to forget, more that he wants them to remember their mum as they knew her—how she was in life, not death. I miss them desperately, but I'm proud of him for stepping up in this and so many other ways, for finally putting them first.

Marcel might not have been in our class, but the arrival of those letters changed his life, changed him, the same way they changed all of us...

I recently learned a new term—"lifequake"—have you come across it? It's used to describe a sudden unexpected shift in the trajectory of your life that initially feels devastating but that ultimately catalyzes personal growth, transformation and rebirth. Now, when I think of us opening those envelopes last year, this is the word that comes to mind. For some, the Richter scale didn't register much. Camille's day-to-day existence is the same as it ever was, except she tells me she feels lighter, unburdened by the secret she'd carried for so long. For others, the effects have been tectonic. In recent months, Belinda has announced that she is going to challenge Robbie for his seat at the next election. She makes a convincing argument: her campaign is centered around the fact that no one knows and loves the place and the people better than she does. That she, with all her children, is personally invested in making the town somewhere the next generation can thrive. I actually think she might win, and that she will make a fantastic MP. Leighton took Belinda's dumping him hard at first—a bit rich, when you consider he spent most of their marriage obsessed with another woman—but now he's pivoted, made it his unique selling point. Apparently he's found a new niche, life coaching freshly divorced people online, and is doing a roaring trade. Then there's Ricky Larkin. Melvyn heard a rumor he turned whistleblower, reported his oil rig for illegally dumping effluent into the sea. Like I say, it's only a rumor, but one I hope is true. I like to think the Surfers Against Sewage part of him still existed deep inside after all; that his letter helped him get reacquainted.

As for me, the aftershocks—good and bad—keep coming, and I suspect will do for the rest of my life. And although I now understand the pull of home—why so many people ricochet back to that pocket of coast in search of comfort, or a sense of belonging that isn't necessarily there—I don't think I'll ever live in Saltburn again. I like walking down Trinity

Street and no one knowing who I am, I like living in a place from which I can travel outwards in any direction, the way I walk taller here, the way I look people in the eye. How I make sure to speak up in tutorials, how I spend hours browsing the shelves in Heffers without once wondering if someone is going to question my being there. How I now take up the space I deserve.

You'll be what, in your sixties, by the time you get out? You said you are struggling to sleep in prison. Well, apparently the halfway house hostels you get put in on your release are worse. Melvyn says they're brutal, so bad he overnighted there as little as possible, choosing to squat in that rotten farmhouse instead. It being full of desperate people, your stuff gets stolen all the time.

Thieves—they're everywhere, Kitty.

Melvyn and I have been together a while now, and although we're often in completely different parts of the country, we're making it work. The more I get to know him, the more I see how good a father he is to his son—the best, actually. How about your parents? Your dad?

Your mum.

Does she come and visit? But then, no, that's unlikely. Polly has a tendency to leave people in holes, doesn't she? To abandon them to the dark and the cold. I wasn't surprised when she denied abandoning me there that night. I'm sure she nurtures the lies to herself, just as she does her denial in the part she played in shaping the person you became, and your eventual fate. Not that she's completely to blame. In the years since losing Miranda, I've started to realize that we are not our parents: that even though they leave doors open for us, we have a choice about whether or not to walk through them.

I heard Jago rented out the cottage as a vacation home. That he's using the proceeds to go on a kind of belated gap year, traveling with the lovely Cordelia by his side. Vacation homes, they are surprisingly lucrative. I bet the tourists love being in your study. Maybe they play cards there if the weather's bad? Light a fire and marvel at the views of the Cleveland Hills. As it happens, my brother and I have gone down the same route with our own house. Brunswick Road is nowhere near as grand as your place, but still it brings in way more than regular rent ever would and is enough to help fund our respective degrees.

It sounds like you are becoming quite the seamstress. Despite everything, I was glad to learn that you're finally getting to indulge in fashion—the one thing you actually always wanted to do, your true passion.

I haven't found my place in the world yet, but I'm getting there. It feels good to put myself first, for once. I feel comfortable in my own skin, but I understand now that this isn't a final state of being; that like snakes, we shed our skins all the time, that being happy with who we are is an ongoing process, something we need to work at for the rest of our lives.

How about you? Do you feel comfortable with who you are? Can you look at yourself in the mirror?

I'm going to finish up now. My phone keeps buzzing—my brother Ned. Their place in London is only forty-five minutes on the train, and so I see them and the little one often, but still he calls all the time. I worried becoming a parent so young would derail him, but in truth it has made them both more determined than ever to succeed.

Goodbye, Kitty. This has been my first and last correspondence with you, so please, don't bother me again.

Yours
Audrey

THE END

ACKNOWLEDGMENTS

This book had a few false starts. Rachel Yeoh helped me pick through the weeds with brilliance and patience. Rachel, I am and always will be so grateful for the role you played in bringing this novel to fruition. Sophie Orme and Jenna Jankowski. This book is a thousand times better because of your sharp, clever notes. I count myself extremely lucky to have access to your editorial prowess. Saskia Arthur for your careful reading and excellent notes. Zoe Yang for guiding me through the final, critical stages toward publication. Jo and her beautiful daughter, Paige. Unlike Camille, Jo has a huge brain; however, I did take inspiration from Jo's extraordinary strength and resilience. Camille is the character I admire the most in this novel. Katy Johnson. The sort of person who, when I needed somewhere quiet, away from a demanding toddler, to edit this novel, came over and built me a desk, far away, at the top of the house. Thank you for this and so many other kindnesses.

Alan, Dorothy, and Charlie. Growing up, I could never have imagined the riches that lay ahead.

ABOUT THE AUTHOR

Deborah O'Connor is a writer and TV producer. She lives in North Yorkshire with her husband and two children. *Dear Future Me* is her fourth novel.